A MURDER OF CROWS

Book II
A City With Seven Gates Novel

STEVEN L. LOVETT

A MURDER OF CROWS

Book II
A City With Seven Gates Novel

STEVEN L. LOVETT

ISBN 978-1-77400-026-7 (print)

ISBN 978-1-77400-027-4 (ebook)

www.dragonmoonpress.com

DEDICATION

To the Head Teacher, Mrs. Vinsome, and the wonderful students of Hunter Hall primary school, those unwitting friends and classmates of Nicolas, who are now true friends of mine.

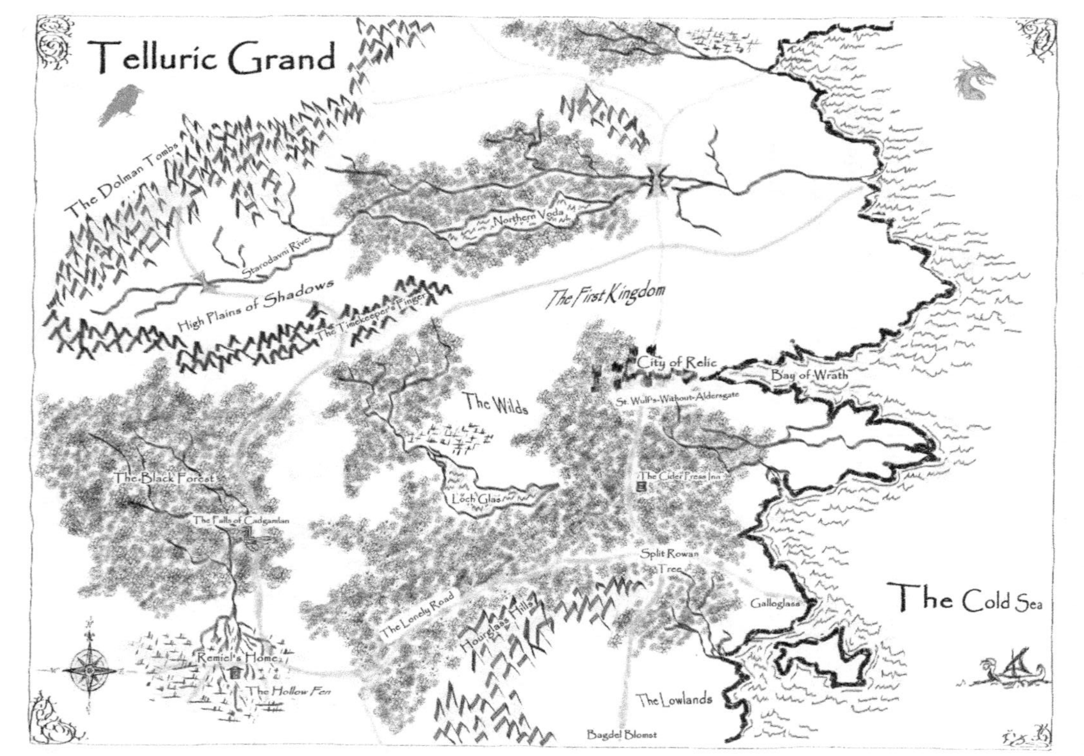
Telluric Grand
The Dolman Tombs
Starodavni River
Northern Voda
High Plains of Shadows
The Timekeeper's Finger
The First Kingdom
City of Relic
Bay of Wrath
St. Wulf's-Without-Aldersgate
The Wilds
The Black Forest
Loch Glas
The Cider Press Inn
The Falls of Cadgamlan
Split Rowan Tree
The Lonely Road
Hourglass Hills
Galloglass
The Cold Sea
Remiel's Home
The Hollow Fen
The Lowlands
Bagdel Blomst

ACKNOWLEDGMENTS

This brief page of gratitude is as important to me as any of the words I've put together in the story that follows; those words couldn't have been written in the way they have been without the inestimable help, encouragement, and genuine support of several people, whom I'd like to humbly thank.

My wife and daughter have been my bulwark of strength and purpose when I felt, on more than a few days and nights, that what I was doing and what I was writing were beyond my capacity to finish and finish well. This book exists because of them.

My publisher, Gwen Gades, has continued to be magnificent, resourceful, and understanding. This book, like the first one, took longer than I thought it would, but every note I ever received from Gwen was reassuring. She also deserves a special thanks for the hard work she put into the cover artwork!

I also want to express my heartfelt gratitude to Kim Durham, the English gentleman who performed the audio reading of the first novel, *A Place With Dragons*. Kim kindly read drafts of this book as it was being written, providing priceless comments and criticisms that ranged from "readability" to character interactions to culture-specific references. My family and I had the immense pleasure of sharing a dinner and a few pints with Kim (and his delightful partner, Flic) at The Guildford Arms in Edinburgh, Scotland, and I discovered I had found a friend as well as a brilliant actor and literary co-conspirator.

Lastly, I want to sincerely thank my readers. Without exception, they have continued to convey their enjoyment with the first book and their enthusiasm for this second book. Their excitement, and above all, their patience, have been both humbling and inspiring. I hope you, my dear reader, will find that this next part of Nicolas' adventure delivers.

PROLOGUE

The highest sea cliff in all England bears the luckless name of 'Hangman Cliffs.'

Its crags consist of a pair of windswept stony bluffs rising up near Combe Martin on the north coast of Devon where the western stretch of the Exmoor holds fast against the violence of a green-blue sea. It is a lonely place. A place of cobalt skies, salt-addled mists, and fierce storms.

A little over a hundred years ago, an adventuresome Englishman described the cliff's two scarps, one named 'Great Hangman' and the other 'Little Hangman,' as a 'cairn of stones,' a 'desolate heath,' looming high above the chop and froth of Bristol Channel's dangerous tides. It's said the Englishman leaned against the weathered and stacked rock wall atop the Great Hangman scribbling his notes in a field book, the lapels of his Callahan frock coat flapping wildly in the cold Atlantic wind as some nameless sheepherder told him the tale of how the Hangman Cliffs gained their dark names.

"'Twas a thief!" started the wizened sheepherder. He spat a gypsy's low curse into the unfriendly wind. The wind spat it back with a briny spray of ocean water. "'Twas a thief that'd come in the dead o' night! 'E seized a wee ewe lamb from the safety of its warm fold, an' 'avin' seized the pretty lamb, 'e stole away, thinkin' he'd made good on his devilish thievery."

"Yes, yes," muttered the English gentleman. The stump of his whittled pencil scrawled furiously in his notebook. "And—

am I to suppose—the thief was thereafter caught by the local constable and soon hung on this hill for his crime?"

"Garn!" the wrinkled sheepherder protested, now spitting out of disgust. His seasoned head wagged; his aged eyes squinted against the blustery wind. "Naught at'll, m'lord, naught at'll. The thievin' scoundrel made away wit' his prize lamb, but after some time the fool stopped to rest, to catch 'is breath, thinkin' he'd outwitted any pursuer."

"Oh?" said the English gentleman, hesitating with his pencil in midair. "Unexpected, that. What then became of him?"

"What became o' him?" the sheepherder echoed smugly. "Well, I'll tell ye what *became* o' him. That thar little lamb he'd stolen struggled to free itself from the 'is shoulders, an' when it did, its halter rope caught 'bout the thief's dishonest neck. Twistin' an' bindin' like a hangman's noose!" The shepherd drew back his head and spat a third time, a final time, this in grim satisfaction. No salt-spray spat back. "The chokin' thief gagged an' fought to loosen the slender cord, but it held *fast*, you see, an' the little ewe lamb hung from the miserable thief's neck like the weight o' Judgment Day, until life was choked out o' him." The sheepherder laughed. "The doomed bastard stole nothin' but Death. 'e nicked 'is own hangman."

The Englishman peered at the crinkly man, his woolen lapels beating against his cheeks. "The lamb, you mean to say? The lamb, the lamb was the hangman?"

"'Twas," came the sheepherder's firm reply.

At that, the weathered man folded his arms and turned his heel, the story now finished. As he walked away, a final, cautious word drifted over his shoulder. A warning almost lost in the sea's wind. A warning the highborn Englishman never forgot. "Lambs," came the sheepherder's fading voice, " Lambs might be offered for sacrifice but *sacrifice*, sacrifice always brings *judgment* with it, m'lord."

With that, the nameless shepherd was gone.

PART I

WELCOME FOR A KING

They went with songs to the battle, they were young,
Straight of limb, true of eye, steady and aglow.
They were staunch to the end against odds uncounted;
They fell with their faces to the foe.

They mingle not with their laughing comrades again;
They sit no more at familiar tables of home;
They have no lot in our labour of the day-time;
They sleep beyond England's foam.

For the Fallen
Laurence Binyon

CHAPTER 1

Heading Home Again

Over a year had slipped quietly by since Nicolas Bennett had found his way to the world of Telluric Grand. Since he'd walked the highways of the First Kingdom. Since he'd seen the great and ancient walls of the City of Relic, met a true giant, had belted a stained weather cloak around his waist, hung a small dagger around his neck, hurried down dark forest roads, or said heartfelt goodbyes to genuine friends, the swordsmith-in-training Ranulf son of Renfry, the boy-thief Benjamin Rush, and the enchanting young Healer, Adelaide Ashdown.

Nicolas had done his best to return to Telluric Grand ever since.

Christmas Eve had finally arrived in Plumpton Head, a small hamlet just north of Penrith, England, along the A6.

This year the much-anticipated holiday had brought an oddly heavy December snow, a gauzy white snow of loose-laced yarn, wind-spun in vague drapes that dappled the moonlight and softened the cold night's stars.

Nicolas Bennett, right at thirteen years and fifty-five days old, sat by himself in a dim corner in the living room of the Bennett family's cottage farmhouse. He was staring absently at sparkles of candlelight caught by the prism-cut, green glass of chilled milk that sat next to a smaller, tulip-shaped glass of creamed sherry which sat next to a petite, dessert plate holding three long, freshly scrubbed carrots and a thick slice of warm mince pie. The pie smelled of nutmeg, cinnamon spice and the distinct musk of cloves. This small spread of food, a traditional refreshment Nicolas' mum always made sure to put out in case Father Christmas arrived in the middle of the night feeling a bit peckish, was arranged "just so" alongside a simple flat wreath enclosing four red and one white candles of advent, all of which were arranged atop an old crocheted runner spread the length of the sideboard that stood behind the sofa. Nicolas leaned forward in his chair and poked one of the carrots until it crossed the other two. He drew a slow finger against the milk glass's cold surface. And in a secret place tunneled so deeply within his heart he only *felt* it instead of understanding it, Nicolas unhappily wished the holidays were over.

He felt guilty for loving Christmastime, had for years, but this year most especially, he wanted the season to pass quickly and with it, the painful mix of hurt and loneliness in his heart.

For the past seven years a miserable blend of sorrow and joy had become so normal with the arrival of advent, Nicolas had begun to associate the arrival of those emotions with the month of December and in particular with Christmastime. Deep within a profound and nameless place inside, Nicolas wished things were different, he wished *he* was different. Selfishly he wished the loss he'd carried for the past seven years would just go away, disappear. It had happened a lifetime ago it seemed. He'd been so young and now, even aged beyond his time, only small pockets of real memories were all that remained. But the ache, the ache renewed itself each December, each Christmastime.

Nicolas' soul wordlessly wished what it had wished so many thousands of times before. It bargained with the endless heavens. It hoped by some stroke of celestial magic, a raw magic summoned by the sheer force of his own will, that Nicolas' older brother, Jack, would suddenly appear. Jack would magically be sitting there as he so often had in the middle of the living room floor, laughing his wobbly laugh, his thin shoulders slumped over, his limp arms resting on his bony knees and his deep, grey eyes wide-open, reminding Nicolas for the millionth time how marvelous it was to sit on the floor, to pretend everyone else were giants passing by.

But no magic occurred. It never did. And Jack never appeared.

Just the same feeling of guilt and sorrow and loneliness.

And Christmastime.

This year, this particular Christmastime, that strange once-a-year blend of heartache and delight was further mingled with an additional sensation. A more-poignant-than-usual sense of being… out of place.

Sighing, Nicolas pushed the thin carrot into its spot, leaned back in his chair and shifted his stare to the empty living room floor. He'd come to understand that some pain remains no matter how long ago the wound was inflicted. No amount of Christmas cheer would ever change that. This year's feeling of being lost only made it worse.

Half an hour before, the Bennett family had arrived home from evening vespers held at the Parish Church of Saint Andrew, a centuries old building of red sandstone ashlar tucked neatly at the center of St. Andrew's Place, the church's snow-decked tower peeking up behind a narrow redstone row of banks, the Penrith Library, a few local eateries, and the Eden District Council's offices.

The Bennett's home rang full of Christmastime noises. From out of the kitchen Nicolas could hear his mum's enchanting Irish accent floating through the farmhouse as she sang, "The Kerry Christmas Carol," a hymn Sarah Bennett would often say had been the same carol her own mother, Kathryn Shaughnessy, sang every Christmas Eve when Sarah was still a young girl growing up in northern Ireland—a turbulent childhood spent in the town of Dungiven folded among the rich green mountains of County Derry. "Leave the door upon the latch," she'd sing, "and set the fire to keep, and pray they'll rest with us tonight when all the world's asleep." Even without looking Nicolas knew his mum was twirling about the kitchen as fiery waves of red hair spilled over her shoulders like the soft doublings of a strawberry shawl. Sarah Bennett's soft but searching voice filled the Bennett's small home like warmth coming from and oven full of sweet pies.

There was also the ill-kept beat of stomping boots. Mr. Bennett's winter boots stamping against the stone floor of the cubby boot room as Peter Bennett busily cleaned away clumps of clinging wet snow onto the stone floor that ran between the kitchen and his small study. Layered against this was the patchy snap and crack of hedge wood burning in the study's fireplace and a subdued radio broadcast of "It's Christmas Time Again" by Louis B. Armstrong and Peggy Lee. Wonderfully discordant, these Christmastime harmonies had always carried a strong sense of *home* for Nicolas.

But this year, for over a year, Nicolas felt something more was missing than just his brother Jack. There was something more he'd lost.

Nicolas felt lost.

A part of him, who he was, *what* he was, had been stolen away. At times this sense of hollowness had made him impatient, cross even; in those moments the eyes of his long-suffering father would darken and Mr. Bennett's mood would fall back into the Bennett family's coal-mining tradition, a no-nonsense attitude that had sustained the hard-working Bennett family even after Wood Pit, the last colliery in their hometown of Haydock, closed down in 1971. Peter Bennett would sternly remark, "Don't ya get shirty with me, lad! You'd better get it sorted out, an' sort it out right, before *I* do the sortin' for ya."

As of late, with the onset of an early winter and Christmas Day now lying around the corner, the restlessness with which Nicolas had wrestled for over a year settled over him like the eventide's snow. A leaden gloom of discontent and crankiness.

For over a year, the once-happy home fires of burning sticks and seasoned wood only served to remind Nicolas of another place, a faraway place and yet one not so far away if one knew where to look. The sound of crackling fires prompted memories of a bookish study other than his father's. A massive gatekeep's private chamber stocked to its brim with teetering stacks of books, parchment scrolls and dark whispers of mystery. It, too, had resounded with the lively splutter and split of a spirited fire dancing inside a peculiarly engraved firebasket. It, too, held a strange but unmistakable sense of home. A *second* home, this one. A home long lost, a home newfound. A sense of home somehow deeper and older than the Bennett's sheltered farm cottage, somehow more profound than the home he'd always known situated in the sheepherder's countryside outside of Plumpton Head, England.

Along with pangs of guilt and grief and Christmas expectation, this year Nicolas felt the added loss of a home he knew very little of. But of the little he'd once come to know, he loved it. A land of mysterious warrior kings, blacksmith giants, fearsome Wisps, and the ancient horror of real dragons. Above all else—in a way Nicolas hadn't felt since before Jack had slipped away seven years before—that faraway place held the promise of true friends. The kind of friends Nicolas greatly needed. The kind of friends who could laugh together, who could travel together, who trusted each other, understood each other, and even in moments of extreme peril, who saved each other whatever the cost.

Friends Nicolas was now convinced he'd lost forever, much as he'd lost Jack so many Christmas's ago.

Before all of that, several years before when Nicolas was a bit younger, the wintry cheerfulness of Christmastime had been among his favorite seasons.

When England's northwestern autumns gave way to winter's roaring gusts of stinging wind and sleet-spiked rains, Nicolas would look forward to the first gauging snowfall, a settling in of cold weather that invited deep mugs of cream tea and mulled eggnog, the woodsy fragrance of pine wreaths, the sheltering weight of woolen mufflers and mittens, the glitter of tinsel and advent candles, and his school's nativity play which always preambled an eagerly awaited holiday from classes and school work. And over the past seven years since Jack's passing, Nicolas had sensed his parents were determined to make Christmas feel like Christmas had once felt but the memory of Jack remained there like the shadow in the corner behind the Christmas tree, always present in the family's hearts and minds, but there was an almost tangible effort to dilute grief with an abundance of Christmastime joy. There were always one or two colorfully wrapped presents that appeared on early Christmas mornings, and every Christmas Day Nicolas looked forward to Mrs. Bennett's famous midday dinner—inevitably served much later than planned, sometime past one o'clock. Roast brown turkey filled with peppered stuffing piled high on porcelain plates. Lumpy potatoes, great spoonfuls of sticky brown gravy, deep red cranberry sauce, steamed carrots, turnips, and parsnips, and brussel sprouts, which Nicolas did his absolute best to avoid at all costs, heaped high in serving crockeries. And for "afters" there were sweet cobbler desserts delicately spooned into small chinaware bowls and saucers, rimmed with chipped gold paint, brimming with boiled Christmas puddin' and brandy butter—every saucer garnished with playful, bright sprigs of holly laid in wreathes around the edges.

Nicolas' great aunt, Harriet Lorretta Cheesebottom, an excessively fat woman with an excessively unpleasant character, always joined the Bennett's festive celebration. Nicolas' father would have to drive to Carlisle to fetch the large, fleshy woman and her annual platter of very traditional Bath buns made from rich egg and butter dough, coated in thickened sugar, and sprinkled with caraway seeds. Aunt Harriet would grouse and grumble the entire drive back to Plumpton Head without uttering so much as a hasty thank you or even a Happy Christmas. And much to Nicolas' constant irritation, would never fail to eat much more than her fair share of roast potatoes and gravy, sopping them loudly off her plate with more than her fair share of warm Christmas bread all the while dribbling fatty globs of food onto the immense curve of her much-too-large stomach. With Jack gone, Nicolas would end up sitting next to Aunt Harriet. This meant when it was time to pop the crackers at the dinner table, he would have to strain to reach his right hand across himself, far enough to grasp the end of the foil tube she held in front of her much-too-large stomach, before pulling the end of the foil and dropping the cracker's surprise contents—a clever joke, a simple trinket, and a folded paper crown—into the gluttonous mess of her plate's left-over meat bits, bread crumbs, turkey bones, and streaks of congealed gravy. Sarah Bennett would cover her mouth, trying to stifle her affectionate laughter as Nicolas dutifully put on his paper crown wetted with meat juice and bejeweled with flecks of mashed potatoes.

At three o'clock sharp, with everyone still groaning from full stomachs, Mr. Bennett would gather the family in front of the telly—the much-too-large Aunt Harriet always taking up much-too-much room on the sofa—to watch Her Royal Majesty's traditional Christmas broadcast. Afterwards Mr. Bennett would retreat to his study, propping his sock feet on his overstuffed footstool and declaring he was going to squeeze in a bit o' a nap before the six o'clock round of cheese and pickle sandwiches, scones with butter, jam, and clotted cream, Yorkshire curd tarts, and steaming black tea in small china cups. The day after Christmas, Boxing Day, Mrs. Bennett and Aunt Harriet—who never stopped complaining about her aching back, the large moles on her fat neck, or the ever-present wart on her finger—would trundle off in the Bennett's dented Range Rover to go shopping in Penrith, while Nicolas played with new toys, read new comic books and delighted in the absence of his great aunt.

But *this* year, this *particular* Christmas Eve, felt different to Nicolas. Like the muted pressure of a storm on a faraway horizon, a lonely sadness even more keen than he usually felt kept pushing back against the holiday's merriment.

In late autumn, he'd surprised his parents, telling them he didn't want a birthday party. He wanted one thing alone. He'd asked to visit the Will-o'-the-Wisp Medieval Fair stashed within the shadows of Yanwath Wood just north of Arkham Hall bordered to the east by the River Lowther. Baffled but in agreement, Mr. and Mrs. Bennett consented. His father, half-joking and half-uneasy having asked, "You alright in the head, lad? This year, yer mum and I can afford to throw a bit o' a party, or yer friends can join us at the fair." Nicolas politely said thank you but no, keeping his thoughts to himself, and on the chilly afternoon of 31st October the three of them made their way through the gate of the fair. With barely a wave goodbye over his shoulder, Nicolas made his way back up the Alewife's Alley, eagerly pushing through the usual noisy crowd of fair-goers, and stopped just short of the Cock & Bull Pub. His heart beating fast, anxious, excited, and restless all at once, Nicolas had been unable to find the overgrown footpath he'd once stumbled upon: a narrow trail that should have been just beyond the thoroughfare's well-trodden edge, concealed within a thicket of wild crab apple trees. Worse yet, a rickety, sagging picket fence now stood between him and the crab apple trees and when Nicolas, in a mounting sense of panic, threw his leg over it, one of the fair's meddling staffers, a towheaded, sweaty man dressed in an itchy brown tunic, gruffly told him to move along and to quit pokin' about in the bushes.

With a miserable and lost heart Nicolas mindlessly made his way back to his parents, looking now and then among the branches of scattered oak and alder trees for the happenchance glimpse of a once-familiar thrush. There was none to be seen.

For the rest of that dreary day, Nicolas had done his best to pretend he was enjoying the shows and food and games but inside, Nicolas—the once-Wren and Dragon Nightfall of a secret and hidden world—felt truly wretched. Helplessly alone.

He'd been nervous about returning but felt like he must all the same. A promise to keep, a feeling of wrong to make right.

Now a deep melancholy lay like a long shadow over his heart and for the next two months his thoughts had been full of ominous crows and coppery leaves, rowan trees, dark forests, and the impenetrable fogbanks of the Hollow Fen. The quiet strength of an orphaned bladesmith. The irrepressible faithfulness of a boy-thief. The haunting passion of a young Healer. He couldn't shake the feeling, anymore than he could a thousand times over the past year, that he'd made a terrible mistake by returning home to Plumpton Head, to his parents and the refuge of his attic bedroom. Nicolas couldn't shake the feeling he'd somehow let down Aldus Ward, the Laird of the First Gate and the greatest among the Commissioners of the Forfeited Gates of the City of Relic. Or that he had deserted Ranulf who'd so bravely stood by him, or Benjamin who had stubbornly believed in him, or Adelaide who had been perceptive enough to see past what seemed obvious and to accept what seemed impossible. Deserting those who'd not just called him a friend but who'd remained faithful even when it seemed Nicolas had betrayed them all.

Perhaps even more deeply, Nicolas felt he was letting down a man he'd barely known. The fabled first king of Telluric Grand's First Kingdom. His own grandfather.

"Nicolas!"

Snapped back to the present, Nicolas hopped off his chair and trudged into the cubby boot room where Mr. Bennett still sat on a low bench, wrestling his wet boots off thickly socked feet.

"Yes, Dad?"

"I left ol' Jasper Carrot outside, lad. He was barkin' all sorts o' nonsense at some long shadows out in the sheep pasture." Peter Bennett smiled kindly at Nicolas. "My toes were beginnin' ta feel a tad frosty. Besides," his father laid a calloused hand to the side of his mouth and said in a mock whisper loud enough for Mrs. Bennett to hear, "I didn't want ta miss havin' a warm glass of yer mum's Christmas wine before she closes the kitchen fer the night." Nicolas heard his mum's teasing *hrumph* from the warm kitchen and grinned back at his father. "Could ya have a butchers an' go find 'im, my boy?"

Nicolas reached for his dark green, lambswool scarf. "No worries, Dad. I'll fetch him."

"Nicolas."

"Yes, sir?"

"Everything alright?" His father's face was tight with concern. "Ya seem so far away, lad. I know this past year has seemed a strange one tho' I'm not certain why. Things always *do* get better."

Nicolas shook his head. "I'm fine, Dad. Really, I am."

Mr. Bennett nodded, reached out and squeezed Nicolas' arm. "Yer Mum an' I 'ave always said yer the kind that carries too many troubles too quietly. Love ya, son."

"Love you, too, Dad."

Nicolas turned away before his brief smile faded and away he went, a miserable and heartbroken Wren. Off into the cold, empty space of a long winter's solstice night.

The sharp air was all frost and bitterness. It made him gasp. He shoved his hands into the bottom of his trouser pockets and plunged his face deep behind his scarf's protective wrap.

"Jasper!" The wool in front of his mouth muddled his voice. A blanket of December snow was settling itself atop the small yard's wooden fence and spanning out across the gentle roll of the sheep pasture. Looking down, Nicolas spotted a snowy muddle of paw prints near the yard's open gate. "Stone the crows!" he muttered. His breath felt warm and moist inside the wool, and as he hurried out of the gate he wished he'd taken a moment more to grab his wool coat and knit cap.

The fallen snow was the worn color of old, grey bone, bespeckled with sparkling gems. The wind was shaping the snow into shadowy ripples that in the moon's diminishing light looked like long skeleton finger-joints lying still on the ground.

Nicolas paused at the edge of the field. A distant look came over his face. The grim colored ripples brought to mind an awful memory, a dark memory of cluttered and gnawed bones and carcass scraps—*human* carcass scraps—littering the soiled floor of an ogre's stony lair. The rancid hideaway of a bent, evil creature named Sultan. A hole of drafty stone tucked near the Falls of Cadgamlan, dark waters that roiled under the sinister canopy of the Black Forest's black trees; a stinking hole strewn with a cruel assortment of chewed bones, dirty and stippled with shriveled bits of ligament and rotten meat—the left-over flesh of several unfortunate travelers whom the ogre had ambushed and rabidly devoured.

Nicolas shivered.

He glanced at his shabby Malham boots, his eyes no longer seeing the snow piling high around him. Instead, clear as the light of the morning sun streaming through his attic bedroom's window, Nicolas could see Adelaide Ashdown's lifeless body. Her pale skin smeared in her own bright blood, being dragged along the ground behind Sultan as if she were a catch of fresh game the ogre had just killed.

He gave his head a forceful shake but the disturbing image didn't easily wear away. It left him uneasy.

Somewhere in the snow-stilled distance, Nicolas caught the quick clip of Jasper's high bark and looked up just in time to see the blur of the black and tan setter bolt out of the shadowed tree line on the far side of the pasture. As soon as the dog appeared, it was gone again, lost within the inky dark. A blotting ribbon of lifeless trees that looked a little too much like the Black Forest.

"Jasper!" he shouted. A cold, quick twist of fear gripped his insides. The barking grew faint and with a last, upsetting howl, died off.

"Stone the crows!" Nicolas said again more out of panic than anger. He stiffened himself against the cold and set out toward the treeline's ominous smudge. Jasper usually responded to his voice but something must've got into the dog. The family's setter was nowhere to be seen or heard.

The late December night lay still, silent as a black roll of soft felt shrouded in white silk.

Nicolas squinted his eyes as he trudged through close rows of undulated snow. Wet flurries tossed his hair and icy wind bit meanly at his ears. Marbled grey bruises of thickening clouds clotted every part of the night's sky. The moon and stars were all gone as if they, too, had slipped stealthily after Jasper, losing themselves among the murky patch of shadowed trees across the field.

Nicolas shuddered.

With a gasp, he tucked his chin to his chest, pulled his scarf up and pushed swiftly across the hushed pasture, his boots kicking through skeletal ripples of bone-grey snowfall. Less than a minute later he, too, was swallowed by the wood's long winter's glooms.

The young English boy from Plumpton Head, lost, hurting and feeling very much alone inside, was finally headed home.

CHAPTER 2

A Cold, Wet Burrow

Several miles to the north of the Bennett's home outside Plumpton Head but not as far north as Brampton flows a gentle river named The Gelt.

The River Gelt, timeless yet not much more than a stream, flows down Geltsdale Middle toward the direction of Cumrew Fell before wending its way through Greenwell and under the Newcastle & Carlisle Railway. Eventually the bywater finds its peaceful way through a modest stretch of secluded woodland, a pleasantly tousled collection of lovely beech trees, oak, and elder trees, a modest woods colonized by braces of wild duck, ghostly flocks of long-legged heron, and clannish drays of grey squirrels. In certain places The Gelt's peaty brown waters run close along a stretch of high walls made of crudely chiseled rock. A hoary-brown rock that once, a very, very long time ago, had been cut by hundreds, thousands perhaps, of war-scarred Roman legionnaires. Rome's imperial soldiers who'd busied themselves building a lean border wall meant to protect the western occupiers from savage tribes of Scots that swept down from the north like mortal winterfrost, howling vengeance and death. A few of those Roman soldiers-turned-stone-masons left behind carved inscriptions in the high walls of hoary-brown rock, their names mostly but also tidbits about their army units, officers, and august emperors who ruled the civilized world from a faraway and long-since dead empire. And sometimes, as Nicolas' father had once found, the soldier-masons would leave a tidbit about themselves, too.

Deep inside the copse of woods on the far side of the sheep pasture next to the Bennett's cottage home, not far from the enormous trunk of Nicolas' favorite English elm tree—the Red Deer Tree—there stood a solitary, weighty stone. It jutted out of the forest floor at an odd angle and stood approximately two feet high. This out-of-place stone was perched near the sloped shoulder of a snaking depression that cut and wound its way under tree and bush; an ambling rut in the forest floor which served as a part-time brook when heavy spring rains fell. When Nicolas was several years younger and Jack was still alive, Mr. Bennett had pointed out the strange stone to the boys during one of his customary Saturday morning long walks, a late autumn adventure the three of them had shared on an unusually quiet October day. It wasn't often Jack or Nicolas went with their father which made the outing all the more special. The stone seemed to Nicolas like a giant's lost tooth, half-buried and crookedly capped with a wet splat of leafy moss sprouting from a crack in its crown, a bit of unchewed spinach the giant had never picked out. Jack must have thought the same thing.

"Looks jus' like Nicolas' front teeth after dinner!" he'd said, laughing his wonderfully wobbly laugh. The disease that had already begun to steal his life away had done very little—then or even a year later when it seemed everything was gone except for his constant smile and silvery grey eyes—to change how cheerful Jack always was.

"No it don't!" Nicolas popped off. A shade before his sixth birthday, he couldn't think of more of a defense than that. Keeping up with his father's long strides, made no less long with Mr. Bennett carrying twelve-year-old Jack's spindly frame piggy-back, had caused Nicolas to be out of breath. "I don't have no spin'ch in my teef," he panted.

Jack laughed and reached down trying to tussle his brother's curly hair. "I meant nothin' by it, Nicky," he'd said, smiling ear to ear. "Yer a wise chap, of course, keeping a bit of yer dinner in yer teeth for when yer hungry later."

Nicolas scowled and wheezed bursts of air out of his nose. "Yer a ninny!" He cast a quick eye toward his father to see if his name-calling had crossed the line. Peter Bennett, an arboriculture professor at the Askham Bryan College's agricultural campus and a historian at heart, was much too excited about the stone to pay any mind to his sons' messing about. Carefully, he swung Jack around to his front and set him down on a matt of elm leaves near the stone. "Look here," said Mr. Bennett, gesturing to the stone's face. "'Tis a bit of ancient history, lads." Nicolas knelt by his father in front of the upright stone and years later was still able to recall the rough feel of the weathered rock as his fingertips traced a series of coarse cuts in its scoured surface. Jack, who was practically buried inside their grandfather's British army greatcoat, fished a skinny arm out of one of its long, heavy sleeves and did the same. The chiseled cuts were in two lines of familiar-looking letters but the words they formed were strange to Nicolas.

"What do they mean?" he'd asked, tracking his small fingers through the worn valleys of each chisel mark.

Frowning, his father tilted his head to one side for several moments. "Well, I can't be sure. Some of the marks are a bit washed out but if my Latin serves to remember, I think it says, *I am free, therefore, I owe.*" His thoughtful frown deepened. "I hope the poor bloke who wrote it wasn't a deserter. I think the punishment for desertion was stoning or being cudgeled to death. There were Romans, you see, battle-hardened soldiers, brought here from far away to fight and conquer the people who lived here before them. They had very strict armies and fought very hard, but some of those ancient people fought back so fiercely the Romans had to build walls to protect themselves. Roman armies didn't travel with any bricklayers so they put their soldiers to work building those walls. Army life was very harsh and there must've been at least a few soldiers who wanted something better, I imagine." Mr. Bennett stared at the quiet forest around them. "Maybe the wildness of Liberty they encountered in the people they tried to conquer weighed on their souls. Maybe it did more to breech their walls than any battle ever could. Maybe it called to them. Maybe it called to them to be free."

Nicolas at the time not entirely sure what it meant to be 'cudgeled' guessed it meant something terrible. He nodded his head in as much somber agreement as he could. "Maybe he got free, Dad. The fella who wrote this." His eyes widened with a thought. "Maybe he lived in the forest."

"Maybe," Mr. Bennett said, lifting his eyebrows. "Maybe he did." Nicolas watched his father glance at Jack who still had his thin hand on the stone. Jack's face was pale in the shaded light and his eyes were closed. "Maybe he did, lad," Mr. Bennett said again but softly, "an' such freedom can sometimes come with peculiar burdens."

Nicolas scrunched his face, trying to think of a person who was truly free, who didn't have any burdens, who didn't have to submit to anyone else. Someone above everyone else. "The Queen!" he'd said triumphantly. "The Queen is free!" His eyes alight, full of self-satisfaction.

"Well, yes, I suppose 'er Majesty is free in a sense." Chuckling, his father ran his fingers through Nicolas' mop of hair. "But as a good Queen, she's also pledged her life to her kingdom—to you an' me, Nicolas. To us all. We're her subjects, my boy. She's supposed to rule for our benefit along with those in Government. I'm not sure if that's real freedom." He rubbed his chin, looking up into the sweep of tree branches above them. "That's her burden, I think, for being free. For being the Queen." Then, in the peculiar way the bookish Mr. Bennett would sometimes do, he rested a gentle hand atop the stone and, raising his chin as if he were delivering a lecture, quoted a few lines of timeworn poetry.

But snarling wolf no longer haunts the fell,
Fit target for the savage chieftain's spear;
Nor bounding hart seeks shelter in the dell.
Once clothed with forest, now a desert drear;

The wild beast dies where treads the step of man;
The wild man dies where treads the step of Time;

The hills alone unchanged from span to span,
In silence lift their granite crowns sublime.

"An' *that's* all I know," Mr. Bennett finished with a sly wink at Nicolas as Jack opened his eyes.

"I like that, Dad," Jack said quietly, staring at the stone. "*The hills alone unchanged from span to span.* I like old things. It's a special stone, I think." He looked down at the slight shape of his withered legs hidden beneath the wrap of the khaki greatcoat. "I think I know how that soldier must've felt wanting to be free." His voice wasn't sad, wistful perhaps but far from self-pitying, and his face broke into a broad grin. "And I think if you're free, you owe it to others who aren't to be as free as you can… to somehow… to somehow take them with you in your freedom." He straightened up as much as he could under the weight of the greatcoat's heavy wool and the even heavier weight of the disease inside him. "That means a piggyback ride home, Dad!" So off they went, autumn's evening at their heels.

In Nicolas' mind, the peaceful woods seemed to hold the echo of his brother's voice long after Jack was gone. An echo that stuck in Nicolas' memory for years to come.

If you're free, you owe it to others who aren't.

In later years, Nicolas would sometimes pretend the ancient stone was the tombstone of a fallen king, or the enormous toe of a buried giant, or the tip of a dinosaur's bone. Something protective inside him wouldn't ever again let him see it as his brother had—a lost tooth with a funny bit of spinach in it.

Most often he would simply sit beside it or he would stare at the rough letters, traveling his fingers along their worn course as he and Jack once had, forever wondering who'd carved them. A deserter, a legionnaire? A lost soul who'd fled from his army unit exchanging the grist mill of hard labor and the harshness of army life for the crude dangers of a once-ancient Britain? Nicolas wondered why the man had said he *owed* something? Was it a debt? A niggling sense of personal honor? A favor to be repaid? Or, as Nicolas' quiet heart privately chose to believe, because the long-dead stone-author felt he must live his life on behalf of someone who couldn't? A chiseled inscription to memorialize a lasting obligation; an obligation to be fulfilled as long as the stone stood, thousands of years and generations upon generations. The stone, shrouded in the woods like a memory buried in the folds of the mind, stood as Nicolas' own private promise to Jack. It wasn't a painful place; it made him feel hopeful and purposeful even if it also held the shadow of loss.

And on this particularly cold, dark Christmas Eve, in the year of his thirteenth birthday, Nicolas thought he'd heard Jasper's bark coming from the direction of the ancient stone.

"Jasper!" he called out again but heard nothing in return. "Sweet fanny adams! Where in the world has he gone to?"

A few snowflakes settled in soft whispers amid the deep gloam of ghostly trees—fat, feathery flakes of frozen damp cold. The woods around him were silent. Even the wind hadn't dared follow him inside the woods. Everything stood still, hushed, and the quiet didn't feel very welcoming. In a place he'd often come to find a private escape from life at school, Nicolas now felt very alone. The merriment of Christmastime, his mother's lovely singing, his father's warm study, the safety of his attic bedroom, and the closeness of the Bennett home were all behind him, lost somewhere outside the shadowed throng of trees surrounding him. *The hills alone unchanged*, he thought. *In silence lift their granite crowns*. High above him, shore-like breakers of gusting snowfall lapped over tree branches like waves submerging barren sandbars until all that could be seen was the white foam of a grim winter's groundswell. Just as they had the day he, Jack, and his father had wondered at the carved stone, the woods lay solemnly muted, submerged under December's cold tide.

"Jasper!" Nicolas urged again in a hissing whisper. He dodged beneath cold snarls of crooked oak and elm branches. "Here, boy!"

Ahead in the dim light, he could begin to make out the greyish tooth of the chiseled stone and within several strides, he was standing in front of it. He looked around through the gloom but Jasper was nowhere to be seen.

Stone the crows! Nicolas swept a hand at the pile of damp snowflakes in his hair. *Where did he get off to this time?*

He took a step back from the grey stone, down along the gentle slope of the waterless streambed. As he had so often before out of habit, he stared for a moment at the grey, chiseled letters. He mouthed the words, *I am free, therefore, I owe*. He thought of Jack sitting next to the stone. He thought of his brother's wobbly laugh that was sometimes so hard to now imagine. And surprisingly, he suddenly thought of Benjamin Rush, the smallish boy-thief telling the story of a Cowbird giving up its chick so it could have a better life; a story that helped Benjamin make sense of why his mother had orphaned him and why Nicolas had done what he'd done when he'd killed the dragon over a year ago. Why he'd *had* to do what he'd done to kill the Shadow Thief, Árnyék Tolvaj, a fourth generation overlord dragon. Freedom, gaining it, giving it, keeping it, was a troublesome thing Nicolas still struggled to understand. "I'm sorry, Jack," Nicolas mumbled through numbed lips. He didn't know why he'd said it.

Instead of leafy moss, a coronet of silvery snow capped the head of the chiseled stone. But something else sat atop the snow. Something he somehow hadn't seen before as if it just appeared or had just come into focus. A most curious thing; a dark ribbony thing. A black scar against the bone-white snow. A single, great, black feather.

Nicolas stumbled backward. A menacing tenseness flooded inside him.

Where is Jasper? he thought, desperately needing to be back in the warmness and shelter of the Bennett's farmhouse.

As if on cue Jasper's bark suddenly jumped out of the impenetrable dimness to his right, somewhere further up the streambed. Eager to be shut of the gloom and the worrisome black feather, Nicolas leapt in the direction of the bark, bending low beneath the whip and grasp of low-hanging branches. After several yards, he caught a teasing glimpse of the family dog's hindquarters just before it disappeared again in the densest blot of blackness, even darker than the shadows surrounding him.

"*Jasper!*" Nicolas insisted in a furious and desperate whisper.

Nothing.

"*Jasper*," he hissed and crept closer to where he'd seen the dog vanish. The charcoal-smudge of shadows in front of him seemed to pour into an even darker hole. It was as if this small eye of the woods—this little bit of the brook's shallow seam—entirely ceased to exist, pulling everything around it into some kind of black nothingness. Nicolas stared and stared, his eyes trying to make sense of the strange void, now wishing he'd brought a flashlight along before charging out of the house and into the snow whipped night.

As if to tempt him further, Jasper barked again but this time the dog's yap sounded far away, stifled. In a sudden snap of common sense, Nicolas knew why. The hare-brained dog had simply chased a rabbit or something like that down inside its winter burrow. The inky stain of darkness was the opening to some animal's home tunneled deep inside the frosty winter's earth. Jasper had crawled in after it, probably stuck in the process.

"Stone the crows," he said, shaking his head and looking up into the blue-black shamble of leafless branches. "Just brilliant."

As aggravated as he was Nicolas honestly felt a masterful sense of relief. He unwrapped the thick scarf from around his neck and pawed around blindly, locating the broken stump of a nearby bough on which to hang it. *Mum's not gonna like this*, he thought, groaning with regret as he dropped to his knees into the clammy litterfall of rotting leaves and snow-soaked mud.

The strong odor of decaying bark and soggy, chilled moss filled his nose. The soggy earth drenched the knees of his trousers and an icy cold crawled up his legs. Nicolas scrambled forward, ducking his head to avoid bumping the lip of the burrow. After a foot or so he was forced to flop onto his stomach, pulling himself along with his elbows and pushing himself forward with the toe-edges of his boots. The burrow's floor was no longer squelchy mud but still felt damp and clammy instead of being the kind of dry, comfortable den Nicolas thought an overwintering animal would make. Instead of soft sand, the ground felt more like the prickle of pitted stone.

"*Jasper!*"

Nicolas' forced whisper rasped inside his throat as he muscled along. *That dog's a daft cow, crawlin' in a dodgy hole like this in the middle of the bloomin' night.* Feathery shakes of dirt and squiggled tails of roots tickled inside his collar. He spluttered and spittered and gave his head a furious snap to keep what felt like wispy cobwebs out of his face. He couldn't see a thing, much less the hind-end of his stubborn dog. Nicolas stopped moving to listen but heard nothing ahead of him. Just silence. Cold, wet, tomb-like, and baffling silence.

Then, with a violent shiver from his curly hair to his cold toes, Nicolas instinctively jerked his chin to his chest as if to protect himself. A sense of certainty struck him like the quick moving violence of winter storms born in the Irish Sea. In the bleak damp belly of that dark and stony burrow Nicolas' nose was filled with a smell distinctively out of place for a small copse of woods tucked away in northwest England. A smell that shouldn't have been inside that earthy burrow at all. His nose tingled with the sharp, brackish tang of *salt water*. And like that, the once-Wren and Dragon Nightfall knew exactly where he was. This time no thrush led the way. No little man with a round belly beckoned him on. Joy and fright and thrill shuddered in Nicolas' fast-beating heart.

Expected or not, the quiet boy from Plumpton Head, England, knew he'd finally *arrived* home again.

CHAPTER 3

Over a Cliff's Edge

An age-worn but familiar voice filled Nicolas' head. *There are places and spaces we share*, it said. *Old towns, old woods, old caves, old castles, old graveyards, and even old storm cellars.*

The voice's grey owner wore a linen tunic under a dark green woolen cloak embroidered with silver leaves and vines along its long hem and collar; a simple leather belt wrapped at the waist. He had one bright blue eye sparkling with flecks of gold and emerald and one dead-eye, milky white and sightless with a scar that stretched from under its lower lid, down a high cheekbone and into the depths of one of the thickest and fullest beards Nicolas had ever seen.

Come now, Master Bennett, said the voice, a memory Nicolas carried of Aldus Ward, the remarkable Laird of the First Gate of the City of Relic, St. Wulf's-Without-Aldersgate, and the greatest among the Commissioners of the six Forfeited Gates. *You and I have much to discuss, I think.*

The recollection of that conversation on that strange, wonderful evening when Nicolas first glimpsed his purpose in Telluric Grand flooded back over him as if he was sitting in one of the high-backed chairs in Aldus' private study watching a lively fire dance away in the fireplace. Aldus spoke again. *I'd much rather begin with* answers *than with questions, my boy. Answers, after all, are tidier than questions because answers know where they belong. Questions, anyway,* most *questions, have no idea where they're going or where they belong.* You, *Master Bennett, have questions because you have no idea where you're going or where you belong. I, however, have* answers *because I* am *where I belong.*

Nicolas smiled and a warm flash flittered inside the cold bulbs of his cheeks. In the same way an *answer* knows where it *is* while a question only wonders where it is *supposed* to be, Nicolas knew the answer to what had happened to the Bennett's family dog. He knew exactly what was causing salty air to fill his nose; why prickly pitted wet rock was beneath his hands. Aldus' voice, as alive as if the great Laird was sitting in a wing-backed chair inches away, told him so. It didn't matter that he'd never been in that exact spot before. Like a mountaineer's first summit atop an ice-sheathed crag, Nicolas undeniably knew *where* he was. And that knowledge kept his chin pinned to his chest for several minutes, bracing for whatever might come after.

Gradually… measure by measure… Nicolas felt the silence around him begin to squirm. The burrow's quietness seemed to writhe like a living thing. It twisted and wriggled and fidgeted. Slowly, ponderously, the thick noiseless coils inside the burrow uncoiled and Nicolas could finally *hear* something—not words, sounds. Sounds like the advancing swell of a coming windstorm pressing through a thousand leaf-rich branches. The restless air came with cool whispers of a curious breeze, licking his cold-numbed cheeks and tussling the curls of his hair. He took a moment to put it all together. The enlarging sound he heard wasn't just wind. The whooshing whorls of sound were the booms and crashes of emerald-dark waves. Their thundering sound rumpled back the burrow's changeling silence as if they were wadding a piece of paper into a scrap of nothingness. This was a shoreside sound never yet heard in the countryside outside of Plumpton Head, England. A striving energy of great volumes of water, sucking and pulling and assembling into monstrous reels that dashed against rock and shell and sand like infinite columns of heavy cavalry stampeding from a fantastical sea. Indeed, from Telluric Grand's Cold Sea. The report and rumble of deep waves rising and falling, disassembling along the bluffs and irregular shores of the First Kingdom, filled Nicolas' ears. The thunderous sound of waves stuffing and heaving inside the burrow's tight space.

Out there, from what was moments before the deadened end of a soggy, winter burrow, lay the magic, mysticism, and legends of an ancient and terrible Cold Sea. Out there, dragons had once waited for him. The depths of the squelchy burrow had magically become *out there*, and out there he began to see the shimmer of millions of pen-lights. Stars' lights in a night sky. Out there, mere feet away from Nicolas, stars and constellations unknown pricked at the fabric of space.

To point our path, and light us to our home.

Like a snare's noose that snatched at the leap of a wild hare, another voice caught Nicolas' thoughts. Immediately the massing sound of tide and surf somehow lessened. *To point our path, and light us to our home.* This new voice, a different voice than the one with the sightless eye, was his father's calming, wistful voice. *They point our path, Nicolas, and light us to our home.* It was part of something Mr. Bennett had always said the night before every birthday Nicolas could ever remember.

His dad would sit on the edge of Nicolas' bed, draw a leg up across the other and would gaze philosophically out of the attic bedroom's small window at the night sky. "Long ago, a much-forgot but great English poet wrote there is a '*tongue in every star*' that speaks to each of us, Nicolas, stars," he'd softly say, "they're '*citadels of light, and seats of gods.*' Each year you'll grow older, my boy, an' each year you'll find out a little more about yourself than you've known before." His father would then sit quietly, sometimes for so long Nicolas would be near asleep before he'd hear Mr. Bennett let out a thinking sigh and almost under his breath, as if he were alone, hear him quote,

From what pure wells
Of milky light, what soft o'erflowing urn,
Are all these lamps so fill'd? these friendly lamps,
For ever streaming o'er the azure deep
To point our path, and light us to our home.

Memories of his father's words, alone in the winter murk of a burrow-turned-door, made Nicolas feel *less* alone. Less lost, belly-down on a rim of magic between two worlds. The dark around him lightened a shade and he began to raise his head. The crashing waves returned; the salted air grew stronger; yet his father's voice continued firmly over it all.

...Let me here,
Content and grateful, wait the appointed time,
And ripen for the skies: the hour will come
When all these splendours bursting on my sight
Shall stand unveiled, and to my ravished sense
Unlock the glories of the world unknown.

Nicolas clenched his jaw. *Even if I can't see the stars, they're there. They're out there somewhere. They'll point my path and guide me home. Home.*

He looked up, and as if looking through the reverse end of a telescope Nicolas could see the far-flung sparkle of stars, scattering slivers of gold-flecked light across a wide, fearsome expanse of watery dread, across the night-black heaves and hauls of the Cold Sea. Nicolas, after all, had crawled into a sea cave.

Beyond it, out there, rose the high sweeps of the First Kingdom's shore. Out there, outside a sea cave that somehow lay hidden inside a gloomy winter's burrow tucked within a quiet copse of English wood, was the mysterious and ancient realm of Telluric Grand.

A place Nicolas' grandfather had once known, long, long ago.

Nicolas felt an inward pull toward the gritty, faint pen-lights. He swayed back and forth on his hands and knees, queerly off balance and, a bit unexpectedly, bewildered. He was where he'd so desperately wanted to be for over a year's time yet he wasn't *exactly* where he'd wanted to be, where he thought he'd be. He lay muddy and wet, trapped in the recesses of a sodden sea cave somewhere above the blast and bellow of waves as they thumped against an ancient shore's stone walls. He was cold and shivering. His ears hurt, his hands were chilled and scuffed. His clothes were soaked. His eyes stung from the sour spindrift of a brackish, coastal haze, a soupy, creeping shroud of foggy droplets that rose like spellbound ghosts from a ragged shoreline far, far below. The shuddering power of spent waves prickled their way through weathered rock, juddering into the flesh of his stiff-cold arms. He licked the salt water's bitter taste from his damp lips. His nose smarted with prickly nips of raw, cold air, fresh yet ageless at the same time.

Nicolas looked again past the sea cave's scoured floor. The view was dim, but he could see the floor of the cave seem to vanish a few yards ahead, opening its storm-chapped mouth into the midnight bruise of the starlit sky. Unseen was the fading moon, pitched high and away from the distant, eastern horizon; its sallow gloss reflecting dimly across the sea's rutted surface, creating a faint but jumbled path of cobbled bricks athwart an endless prairie of greenish-black water, pointing the way toward a coming sunrise.

Spread before Nicolas in a hued panorama of greys, black-blues, and bottle greens, all beneath the glowing, sparkling crystals of countless strange stars, was the haunting and terrible vastness of the Cold Sea. A wave-chopped and treacherous borderland that lay between the First Kingdom's ordered realm and distant barbarian chaos. A watery border between peace and war. From here, where the First Kingdom's soaring, sandstone cliffs repulsed the clamor and confusion of dark, deep waves for centuries, had sometimes come brutal clans of hellish War Crows. The Crows came like sea-wraiths borne out of salt-mist and landless horizons, scavenging, thieving and murdering without mercy, until, blood-sotted and gorged with treasure, slaves, and the souls of those they'd killed, they would vanish again somewhere into the far eastern ocean.

Nicolas the once-Wren and Dragon Nightfall had unwittingly and unintentionally crawled out of a quiet English Christmas Eve. Not as he once had, through an iron door at the end of a wooded path of mossy grey crab apple trees and into the thin, wet edge of a long-fought and desperate struggle between the civilized rule of law and the chaos of savage madness.

There are places and spaces we share, the grey voice in his head again repeated, it was the kindly voice of Aldus Ward. *Old towns*, the old man whispered, *old woods, old caves, old castles, old graveyards, and even old storm cellars.*

And see what I've done, thought Nicolas, *I've found an old cave*. When he shivered this time, it wasn't because his arms or legs were trembling from the salt-wet cold. For a while, Nicolas, the grandson of a warrior-king, simply stayed where he was.

After a time, the thirteen-year-old Wren from the quiet countryside outside of Plumpton Head pulled himself together. He folded his wet, chilled legs beneath him and crossed his arms tightly about his chest. He licked coarse salt from his lips and watched as wafts of curling clouds veiled the fragile, pale light of the moon. Lost in thought, he listened to the doomed march of waves as they hurled themselves against the hard stones below, and every so often he would glance over his shoulder into the dark recess of the burrow-cave. It remained black as roof-pitch. There wasn't anything he could see that looked familiar or that looked as if it might lead back to the dry creek bed, the chiseled stone, the Bennett's farm cottage, or back to the snow-frosted Christmas Eve unfolding in a quiet corner of England.

The open mouth of the cave was all he could see. All that seemed left.

Its dimpled lip of rock dropped off into empty sky and, aside from the Cold Sea below, Nicolas couldn't hear anything that might suggest what lay outside the cave. What might suggest the presence of a friend or foe. Not the creak of burdened cartwheels rolling along some nearby path. Not the snap and crack of a ship's stiff sails straining against a taut mast. Not the bellowed warnings of a gatekeep's night watchman. Not the wind-carried cries of hungry gulls. Nothing but the Cold Sea as it flung its immense shoulders against the stubborn bulwark of the cliff's sandstone shoals.

Like the persistence of the dark water below, year-old memories surged against his worrisome thoughts, wearing away their concern. Memories of the City of Relic, of Aldus Ward, of Nicolas' three, adventure-sworn friends, of a sacrificial, dying Wisp; memories that leapt back to life inside his head even as the memories of his own attic bedroom, the Bennett's glittering Christmas tree, and the caroling voice of his lovely mum, slipped quietly away into the inky blackness of the cave's dark belly—these searched for a home, somewhere through the snowy branches of the still woods next to the sheep pasture littered with Jasper's pawprints. Like a broken bone mended even stronger than before, the bloody act Nicolas had once committed over a year ago had changed him profoundly. It recast him in some deep ways and in spite of a skulking sense of apprehension, he longed to see the mysterious and dangerous world of Telluric Grand again.

He felt pulled into the world in which he now sat but he felt unsure all the same and this surprised him. Telluric Grand, with all its dangers, all its wonders, where he'd done the most horrible thing for the greatest good, was where Nicolas had dreamed of returning. Even beyond the newfound friendships he'd gained, the powerful sense of closeness he'd felt as he, Adelaide, Benjamin, and Ranulf had traveled, eaten, laughed, and cried together. Nicolas had an intense desire to redeem himself. He wanted to prove to himself he was his grandfather's heir, wanted to show he possessed the blood of a king—the *first* king—in his veins.

But he couldn't shake the lingering sense of being alone. Perhaps it was the melancholy of Christmas time, a season haunted by sadness for a lost brother.

Now that he sat in a cold, wet cave, somewhere on the cusp of two worlds, Nicolas felt hesitant, fearful even. Afraid of failure even as he was pushed by the untested echo of his grandfather's legacy. No one stood to judge him or encourage him or hold him back. He thought of his classmates at Hunter Hall, romping about, playing schoolyard games of wizards, knights, witches, and make-believe spells. He wondered what they'd think if any of them were here, if Willa, Carson, Minnie, or Raphael found themselves sitting inside a sea cliff cave tucked high above the Cold Sea's pounding volleys of violent waves. What would they do? Would they crawl back looking for home or would they find out what lay beyond the encrusted lip of salty rock? He didn't know. But in his heart, Nicolas knew what *he* should do. Wet, cold, alone, and uncertain, he knew what he was *going* to do.

He sat there looking out of the unpromising mouth of the cave and without intending to, without any great fanfare or assurance of what might come, he quietly but firmly said those words he'd not said in a long, long time. "I'm a *wren*. I *am* a wren."

Nicolas hadn't said those three words in over a year. They felt graceless in his mouth like drawing an old sword from a rusty scabbard, but even though the sound of his small voice was lost amid the noisy sea, he'd said them.

And he meant it.

After what felt like a long time, Nicolas began to focus on his nearby surroundings. Shallow troughs in the cave's floor held spoonfuls of stagnant water, half-a-dozen gooseneck barnacles, several empty shells, and scraggles of rotted driftwood splinters. Aside from this, the sea cave held little else. Its walls and ceiling were gritty but smoother than its floor, and Nicolas guessed the cave had been carved out of the sandstone over eons of time, little by little, by endless ranks of tides and storms that had scaled the sea cliff's walls.

Nicolas rocked his weight forward to stand up, or bend slightly over as it were, and eased himself to the cave's edge. The cold bite of the seaborne breeze on his face tightened his skin as salt water seems to do. He closed his eyes and took in a deep breath. Like an unuttered promise. A private vow. A deep breath of the air of Telluric Grand. A secret realm, a nearby but hidden history, and a place his grandfather had once helped to shape and rule out of the grasping tentacles of destructive ferocity of clannish war.

Gradually, Nicolas opened his eyes. There was a physical intensity in the constellated stars, the waning cream-light of the moon's crescent, and the ruffled spread of the Cold Sea's chop. He felt wonderfully *awake*. Something deep inside had been stirred up and rediscovered. He felt energized, quickened. Nicolas gave his head a vigorous shake, glad of the night's chilled breeze, carelessly shaking his hair in tangled knots. For the slightest moment, an irrational moment, Nicolas felt like taking a swan's leap out of the cave and into the depths of the water thundering below. Instead, he stretched out his arms, his fingers tingling as each tip pressed into the soft belly of the seaborne wind. His neck muscles relaxed. He tilted his head back and took another deep breath.

England was gone. Nicolas was home.

Home? Nicolas thought with a laugh. So far away, yet so nearby. So mysteriously distant. But *home* nonetheless. Where his grandfather had once lived and served. Indeed, where he'd *reigned*.

Nicolas looked around for a way out of the cave—a way *in* so to speak—a way back to Relic, to Aldus, and most especially, to his friends. There, near his feet to the left, around the slight bulge of a sea-splashed rock he spied the pale thread of a grey path, a ledge really. A narrow, spindly, rough-cut course of rock, crudely hewn and not much more than a jutting scar carved into the uneven cheek of the cliff's face.

Nicolas hardly gave pause to the danger. He turned to the left side of the cave's opening, swung his right leg over a knob of algae-dressed rock and pushed himself out into space, out onto the ledge. And like that, he was outside the cave.

The sound of the waves swelled, clouting angrily against the sandstone below. But the moon's light, waxy, dull, but still the warmest mystery of the endless heavens, responded helpfully.

It pushed back an interfering pall of clouds and illuminated the path's thin scab of rock. Nicolas clung to the cliff's wall. Step by step he traversed several yards of the narrow ledge. He kept his face tightly against the rough stone until the outcrop widened just enough to allow him to turn his body in the direction he was headed. His left shoulder squeezed against the cliff; he moved forward and, gradually, *up*. The ledge, nothing more than the jutting lower lip of a great split stone, worked its way in a slow grade up the face of rock and within a few dozen shuffled footsteps, the top of Nicolas' head was even with lip of the cliff.

Hesitating, he took several, shallow breaths. The boldness of what he was doing had begun to sink in and he wasn't entirely sure he now wanted to peek over the crest. He could still turn back, no one the wiser.

There are times and spaces in a person's life when a decision *not* to do something remains forever personal. If he decided to return to the Bennett's farmhouse, no one would know, everything would be the same as it had been for the past year. No one would know except him. *He* would know. Nicolas would know. *What you do when no one is looking is who you are*, his mum would often say. And that, in the end, was enough.

With that he again said the words he'd long left unspoken. They came out of his mouth with the same firm determination as they had on that early Saturday, birthday morning in October more than a year before. Words he'd said when leaving the quiet of his attic bedroom not yet knowing he was bound for a place with dragons. Words he'd said moments before while on his hands and knees, looking out into that same strange world.

"I'm a *wren* today!" he shouted.

This time these words flung themselves over the thunder of the Cold Sea's waves, out into the vastness of the endless heavens. The high exclamation of a court's herald, announcing the heir to a king finally come home.

So up he went, Nicolas the Wren-once-more, pulling himself over the cliff's edge, the failing black of night to his front and the first, stealing shades of dawn at his back. Up he went. Bold. Content at heart. Up and over the cliff's edge, a daybreak's new sun beginning to throw back the grim night of a sea-lashed shore.

CHAPTER 4

The Shadow of a Crow

Nicolas' decision to launch himself over the sea cliff's edge, into a land of myths, giants, death, and ancient dragons, hadn't begun very well. His focus was on scrambling to his feet and not pitching backward over the cliff's jagged edge. Because of that, he didn't at first realize the circumstances into which he'd leapt.

The graveled cliff's edge was distracting and kept Nicolas concentrating on finding a steady grip in scallops of weather-gouged rock before hauling the rest of his body up. As his feet left the ledge's narrow shelf, he kept his body's center low, instinctively thrusting his chest forward, then his hips, then his legs over the ashen sandstone's grainy surface, scrambling until there was a level solidness of stony earth beneath him. With that, Nicolas popped himself upright the way a boy does, a damp easterly wind at his back, pushing him forward away from the dizziness of empty space.

Looking up, he slipped.

His left boot had come to rest on a black swatch of slick moss, and when he shifted his weight, his leg shot out from under him as if it were on a patch of dodgy ice. With no small bit of luck he fell forward, dropping down on his left knee and throwing out his hands to catch himself. With the almost effortless, natural reaction of youth, Nicolas again popped to his feet, this time taking a prudent half a step forward onto barren, worn rock. He set his feet cautiously and drew up to his full height… and for the first time, he actually looked around. And *that's* when he saw them.

There were three of them, all standing only a few yards away.

The first to catch his eye was a dreadful, huge, pale man. Heavily bearded with coarse, wiry hair that sprouted to the tops of his ears but otherwise bald, with no other hair across his shirtless chest. He was at least a full head taller than Nicolas' father and twice as wide. Shadowy stains of lettered tattoos twisted and snaked across the huge man's bare scalp, down the sides of his thick neck, over his broad shoulders, and spiraled around his enormous forearms which were bound tightly behind his back with dozens of lashes of knotted cord. Fleshy slithers of pink scar tissue crisscrossed his chest, some slight and some as wormy and as long as pigtails. Heavy ringlets of burnished copper drooped from his thick earlobes like windchimes. Worn belts of scraped leather, coiled with armlets of silvery bands, were wrapped around his thick, right wrist, although the man's left forearm ended abruptly in a handless stump; in place of a wrist was a mean sleeve of cracked leather punched through its end by a dull spit of chipped metal with a slight curve. Nicolas could see scratches, abrasions, and one or two deeper cuts in the pale man's scalp and across his knotty back and shoulders. These had left smears and streams of blood all over him, some scabbed and old, others fresh and bright red against his fish-belly white skin. His face was like the Halloween mask of costume gore. One of his eyes had been smashed and was a barely visible slit within a bulging, purplish bruise of tight skin, yet the huge man's cracked lips were stretched back in an uncaring, wicked smile. Blood-frothed spittle bubbled in the corners of his mouth while darker gutters of blood creased the defiles between his unhealthy, dull-yellow teeth. His face's rough, colorless skin looked stretched like wet cow hide, pulled back into deep creases at the corner of his undamaged eye. That undamaged eye was flat, narrow, and evil-looking. "Pinched like the devil's," Nicolas' mum might have said. The man was more brutal and more wretchedly cruel-looking than any man Nicolas had ever seen. He made Nicolas instantly afraid.

When the bound man spotted Nicolas hauling himself over the cliff's edge, his tightly strained cheeks slackened and his toothy, grinning mouth sagged open like the cavernous maw of a primeval bear. Whatever trace of color might have been left in his pallid skin drained away; his good eye widened and an elongating string of blood-mixed drivel suspended itself from his lower lip, moving back and forth like a clock's long pendulum. The huge man's tongue had been cut-out long ago, so he made nothing other than a gurgling noise.

Another man of more normal height stood a feet away from the huge man, topped by a simple steel helmet with a bent nose plate, a soiled leather shirt, mud-spattered boots, and filthy stained breeches. He wore a crimson colored coverlet belted at the waist which, in spite of its shabby appearance, boasted an ominous piece of embroidered work that had begun to unravel. The sewn image of a dreadful, clawed hand rising up from an ocean's deep-blue depths. The clawed hand was enormous compared to the small figure of a man swimming on the water's surface. A battered shield hung on the helmeted man's back, and a sword, jammed inside the length of a dented, dull scabbard, was shoved carelessly into his thick belt. This man held the end of a long, fat-linked chain; its other end was looped around the huge, pale man's raw neck, locked in place with a blunt pin the size of a coat peg. Even in the foredawn's first stabs of light the helmed man's prunish skin looked unwholesome, drab, as if he'd commonly spent most of his time hidden from the sun. His face was sour, scattered with bits of bristly hair, and Nicolas' first impression was that he looked somewhat like a blind shrew.

Indeed, this man didn't see Nicolas at first. His smallish eyes, blinking snappishly from under the lip of his helmet, were fixated on his large and sinister prisoner. His fists clenched the chain and his elbows were tensed, bent, ready to jerk the weight of the chain into his shoulder if the huge man made any threatening moves. The sudden and clear change in the huge man's demeanor bewildered the shrewish, armed man. He hauled hard at the prisoner's chain, bringing it tight against his chest as if expecting foul play. But when Nicolas slipped on the moss, the quick snap of motion caught his eye and he spun his head in Nicolas' direction with a look of disbelief. A disbelief that budded into panic.

There was a third man, too. This one was kneeling a few feet from the armed man's muckish boots. Whether it was because he was kneeling or because of his naturally scrawny build, he appeared much smaller than the helmeted man and much, much smaller than the huge tattooed man with the bloodied face. The kneeling man wore the same grey coverlet as the armed, shrewish man. He also wore a simple helmet and from under the helmet sprouted matted snarls of dirty brown-green hair that lay over the collar of the man's tunic. His frowzy splay of hair looked like grasses of dried seaweed. He was occupied with settling a large stump of wood, a high block of abused, scored, and viciously sliced wood. In those places where the wood block wasn't stained with swaths and sullies of old rust color, it was bleached white like an old, weathered giant's bone. The stump stood two feet high and sported a crude scoop chopped out of its opposite side. It was, Nicolas suddenly realized with a sick knot in his stomach, an executioner's chopping block. A crudish stump of mortal ruin. A rejected scrap of tree, soaked in the blood and gristle of doomed necks.

The huge chained man was about to breathe his last across the stump's notched and blotted surface. He was about to have his head cut off.

Most boys have never witnessed an execution, and Nicolas, of course, was like most boys.

But in some ways, he was not.

Most boys had never killed a Wisp, and Nicolas, of course, had.

Once, perhaps a year before while sitting in the window seat of his father's study looking through one of his father's many books, Nicolas had stumbled across a telling about the violent death of Mary Stuart, Queen of Scots—how she'd met her ghastly end on the hewn surface of a chopping block much like the one being lurched into place by the kneeling man. Mary's beheading had been a shocking affair. The first swing of the axe missed its mark on her neck and caught the throneless monarch in the back of her head, splintering bone and mashing soft brain matter. The second chop was no more adequate than the first. The frustrated executioner being forced to saw through a last bit of still-attached sinew before the Queen's delicate neck came free of her body.

As dreadful as the details of Mary's death had been, Nicolas had been even more sickened by the sad story of young Lady Jane Grey, a great-granddaughter of His Royal Majesty, King Henry VII, whose own miserable execution was tied as an almost forgotten footnote to Mary's demise. In October 1537, having been condemned as a supposed enemy of the soon-to-be ill-fated Queen of Scots, Lady Grey had her own date with the chopping block. Nicolas recalled the blunt sense of despair captured by a black and white drawing in his father's book, depicting the brave and blindfolded sixteen-year-old girl clutching her slender arms around a large block of wood. A moustached man, wearing a buttoned and belted vest, was poised above her, raising a great axe in the air. Those last gruesome moments of Lady Jane Grey's brief life were left to Nicolas' own terrified imagination.

Aside from these bookish memories, executions, beheadings or otherwise, weren't something Nicolas knew much about. And yet, in the uncertain light of a flowering sun, he instantly knew exactly what was about to take place in front of him. He had crawled through the gut of a soggy burrow, hailed the expanse of the Cold Sea, beheld the glimmer of beckoning starlights, and had leapt atop a sea-battered cliff just in time to witness the morbid strike of swift death; a man's head about to be separated from his body.

But here, instead of a great sword or axe, a more baleful killing tool waited to be used.

Lying next to the kneeling man's grime-spattered boot lay a butcher's hatchet. An absurdly large meat cleaver. The heavily forged blade, a dirty, discolored wedge of notched steel, was the size of a large schoolbook. On the near side of the chopping block, the side nearest the Cold Sea's up-spray, the kneeling man had further arranged a rough-cut trough with its gutter adjusted in the direction of the cliff's edge, pointed in fact toward the same edge over which Nicolas had just scrambled. The cliff face was intended to serve as the final drop after the final chop, parting a doomed man from his doomed head as it tumbled down into the scrambling, hungry waves below, into a salt-sodden tub where crabs and fish would nibble and peck at sightless eyes and soundless ears.

"*Wait!*" Nicolas shrieked. His voice unusually stretched was unnerved, barely managing to squeak its frightened way above thrumming gusts of an easterly wind.

The word had erupted out of him. It sprang uncontrollably out of breathless lungs. Nicolas hadn't had time to think before he'd screamed out, and he wasn't even sure of what he meant or what he intended should happen. In fact, if he'd taken the time to think he might have admitted he shouted *wait* in the same way a person instinctively recoils from a fist flying at one's face. The word was impulsive. A frantic reaction. Nicolas, most decidedly, was *unready* to witness the savagery of a head being violently hacked away.

"*Wait!*" he screamed a second time. This time Nicolas waved his arms in the air, his cold fingers thrashing about in the morning's cold wind. Every muscle a whip of braided wire. Senses painfully alert—nostrils flaring, filled with the brace of sea salt, his skin chaffed by rock and salt, eyesight misted by the hazy dawn's first light, and a mouth sponged dry by *fear* Nicolas could feel in every rib of his chest. A physical fear that slapped and whipped at the pleats of his trousers, the folds of his heavy sweater, and the locks of his wild hair.

Something like when he'd thrust that horrible knife into Remiel… A cold, sick fear.

The moon hung like a dying sickle low on the horizon in front of him. Silently, it sank down behind the three men, and at Nicolas' back the resurrecting sun flung its first, long, bloody beams through a grim, purplish sky. Stretched out on the ground in front of Nicolas was his own morning shadow, a distorted look-alike, a distended ghost of himself cast by the sun's emerging light. Bizarrely, as if transfixed by an absurd dream, Nicolas watched the misshapen shadow of his own head stretch across the chopping block's whittled surface as though he, too, was waiting for the ugly cleaver to hammer wickedly through his neck. Cold beads of sweat formed on his forehead and for the third time but now in a guttural tone, he heard himself say, "*Wait.*"

This time the word dropped out of his mouth like a ship's leaden ballast. The word came dead-calm, composed, fixed. In spite of the shock and fear misting around him in the winds from the Cold Sea, Nicolas felt a sudden anger rising, an intense resolve from somewhere deep inside, from the same place where he'd once found the strength to kill a Wisp and face an overlord dragon. It was as if his soul was moored to a greater anchor than fear. The shadow of his own head on the chopping block, death drawn near, immediate, had shocked this determination into a cold, stubborn existence. If he wasn't ready for death to occur, then occur it *wouldn't.* Nicolas had spoken the word as if it were a steely order to be obeyed.

And that wasn't all.

Other words, strangely filled with the incensed confidence of absolute authority, came out of his mouth. "Stop!" he said. "There *will* be *mercy.*"

It didn't enter Nicolas' mind as to whether he was speaking to the guard or the executioner or the prisoner. It didn't matter. He'd uttered a royal prerogative of mercy; whether from out of terror, mad resolve, or haste, Nicolas, the Wren-come-again and Dragon Nightfall, was fully committed. As other-worldly as the words might have sounded to his own ears, he meant for them to be *obeyed.*

What followed seemed like a long silence.

Strained seconds passed. Nicolas stood there unyielding, his arms still high in the air. The three men as unmoved as statues. Then, like the startling crack and pop of thin ice on a frozen lake, everything *moved.*

As one, the huge man, the armed man, and the kneeling man exploded in movement.

The chained man, his bloody mouth agape, and his helmeted keeper reeled backward together, the huge man spinning on his heel, lurching awkwardly away, gurgling miserably, his massive legs moving as quickly as they might. The armed man followed suit without pause. He cast the fat-linked chain away as if it were a hot pan and pawed his way past his former prisoner, both of them in some kind of mad footrace to get away from Nicolas. Within moments the two men had very nearly disappeared over a gentle rise of earth in the distance and had faded into gritty shadows. The kneeling man, distinctly disadvantaged from the other two, threw his arms over his head and fell weakly on his side, mewing and crying like a lamb before a snarling wolf.

Nicolas stood there, his mouth hung open, more bewildered by the swiftness and completeness of their reactions than he was relieved. Having unexpectedly been obeyed, he didn't much know what to do. His arms remained tensed and out-stretched, a lung-full of breath waiting in his chest, his eyes transfixed on the hasty flight of the huge man and his armed guard. Nicolas hardly dared to breathe.

Then he, too, felt a renewed flood of panic course through his chest.

But instead of running or throwing himself down, Nicolas ducked and braced himself for the worst.

Without warning, an enormous, malformed winged shadow had appeared, engulfing his own. It spread out on the ground in front of him, casting the sea cliff into stark shade, darkening the cliff's tuffs of mugwort, its shocks of shrubby hare's ear, its clumps of bouncing bess, and its stands of sea holly. These, it all blocked from the rising sun's first rays. Indeed, the great shadow grew gigantically, but just as abruptly shrank as the body of an enormous sea hawk vaulted over Nicolas' head, landing gracefully atop the executioner's block in a fierce burst of beating wings, as if it were a somber circuit magistrate who'd come to hold court by the Cold Sea.

The golden irises of the bird's hooded eyes flickered sharply between the odd pair of fleeing men, the cowering man on the ground, and Nicolas, finally settling on Nicolas with an unblinking stare. The raptor's tapered head was pure white, interrupted by a black visor of feathers reaching around the long flanks of its neck and across its sloped eyes. Its chest and legs were also white, streaked with chestnut brown, its feet coal-black. The bird's upper parts were glossy, hued with tans and greys except at the joints of its wings in which there were faded bands of deep scarlet. The great bird had a relatively short tail but the span of its wings stretched over five feet, each with four, dramatic finger-like feathers and a shorter fifth one. Most distinctly and strangest of all, the noble sea-hawk possessed one sharply taloned foot and one webbed foot.

Nicolas, numbed, stayed as he was.

"Please," the man on the ground whimper. "*Please*," the man begged again with an upraised and quivering hand. He thrust his sheet-white face to the ground.

Slowly, the great bird took its eyes off Nicolas and swung its slick head toward the cowering man. It pushed its hooked beak forward and shrugged its patagium—the length of wing between its shoulders and wrists—upward while sweeping its large primary feathers back in such a way it looked unnervingly like a cloaked villain about to strike a helpless victim. The upper cutting edges of the bird's hooked beak separated from the lower mandibles, but instead of emitting a more common series of quick whistles, the immense sea hawk expelled out an ear-shattering *cheereek!* The bird, seemingly satisfied, drew in its immense wings, raised itself upright, and once again shifted its glowering stare to Nicolas.

The man on the ground, now sniveling and moaning, said in a shamed whisper, "I've soiled myself."

Nicolas didn't move.

His feet felt rooted to the earth, but as he stared at the hawk's coffee-colored eyes he somehow became… entirely unafraid. The bird's third eyelid, a near-translucent pale blue, blinked rapidly; its cerulean eyes glistened like polished gemstones in the light of the rising sun. It cocked its head knowingly. The raptor seemed to approve.

"Run," Nicolas said. He didn't remove his eyes from the bird. Why he told the cringing man to run, he didn't know, but he *did* know the word had come out more as a command than a suggestion. "*Run*," he said again.

Run the short man did.

Straight up on his feet like a wood pigeon startled from its roost, like a roe deer darting frantically away from a pack of hunting wolves, the man's bony legs spun fleetly over the same subtle rise of earth the armed man and the huge man had traversed moments before, his soiled breeches slapping his thighs in sloppy wet smacks. Within seconds, he was gone.

Nicolas who was still staring at the noble bird's flashing eyes said, "thank you," in the same odd voice with which he'd told the man to run, and having said that, dipped his head. It was a ridiculous thing to say and do but it also felt exactly right.

The highborn bird slowly lowered its head in equally good form and looked up at the brilliant, now-risen sun. Its massive wings fanned out, sensing the nature and shape of the sea-salted wind. With a sudden pushing, forceful fury, its wings launched the bird up through the slight eddies of ground-level breezes and into the great billows and cribs of the Cold Sea's stratospheric winds.

Having held court with Nicolas, who unwittingly had granted what was known in the First Kingdom as the 'King's Grace' to a prisoner doomed to die, the hawkish magistrate was abruptly gone, nothing more than a hazy silhouette dissolving into the light of the morning sun. Nicolas stood for a moment shading his squinting eyes against the dawn and watching as the bird wheeled and banked until it was too high, too far, to see.

Without another thought spent on how remarkably peculiar the last few moments had been, the boy from Plumpton Head turned on his heel, bubbling with the grand feeling of long-forgotten hopefulness, swells of chance and joy filling his heart. Nicolas leapt into a headlong sprint away from the cliff's storm-chewed edge, away from the rolling tumble of dark waves far below, away from the Bennett's quiet farmhouse and the safety of his small attic bedroom, until he, too, had disappeared over the subtle rise and into a place with dragons.

CHAPTER 5

BILGE WATER

The last trace of Christmas Eve settled like wintry snow into the gloom of his subconscious. As if Nicolas had shuttered his mind against its cold, it would remain there for some time, overlooked, still.

Nicolas was fully in the present, *his* present, and it was marvelous. He felt thrilled and nervous all at once. A delicious feeling of high adventure, a jittery but brilliant desire Nicolas had not known since stepping through the iron door inside Baatunde's humble tree-home over a year ago. His eager legs propelled him forward as fast as they'd go. He was truly free. Having stood on the edge of a high cliff towering above the fearsome waves of the Cold Sea; within splattering distance of an executioner's block; eye-to-eye with a great sea hawk; indeed, having stood *his ground*; Nicolas was wonderfully exhilarated. He ran with abandon as if it might be possible to outrun the shadows shaping at his feet by the newly risen sun. Shivering, he ran and ran.

With the sea's baritone waves soon fading behind him, the First Kingdom's wide expanse stretched before him. Somewhere out there was Aldus Ward, Laird of St. Wulf's-Without-Aldersgate, the stalwart Ranulf, the irrepressible Benjamin, and the determined Healer, Adelaide Ashdown with her pet goat Cornelia at her heels. Nicolas' legs and feet peddled wildly beneath him quickened by the silly feeling he might see them, see them all, waiting for him just over the next rise.

He didn't of course.

But what he did see, seeming to pitch and yaw atop the ebbing grey of the northwestern horizon, was almost as thrilling.

Far above the groundswells of stubborn sea mist, like the powerful main-mast's rigging of a square-sailed man-o'-war, rose the topmost battlements of an enormous gatekeep, one almost as vast yet far more grim-looking than St. Wulf's-Without-Aldersgate. Nicolas, both surprised and delighted, pulled up to a dead stop. For the first time in his life he was staring at the ancient battered ramparts of the Second Gate of the City of Relic, the fabled, seaside Gate of the Deep. The gatekeep had been built as if it were a ship's colossal bowsprit, excessive and thrusting out beyond mammoth strakes of quarried cliff-face into the deep-watered Bay of Wrath, a violent, natural harbor that spewed salty spin-drift upward like a nest of spitting snakes. The Gate of the Deep served as the City's key, seaward lookout and shipping anchorage, balanced high on the extreme shore of the First Kingdom with dozens of storm-frayed banners and standards beating along its soaring parapets, waving and snapping in the briny, easterly winds.

The three men who'd fled from Nicolas were nowhere to be seen but a short distance in front of Nicolas lay the narrow zigzag of a rudely beaten path. It looked as if the rutted turf led straight to the mist-shrouded gatekeep and even though the path's borders were wild and overgrown Nicolas thought it the best gamble to take; he'd been Laird Aldus' friend and he was sure he'd be welcome to enter the City, make his way to St. Wulf's-Without-Aldersgate, and with that, find the quickest way back to his friends.

Off at a skipping jump, Nicolas again took to his heels and raced along the seaside trail. He plunged and dodged his way amid sand dune dips and turns and sea-grass coves that were emptying themselves of the night's coastal hazes, onward toward the looming specter of the second of the six Forfeited Gates. Onward toward the ancient city's only access to the fabled dangers of the Cold Sea.

The door to which Nicolas finally came, however, was an odd one.

A broad, ragged, gravel apron spread in front of it, at the back of which a blunt series of seven chiseled stone steps led up to a salt-pocked and black-moss threshold. The door itself was made of weather-beaten but dense, wood staves bound tightly together by a confused mess of flaking metal strips. Roughly head-high, a large square casement framed the door's center; it, too, was covered by a latticework of metal strips and within the casement were closed shutters. *What a curious, giant peephole*, Nicolas thought, smiling to himself as he climbed the steps, his chest heaving from his morning sprint.

At the top step, he found himself eye-to-eye with the door's peculiar knocker, a short pole of tarnished metal. More the same-looking kind of metal as what criss-crossed the door and jutted out from the door's face. The grotesque likeness of a hung man hung from a large ring hooked through the tip of the metal spar. The man's neck bent at a lop-sided angle from its contorted corpse. Circlets of coarse iron bound his body around his torso, arms, thighs, and ankles. One of his feet was shoeless, his trousers torn open pitifully at both knees, his ill-fitted shirt drooped loose and ragged, and in spite of the bindings, Nicolas could see the fingers on each of his hands rigidly spread open. The hung man's face was hidden underneath a coarse looking, pleated hood, but Nicolas could see the impression of his gaping mouth and the man's sunken eye-sockets, a perpetual mask of utter horror, a man choking to death with empty, burning lungs, bursting muscles and the mad helplessness of a terrified mind. The ghastly knocker swung gently in the morning breeze, rhythmically tapping the iron cleat bolted on the wood behind it.

"Who are *you*?!"

Nicolas jumped as if the little metal corpse had come to life, and stumbled back a half-step, almost losing his footing on the threshold's slick, top step.

A sweaty fat face glared down at him from the within the shadows of the open shutters. The face's two eyes were a lackluster dirt brown, narrow and pulled together with a single, great bushy eyebrow. "I *said*, who are you?"

Nicolas felt as if he were two years younger, standing in front of the Head Teacher at Hunter Hall for not having finished his lessons. "Nicolas," he mumbled timidly.

"Huh. An' *whose* Nicolas are you?" the greasy man snorted, his round nostrils flaring and fuming.

Confused, Nicolas repeated himself. "I'm—I'm Nicolas."

The pig-face in the shadows grunted annoyingly. "I *know* yer Nicolas, ya snot-nosed cumberworld. Ye've already said as much. I'm askin' after yer heredity. Yer family stock, boy. *Whose* Nicolas are you?"

Nicolas almost said *Bennett* but that seemed foolish. His last name wouldn't make any more sense to the piggish man in the window than his first name. "I'm…" Nicolas tried to think of what might make sense. "I'm—I'm…" Nicolas thought hard. "I'm… *Renfry*. The son of Renfry," he said, borrowing Ranulf's surname.

The pig-face grunted again but this time seemed a tad less scornful. "Renfry, eh? Don't know any Renfry's except the *one* Renfry." The oily man snorted again, a snort that spat out like a footballer's kick, this accompanied by a ghastly bloom of white spittle and snot. "An' *you* don't look like *that* one. 'Aven't seen 'im, but I've 'eard *that* Renfry's at least six feet tall w'th shoulders as broad as an ox-yoke, an' 'e carries a blacksmith 'ammer the size o' an anvil." The man's boorish face squished against the bars of the lookout window as he glowered at Nicolas. "I'm not some hedge-born fopdoodle sot, ya three-inch toad boil! You'd better be playin' straight with me or I'll carve ya into pigeon liver'd bits and feed ya raw to some devil whale."

Nicolas felt the warmth of the sun on his back; relief the watchman had at least heard of Ranulf. "I am! I am!" Nicolas insisted. "I'm Ranulf, er, I mean Nicolas, son of Renfry. I'm a friend, er, I mean a cousin to Ranulf son of Renfry. Might I come in?"

The man paused and narrowed his eyes until they were black slits. There was an irritated snuffle and the shutters banged shut. The large door opened inward with a discordance of shrieks wrenching their way out of its metal hinges.

This little-used entrance to the Gate of the Deep was barely large enough for two men to walk through it abreast of each other but for the moment, it needed only be wide enough for a slight Wren. Nicolas stepped inside and was swallowed whole, out from the sunlight and into the belly of Jonah's great fish.

Behind him the rusty strapped door slammed shut, the hanging man screeching, striking hard against the iron cleat.

"Watch yer clapper-clawed steps an' try naught ta slip," bellowed the blubbery watchman. He was leading the way down an ill-lit, dank corridor, waving a sputtering torch from side to side. In the darkness, Nicolas could hear the scrape of tiny feet scurrying out of their way. *Rats*, he shuddered and kept a sharp lookout where he put his feet to avoid tramping on any careless rodent. "It bloody well stinks!" Nicolas exclaimed aloud, clasping a hand tight over his mouth and nose. "Smells bloody awful. Like someone blew off!" The passageway's clammy reek of fetid seaweed had suddenly filled with an even more rancid smell. Nicolas thought they might have stepped past some sewage grate in the dark.

"Apologies, m'lord."

Nicolas could hear the fat watchman snicker sarcastically.

"I've 'ad nothin' but brown bean porridge an' brown bean cakes with bacon fat fer weeks. Makes me trump in my breeches, that, like horns of war." The confession was barely made before another fart abruptly discharged, this one thunderously loud and ending in a queer sound that reminded Nicolas of pulling a wet boot out of sucking mud. "Ahhhh," the piggish man sighed with genuine satisfaction. "*That* one's been bakin' fer a while! Feelin' much better now."

Nicolas gagged. It smelled like three-month-old, curdled bean soup. The moldering dark and the darting rats kept him much closer behind the fat watchman than he cared to be. He kept turning his head from side to side, snagging quick shreds of breath, hoping the air was a little less rancid than the foul draught filling the watchman's wake.

After a several minutes the pig and the Wren emerged from the passageway into a dimly lit antechamber where several other dark corridors intersected their own. The fat watchman came to a jiggling, wheezing halt. His loud breath echoed in a bizarre way inside the stone-arched chamber, causing his labored rasping to sound something like the forced push of a faraway train. "Sergeant Billibeck and Mr. Killick seemed to think yer some kind of sea-spirit come to kill us all," he said without looking at Nicolas. "They came hollerin' back from their lawful killin' duties without their prisoner or a scrap o' wits between 'em. But *I* know the ropes better than either o' those onion-eyed sots! *You* ain't no sea-spirit, an' those two are likely to catch the whip fer not havin' taken the vile head o' that wretched vermin Crow." Nicolas watched the man's bulbous head sway left to right as if he was wondering in which direction to go. "Those two upper-decked, pox-marked, clay-brained, mewling minnows don't know their fart-holes from their snot-holes. But *I* know the ropes, mind you, an' you *ain't* no barnacle-breeding sea-spirit. Ya might be no *Renfry* neither, I suspect. Probably some gutter snipe livin' like an animal or a runaway apprentice tryin' to wag off yer lawful duties. An' that's why I think… I think…" His puffing voice trailed off. Nicolas heard a grunt and squeak and the sizable watchman expelled an astonishingly long rumble of wind that created an echoing reverberation equal to the blast and fury of a man-o'-war's broadside. A sprinkle of dirt fell from the ceiling. Nicolas pinched his eyes shut and held his breath until his lungs burned.

Fittingly, a memory of standing with his father in the ticket hall at Preston station popped into Nicolas' air-starved head. It had been the end of a vibrantly lit Saturday afternoon two years before; an early spring day spent with his father at the Bowland Wild Boar Park. Mr. Bennett had delivered a guest lecture under a neatly-staked pavilion in the Myerscough Gardens on the west side of Myerscough College. He'd spoken about the methods of detecting decay in trees and how a meaty-looking fungus called Ox Tongue could cause heart-rot in oaks. Afterward he and Nicolas had stood in a queue to purchase last-minute tickets for the short rail ride home when an extremely large and gasping woman charged in front of them. She immediately began scolding the man at the ticket counter as if he had personally caused her to miss her train to Farmby. She'd been clutching several shopping bags in each hand and had managed to drop her coin purse at the height of her tirade. Before Mr. Bennett or Nicolas could move to help the obnoxious woman, she had bent over to retrieve the purse and had let go a fart that sounded like a quick pull on a long zipper. Mr. Bennett, in an instant, said in a showy stage-voice, “Blow, winds, and crack your cheeks! Rage, blow!” The hefty woman had whirled on them, red-faced snootiness and accusation flushing her round face, but before she could let go any complaint Nicolas’ father looked straight at Nicolas and, placing an educating hand on Nicolas’ shoulder, said in his professorial voice, “An’ *that*, lad, is what the mad King Lear said when his daughter tossed him out in the middle of a storm, at least according to Mr. Shakespeare.” The scarlet-faced woman, now unsure of whether her expulsion had been the butt of a joke, turned suspiciously back to the ticket counter while Mr. Bennett and Nicolas did their absolute best not to die from holding in their laughter.

Nicolas laughed in spite of himself; whatever else his last adventure in Telluric Grand had taken from him as a boy, it hadn’t taken his boyish sense of crude humor. He gasped a jiff of fouled air and battled a burst of coughs as he fought between the need to breathe and the effort not to smell the piggish man’s stinking outburst.

The fart’s din finally quieted down.

“I think,” wheezed its inconsiderate creator as if nothing had ever happened, “that it’s best to put you in the *bilge* whilst I see what’s about what. Yes, yes.” He pushed a stout finger against one nostril and blew a mist of snot out of the other. “That’ll do jes fine.” Off he went to the left, ducking down to fit his bulk inside a tighter corridor than the one from which they’d just come.

Nicolas, now more disgusted than bemused, but not wanting to be left alone in the dimness of the antechamber, hurried after him.

The air did not improve as they went.

A distinct smell filled Nicolas' nose as they descended the passageway, snaking and turning ever-downward—the pungent odor of a stagnant ditch, soured and diseased. It wasn't quite the smell of sewage but that was at least part of its stink blended with the brackish rubbish of moldering seaweed. Slowly, troublingly, it occurred to Nicolas the strongest stink was of flesh-rot, a sickly sweet stench of putrefaction.

Years before he and his father had found an old ram lying dead within the first stand of trees across from the Bennett's sheep pasture. The sheep, most likely aged and sick, must've become separated from a neighbor's nearby flock and had wandered into the trees to die. Nicolas' father thought it might have been a Welsh Mountain ram due to its long tail but he couldn't be sure; the ordinary thickness of its wool was patchy and thinned in death. The ripe corpse had just begun to swell and a horrible smell drifted over it. Handfuls of burying beetles scutted around its tongue, bickering and quarreling over minute bits of the lifeless flesh. Small splits had appeared in the blackish, puffed-up flesh of its stomach and hundreds of flies had massed on them, queer jewels of light reflecting from their shiny, metallic-blue abdomens. Nicolas remembered the feel of a watery queasiness in his stomach. When he'd finally looked up from the horrid scene, he'd noticed his father wasn't looking at the dead sheep at all; he possessed a distant air about him. Nicolas followed his father's gaze through the breaks between the trees to a faraway line of storm clouds settling along the downs from the northeast. A cool breeze's first trace swished among the elms, feathering against Nicolas' cold cheeks.

"The low sky has finally come," Mr. Bennett said as if to no one, a sad look on his face. "Bands of grey to pass through.

And then… light. Silvered. Never-ending. But for now, the low sky… the low sky has finally come." At the time, Nicolas had thought it must have been some fetched-up quote, but Mr. Bennett said no more than that, and he wasn't sure of it. They'd silently turned back toward the sunbeams that still filled the family's sheep pasture, leaving behind the smell of corruption and death under the shadows of the trees.

His father's strange melancholy and the working of death had stuck with him long after.

He found those same feelings again inside the tight corridor deep beneath the stronghold of the Gate of the Deep. They hung heavy in the air and Nicolas wished he'd remained on the sea cliff, scrubbed clean with salt spray and the flushing affection of a living sun.

Within yet another antechamber two grease lamps cupped high against a wall spitted and popped, providing a shaky, butter-yellow light. This with a lower ceiling than the first and a single, visible passage at its far end.

Nicolas stood there alone.

Moments before, the wheezing, fat watchman had abruptly said, "Stay where ya stand, ya worm!" and Nicolas had jerked to a halt. "Here you'll be 'til yer told otherwise. I 'ave inquiries to make. Inquiries! Sort this madness out. Find out what's about what." And, without any more instruction or the chance for Nicolas to ask any questions, the brute had clumped off on his own, gasping and grousing in mean mutters until his great outline had been swallowed by the inky gloom of the passage's far-end.

Nicolas was left standing in a large puddle in the middle of the chamber. The entire floor seemed to be covered with an oily slick of gummy black-water, but the sole seams of his boots held fast and since there didn't seem to be more than half-inch of depth where he stood, his feet remained dry. He could hear faint and repeated thuds somewhere far overhead, not directly above him but somewhere above; low-pitched noise that fed its was down through the stained walls like padded battle-rams thumping against the gatekeep's stony bulwarks. Closer by was the constant scrape, scuttle, and splash of rats' claws accompanied by the sound of something being drug along, likely a prize-kill of lizard-meat or of a smaller rodent or of some other awful thing that might live deep inside that black vault, things Nicolas dared not think about.

He then heard breathing.

Slight at first and several feet away from where he stood.

As best he could see in the blurred light, the chamber's walls had several curved openings, each covered by a heavy grate of crossed bars. The breathing sounded as if it came from within one of those openings. Like a hammer strike on the head of a nail, a nasty thought struck Nicolas between the eyes, the crossed bars were cell doors. Prison gates. He was standing in a dungeon, a stygian, dungeon of stink, wretchedness, and despair.

The cold frost of complete fear checked his breathing, froze his soul.

"Who's there?"

More breathing. Definitely more than one person, or thing, *breathing*.

"Who's there?" His words weren't bold and they didn't sound it; they were feeble and nervous, far removed from the confident orders barked an hour before on the sea cliff.

"*Weeeeee arrrrrrre.*" Two stretched, splintery-sounding words. Heavily accented, cruel.

Dozens and dozens of thickset, hand-tapped tattooed fingers pushed out of the dark cells and wrapped themselves around the crossed bars. Dozens and dozens of fisted fingers gripped the bars as if they were shafts of iron hammers. Nicolas could see no arms, no bodies, no faces, only jointed stubs of clenching fingers, several hundred or so of them, some bent and disfigured, some missing, cut-off, torn away. And hidden behind the fingers, unseen mouths breathing, rasping. All ragged, hoarse, guttural.

He couldn't move.

The same disembodied voice spoke again. "*You* saved one of *usssssss*; one of us, didn't *you*? One meant to be chopped. One meant to join the great Murder. The walls whisper, pet; they've told us what you've done. *You* gave a King's Grace? *You*???" The voice was prying. Then, a dreadful pause. Breathing. A mischief of rats afoot, splashing and darting about less carefully than before. Something larger causing heavy ripples in the sticky bilge-water lapped at Nicolas' boots. "Are you *it*? The dragon-demon reborn, come again? *Are you it*?" The faceless voice's tongue clicked against wet teeth. Eager, dreadful clicks. Another awful pause; a last question. A searching question, one that wound Nicolas' insides into hardened, cold twists of fear. "*Worm... Worm of Crowssssses*?"

Nicolas' petrified mind was seized by the fragment of a distant conversation, a conversation from more than a year ago, a conversation from a time when he was within the walls of another gatekeep. It had been about an evil history of hungry terror. The monstrous horror of a long-dead overlord dragon. *It favored the earth more than the sky*, came the aged voice in Nicolas' aching head. *It carved out a deep lair in the cliffs overlooking the Cold Sea. The War Crows called it the 'Worm of Crows.'* Nicolas shook in the dark. *They thought they could parley with the dragon*, whispered the voice, *but overlord dragons do not covet kingdoms.*

"Who are *you*?!" Nicolas screamed at the gripping fingers, his voice cracking, but the scream didn't silence the voice in his head. *And it took its time, picking the War Crow's bones clean.*

"*Who* are *weeeeee*?" mimicked the faceless voice floating somewhere within its black cell. It laughed a crude, tattered laugh. "Murder! Crows! We are Crows in a cage!" The laughter sank into something like the panting of a dog. "And *you*?" A wicked question—interested but almost sure of itself—became a statement. "You! *You're* the Worm of Crows?!"

Nicolas didn't answer. He did the only thing he could think of.

He ran.

CHAPTER 6

Things Gone Wrong

Nicolas was in a dread-driven full flight.

His hands were scraped and cut from having them stretched out as bumpers against weeping limestone walls. Greasy water and mold had left large wet blots on his boots and trousers. Sweat from fear and physical exertion soaked his sweater. He was out of breath, gasping for air in the suffocating closeness. His terrified imagination had kept his legs moving at top speed, vividly alive with thoughts of brutal War Crows, those same butchers who'd killed Ranulf's parents long ago, feather-bedecked demons clawing at him and plucking him back into the sodden doom of the bilge-dungeon below. Nicolas had run blindly. He'd run like a radge rat caught in a sunless trap. He'd sailed headlong into dead-ends of confusing turns and twists but kept running; running even after his lungs felt rasped and on fire; even after his legs seem to flop beneath him, sapped dull and sluggish.

At last Nicolas saw a misty hope of light from somewhere ahead and he bent into his frantic pace, forcing himself upward, lifting each leg with a will to live, away from whatever was imprisoned below, upward toward people who might know his friends, who might allow him to wait in a less horrid place, who might be kind enough to help him, to save him. But when he'd at last come hurtling out of the groping darkness, his eyes were blinded, cowed by the abrupt flash and glimmer of large torches, oil lamps and, most welcome of all, a bright sluice of grainy sunlight that burrowed into the corridor's deep shadows.

The passageway had suddenly opened into a broad and ingeniously constructed, partially covered shipping port of enormous size built beneath the Gate of the Deep. This was the gatekeep's wide-famed Portus, the Cold Sea's sole entry into the City with Seven Gates, a wide channel of black seawater, dredged through the heart of the Bay of Wrath and ending in a Stillwater harbor deep inside the gatekeep's girdling walls. The Gate of the Deep's stone quays guided the green-black water as if it were a podgy worm wriggling its way into the heart of the earth. Bow waves slopped lazily against high dockworks where king-ships, merchant sloops, and coastal skiffs of all different tonnage and styles were moored securely to massive, iron rings or were being hauled up the middle of the sheltered waterway by monstrous iron pawls, giant gears, and block-n-tackle pulleys the size of a man.

Above the clamor and commotion of sailors and ship captains, a harbor master could be heard bellowing slates of orders and instructions to a dozen channel keepers who churned about the moored and moving boats in busy, willow-framed coracles of oiled bullock hide. The harbor master sounded like an obnoxious natterjack toad, and like lesser toads, the channel keepers shouted their own missives, harassing deck officers and their crews with inspection requirements, custom collections on sundry goods, and lengthy recitations of the authority of the Laird of the Gate of the Deep to impound ships, detain crew members, and punish offenders as a high officer of the King's Bench. Knots of sailors on liberty from king-ships eagerly shouldered their way through the bustle, heading for the marked corridors that led past defense checkpoints and eventually into the City, while bands of idle gatekeep soldiers, scattered up and down the length of the great port's docks, huddled in sally ports waiting for the gatekeep's drummer corps to signal the second-quarter watch to duty. Sentries stood silent posts beside closed doors or, as was the case with the corridor out of which Nicolas burst, beside the open entrances to half-a-dozen posterns and access passageways leading into the belly of the gatekeep. The massive shipping port—an undecorated but functional affair walled in by immense, staggered coursings and lofty arches of grainy, brownstone—had no windows to illuminate its drab sandstone interior. Instead, seventy-two torch-rings and a healthy sized crack in the hall's high-and-away ceiling allowed in enough sunlight to push back most of the tall shadows.

As Nicolas came spitting blindly out of the narrow corridor, a hard staff of ash wood struck him on the back of his skull out of nowhere. Even if Nicolas had seen it coming, he was so spent, rabid with horror and physically shattered, there would have been little he could have done to avoid it. The alert sentry who laid the hickory staff of his half-pike across the back of Nicolas' head did so just enough for a clipped knock but not quite enough to crack skull bone. The sentry's quick action and the precision of the blow suggested a skill-level gained from long hours of martial training, but for Nicolas it meant nothing more than having raced out of darkness and into light only to plunge back into a greater darkness as he collapsed on the stone floor a dead man, completely unconsciousness.

"Nicolas?"

Floating, murmuring voices. Receding, swelling, and receding again.

"Nicolas?"

In the sworls of his foggy mind, he could hear her delightful voice. *When someone dies, the Healer comes to the door carrying a sorrow basket in her arms.*

"Nicolas?"

Am I dead? he thought. The question was a curious one. He turned it over in his mind in the same way he might have studied a firefly caught in a jar. He didn't *feel* dead but perhaps death didn't have a precise feeling. *I don't see a low sky*, Nicolas thought, using the memory of his father's voice to poke at the firefly question. *In fact, I don't see anything at all.*

"Nicolas?"

The firefly in his mind transformed into a shard of white light. One eye nicked open, then the other. Nicolas wasn't dead, of course, but his head hurt like the dickens.

"Ahhh, there you are," said the wonderfully soft voice, very real and close. A breath's hint of honey and sweet parsley. "There you are." Stiffly, he turned his sore head, and there *she* was.

His Adelaide.

Adelaide Ashdown.

"Adelaide!" Nicolas cried, a choke in his voice as he tried to sit up. Pain shocked through him from head to foot. He shuddered and fell back with a gasp.

"Easy now. Easy, Nicolas," Adelaide laughed, her own voice lightly catching. "You've taken quite a whack on the head. I honestly thought you'd been killed dead at first, you know. You were as limp as a boiled eel and everyone was just standing there, nodding their heads over you like you were a blind hatchling fallen out of its nest." She gave her head a determined shake causing the sandy-brown locks of hair to bounce against her shoulders. "I made 'em stand back. Told 'em to give you some room, I did, and thank the endless heavens I saw you were breathing!" A sudden flush of hot tears welled in the corners of her bright eyes, but she brushed them away. The resolve in her voice never changed. "I told them they'd better carry you in here and be glad you're not dead. I told them I'd tell Laird

Aldus Ward what they'd done. They didn't like it one bit but at least they listened."

Nicolas did his best to smile, winced, and slowly looked around. The two of them were alone in a fairly small and murky room. He could smell the staleness of old sweat, linseed oil, moldering oats, black beeswax, and the tidal dankness that soaked the entire gatekeep. On the walls there were standing racks that held various weapons, trappings, and wrist-size hoops of metal with odd assortments of polished keys, those items necessary for the gate's defense, along with a sagging wicker basket that sat atop two bulging sacks of pot barley. The basket contained a few dozen turtle eggs and hanging on a hook above it was a single cooking crock for barley custard, an egg-thickened puddin' for roving sentries to eat during long night watches. A shaky grin kept tugging at the corners of Nicolas' mouth but it hurt to do much more than that. More than anything, he felt an enormous sense of relief. Everything was finally going to be alright. "Brilliant, Adelaide," he said quietly. "I bet you set them all to rights."

"Of course I did, silly." The young Healer was sitting on the floor next to him and she held herself up for a moment, her chin lifted, her back straight. "You've been as still as a boundary stone for hours! My legs are tingly from falling asleep but I suppose turn-about is fair play. The last time it was *I* who gave you a good scare about dying." She looked away and absentmindedly touched the scar that cut down from her forehead and through her right eyebrow. It was even paler than her light complexion—the smooth gloss of unevenly mended skin; an unpleasant reminder the length of a long straight-pin left by the carving claw of a flesh-eating ogre.

"But you *didn't* die. You didn't die, Adelaide. I thought for certain you were dead but you didn't die. I… I couldn't have beared it if you had." Nicolas could hear how absurd-sounding his words were but he couldn't help it. His thoughts were like clouds and mist and it was as if he needed to reassure himself she was real, she was alive, she was really there.

Adelaide didn't seem to think it was absurd. She cupped his cheek in her soft hand and very gently gave him a light kiss on the forehead. A rich smell of vanilla bean and peppermint filled his nose as her hair fell in his face. When she sat back, her smile was bright and cheery. "Oh! It's so *very* good to see you, Nicolas!" With a not-so-gentle dive and twist she wrapped him up, hugging him like a newfound toy. A tined fork of pain punched from the back of his head to the back of his eyes but he hugged her just as hard in return. For a moment it was as though he'd never left; she was warm and wonderful. Part of his heart mended.

"How did you find me? Why are you here?" he asked weakly.

"Oh!" Adelaide sat up again, her face suddenly overcast with worry. "I didn't really *find* you, Nicolas Bennett. I've been living here inside the gatekeep since the wane of the past full moon to help with some of the wounded soldiers and," with this, her voice began to fade "a few of the more… harmless prisoners." Adelaide's eyes dropped. He couldn't tell if she were ashamed of something or if there was something more she didn't want to say.

"That's brilliant," he said, lightly touching the back of her hand. He thought a tingle passed between them. "It's what you've wanted, right? To heal? To be a Healer and help people?"

Adelaide shrugged. "I guess. I was one of the apprentice Healers sent from the City's Barrow Cloister to come help." Her shoulders slumped and she hung her head, but Nicolas could see her jaw was set tight. "Not really 'sent for' if I'm being honest, I suppose. The Timeworn Sofren, she's the Cloister's

Healer of the First Order, *she* said I was a waste of time—said I'd never become a *real* Healer, a real *Bendith Duw*." The girl's nostrils flared and her chest rose and fell, her face flushed. "The next thing I know, they—they wanted to be rid of me, Nicolas! I was told to come here with a few other 'refusals,' other failed apprentices meant to be turned out by the Cloister. I was told I could earn a fortnight's keep if I agreed to help the gatekeep's wounded." The tremor in her voice was bitter and before she could rub them away a few angry tears spilled down her pale cheeks. "It's not right!" An indignant fist slammed against her thigh. "I have the *gift*. I know I do! I do—I know I do." She said faintly and looked at him. Her moist eyes were pleading, helpless almost. "I *do*, Nicolas. I've known it since I was a young middling. I left everything behind …" Her delicate jaw set itself again. "My heart's been fixed before Time began. I'm a *Healer*," she insisted.

Nicolas gently took her arm. He felt jittery and his head throbbed, but he laced his fingers together with hers and gave his best squeeze. "Of course you are, Adelaide Ashdown. You weren't ever meant to be anything else." Her chin quivered. She sniffed and nodded, relieved. "Just look at *me!*" Nicolas said with a flashy sweep of his hand. "You've brought *me* back to life!"

She gave a laugh and rolled her eyes, wiping her tears with the back of her dirty hand. "Thank you," she said. Her wonderful smile returned.

There was a brisk pounding on the door.

"Hurry up! The drum's beating to fallow quarters an' I'll not 'ave a clouted sandcrab makin' his private accommodations inside an arm's room." The door's thick planks did little to muffle the brutish authority of the man's voice on the other side. "Hurry up, I say!"

"Quick now, let me help you up, Nicolas. That's one of the high-gaffers of the watch. I think they spend their whole life nitpicking and being mean to others." Adelaide scrambled to her feet and looped an arm through one of his. Slowly, with his head pounding, Nicolas pulled his feet underneath him and pushed himself upright.

"We're coming!" She shouted at the door. "Can you stand?"

"I think so." He gingerly touched the back of his head. There was a good-sized bump hidden under his mess of curly hair. "Ouch!"

Adelaide smiled. "I bet it hurts. Getting conked about isn't any fun; I should know. Here, drink this." She withdrew a leather flask from inside a deep pocket within the folds of her russet-colored kirtle and put it to his lips. The liquid was cold at first but left behind a tickling warmth that refreshed his mouth and throat. He swallowed several gulps and the throbbing inside his head almost instantly improved. "C'mon," she said in a firm tone but patient with encouragement. "Let's get you down the hall where I can hand you off to young Diggory. He's one Second Watch's pages; a little simple, he is, but he'll know better what to do than one of those bad-tempered soldiers."

Nicolas grabbed her wrist. "Wait! You're leaving me?"

A troubled look passed across Adelaide's face. She paused and leaned close. The scent of her breath again reminded him of crushed parsley. "I'm *worried*, Nicolas. Things aren't—they aren't *right*." Her sea-green eyes were wide, close to his, earnest; she hushed her voice further. "Benjamin's here, too."

"Benjamin?! He is? Where?"

"Shhhh!" She glanced nervously at the door. "Hurry!" she pressed him in a whispered voice. "We *must* be careful." Then, in a louder-than-necessary voice, she yelled, "Pull yourself together!" and looked at the closed door. Outside there was a tramp and shuffle of moving feet along the great hall's flagstones interrupted by muffled barks of annoyed watch gaffers and higher officers issuing orders.

Again, a forced whisper. "He isn't a *guest* here, Nicolas. I don't know what they've done with him." Her voice caught. "I saw him briefly two days ago but he's been moved since." Part of Adelaide's stubborn spirit left her slender body. "I've been told the City's bailiff men arrested him a week ago and, for some reason I can't gather, they sent him here. They had—they'd *beaten* him, Nicolas." She paled and her eyes had the vacant look of tremendous sadness. Adelaide shook her head. "There is something terribly *wrong* with all of this," she said, waving her arms about. Her red lips were pinched; she seemed at a loss to find a better explanation. "There has been something *wrong* almost since the moment you left us. Things have… have been *strange* and now I think they've even become *dangerous* for us all but I don't know why."

Nicolas felt sick. His head hurt. His cheeks hurt and his tongue was dry. "What about Ranulf? Is he okay?"

Adelaide let out a long sigh. Her shoulders fell. "Ranulf?" she said with a wistful curl. "Ranulf? He's okay, I think. At least I suppose he is." With that, she squared herself and pursed her lips in a hard, impatient line. "Really, Nicolas Bennett, I *don't* have all the answers. I haven't seen Ranulf in months. I've been doing the best I can on my own. I've only heard things about him. Rumors, if you care. They all sounded like dirty dishwater to me. Some say he's a Dragon Nightfall. Some say he's the 'King-to-be.' Others say he's permanently disappeared. Spirited out of the City by Âld Elves is what most of the gossipy fishmongers like to say to those that'll listen, to someplace magical, I suppose. Worst of all there are a few bloody natters who claim he's left the City on his own and journeyed beyond the Northern Voda, That he crossed the ice water under the Harrow Bridge," she shivered, "and was enslaved by northern orcs; what poor northern folk call the *Hladný*." Her voice changed. Angry. "But the most evil chinwags of all say Ranulf was seen a month ago traveling with a band of raiding War Crows to the south in the Lowlands but that *can't* be right, Nicolas. Those monsters killed his parents! You *know* Ranulf hates 'em, and I hate all these tittle-tattles! Ranulf *must* be alright," she said, unconvinced, worried. "I *guess* he's alright, but I don't really know. I don't feel like I know much of anything anymore." Defeated, Adelaide shook her head and in an angry whisper said, "Why did you ever leave, Nicolas?! Why did you *leave us*?" Her small fists were bunched on her waist and hot snorts of breath jetted from her slender nose. She was holding back more tears.

"I—I… I'm sorry."

More irritated cuffs flurried on the stout door.

Adelaide waved a hand across her face, shook her head, and took in a great breath of air. Her face softened. She sniffed. A tired smile reappeared. "It doesn't matter. It really doesn't matter anymore, Nicolas. You're here now."

Another violent round of knocks beat at the door.

"Please," Adelaide begged. "Please, there isn't much time." She placed her hand on his shoulder and took another deep breath. "I need for you to be patient, Nicolas. I've found a way to send for Aldus even before I knew you were here; hadn't any other hope really. Hope he's on his way. I'm sure he'll set things right again. Until then, please do whatever they say. I think they're unsure what to do with you until the gatekeep's Laird gives you a formal audience. I'm afraid you appeared as—as…

someone or something quite unexpected." She laughed. "That's not a good thing these days."

Adelaide gave another quick giggle and covered her apple-red mouth. Her half-hidden smile now emanated pure warmth, everything Nicolas remembered it to be. "It's so *good* to see you again," she said and gave him a light peck on the cheek. Then, with an arched eye toward the door, she shouted. "Get up, you lazy fool! Quit complaining!"

The young Healer winked slyly at the Wren as the thick door crashed open.

PART II

Black Feathers and Salt

The fighting man shall from the sun
Take warmth, and life from glowing earth;
Speed with the light-foot winds to run
And with the trees to newer birth;
And find, when fighting shall be done,
Great rest, and fulness after dearth.

The kestrel hovering by day,
And the little owls that call by night,
Bid him be swift and keen as they,
As keen of ear, as swift of sight.

The blackbird sings to him: "Brother, brother,
If this be the last song you shall sing,
Sing well, for you may not sing another;
Brother, sing."

The thundering line of battle stands,
And in the air Death moans and sings;
But Day shall clasp him with strong hands,
And Night shall fold him in soft wings.

-*Into Battle*, Julian Grenfell

CHAPTER 7

THE PASSAGE TOMB

Stone isn't fit for sleep. Stone might be used as blunt weapons for brutish men, but they're not meant for sleep. Not for the living anyway.

Stones are the dense walls of castle keeps, they are grinding wheels, rough weights, pillars, the bones of mountains, the dams of dark burrows for those long deceased, or the cold hollows for much darker things, ghastly, deformed things, things that have business with the dead.

In whatever way a tired person might toss and turn, stretch and twist, or fuss and gripe, *stones,* those primordial knots of petrified earth, do not function well as beds for the restful slumber of human flesh and bone. Stones push. Stones poke. They prod. They cut. Even cobbled stones, no matter how many screws of time may have tumbled and worn their edges, do not make for a comfortable bed. While *most* people don't have any reason to think on this simple fact, to be sure, there *are* a few who *do*: forgotten prisoners wasting away in forgotten cells and holy monks praying away in holy cells. But aside from these luckless few, not many people ever find themselves sleeping on beds of stones.

Nicolas Bennett was no different than most people.

Almost every night Nicolas could remember had been spent wrapped in the warmth of the old, hand-stitched quilt that lay atop the lumpy mattress on a rickety heirloom bed frame made of stained alder, tucked safely away in his attic bedroom. Most every night spent, Nicolas had slept in the reassuring shelter of the Bennett family's farmhouse comfortably nestled alongside a seldom-used lane. A peaceful street that gives way to a minor road that, itself, connects to the A6 and the B5305 near Skelton, Cumbria, a rugged province of northwest England, a land dominated by an ancient range of wild mountains, cold lakes, and stretches of forests bordered by the Scotland to the north, the Irish Sea to the west, Lancashire to the south, and Northumberland to the east. Among these ageless crags and deep lochs, the Bennett's old farmhouse and Nicolas' homey attic bedroom has stood for the breadth of at least two centuries and in all that time not one of its gentle inhabitants ever had to make do with a cold and unyielding bed of stone.

Except on *this* night. On *this* night, a dark nightfall spent far from that predictable English home, Nicolas found himself doing just that.

On *this* night, the bed on which Nicolas tried to sleep wasn't inside his snug attic bedroom. It wasn't inside the peaceful farmhouse standing outside the quiet shelter of Plumpton Head parish. It wasn't among the crinkled peaks of Cumbria. Indeed, it wasn't even in England. On *this* night, in a place faraway from England, yet nearby all the same, Nicolas was obliged to make his bed on rough courses of chipped and stained stones.

On *this* night, a night in which his hair, his clothes, and his skin were as chilled as pickled cabbage and the thin woolen blanket wrapped around his shoulders stank of unwashed horse hair, manure, and old sweat, Nicolas lay curled on the stone floor of a monstrous tunnel. A passageway. A great hall routed through an even more monstrous gate. A monstrous gate that led to an even more monstrous city. On *this* night, only a few hours after Nicolas Bennett had at long-last returned *home*; home again to Telluric Grand; home again to the strange lands of the First Kingdom; home again to the walled City of Seven

Gates, to the City of Relic, he spent the witching hours of a cold and miserable night trying to sleep on the unwelcome stone floor of a hellish corridor deep inside the belly of the Gate of the Deep.

Worse even than the suffering the stones beneath him, he spent those wretched, dark hours convinced he might be dead in the morning.

From the moment Nicolas had parted ways with Adelaide, his day had taken a series of turns for the worse.

Leading the way, the harmless page-boy Diggory weaved Nicolas in and out of the path of more gatekeep soldiers, barter-women hawking stick-cages full of chickens, pigs, and goats, and burly longshoremen off-loading ship-borne goods of cloth bolts, sacks of grain, spice tins, large jars of tallow, pickled vegetables, and berry-jams, and casks of malt-roasted ale made with wild yeast, or on-loading sturdy barrels of salt pork, cured beef, ship's biscuits, fresh water, and weevil-infested flour.

While attempting to sidestep a clutter of poorly stacked grouse cages, the toe of Nicolas' boot caught the lengthwise end of a pile of spare sail-spars resting near the stone wharf's edge. He was able to keep his balance until, at the last moment, he grabbed the first thing near-to-hand—a fistful of stodgy canvas. The canvas happened to be the roughly stitched dirty sea jacket of a dodgy-looking deckhand who hailed from a single-masted cutter moored nearby. The old sea hand whirled upon Nicolas as if he'd caught a pick-pocket and cuffed him hard enough behind his ear to send him sprawling into the grouse cages like a tenpin bowling ball. Dazed and fighting through the thundering pain in his already-battered head, Nicolas pushed himself back to his feet only to be roughly shoved along by the barter-woman whose birds he'd sent into a nasal-squealing fright.

"Hard cheese, that," Diggory said with an impressed nod of his head. He'd stood there with a crooked grin on his face doing nothing to help or intervene. "Gettin' walloped on yer head an' whacked 'bout yer ears all in the same day! Hard cheese, I'd say. I usu'lly don't earn a thumpin' more than once a day 'less the watch's gaffer catches me takin' an extra crust o' bread with my porridge." He smiled.

"Don't lemme kitch ye wharf rats grabbin' at me fine jacket agin!" growled the deckhand with the shake of his filthy fist. A nub of scar tissue served for what was left of his right ear while a large hoop of metal hung from his left one.

"Shut yer water-logged mouth!" shouted one of the channel keepers whose skiff was tied-off to the nearby, moored cutter. "Get yer stewed guts back on yer weather-bitten vessel before I 'ave the watch-men drag yer pox-breeding skin down to the Bilge. There'll be no mischief on my wharf!" The deckhand, about to let loose a reply, caught sight of a trio of soldiers armed with boarding pikes glaring harshly at him. He immediately set a smart knuckle to his forehead, spat a brown gobbet of spit on the wharf, and backed away toward his ship, his chin tucked neatly against his chest.

Diggory grabbed Nicolas by the elbow and set off again at a brisk weave-and-bob trot.

"I thought that fella was going to kill me," Nicolas said, his head and ear pounding.

"What?! That sea-plowed pillock? Nah. Them sort o' sea-lags are all mouth an' no trousers; they're afraid o' us," he said proudly with a whip of his finger. "Ya don't 'ave to worry about a legless tosser like that. It's the soldiers, an' *him*, you've got to keep a quick eye an' foot out for," Diggory said with a sly nod as they passed an exceptionally monstrously sized man who stood quietly by himself, half within the shadow of a scalloped recess carved into the seaport's stone wall.

Nicolas glanced at the man and was instantly reminded of another, almost identical, man. An immensely large, war-helmed and plate-armored man he'd once encountered outside St. Wulf's-Without-Aldersgate along with his equally enormous dog, Basileus—the ancient gatekeep's Master Grimlock who, aside from the Laird of the Gate, was the man entirely responsible for the well-being, defense, and security of the gatekeep. The huge, shadowed man standing quietly amid the din and clatter of the Portus' anchorage appeared identical to the one whom Nicolas had met so long ago except that his knee-length vest was a dark blue velvet. Like his counterpart, he also wore a substantial chain around his neck from which hung a large, flat, iron gear-like disc, and as had the other man from so long ago, his helmet's single narrow eye-slit was trained toward Nicolas, staring at him. Nicolas ducked instinctively but as he did the Gate of the Deep's Master Grimlock gave an almost imperceptible nod as if he approved of, or at least permitted, Nicolas' presence.

Gusting sea air pushed salty fingers through Nicolas' curly hair and for a moment, he felt hopeful things might become a little better. They didn't.

Minutes before, with nothing more than a brief wave, Adelaide had faded into the gloom along the arched sides of the great shipping port, following closely in the tramping wake of a heavily armed troop of billmen. Their fanged billhook weapons bobbing up and down in the air like a well-ordered cloud of blackbirds. In an instant, Nicolas missed her and wished he could follow her, but there was no stopping the forward momentum of his gawky-limbed, hurried escort.

Diggory now led them together into one of the many broad corridors leading out of the swill and stench and hullabaloo of Portus' harbor, a much drier corridor from the one Nicolas had recently escaped. This one, in fact, had a gradual slope upwards interposed by several short stages of winding stairs.

"I haven't any real orders," the page-boy panted. He'd been running back and forth delivering messages long before Nicolas had been handed off to him and the gangly fellow never seemed able to catch his breath. "Sergeant Miles didn't say nuthin' more than to take ya to the Second Watch's wardroom." His threadbare clothing flowing behind him, all ill-fitting, too large for his skinny frame, stained and shabby. "The wardroom," he repeated. "Don't 'ave much call to visit the Second Watch's wardroom these days. Not the haunt of page-boys, ya might say! All high officers an' sech, eatin' their sweet kelp with jellied eels, stargazy pie, an' cod steaks off stacks o' silver plates with silver eatin' picks an' all. No salted barley puddin' an' turtle eggs for those gents!" he exclaimed with a pleasant laugh, not a trace of bitterness in his voice.

"Could we slow down a bit?" Nicolas begged. Their half-jog pace had changed the dull press of his headache into an almost unbearable ache.

"Eh? Wots that? Slow down, ye say?" Diggory's gasps erupted in regular bursts. He wagged his narrow head, an understanding look on his face. "Aye. I bet that whack laid ya on yer beam-ends, though I can't say I've ever been much fer 'slowin' down," and on he went, his rangy feet padding up another flight of stone steps.

Before much longer and to Nicolas' relief, they found themselves entering a large apartment. An airy room with two windows flooded by the late afternoon's sunlight. Fresh sea air disturbed the thick tapestries that hung from the room's high walls. Long benches lined either side and its floor-stones were covered with colorful, braided runners. Suspended from its vaulted ceiling on an ornately carved rod of burled wood was a great drape of the same coverlet Nicolas had seen worn by the two soldiers near the edge of the sea cliff, except instead of crimson, this standard had a field of royal blue. The banner's design, however, was the same. A clawed hand rising toward a swimming man, the stitching and needlework well-defined and neatly done. Nicolas could distinguish a changing hue of color from the deepest water, a purple-cerulean shade to an almost-white sunlit blue just below the water's surface. He could make out a gnarl of sinews, veins and knuckles on the clawed hand, its gaunt fingers tipped with unnaturally long, dagger-like nails. There was stitched froth, the surface-water's chop of whitecaps, the splash of the swimmer's kicks, and even a distinct sense of where the unwary man was looking, to the sky, oblivious to the stalking nearness of the terrible threat below. Above this scene, separated by the image of a broken chain, was a picture of another large hand holding a chalice while drops of liquid spilled over its tilted edge. The drops were colored with scarlet thread, a much brighter red than wine. The sea breeze from the two windows caused the hanging banner to ripple in such a way Nicolas thought the clawed hand, the swimmer, and the spilling drink moved in slow motion. He blinked hard as he tried to clear the pain out of his head.

A pair of oak doors stood at the far end of the room, one open and one closed. Out from the open door poured sounds of unrestrained merriment, a mix of jokes and amusements from those whose rank and position provided for better draughts of honeyed wine than the bland piddle mess-stewards ladled out of grog barrels several decks below. Nicolas could smell spit-roast duck, pasties of spiced meat and potatoes, steak and kidney pudding, and vegetable pottage of cabbage, leeks, turnips, carrots, and onions. His empty stomach growled.

"A moment, if you please!" cried Diggory, waving a skinny hand at Nicolas to stay put before he slid like a rat through the open door. The general sound of laughter abruptly stopped. Nicolas heard a voice muttering, *Diggory*, answered by what sounded more like irritated grumbling than spoken words.

"Yes! I *said* the *passage tomb*, you pribbling, rump-fed, measles sore!"

Nicolas jerked as a metal plate crashed and clanked against a wall inside the room. Boorish guffaws of laughter and insults followed, and Diggory, meekly backing out of the wardroom's doorway with his head bowed, didn't bother to pick the morsels and bits of jellied ham out of his hair until they were legging it back down the same corridor from where they'd come.

"What—what happened?" Nicolas winced as the pounding in his head deepened.

"What? O' that? Ha!" spluttered Diggory, smiling merrily as he flicked a ruddy glob of pork fat onto the floor. "That was nuthin'. That was the good Captain Gybon's mannerly way o' tellin' me where to put you for the night."

Nicolas eased his way down a short flight of stairs, trying his best to keep up and nearly losing his footing on the rubbed edge of the last step. "And where… where did he say to put me up?"

Several minutes later, Nicolas found himself left alone for the second time since he'd entered the Gate of the Deep.

He and Diggory's headlong rout from the second watch's wardroom had ended in yet another wide passageway, this one deserted and much lonelier than the great seaport where so many sentries and soldiers had been. The corridor was incredibly long as if it ran the entire width of the gatekeep; so long, both its ends disappeared in a darkness not penetrated by any light. It was narrow too, with a low-vaulted ceiling, rough-quarried walls, and only a few sporadic torches that barely illuminated its middle. It was a shadowy place. An abandoned place. Ghostly.

"Here you'll sleep fer the night," Diggory said without looking at Nicolas, his fingers interlaced as if he were apologizing. "I was told ta tell ya that yer not,... not a prisoner, but—" the page-boy hesitated, "but ya also can't leave. I'm sure they'll be by ta fetch you in the mornin' an' give you yer breakfast an' such." He said this last bit quickly, matter-of-factly as if would ward off any awkward questions Nicolas might have. Then, for several moments, Diggory stood uncharacteristically still. Only his eyes flickered nervously.

"What is it?" Nicolas finally asked, trying hard not to sound exasperated or afraid.

"There's to be a trial, I heard," the thin-lipped boy whispered.

"A trial?" Nicolas felt a rising sickness in his stomach and chest.

"Aye, well that, or an ordeal. I don't really know which but—but I hear they've taken neck-ropes to the suthren Hangin' Point."

"Oh." Nicolas didn't know what else to say. He felt sick. His mouth was dry and his face twitched; his eyes wetter than he would've liked for Diggory to see, he clenched his jaw and balled his fists. "Well it *can't* be a trial for me," he said with almost a snort. "I haven't done anything wrong."

Diggory looked up, his eyes bright as if Nicolas' innocence hadn't yet occurred to him. "Right o'! Might not be you at all!" The page-boy stared at his dirty bare feet. "I'm sorry fer all this," he said. "Ya seem like a nice lad."

Nicolas closed his eyes, willing the pain in his head to disappear. He took a deep breath. "It's alright. It's alright. It really is *quite* alright," even though nothing felt alright. Nicolas was simply repeating this to himself more than he was saying to Diggory. As if his father were standing over him reminding him of his manners, Nicolas forced his best smile. A surge of pain flashed behind his eyes. "Off with you now!"

Diggory opened his mouth about to say something, thought better of it, snapped it shut, opened it again and with a sigh, closed it. He pulled a tattered and stained blanket from under his thin coverlet and tossed it to Nicolas. Giving a quick nod of his head, he touched a knuckle to his brow, turned and sped away.

Nicolas watched as his brief companion dashed back the way they'd come, his thin clothing aflutter in his wake like a nervous scold of flapping brown jays.

"You've gone an' made a dog's dinner of *this* adventure," Nicolas muttered to himself, angrily smashing a fist against his thigh. "Left in a dungeon, conked on the head, not once but twice! Run up a tower and down a tower like it's a doddle, never a bite to eat or a kind word, and now this bloody place to bloody-well wait for some kind of bloody trial! *That* takes the biscuit, Nicolas Bennett! That *really* takes the biscuit." The cruel echo of his voice sounded hollow and lost and hadn't made him feel any better. There was little left to do but look around. Strangely, the passageway didn't seem to have the same tidal-dank, sea water tang as did much of the rest of the gatekeep, but it also didn't have the drier, breeze-washed scent of the waiting chamber outside the second watch's wardroom. The long, tunnel-like chamber was relatively dry but filled with a nasty, foul odor like burned, sour earth. Smack in the middle of the passage Nicolas noticed a very large hole, large enough for ten or fifteen men to be lowered into it at the same time except the hole was covered by an even larger grill of copper-sheathed bars.

Nicolas wrinkled his nose and snapped Diggory's blanket open. It also stank and Nicolas held it at arm's-length. Its stench was of more familiar smells—earthy manure, day-old sweat, and a damp barnyard's moldering hay. Far preferable odors, these, to the sulphuric, blistered stench that permeated the long passageway.

Nicolas shivered. The corridor was cold.

Chilled lines of anxious sweat rolled down his back under his armpits and at the back of his knees. He wrapped the scruffy blanket around his shoulders. His feet ached. His head ached. He wanted to sleep. He wanted to hide. He roamed a short way up and down the cracked and burnished flagstones, looking for a tucked away corner, some kind of alcove or recess that might feel warm and safe. There were none. His tired feet eventually took him near the great hole he'd seen. The stink saturating the rest of the long hall seemed to come out of the hole and so did a curious flow of warmed air. Nicolas pulled his clammy sweater over his nose and collapsed a few feet from the grimy green patina of the copper-covered grating. He ran his hands absentmindedly over the rough floor, picking up bits and bobs of chipped stone and pebbles. He began arranging them into a very specific, yet peculiar, design. The impulse was an unconscious and eccentric habit Nicolas never really thought about; it didn't happen very often.

Shortly after Jack's death six years ago, one of Nicolas' teachers, an observant, elderly lady named Ms. Drum, had brought it to Mr. and Mrs. Bennett's attention after noticing Nicolas repeat the unusual routine on a daily basis during his class's outdoor free time. At the time they all agreed it was likely a way Nicolas was coping with the stress and grief of his brother's loss. The odd design he made never varied and over time the frequency of the bizarre habit lessened. On rare occasions in the years that followed, occasions during which Nicolas was under extreme anxiety or pressure, Mr. or Mrs. Bennett would notice the same behavior; identical every time; Nicolas would sit on the ground, stare off into space, and reflexively gather bits and bobs of things while arranging them in a very particular way. The act seemed harmless enough and neither his parents nor Nicolas ever said anything about it.

As Nicolas sat there on the stone floor, he thought of Benjamin, wondering where he was inside the gatekeep and why he'd been arrested and mistreated. He thought of Aldus and his blind eye, hoping desperately the Laird of the First Gate would come in the morning and sort things out. He thought of Ranulf and the steadiness of his character, wishing his strong friend was with him to laugh and light a fire. And he thought of Adelaide; Nicolas thought of her the most, his eyes nearly closing in a dream. Her fragrant hair, her determined yet beautiful face, and the earnest closeness in her embrace.

He stretched himself out on the broad flagstones, granite stones better meant for thick walls of castle keeps, for grinding wheels, for rough weights, pillars, and the bones of mountains. His bed of stones pushed uncomfortably against his back so he flipped to his side. He thought of the shouted order he'd heard coming out of the second watch's wardroom, '*the passage tomb!*' and Nicolas thought of gravestones. Stones that marked where corpses lay. Stones that walled ancient dark barrows of people long-dead. Even more troubling, Nicolas thought of the blood-black stones of the ogre Sultan's hovel deep inside the Black Forest near the Falls of Cadgamlan, a sickening place where he once believed Adelaide had died, a place in which he'd believed he might die as well.

His sleepy and uneasy imagination thought of stony places for much darker things, ghastly misshapen things, things that have some frightful and wicked business with the dead. Nicolas wondered if he was spending the night in such a place as that. A stony bed-turned-tomb for his last night of sleep before being unfairly tried like some criminal. Maybe they would hang him; after all they'd hurt small Benjamin. Why would they care to treat him any differently?

His sleep-heavy eyelids sagged closed. Opened. Then closed again. The painful thump inside his head was a little less than it had been.

Like a dull prisoner gazing out of a small cell window, the slipping consciousness of his mind plunged back to a snow-blanketed Christmas, to dreams of his attic bedroom, and just as he fell into the deeper waters of oblivion, he thought of a black feather's plumes from long ago. The feather's image became a doorknocker. The doorknocker became a hanging corpse. It swung against a vast, door with a large square of iron on its face, covered in strange writing.

We are the dead, he heard a legion of mournful voices say.

CHAPTER 8

The Trial of a Blood Horde

"You there!"

Shocked to the edge of consciousness, Nicolas tried opening his eyes. He could feel his eyebrows lifting, doing their best to pull open his eyelids but his eyes remained stubbornly shut, glued together. *Poppycock,* his thoughts a stewed grog of deep weariness, *that such a short wink of sleep is called a long night. Not a long night at all, that. It was a short night. Too short. I don't think I managed three winks of sleep the entire time. I've barely had a kip!*

Nicolas' bed of hard stones, made even more uncomfortable by the anxiety and pain drumming inside his head, had caused him to wear away most of the night half-awake. Worse yet, there had been a nicking current of cold air fingering its way through the passage, shaping a circle around the warm stench filtering up from the grated hole. Diggory's reeky, shabby blanket had provided scant comfort but the rise of heated air, as horrible as it smelled, had kept the chilly draught from turning Nicolas' tense night into a truly miserable one.

"Feels like ten to five in the mornin'," Nicolas said as he stifled a yawn. "I don't think I can open my eyes." With his head still aching and with fear of what the day may hold, he didn't much care to.

"You boy! Get away from there!" As had the first shout, this bellowed order came from somewhere faraway, a smart stone's throw down the length of the long passage. It seemed to carry as much alarm with it as authority. "Come away from that infernal hole, ya idle-headed foot-licker!"

The foot-licker accusation reminded Nicolas of his thirst and hunger, and he ran his parched tongue along dry lips and gave his head a brisk shake. "I'm awake! I'm awake!" he croaked as if responding to shouts from his mum on an early school morning. "What's o'clock?"

A pause of confusion followed. "Eh? O'clock?' What in the infernal? Yer as barmy as a stock-fish. Quit yer fopdoodlin' talk an' get yer loiter-sack away from that unlucky hole!"

"An' *you* quit whinging like a baby," Nicolas said stiffly under his breath. Wriggling both hands beneath him, Nicolas pushed himself a few paving stones away from the edge of the hole's gummy grate. He drew up his knees, heaved onto all fours, and with a lurch, wobbled to his feet. "I'm awake!" he croaked again but this time with what his father would have said was ill-mannered annoyance.

His aggravation was met with a sarcastic chuckle. "Fine, fine. Don't get yer spar-lines in a twist." The man's voice had a single volume: loud. "I've never seen nor heard o' any soul with any life-preservin' instinct get near that damned hole. I've got no idea who told ya to sleep so close to it, it's a goblin's curse just to be in this deserted place at all."

Nicolas pulled his sore shoulders back and stretched. Every inch of him was hurting, even the inches that hadn't been poked or pushed by the floor stones. He was as thirsty as desert dust and he squirmed his face muscles about, doing his best to force himself fully awake. The bump on the back of his head didn't feel quite as tender as it had the evening before; neither did the slight bruise behind his ear. Not wanting to show any weakness, Nicolas began heading for the sound of the loud voice even before his drooping eyes had fully adjusted to the blurred light of the dim passage tomb.

A half-squad of eight soldiers, four armored spearmen in leather caps and shirts of round-linked mail, and four more heavily-armored swordsmen wearing open-faced helmets with aventails to protect their necks, steel plate-mail over chain-link on their bodies, and leather breeches with hardened leather greaves on their legs, were standing in a loose square formation. Their sergeant, a larger, muscled man with a brightly polished belt-buckle and a helmet notched with axe scars and hammer dents stood at their front. His thick arms were folded over his broad chest, partially masking a coverlet with the same deep blue background Nicolas had seen the evening before.

"The weak-kneed Mr. Killick from the First Watch 'as been spreadin' scuttlebutt all over the gatekeep that yer as tall as an archangel! By 'is description, yer supposed to be nine feet tall w'id smoked wings, a beak made o' iron, an' a single, web foot." The sergeant laughed until tears welled in his eyes. He wiped them away and with a sneer, glared at Nicolas. "I don't see no webbed foot, an' ye ain't any taller than poor Esmond." He jerked the stump of a missing thumb toward one of the shorter spearmen who stood at the back of the square. The sergeant's eyes landed on Nicolas' Malham boots. "Ya certainly ain't no seaborne beast. Can't be; not with those 'eavy limbers of leather on yer feet."

Nicolas, perhaps because of the anxious night, perhaps because of the ache in his bones and muscles, or perhaps because of the cuffs of pain rapping at the back of his eyes, leveled a narrow gaze at the sergeant. "I'm *not* seaborne," he prickled back. A low, dead tone, surprising even himself. His ears red with embarrassment and anger. "I'm—I'm a *Dragon Nightfall.*"

Two of the younger, pimple-faced soldiers gasped, low-rank sappers roughly Nicolas' same age who knew little more than to point the tips of their spears in an enemy's direction. The sergeant snapped his stony face around and gave his crew a bitter look before turning a malevolent hawk-eye toward Nicolas. "If *that's* the truth of it," he said, his voice a cagey, thin scrape that scared Nicolas more than his loud shouts, "I'm *sure* Laird Halen will know. Form up!" he roared. The soldiers jumped, jostled, drew to order, and away they all went, the nervous Wren and weary Dragon Nightfall trimly bordered by a ring of the gatekeep's soldiers, feeling very much like a condemned felon.

Nicolas was out of breath and his throat burned by the time they came to a halt. By then he was too tired and whipped for irritation or anger.

Once leaving the long passageway, they'd climbed flights of stairs more numerous than he could count. Crooked stairs. Straight stairs. Narrow stairs. Broad stairs. Stairs with dry and sandy footing, and stairs with slippery mildew and spotted toadstools in their cracks. Stairs that twisted and snaked and screwed and unscrewed, but always they climbed, higher and higher, until Nicolas was certain, in brief thoughts pinched betwixt gasps for air, they must eventually run out. And finally, they did.

"Hold here," the sergeant growled, also slightly out of breath.

Beads of sweat trickled down Nicolas' temples and he could feel a spread of cold wetness in the small of his back. His thick sweater was terribly warm and his boots had grown heavier with each new flight of stairs. Around him the soldiers panted but said nothing.

Their brisk march had brought them to a spacious, terraced landing of cleanly chiseled stone with such finely fitted joints no mortar had been used to build it. Tall window slits ventilated ash-grey walls, allowing crisp, sweeping fins of late morning light to slice through the air like giant sickle blades. Above an outsized set of iron-strapped doors on the far side of the landing and at the head of two broadly spaced stairs, hung a single decoration, a discolored and frayed standard, the horrible clawed hand crudely stitched into rough sailcloth, stained dark red. Six, stately archers, all sinewy, towering men with hard jaws, deep-set eyes, broad shoulders, and muscular hands covered in metal-studded gloves, stood in two, unmoving groups on either side of the large doors. Longbows of mated elm and lemonwood, strung with woven cords of flax and silk, lay against their chests or balanced in the crooks of their arms.

The muscular sergeant hesitated for a moment.

Nicolas had the distinct impression he was taken aback by the archers' presence but any indecision in his step was imperceptibly brief; he stomped over to the closest archer, a seventh man, one who stood apart from the other two groups as if he'd intended to set himself squarely between the approaching soldiers and the large set of doors. This seventh archer, slightly taller than the others, wore strange crests the size of tea saucers. Silver circlets containing discs of banded agate stone engraved with a twin of holly leaves on either side of the drooping bell of a snowdrop flower. The large crests clasped the archer's deep purple cloak to his sculpted leather chest guard. Everything about him seemed purposeful; splendid as it was and noble.

"What business might you have?"

His question possessed a low, studied pitch, challenging but not yet unfriendly. His words were accented differently than the rest of the men Nicolas had encountered; each word neatly formed as if the force of his breath individually unwound them one-by-one from some kind of spool hidden inside the archer's drawn cheeks.

"We 'ave the boy, the one 'ho came in through the suthren door," the sergeant said flatly.

The seventh archer had no reaction; his measured look rested briefly on Nicolas, then to the square of soldiers surrounding him, and back again to the barrel-chested sergeant. He seemed unsurprised to see Nicolas. Again came an unwinding of flawlessly refined words. "If you would be so kind—*where* has he been?"

The sergeant shifted his weight. He and the archer did not appear to know each other. Nicolas couldn't see the sergeant's face but he could see how the sergeant stood like a rugby player about to bind himself in a scrum. "Why in the passage tomb, *that's* where, if ya must know! That's where we were ordered to fetch 'im from."

"And if I may impose upon you again, sergeant. It is sergeant, isn't it? *Who* told you to fetch him, as you say? Why was he overnighted in the passage tomb?" The archer's words were all spoken in the same untroubled tone but in them, a whisper of accusation crept about the edges of the last question.

"Cap'in Piers, First Officer of the Second Watch. He gave the order. I… I don't know *why* the boy was there. I suppose a watch officer sent 'im there." The sergeant straightened his back with an air of veteran impudence. "An' just as kindly in return, *who* might you be? I can see yer a pack o' *Eodur Nihtweard*, king-guardians an' all that, but *who* are ya, an' *why* are ya standin' as if yer post is to be outside my own Laird's deck?" His bullish head thrust forward, his hand on the grip of his sword, and with graveled, combative menace he asked bitingly, "An' *why* are yer war bow's *strung* while ya stand *inside* a forfeited gatekeep o' the City?"

For a long moment, the seventh archer stood there silently, regarding the sergeant. Then, like the viper that dripped its venom over the Norse god Loki, words dropped evenly out of his mouth with a ferocious assertion. "*I* am *Ansgar. I* am an islander-come-home like my father, and his fathers before him, and their fathers before them. *I* am a Throne Shield. A Sovereign Protector. *I* am *Eodur Nihtweard* of the First Kingdom. My bow bears my oath and my arrows are its prosecution! The High Chancellor, deputy of the empty throne, sits within your Laird's courthall. *That* is why we are here." By the time Ansgar, a rare and high Captain of the King's Guardians, an ancient order formed at the dawn of the First Kingdom, finished, the gatekeep's sergeant had taken a step backward. His back was still straight but his chin was drawn to his chest as if tucked against a slanted rainstorm. Ansgar's tone had been black, powerfully restrained yet filled with veiled counsels of authority and timeless doom. Nicolas could almost sense the soldiers around him tremble, even the swordsmen, those stout men born to war and to the Gate of the Deep's mortal defense.

Yet Ansgar's commanding words hadn't troubled Nicolas.

Nicolas found a bizarre sense of authentic peace as Ansgar had spoken, the kind of restful calm he often felt when Mrs. Bennet would turn off his night lamp, kiss him on the forehead, and in her beautiful sing-song of an Irishwoman's lilt say,

May yer thoughts be as glad as the shamrocks.
May yer heart be as light as a song.
An' may the angels bring bright an' happy dreams ta stay with ya all night long.

Nicolas missed his mum, desperately missed her. He missed the familiar homeliness of the Bennett's farmhouse, the squeal of the sagging gate's hinges in their small yard's fence, the sheep pasture's friendly green span, and the cool copse of trees on its far side. Nicolas, exhausted and still sick at his stomach with anxiety, felt a renewed stab of pain from the lump on the back of his head as he realized he missed his parents' home. A different home than this.

In the same moment, Nicolas also realized the tall, seventh archer, Ansgar, was staring at him, a most bemused expression on his face. Ansgar threw his head back and along with the six purple-cloaked archers standing behind him erupted into lively explosions of laughter. The sergeant glowered at Nicolas as meanly as he could, and the square formation of soldiers around him loosened, all of them also staring at him, some a bit confused and others amused. The tension that had filled the landing like a lightning storm about to burst had almost entirely vanished. To his everlasting embarrassment, Nicolas abruptly realized he must have said his mother's evening benediction aloud.

Ansgar wiped tears from his eyes. "The rumors have all said he gives the King's Grace in moments of execution, but no one has said anything about the boldness of his levity in moments of near-battle. Perhaps we fools should have let the boy speak first."

The less-than-amused sergeant spat on the floor in disgust. "Hrmph! He 'asn't got the wits of a pollywog, this one! I spotted 'im sleepin' next to the passage tomb's murder hole."

Immediately, all laughter died away.

"What do you mean?" Ansgar's eyes were thin splits of dark coal.

"I mean when we woke 'im up this marn, he was nestled like a loon next to the grate coverin' the murder hole."

"Is this true?!"

Nicolas, caught off balance by having been the object of laughter one moment and the target of a blunt question the next, wasn't sure how to respond. "I don't know what he means by 'murder hole.' The passage was… was *cold.* I was cold. There weren't no bed, nowhere to go. I didn't sleep much at all anyway, but yes, I slept next to a large grate on the floor. It was the only place I could find that had a bit of heat." Nicolas looked at the quiet faces surrounding him. "It did *stink,*" he added meekly. "Smelled like a dead lizard rotting in the sun."

The archer's face became quizzical. His voice was gentle. "You weren't afraid, lad?"

"No—no, I wasn't afraid of the grate."

"I didn't mean the grate."

"Oh. No, I wasn't afraid of the hole either, the murder hole, if that's what you mean." Nicolas looked from Ansgar to the sergeant, and from the sergeant to the soldiers, and from the soldiers to the other archers. All of their faces held a mix of bewilderment and shock. "Should I have been?" He wondered if he'd said or done something wrong or stupid.

"Perhaps," said Ansgar more absentmindedly than agreeable. "Perhaps not." The tall archer gave his chin a shake and looked sharply at the sergeant. "Thank you, sergeant. I'll take him from here."

It looked as if the sergeant might challenge the tall archer. Dark defiance shown on his face then faded, finally sliding into sour contempt. "Fine! Take the little lubberwort if ya'd like. My orders were only to bring 'im to the Laird's deck. That we've done." He spit again. "Away to stations," he bellowed and away he and his men went, leaving Nicolas alone with the archers.

The trial, as it was, was a dreadful and frightening affair.

Even before Nicolas entered the judgment court—that stately seat of Halen Ward, Laird of the Gate of the Deep, the Second Gate of the City of Relic, and Deputy Viceroy and council member of the Commissioners of the Forfeited Gates, who was also a sworn judge of the Kings' First Bench—the trial had gone very badly.

Once his soldier escort had marched away, the six archers reacted in unison and opened the iron-strapped doors and formed together in a half-circle behind Nicolas. Ansgar waited until their silent movements were complete before turning and leading all of them into the large chamber beyond the doors.

Those who lived and worked in the gatekeep referred to the space into which they walked as the angel's seat. Its official name was Courthall of the King's First Bench,' a designated area or room common in each of the City of Relic's gatekeeps in which the laird of each gatekeep performed the office of a judge, second only to the vacant throne. The arrangement of each courthall was varied according to the traditions and habits of each gatekeep and its laird. The angel's seat in the Gate of the Deep served a twofold purpose for Laird Halen; one as a court and the other as a high lookout and strongroom. The chamber had earned its nickname because of its incredible height, nearly the loftiest room in the gate, and its unrestricted view of the faraway, seaward horizon, a magnificent panorama of sky and ocean beyond an open and exposed esplanade running along one entire side of the large chamber; a vast window that could be closed with great sail-drapes of waxed canvas to keep out violent, seaborne weather. Like the outspread lip of a monstrous stone giant, the gatekeep's suspended walkway served as a manmade cloud's perch far above the blustery, green chop of the Bay of Wrath and the expanse of the Cold Sea. Halen Ward's dais and seat were on the opposite side, flanked by two great fireplaces with mantle shelves that shouldered the bases of stony, lancet arches vaulting across the ceiling of the dais. The rest of the chamber was commonly lined with sitting benches, long racks of map cylinders, boxes of signal flags, writing desks, and in the room's center, an immense oak table where the Laird's high officers and advisors would gather for occasional ward suppers or the sober assembly of war councils.

For that morning's trial, an exceptional trial compared to routine matters of entry into the City, petty theft, or deciding whether a grain merchant on his way to market had mixed his oats with sawdust to swindle unwitting customers, the oak table had been removed in three substantial sections. In its place, stood fifteen very large, very wicked looking men.

They were all much like the huge, tattooed prisoner Nicolas had encountered by the sea cliff, heavily bearded with heads completely or partially shaven. They were muscled but rabidly lean, reminding Nicolas of a rangy pack of filthy, starving wolves. Each of them appeared half-mad with fierce smiles and pitiless leers that further disfigured their hard faces. One of the men bled freely from his scalp, his face a ghastly mask of dark blood. As rivulets moved past the corner of his mouth, he stuck out his tattooed tongue and licked them.

The men were bound with black manacles around their ankles and wrists, but they were not stooped and submissive as ordinary prisoners might be under the weight of such heavy shackles. On the contrary, their postures were cagey, primed as if to ambush. Nicolas noticed they all seemed to be slightly panting as did the gatekeep's swordsmen who enclosed them in a half-circle. From the four dead bodies lying in the middle of the floor, it was clear the threat of bloodshed had become a shocking reality mere minutes before Nicolas and the archers entered the angel's seat. Three other tattooed and bound prisoners, their lifeless lips drawn back in depraved contortions of pain and spiteful satisfaction, alongside their one victim, an unlucky guard, hardly older than Nicolas he seemed, his eyes locked open in the last moments of mortal fright;

his death swift and vicious. The tattered livery of the young guard's coverlet, torn and ripped open by the dead prisoners' hands before they'd ripped into him with concealed shards of splintered stone, was sodden with the murky blood that oozed from his recently gutted liver.

These dead, and those who now waited to die, were War Crows.

Merciless, clannishly bred to savagery and physical audacity, they used the ocean as feathered crows use the open sky, to sail from across the Cold Sea's eastern horizon from the Land Beyond the Fogs, flocked in black ships of fired blackwood, hoisting black sails stitched with knotted black hair, ornamented with great, black feathers. "Blood hordes" were what landsmen called them in frightened whispers; brutish invaders who sacked the shore towns of the First Kingdom in random flotillas of five to ten longboats, competing for quick-stolen riches and slave-raiding, believing there were only two ways for any War Crow to properly die, by violence or by drowning.

No great invasion of War Crows had ever occurred but for the early spring of 963 R.R. [the R.R. is an annotation for "Relic Rule," the official calendar of time for the First Kingdom first sanctioned by King Widofell in 294 R.R.]. That invasion, as it was, a fog-bourne fleet of at least fifty, black longboats, carrying a thousand carnage-eager Crows, had beached their scored hulls south of the merchant port of Galloglass, south of the eastern tip of the Southern Fells, along the wide, gently-sloped, and dune-hillocked beaches of the Lowlands. The great blood horde, a loose confederation of ancestral rooks, had swept inland like a reckless, rogue wave, burning, killing, thieving, and savaging market towns and farms, murdering the few who dared resist. Three cohorts of the Fourth Grey Legion's old guard, Talon Knights and men-at-arms, had marched without rest from the City of Relic's fourth gatekeep, Sire Long-Knife's Gate, believing the unchecked blood horde might turn its brutal attention northward once it tired of easy slaughter. Shrewd strategy had succeeded in baiting the leaderless Crows up against the lower reaches of the sickle-like Hourglass Hills, and like a great hammer smashing against an anvil, the gatekeep's regimented cohorts had crashed its ranks of heavy cavalry, sharpened long pikes, cleated maces, fearsome war hammers, and two-handed swords against the unready and fragmented blood hordes of Crows until not a dying groan was heard across the killing field.

Hundreds of tattooed corpses were heaped into horse wagons and hay carts and hauled back to the sea. There they were scattered across the shore's cold sand, abandoned among bearded clumps of bent seagrass as grisly warnings to any blood horde that might follow.

Gammeldags, those sloe-eyed nomadic families from far corners of the Wilds, arrived a few days later to burgle the dead Crows of their gold teeth, silver rings, and iron axes but found nothing left among the silent dunes except blood-gored sand, a few crab-chewed legs and arms, and a score of severed tongues. Word spread quickly throughout the First Kingdom. In frightened whispers it was rumored the War Crow corpses had cut out their own tongues so their story of defeat would never be retold and then sailed back across the Cold Sea in burning longboats of pitch and sulfur.

The surviving members of the much smaller blood horde who now stood before Laird Halen Ward had defamed the noble courthall of the Second Gate by turning the august chamber into a murderous sepulcher.

The atmosphere felt oppressively tight, cloying, and reeked of sweat and blood.

Nicolas, near-panicked by what he saw and by memories that rose up like the ghosts of the corpses sprawled out on the floor, was fixed in place. Every muscle felt knotted and cruelly pinched. His mind's eye was filled with the sight of a bludgeoned tinker dying on a dark forest road, an ogre's blood-wet, razor-sharp fingernails dragging in the grass, a dying Wisp gasping and sinking to his knees, and worst of all, an empty chair at the Bennett's kitchen table, tragic thoughts of Jack.

Indeed, Nicolas felt Death was coming.

Tantallon Castle, one of the last of Scotland's great keeps, a once-upon-a-time, curtain wall stronghold of the Douglas family, brought to wreck and ruin in 1651 by swarms of anti-Royalist soldiers, now stares across a vast span of cold water with hollow eye-sockets of abandoned windows, empty doorways, useless crenel arrow slits, and rubbled parapet walks. The castle sits next to the outermost waters of the Firth of Fourth, the dark water's swells and chops colliding with the raw bitterness of the North Sea and with Bass Rock, a rare volcanic rock-island soaring over three hundred feet into the air.

Nicolas had a handful of blurred memories of this decayed castle, the massive rock, and the shadowy green waters between them that were left-over from a weekend holiday taken when he was only five. They were memories he rarely let himself revisit. They slept in the back of his mind, shrouded under a single, clear memory of pain and fear.

Peter Bennett had spoilt the family with an overnight stay and dinner at the enchanting Open Arms Hotel in Dirleton just off the A198. They'd been booked in one of the garden suites and enjoyed an incredible dinner in The Library. Carrot and honey soup, pan-fried border beef with creamy mash and parsnip puree, and for dessert Jack had eaten a vanilla and raspberry custard tart while Nicolas stuck with salted caramel ice cream covered in a chocolate fondant. Nicolas recalled a lot of laughter at the table although he couldn't remember anything that was said other than Jack repeating "scrummy!" throughout the entire meal like a nutcracker, his grey eyes wide, a fork in one hand and a ready spoon in the other.

The following day had been all about castle visits—Jack's passion. Mr. Bennett let him set their course for the day's adventure. There was, of course, the Dirleton Castle to begin with, a stout fortress of brown, drab rock heavily damaged during the Wars of Scottish Independence; then south to Yester Castle outside the village of Gifford to see its undercroft room called Goblin Hall, where it was once believed a powerful necromancer had summoned armies of hobgoblins; afterward turning east to Innerwick Castle and a muddy walk up to its failing walls and barrow-like arches, built on the sharp edge of a high crag overlooking a wooded glen carpeted with rare ferns; then northeast to Dunbar Castle, said to have once been burnt by Kenneth MacAlpin, Kenneth I, the first King of Scots; and finally north along the coast, past Seacliff Beach to the bony remains of Auldhamme Castle, a supposed grave for the corpse of Saint Baldred of Tyninghame. From there, as dusk began to close in, the family made their way a little further to Tantallon Castle and its sweeping view of the Firth of Fourth.

That August evening faded fast as warm, weatherly winds from the east helped the sun find its resting place. It had been a long day but everyone was in a fine mood, *right chuffed!* as Jack put it with a silly smile on his face. Aside from the sandstone Castle of the Kings, in Castle Park, on the southern edge of Penrith, these were the first castles Nicolas remembered seeing and for years thereafter 'castle-spotting' became an enduring Bennett-family tradition; an homage of tender pilgrimages, never discussed but understood, to the son and brother they were soon to lose.

"Pick me up, Dad," Jack had said at once with his slender arms out in front of him. Mr. Bennett had swung Jack atop his shoulders. "I want to see if I can see the castle on The Bass." The rock island's castle ruins of basalt and rough rubble were too far away to see, but Jack's grinning delight was indomitable. "Birds! Look at the birds!" he'd shouted, pointing wildly as the world's largest colony of Northern gannets rose from the rock in heaving squabbles and from on high, speared themselves into the sea in search of food. Nicolas remembered his brother's broad smile and he remembered minutes later when the smile faded, abruptly replaced by wide eyes and a distant, pale look of deep anxiety.

"Put me down, Dad," Jack whispered, his voice hoarse. Nicolas' older brother looked especially thin and vulnerable silhouetted against the lowering sky. "*Death* is coming."

It was the only time Nicolas ever recalled his brother using the word 'death.' It startled and frightened him. He looked out to sea where Jack's gaze had been. The most colossal press of bone-white fog Nicolas had ever seen. A sea fret as the Scots would say—was rolling in from the North Sea as if it were a ghostly sandstorm. He watched as it easily swallowed The Bass. The gannets' remote wet croaks soon weakened and sounded like the garbled cries of drowning men. The bizarre fog, a rarity anywhere else in the world, closed in the sky and with it came a terrible silence.

Jack had four months to live.

The same menacing, grave silence now swathed the angel's seat as if it all sound inside the chamber had been consumed by that same thick *haar*, the impenetrable sea-fog bred by the North Sea. The air was dense and dangerous, a squally headwind had driven a pocket of dead calm into the Laird's Courthall of the King's First Bench. Nicolas' mouth and throat were dry. Dread wrapped its wiry fingers around his heart and Fear kept him from breathing. Death garlanded the air and made it smell sickly sweet with a hint of metal, the stink of iron from spilled blood.

Halen Ward, a corpulent but powerful man, sat still-composed in his stone chair, silently spiking his hard fingers against its cold arms. He was dressed in an imperial robe. A thick golden chain was draped around his neck from which hung a large golden key inlaid with two, swirl-grey stones. He stared intently at the nine hellish men chained in front of him and his piercing look never strayed even when Nicolas entered the chamber. He seemed to take no notice of the English boy or his archer escorts.

But the foremost prisoner did.

"*You*!" The prisoner hissed, spewing gluey spittle through the heavy air. The Crow's lunatic smile revealed jagged, broken teeth and a dark mouth wetted with fresh blood. "*You*," his gory voice an accusation, "*you!* Are you the king-come-again *or*," his black eyes narrowed wolfishly and his breath came in violent bursts through his nostrils, "are you the *Worm of Crows*?"

Nicolas recognized the prisoner's voice. It was the same voice Nicolas had heard in the watery bilge-dungeon far below. His fingers and toes went as cold as brittle frost, cold as if he was standing barefoot and gloveless in the rippled snowdrifts covering the sheep pasture. Terror clenched his heart and his dry mouth was shut fast; he hadn't any idea what to say.

"*Speak!*" demanded the prisoner. Nasty ribbons of black saliva slung from his black mouth. A powerfully built guard lunged forward and drove the iron-capped haft of his halberd into the man's rib bones. The prisoner grunted, doubled over and wheezed mists of sputum onto the floor before defiantly rising back to his feet. He kept his wicked eyes on Nicolas.

The Laird of the Gate of the Deep, a judge of the King's First Bench, stood and folded his long arms across his broad chest. As he did so, a roil of high nor'easterly breeze reached into the back of the chamber and washed out the stifling stillness, stirring the deep folds of his robe. Absolute sentence was to be passed and the crossing of Halen Ward's arms was a traditional sign of no chance for higher appeal by the accused. A decision had been made.

The Laird's voice, scraping, grainy like coarse sea salt ground against rock, was deliberate. "Having heard the crown's witnesses; having weighed the evidence; and having entertained fair audience of those accused of various crimes against the harmony and goodwill of the First Kingdom, the King's First Bench is prepared to enter just sentence on those brought before the bench under charge. All those," he gave a first brief glance toward Nicolas, "*except* those brought here under pardon or as guests, step forward and hear your sentence. For the crime of invasion, the sentence is death. For the crime of breach of the King's peace, the sentence is death. For the crime of banditry, the sentence is death. For the crime of rogue cruelty, the sentence is death. And for the crimes of hostile manslaying and blood-thirst, the sentence is death!" Halen Ward paused, but none of the prisoners reacted.

The prisoner at the front, still wheezing from cracked ribs, had never stopped staring at Nicolas. Laird Ward pointed to the man. "You there! For the last time, the Judge of this Courthall demands to know who is the leader of this vile blood horde? What is your name? Why have you come?!"

Silence.

At last the foremost prisoner peeled his maniacal stare away from Nicolas and looked daggers at Halen Ward. Thin bloodlets bubbled in the corner of his mouth and fizzled down his chin. He let out a harsh, hacking laugh. "*I* am the Murder," he said in slow, cracked speech. "*We* are the Murder. There *is* no king and the Murder brings *war*!"

The face of the Laird of the Second Gate hardened to the color of grey flint. His voice callous, he said, "Very well then. For the execution of these sentences, the hangman's tower has been prepared. But—" the Laird's unwavering eyes narrowed into a pitiless expression; he leaned forward, "—as you've made so brazenly clear, you and your blood horde are nothing more than murderous *crows*. And Crows—Crows *fly*!" With that, the Laird ordered each prisoner thrown from the soaring heights of the chamber's open esplanade. The prisoner who had spoken was the last of the condemned War Crows to be flung to his death. At the last moment he ripped himself away from the guards' grasps and hurled his filthy body into the sharp, cobalt blue of the morning sky. He let out a guttering screech as he fell, a hateful and shrill scream that ended a few, short seconds later as shore stones of the First Kingdom cracked his tattooed skull open like a limpet's bony shell.

Except for the edgy breathing of the guards who'd carried out the executions, the angel's seat again fell quiet and finally, after a long, vacant stare into the open sky Halen Ward turned a more composed face to Nicolas. "And *you*—" his voice now shrewd but braced to impose the same mortal sentence on a thirteen-year-old boy "—we must now settle who *you* are. Are you a friend of War Crows? Hmmm…" His eyes were searching. "I doubt it. A long-dead curse come to life? I also think not. Perhaps, and this possibility I like," there was a touch of sarcasm "a king-to-be? Or most likely of all," Halen Ward scratched his stubbled chin and settled stiffly into his stone chair "you are *nobody*, a no one. In any case, I deem you as a guest of the gatekeep... at least for the moment, boy."

"If I may," offered a wonderfully familiar voice coming out of a deep shadow by one of the fireplaces that flanked the Laird's stone chair, "the lad's certainly *not* a crow. And if he's a *curse*, then I'm nothing but a toadstool fit for a bowl of mud-toe soup."

Nicolas grinned so widely his cheek muscles hurt. Hot tears warmed his face. He didn't care; he knew everything was about to be set right.

"And as for your third proposition, my esteemed and fellow Laird," the familiar voice continued, "might I counsel patience and an opportunity to speak in private? After all, each of us remains a *no one* until our purpose reveals us as *someone*. For the moment, this 'no one' standing before you is only a cold, tired, and misunderstood boy. And," said Aldus Ward, a shadow-against-the-wall-stepping-into-the-light, "I'd wager he is a most exceptional boy as well."

The Laird of the First Gate was, of course, right on all counts.

CHAPTER 9

The Direction of Footprints

Aldus Ward, Laird of St. Wulf's-Without-Aldersgate, the First Gate of the City of Relic, and the greatest among the Commissioners of the six Forfeited Gates, But perhaps most meaningful of all, a dear friend and counselor to Nicolas Bennett, was busily acting more like a distraught chamber servant, hurrying about, fretting over what should have been a simple of chore of lighting a trimmed wick of a fat, beeswax candle.

Twice the aged Laird had charmed a fragile bud of flame to dance at the end of a long, thin, pinewood taper, but both times draughts of bolshie air had snuffed them out before he could move the taper from the fireplace to the candle. "Not good, not good," he muttered a third time as the taper's feathery flicker died yet again. "I'm not much of a *dewin* they'll say, makin' such a muddled hash of lighting a candle!" he gabbled to himself in increasing frustration.

On the fourth attempt his aggravation trumped his wellbeing and Aldus cupped a vigilant hand close around the temperamental flame, painfully mumbling 'oh!' and 'ah!' and 'crisp, crisp!' as he slowly brought it against the cold wick. At last, the stubborn little flame did its job and caught the braided cotton wick on fire which quickly began waving its own ribbony ballet of happy light. Happy light in a chilled, grey chamber.

"Drat the foul damp of this abominable gatekeep and these worthless wet wogs of wormy wood!" Aldus bull-whipped the pinewood splinter back and forth with a splutter and attempted to jam the taper back into the iron spill-vase sitting atop the mantle piece. Irritation upset his aim. The maligned sliver of wood sprang off the curved rim of the spill-vase and lodged itself deep inside the thorny curls of his thick beard. "What, what?!" He excitedly whacked his hands against himself and tried in a vain panic to pinch the long piece of glowing-ember-wood by its slender tail. Wafting plumes of burning beard oil caused the old man to expel an enormous sneeze which, as kind luck would have it, jettisoned the smoldering taper halfway across the room.

Nicolas couldn't hold back his laughter.

The ridiculous buffoonery of the wizened Laird of St. Wulf's-Without-Aldersgate was too delicious. Relief, release, and genuine hilarity had him laughing until he couldn't breathe. Somewhere in the midst of his hysterics, Aldus, flustered at first, looking much like an insulted clergyman wreathed in incense, joined in, hooting like a white-faced owl. After fits and starts of 'wahoo's' and 'ahhh's' had calmed the persisting snickers of the two unusual friends. Many, many years and two worlds apart, they looked at each other intently and hugged tightly. The rough fibers of Aldus' outer robe smelled of rummaged vellum, leather, and the faint, tannic bite of common black ink while the old man's long beard held a skunky blend of waxy lemon rinds, oily wool, and scorched hair.

"It's *so* absolutely delightful to see you once again, Nicolas. Surprised, I'll admit, but I thought you might soon be coming our way," he said with a twinkling eye.

Nicolas muffled "me too," trying not to inhale a mouthful of whiskers or a fibrous fold of robe.

The old man held him by both shoulders and examined him over from head to foot. "You wear well, Master Bennett! Some dirt here and there… but alive nonetheless. And what looks to be a full year older! A little less time than here, I imagine," he half-mused, cocking a wild eyebrow over his good eye and studying Nicolas' face like a physician. "Concern, too, I see. You've a stew of worry under that mop of hair." The Laird of the First Gate roughed a lean hand through Nicolas' messy hair. His voice was warm and comforting. "*Worry*, Master Bennett, is nothing more than a false prophet disguised as Watchfulness. Worry bleeds a man Today for injuries that Tomorrow is unlikely to inflict. Don't spend your life believing in false prophets, my boy. They promise fruit from dead trees." He tugged at his beard while a wheel of private thoughts spun across his scarred and wizened face. Without looking away from Nicolas, the Laird of the First Gate pointed a long finger at the candlestick and the fat, buttery candle sitting atop it. "Lighting that ridiculous thing should put Laird Halen in a more pleasant mood when he arrives."

The candlestick was an unusually large one, fashioned out of the elbow of some great branch of mottled driftwood; in fact, had it not been for the many melted layers of swaddling wax covering the candlestick's fat stem, Nicolas might not have known the specimen was a candlestick at all. It looked more like a small statue. The piece was dominated by a superbly carved likeness of a sailor frozen in mid-caper, a pose that reminded Nicolas of an old picture he'd once seen of British naval cadets dancing a hornpipe on the deck of the HMS Warspite after the First Great War. The wood-carver's skill had shaped a stocky figure dressed in a fitted jacket of some sort with a half-cape, loose breeches ending above the ankles, and a woolen or leather cap. The miniature mariner's feet were bare and the ridged stalk of his beard was permanently curled up by an invisible wind. A short-stemmed pipe jutted from between his thick lips, and he seemed to have a look of dismay on his small face. He clutched a barrel-headed caulking hammer in one hand while the other hand, and the toe of one foot, were joined to the candlestick's stem; this had the practical effect of providing the candlestick with an elaborate half-moon handle.

"The Laird of this particular gatekeep is an intelligent but superstitious and simple man who sees things in a straightforward way, affixed between two horizons. He has a sailor's heart in a landsman's existence, Nicolas my boy. Lighting that candle will draw his attention to the curious little tar carved into the candlestick and *that*, I believe, is a good way to begin our introductions. I dare say Halen Ward attaches some sort of imagined good fortune to the little figure's presence although I'm not entirely sure why."

Aldus again mindfully tugged his beard.

"He'll be joining us shortly; at the ring of four bells, if I correctly remember the manner in which his gatekeep fixes its hours. We haven't much time. Come, come. Have a seat near the fire."

Minutes before, a guardsman had led Aldus Ward and Nicolas from the large chamber of the angel's seat through the narrow door tucked behind the Laird's stone chair, up through the single twist of a short, tight stairwell and through a heavy-beamed door which led into the room in which they now sat.

Here they were left alone to wait in Halen Ward's private office.

The Laird of the Gate of the Deep kept a room that in some ways appeared to Nicolas to be very much like the great cabin of an old ship of the line; a square-rigged, three-masted, man-o'-war. Brass lantern lights were suspended from the raftered ceiling as if to account for the lean and pitch of a sailing ship's roll; several chairs were scattered about the room, all made of stout wood, cushionless with half-moon armrests as if to prevent occupants from tumbling out as groundswell waves heaved beneath them; a wide bay of thick, slanted windows, diamond-latticed traced with fat lines of soldered lead, occupied one wall of the room from waist-to-head-high to gave a distorted, bluish jade view of the Bay of Wrath. Sitting to one side of a fireplace, which was most certainly *not* a feature of a ship of the line, was a large but plain writing desk littered with a broad-bottomed inkwell, a collection of messily stained quill pens, and various parchments and papers, all in assorted states of authored completeness. What looked like a sailor's loggerhead, a smooth iron ball attached to a long, wooden staff, resting against the desk's edge. Sitting somberly in a dark corner was an oaken sea chest, a strongbox large enough for Nicolas' broad-shouldered Uncle Winston to have folded himself within, which seemed to serve as the room's stone ballast. Strangest of all, on large hooks above that were all fastened in an orderly row, were several brightly polished skulls; six of them—three of men with boorish foreheads and deep eye sockets and three of beasts unknown to Nicolas, sea-like if he had to guess but ruthless and cruel-looking as though legends of ancient krakens might be true. There was the smell of fresh-charred wood, caustic tar, and brined wind that saturated the room's close atmosphere. Nicolas had such a sharp impression of being on board a ship that if the floor beneath his feet had begun to plunge and pitch, he wouldn't have been the least bit surprised.

When Aldus had invited him to sit when they'd arrived, Nicolas had instead first stood boot-toe against the fireplace's broad hearth of rough-quarried limestone. The whip of the fire's heat felt good on his cold and tired face; he let its warmth pink his skin and dry his sweater and the dirty knees of his trousers before he settled back into an empty chair Aldus had pulled near his own. The Laird of the First Gate extended his long fingers to soak up the flames' heat.

"By the king's throne, this is the coldest gatekeep in the city's wall! It has more queer gaps and holes and hollows than a fisherman's net!"

The old man clapped his hands together and rubbed them briskly, remarking more to himself than to Nicolas, "At least Halen's narrow sense of hospitality manages to keep the logs dry and the fires ablaze for the occasional guest." He chuckled and winked. "Quite the host to strangers, I'm sure you know. Afraid hospitality isn't something you've had much of since your arrival, my boy. Wouldn't much count as hospitable to have a guest sleep in the passage tomb, although I've known Halen's officers to do much worse when they've dealt with long-haired corsairs, sea-lane brigands, and ocean-dripping outlaws. I suspect *you*, Master Bennett, were too peculiar a duck for them to be certain as to what to do with. T'sk, t'sk. Even so," he said, a quizzical look beneath his snowy beard, "there was something a bit *sinister* in all of this and how you've been so roughly handled. Too quick to judge perhaps. Much more ado than should have been done."

Nicolas hunched his shoulders indifferently. "I suppose so," he replied, feeling a bit weak. Truth be told, he wasn't much in the mood to guess at vague plots or high intrigues. He wanted to find out why the long tunnel from the night before was called a passage tomb and why both Aldus and Halen shared the title or name of Ward and why those War Crows had been on trial in the first place, but there were other things that weighed on his mind even more. Several things, in fact. He wasn't sure where to begin. And then, once more, it was Aldus' long-ago voice that spoke to him.

Begin with answers, the kind Laird had told Nicolas over a year before in the quiet of his own gatekeep's private chambers. *Answers, after all, are tidier than questions, Nicolas. Answers know where they belong.*

Nicolas grasped for the first time since he'd scrambled out of the sea cave and back into Telluric Grand. The realization of a cold and unwelcome self-admission, that he was *unsure* of where he belonged. Everything kept feeling terribly amiss, not right at all, and the miserable feeling stabbed at his heart.

Answers know where they belong, he thought anxiously, *But I have too many questions. I want to* belong. *What is an answer that knows where it is?*

And so it was that the first answer to find its way into words was where the boy from Plumpton Head, England, began with an 'answer.' An answer that prickled in his mind like a guilty confession during a murder inquest, something Nicolas had felt the need to share aloud with someone almost from the moment he'd darted over the crest of the sea cliff the previous day; to unburden his mind in some way of at least one great weight. A thing about an *end*, not a beginning. Indeed, a thing about death.

"I saw a man about to have his head chopped off," he burst out. 'Twas an answer, a declaration, not a question.

The words were clumsy, graceless, crude, too dull and flat to justly describe the bloody shock of comprehending that one human being was about to hack his way through another's neck. To hack his way through with a large cleaver.

Aldus' look was even. Unaffected. He didn't speak. He waited patiently.

Nicolas shrugged as if he too was impassive, but the look on his face gave him away. The words tumbled out. "He was a prisoner of some sort, I think. I'm still not sure, and I'm not exactly sure what they were about to do but it looked like they were about to kill him. Anyhow that's what it looked like to me. Maybe that was right, maybe it wasn't. Maybe I shouldn't have said anything, it all happened too fast, Aldus. I didn't know what to do. I was afraid and *that's* when this huge bird showed up. I don't know if my feeling changed from fear to anger or what but something… *enormous*, yes, something enormous happened inside me and I popped off. Botched it proper, I guess—"

As sudden as it had begun, his ranting stopped.

Nicolas stared into the flames in front of him, and after a deep breath, began more quietly. "That man, the one about to lose his head, he looked like those other men who—who were thrown off the ledge just now. He was a… a War Crow I suppose…" Nicolas gritted his teeth. "I still don't know *what's* going on! What's supposed to happen! I don't know what to do. I *didn't* know what to do. I feel—I feel—I can't—" The rushed jumble of words suddenly stopped, mired down in Nicolas' own confusion and indecision.

He wanted to *get it all outta yer system* as his mum would say whenever he was upset, but doing that right now was making him feel even more miserable. He didn't want Aldus to think he was a sad twit, some kind of nesh wimp, unfit to be in Telluric Grand. But Nicolas couldn't seem to control how frustrated he was, how wretched and frightening and alarming his return had already been, so unlike what he'd imagined, what he'd dreamed of and wanted for over a year. A feeling of disillusionment bit at him sharply, chewing at his insides like a rats' teeth on a ship's cable. He straightened his back as if doing so would straighten his thoughts.

The woodsy scent of burning hedge and elm kindling didn't help; it reminded him of his father's study; made him feel oddly sick—homesick.

Nicolas realized, unexpectedly, that he missed home. *My other home*, he thought miserably.

He set his chin. "I interrupted what those two guards were doing but I didn't *mean* to, Aldus. I—I just didn't want to watch it happen. And… and those *other* men—those other prisoners. They were just *thrown* off the ledge! There was the dead guard and then that mad man who jumped to his own death screaming, and I—I," Nicolas' teeth chattered as if he were cold. He lifted his hands palms-up in defeat. His thoughts and feelings were like the crooked spire of the Parish Church of St. Mary and All Saints in Chesterfield— "The devil wrapped his tale around that church's spire," Peter Bennett had once said to Nicolas and Jack while watching a match held at Saltergate between Chesterfield's football club and Carlisle United. "You can see a sweepin' pinnacle on Chesterfield's patch jus' like it. That's why those lads are called the Spireites. They say the townfolk rang away at the church bells, scarin' the devil but 'is tail caught on the spire, twistin' it, an' makin' it all skew-whiff, that. We'll go see it someday, boys," but they never did. Yet now Nicolas could feel his thoughts screw themselves into the same twisted, leaning, lead-weighted deformation as the spire atop Chesterfield Parish Church. He couldn't make any more sense out of what he'd seen… much less how to describe it to Aldus.

In spite of this, as if he was the post-captain of a three-decker warship, he smartly tacked against the wind.

"I saw Adelaide yesterday." He kept his voice matter-of-fact. "It wasn't good. I mean, it *was* good to see her but what she *said* wasn't good. She said things aren't *right* here, Aldus. She said the same thing about Benjamin. She said he'd been arrested.

She said they'd beat him. Who would *hit* Benjamin?" His voice changed—thick and trembly for a moment.

Exhausted and near tears, Nicolas gave in, stuttering out the very thing he hadn't wanted to say. "I've—I've wanted to come back here so *badly*. I wanted to see you. I wanted to see Benjamin and Ranulf and Adelaide. I tried to find a way. I swear I did. Hundreds of times, but I failed every time until I finally stumbled across one completely by accident. But—but it hasn't been what I thought it would be. Not at all. I don't know. I don't understand any of this. I miss—" Tiredness quieted his voice, "I miss my home, Aldus; my *other* home." Nicolas hurried this last as if what he'd said might have caused hurt feelings. "I don't know—I don't know." The final bit of momentum died inside of Nicolas. His messy thoughts gave up. They all direction, gumming themselves down into queasy pits of remorse and fear. He didn't want to say anything more, answers or otherwise, and even if he did, he didn't know what more he could say that would make sense.

The gentle boy, come from a quiet farm cottage on a peaceful Christmas eve, bent forward and placed his forearms heavily on his legs. He took a deep, settled his quavering breath, and sadly watched the fire's flames wiggle, jump, and leap like vivid spooks. Nicolas felt very, very alone.

Aldus Ward, the aged Laird of the First Gate, spent several minutes looking caringly at the boy who was staring into the fire, but the wizened man kept his own close counsel. He remained silent, saying nothing in return and instead sat there towing at his long, curly beard again and again, aswim in the deep waters of his own thoughts.

"Nicolas," he finally said sometime later.

"Yes."

"Have you an older brother?"

Aldus' peculiar question caught Nicolas by surprise. The leading tone of the old man's voice sounded as if he already knew the answer.

"Yes. Yes, I did. Once."

"Long passed, is he?"

"Yes."

"And if I were to ask you, as difficult as it might be, to describe your long-passed brother, what might you say?"

Nicolas wiped his nose and thought hard. It wasn't something he'd ever really thought about even though he'd somehow always had a sense of what the answer might be. "I'd say Jack was brave, or funny. No not funny but full of life. I don't know. Bravely full of life, although that doesn't sound like it makes much sense."

"Oh, yes, yes it does, my dear boy. Your brother was brave *in spite* of what he suffered and *because* of what he suffered, I'd say. Brave. Bravely full of life when, of all people, he had an excuse *not* to be brave." Aldus patted his beard. "Brave on *your* behalf, Master Bennett. Bravely showing *you* how to live even though he did that best through dying." As caringly as they'd been said, Aldus' words were painful to hear.

"I suppose," was all Nicolas could manage. His mind held a chest of tender memories, those of Jack when Nicolas was still very young and memories he did not wish to share with anyone; exceedingly delicate memories of an older brother who'd played with him, taught him things, made him laugh, made him feel very special. A brother he still loved and admired and, shamefully, more and more often forgot.

Aldus lifted the poker by the fireplace and jabbed at one of the charred, flame-eyed logs. He half-turned to face Nicolas. A humble rushlight of a flame was trapped inside his intense eye. "All of us are *called*, Nicolas. Tested to see beyond our own selfish ends. To put the needs of others above our own; siblings to each other, parents to offspring, councilors to those counseled, masters to apprentices, lords to peasants. We all succeed and fail to various degrees, *but*, Master Bennett, my dear, dear Wren—" here Aldus paused and thumped the cherry-charred log, sending up a livid rupture of bursting cinders, "the weight of *empires,"* Thump. "The rise and fall of *kingdoms,"* Thump, "Indeed the survival of all that is *good*, and Iall that is *worth,"* Thump, "*Saving,"* Thump, "depends on a much *higher* calling, a much greater test, one to which only a few are elected answer." As he said these things the well-thumped log caught fire; fresh air whipped and whelped its raw embers. "It isn't just the setting aside of one's own delights and desires; it's the willingness and the courage to set aside one's *life,* not just ending it for the sake of others, but *living* it for the sake of others in spite of however it's to end. As grievous as it might be for those who remain, death's *true* effect, my dear boy, is but to judge the effort a person has made in life. The quality of the memories that survive tells us whether a person's life was lived in such a way that it emboldened others to live." Aldus let out a long, deep sigh. "That is why sacrifice in death can be the greatest act of living. And by the endless heavens, Master Bennett, I'd say your brother's life was lived for *you*."

Nicolas' mind was trying hard to keep pace with what Aldus was saying but the fragile ache in his head and heart didn't help. Suddenly, Jack's face appeared in his head as clear as a reflection in still water. Jack was smiling hilariously. Laughing at giants.

"I'm—I'm not trying to be selfish," Nicolas said, his voice choked. "I just—I just."

His heart was rubbed and raw. Aldus' words had thumped away at him just as they'd thumped at the log. They struck at something buried inside him; showers of sparks from an irrepressible revival of purpose, of high adventure, of surprise and delight and fear overcome caught new wind. Nicolas' soul began to burn again. Scales of charred confusion fell away from his tired spirit and a restoring sense of resolve, of *belonging,* kindled warmly in his chest.

"I'm sorry," Nicolas said, firm but quiet. More to Jack perhaps than to Aldus or even himself. "Everything has just seemed all sixes and sevens."

Aldus held his head back and laughed aloud, slapping his knees, and wagging a finger at the boy. "You're not selfish, my boy, an' you don't need to be sorry! You're human; you've high blood in you but you're just as human as the next man. You're feeling what we all feel when things don't go our way, when things around us are cockeyed too far to the left or right. We feel frustrated. We feel lonely and we look for a way out. But *this,* Master Bennett, is precisely the point at which you're also *different* than most others; *you,* the Wren and Dragon Nightfall foretold in prophecies of old. Remember what Straight Hammer, the giant whom you once met, told you: *You are on the surface now, visible, and moving like the sun across a greying winter's sky.*"

"Now is the time at which you look all about yourself and say, I must *live,* perhaps die, for everyone else around me, for everything else around me. Much greater than just two or three or even a hundred, whatever the cost. Beware, my tired boy! The rise and fall of kingdoms, Master Bennett, the rise and fall of kingdoms.... And *this*—" he said wildly waving an arm in the air, "*this* is your *grandfather's* kingdom. You belong here. There is a remnant of him inside you."

The great Laird of St. Wulf's-Without-Aldersgate sat back and hauled again at his unruly beard as the scolded and burning log popped and cracked in two.

The crinkly old man leaned inward over his armrest. "And, mind you, there's the spirit of your long-lost brother, as well."

Aldus smiled but this smile was uneasy. "Make no mistake, you're right as a spring rain, Nicolas, things *are* amiss in the First Kingdom and far beyond our realm. All the more reason for you to have come back. Everything has grown even darker since you left us over a year ago. I'd hoped it would have changed with the death of the overlord dragon, Shadow Thief, but it didn't. Not yet in any case. To the contrary, an ancient menace of some sort has crept forward like rot in a hayloft. I cannot yet see who or what it is, but there's descended a persistent, spreading gloom from which I fear none of us may recover."

Distressed, he shook his grey head. "That cursed dragon, even dead, somehow began the turning of a key to something more powerful, some *greater* doom, even more monstrous and terrible than before; something not yet revealed; something I couldn't see. Something, something I didn't account for—" His voice trailed off and he sat there wordlessly.

Aldus then started up with the most dissimilar thing, as if the two of them had been doing nothing more than waffling on about the mundane, bath-time drudgery of having to clean behind one's ears. "This quite reminds me of a story, Nicolas! A story I overheard Benjamin tell Ranulf shortly after you'd left us. Would you like to hear it?"

Nicolas, his eyes brightening with the mention of his friends, gave a quick nod. "Yes! Please!"

"Right then. I'll do my best not to muddle the details too much. I heard him tell it on the third morning after you'd left. I was mulling over some purchase lists my clerk, you remember Master Brooks, do you not? Had heaped in front of me after breakfasting while those two boys were busy putting their kits together in preparation for leaving the gatekeep. I'd told them they were welcome to stay for as long as they like, but it didn't stick I suppose. Adelaide had left in the early morning the day after you'd gone. She hadn't said much. Kept to herself really. She was pained, I think, but that's my own thoughts on the matter. Not something to chin-wag about.

"Where was I? Oh yes, the boys. They were discussing where they'd be off to after leaving the gatekeep and as I recall, Ranulf was talking about opening his own ironworks shop under Straight Hammer's shingle. A bit of a daydream, I suppose. I think Ranulf might have been feeling his oats a shade much after helping you with the Shadow Thief, but Benjamin was gabbling back, encouraging him while not offering much in the way of what he himself was planning to do. Finally, our dear bladesmith paused and asked the snatcher-boy, "What about you? Will you head back into the City?"

"Benjamin must have had two cheekfuls of honeyed oatcakes drowned in clotted cream when Ranulf asked because it took him a long time to reply and when he did, I could hear him gumming away on something like a squirrel with a nut. By the king's throne, that boy was always eating!"

Aldus let out a hearty laugh and gave a tickled pull at his beard. "I'm quite convinced he must be part magician, spiriting away entire platters of piled pork roast, boiled eggs, toasted almonds, and sugared figs; where can all that food possibly go?" The old man's belly-laughter brought a broad smile to Nicolas' face. As quick as the tide of hopelessness had risen inside of Nicolas, it was decidedly beginning to slide away; not entirely gone but slackened; a despairing riptide easing into a mild current.

Aldus wiped tears of laughter from his eyes. "Dear me, the older I become the more *jolliness* I find in those who are young—oblivious to it, they are, thank the endless heavens! Otherwise they wouldn't be so innocently wonderful." He lifted a last tear away and flung it into the fire. There was a sizzle and a surprising pop of golden-blue color. "And *tough*, I'd say. One tends to find the most iron in those who are pocket-sized." His good eye's bright blue color sparkled shards of gold and emerald. He paused and gave Nicolas a curious look. "Yes, *iron*," the old man muttered, losing his thought until, as if someone had tapped him on the shoulder, he blinked his right eye rapidly. "Apologies, Master Bennett. I seem to have mislaid my story. However! It comes to mind that I'm prattling on about food an' I imagine you've had none. Is that right?"

"Not a bite," Nicolas said, his stomach suddenly tied in knots.

"Shameful," Aldus tssked. "We'll need to bring that to Laird Ward's attention as quick as we can. I'm sure there's something near-edible somewhere in this bat-fouled, barnacle-encrusted gatekeep.

"In any event, between bites of food Benjamin finally says to Ranulf the most curious thing as if it was an everyday common expression that anyone ought to know. 'I'm not sure where I'll go,' that boy says. The City seems like a dark place to me *with all the footprints going in one direction*.'"

Aldus' bushy eyebrows knitted into one and he pulled himself a bit nearer to Nicolas. "When Benjamin said this, I laid down my writing quill and paid close attention. I'd wager you once noticed the same thing when the four of you were traveling together: that simple boy has an unnatural store of wisdom inside him, perhaps even deeper than his appetite. I doubt he's aware of it. When he said the City seemed dark because all the footprints go in one direction, his choice of words struck me as peculiar enough to deserve a few moments of close consideration." Aldus nodded to himself, appearing to gather shades of the memory back into lifelike relief.

Nicolas watched as the old man's good eye looked through him as if he wasn't there anymore. The Laird of the First Gate adjusted his back, cocked his head to one side, and began murmuring something to himself as he reached inside one of the sleeves of his outer cloak and drew out the same long, straight-stemmed pipe Nicolas had first seen him smoke long ago. Delicate threads of spun copper and silver that were wrapped around the pipe's stem sparkled in the firelight, and out of long-practiced habit, Aldus soon had billows of smoke floating out of its bowl. He settled reflectively back in his chair where his low murmuring soon ceased and his eye seemed to catch sight of Nicolas again. He chuckled, wagging his beard. "Again, my apologies, Master Bennett, my apologies. These days I sometimes prattle on to myself like a corncrake at night, forgetting how impolite it might be to others around me. In my humble defense however, I'd say our little Benjamin Rush continues to be a riddle I haven't quite figured out."

Aldus Ward tapped the mouthpiece of his pipe against the palm of his hand. "That morning, Ranulf seemed to share the same puzzled reaction I did to what Benjamin had said. *What in the First Kingdom does that mean? he says*, and Benjamin, mind you, still chomping away mind, tells him this next thing as plain as if he was asking for a dollop of cream: *Do you remember the old hag the City bailiff men took out of the Dreggs and burned to death last year?* Well, I knew her and I know *why* she was burned. She'd been cookin' and eating my friends like that nasty ogre tried to do to our wonderful Adelaide. Not at first of course." Benjamin goes on between mouthfuls. "At first, the old hag sold bowls of pig-ear broth for two pecks apiece. It wasn't bad broth really, I liked it. She must've made it from butchers' rubbish, an' me and my mates would eat it almost every day in the wintertime; we'd mix it with sour grain we'd stolen—I mean *borrowed*—from the brewers' stalls.'"

Here, Aldus paused to shake his head sadly and wince. "I swear, Nicolas, Benjamin said those words as plain as you like—it was as if he was describing a grandmother and her pies. I'm afraid that small lad has seen more of the stomach-turning side of life than most of us would ever care to imagine." Knocking some loosely flaked ash from his pipe bowl, the old man blew another enormous puff of smoke and carried on with his story.

"One day, the old hag—she was a wartish, wicked scab really—became too sick to come out of her hovel. She tried to keep sellin' broth but one of the boys said it began tastin' infected and had bits of rat tails in it; I guess she couldn't make the rounds to get pork-ears from the butchers' scraps no more. Most of us didn't much care. Spring had come and we were able to find better food by sneakin' eggs out of nests and snatching turnips out of carts. When we'd pass along the gutter-rut by her shed, we'd hear her inside, wailin' at us like some wretched crone, 'I've cau't the sweats, boys! Poor, dear me! I'm dyin'! Won' ya step in an' see a sick ol' woman for a bit. Liven my miserable spirit? Ya know I loves the lot o' ya an' I've always been good to ya,' so she'd say.

"One day, a rough lad I didn't know well brags to the rest of us, *I'm goin' in ta see her, an' you'll come too if yer brave lak me. Maybe she's got worms comin' outta her eyes!* Well I didn't care to see it. Sounded awful, that. But some of the others did and in they went. They all came out yellin'. It was quite the spoof, except for days after that, several of them kept visiting her. Macon, another lad I knew, said it was because she offered to pay a peck to anyone who would bring her food, but I didn't like the smell of her place so I stayed away. Several weeks passed an' I noticed there were fewer of us left. It's true that lads like us disappear all the time but this seemed different somehow. One day, me and Macon were passin' by her terrible little hovel an', crackin' smack, there she *is*, standing outside it like a smarty driggle-draggle! She's standin' there, grinnin' like a well-fed toad in a robe and not looking anything like she was about to die. She calls out to us and says, '*Come 'ere, sweet lads! I've got new fat soup fer young boys! Come in an' 'ave a sip or two.'* But when she says this, Macon stops as cold as dead teeth; he grabs my sleeve like a terror and drags me in the other direction. "What's what?' I said, not understanding what he was doing. I was hungry and a spot of pig-ear soup sounded good. *'The footprints!' he says to me all shivery. 'Did ja see the dirt on the other side of the gutter-rut, Benjamin? All the footprints in the dirt are goin' in but none are comin' out!'* He went straight and told the bailiff men. Sure as rain makes mud, Macon was right, an' the bailiff men found the boiled bones of boys in there. That old hag killed our mates, cooked 'em, and made broth outta them when she couldn't get the butchers' scraps no more. Guess she ate it too an' gained her health again.'"

Aldus Ward shook his head and leaned over the arm of his chair toward Nicolas. "After saying all this, Benjamin stopped chewing and in a whisper I probably wasn't supposed to hear, he repeats to Ranulf, All the footprints going *in*. None coming *out*. *That's* what the City feels like to me, Ranulf son of Renfry. Somethin's changed. I'm *not* going back in.' And he didn't. Later that day, Ranulf went over the gatekeep's archway back into Relic, but Benjamin remained true to his word and left the gatekeep headed in the direction you'd gone. I didn't hear anything about him for a long while after that; not until a few days ago in fact."

Aldus leaned back and stretched. He knocked charred crumbles of ash out of the upended bowl of his pipe and rested his arms on the chair's smooth armrests. "That small boy has uncommon wisdom, Nicolas. When all the footprints go *in*, and none come *out*,' then *that's* a sure sign all isn't well. Your sense of uneasiness and feeling adrift make perfectly decent sense in that light; like our friend Benjamin, you're wise to take heed of those feelings. Feelings shared by Adelaide, those footprints, if you will. I'm afraid all *isn't* well, hasn't been well for a time if I'm honest, whether in the City, throughout the First Kingdom, or in all the Outlands." He looked sharp at Nicolas. "My private intention is to see that you get in and out of the City as quickly and as secretly as possible. There are things to be done but we can't lose you to old hags or dark conspiracies. There are other things needing urgent attention elsewhere outside the City, and I'm convinced you're the perfect one to attend to them." With a long sigh he stared into the play of flames and quietly added, "Those things lie to the south of us, Nicolas. I wish I could say the way south leads to safety, but alas, it doesn't. Few places lead to safety these days."

Nicolas didn't have time to think of anything to say in reply because at just that moment, the chamber's door was thrown open, but instead of Halen Ward joining them, Lord Sulla, the High Chancellor of the City of Relic, stalked inside.

CHAPTER 10

An Owl and a Stoat

Three years earlier on a quiet, breezy afternoon, full of May's spring sunlight and the sashay of blue, meadow clary petals that decorated the Bennett's sheep pasture, an English springtime afternoon, long before Nicolas was to find himself sitting in front of a fire inside a cold, wet gatekeep within a world he barely knew, Nicolas had been sitting at the Bennett's chipped, blockwood table in the kitchen, pouring over his school spelling lists. At the time, upper school examination week was only four days away for Hunter Hall, a well-regarded preparatory school situated in Frenchfield Farm outside of Penrith. It had been Nicolas' first year to attend and the stress of secondary school entrance examinations, his eleven plus exam, coupled with the daily strain of meeting new friends and adjusting to the politics of a new schoolyard, had put Nicolas' brain into a hazy, apprehensive fog. He found concentrating on his studies increasingly difficult. Efforts to focus felt like trying to find a whole pea hiding in a bowl of split-pea soup. While spelling had never been Nicolas' strong suit, it was more than aggravating to forget how to spell something as plain as one of the days of the week.

"Mum!"

Sarah Bennett was outside in the cottage garden, planting blue diadem cornflowers, snow carpet alyssums, and Queen Sophia marigold French seeds. She was keeping herself company with the Irish folk song "Carrickfergus" and, at first, didn't hear Nicolas calling through one of the kitchen's open windows.

"Mum! How do you spell Thursday?! Is it an e or a u?"

"*But the sea is wide an' I cannot swim over / And neither have I the wings to fly*," Mrs. Bennett sang.

"Mum! Mum! How do you spell Thursday?"

Acting as if it was the wind who'd asked the question, Mrs. Bennett squatted back on the heels of her rubber wellies, used the back of her wrist to push a thick lock of auburn hair out of her face and looked at the springtide sky. "T-h-o-r-'-s-d-a-y!" she said in a loud, matter-of-fact voice.

Nicolas, putting his pencil to his lips, nibbled at its eraser. That certainly didn't *seem* right. He mouthed out the spelling his mother had provided. "Mum!" he demanded when done. "That can't be right! Thursday has an *er* sound, not an *or* sound."

Sarah Bennett responded with a lovely ring of laughter, stood up, took off her gardening gloves and came inside. "Well of course that's how Thursday's spelled, my love." There was mischief in her Irish smile. "That's how the greatest-grandfather of all your grandfathers on my side of the family would have spelled it. Was he here right now he'd say it was *Thor's* day, named after the Northmen's god of thunder. I didn't know you were studying Norse mythology." She poked him playfully in the ribs. The look on her face gave it away.

"I'm not, Mum," said Nicolas trying to sound cross, but his irritation was beat out by curiosity. "What's Norse mythology anyway?"

Mrs. Bennett didn't say anything; instead, she headed into Mr. Bennett's study, and out of one of the top bookshelves, she withdrew a yellowed and rather tedious-looking paperback book. She flashed the ratty old cover at Nicolas. It had black-

and-white drawings framing the title, "The Heroes of Asgard and the Giants of Jötenheim."

His mother was far more excited than Nicolas thought the dull-looking book deserved. "Norse mythology is a marvelous stewed chowder-mix of gods an' mortals an' evil giants. There are elves an' snakes an' dwarfs! It's part of yer family's history, Nicolas. It's part of us island folk, the Scots, an' Irish, an' Welsh, an' English, too. It's part of who ya are." Sarah Bennett looked wistfully at her son. "I know this year's been a bit hard for ya, love. I do. And I know yer busy with studies, but sit still for a moment. I want to read a passage my Mum used to read to me when I fretted with worry."

The brown edges of the book's worn-out pages fluttered against her thumb until she'd reached a little past the middle of the book. "Here 'tis." She spread her slender fingers on either side of the book's gutter. "'Reflections in the Water,' it says, and this, this is how it goes."

Iduna sat down and looked into the deep water. Besides her own fair face there were little, wandering, white clouds to be seen reflected there. She counted them as they sailed past. At length a strange form was reflected up to her from the water: large, dark, lowering wings, pointed claws, a head with fierce eyes, looking at her.

Iduna started and raised her head. It was above as well as below; the same wings, the same eyes, the same head, looking down from the blue sky, as well as up from the water. Such a sight had never been seen near Asgard before; and, while Iduna looked, the thing waved its wings, and went up, up, up, till it lessened to a dark spot in the clouds and on the river.

It was no longer terrible to look at; but, as it shook its wings a number of little black feathers fell from them, and flew down towards the grove, As they neared the trees, they no longer looked like feathers. Each had two independent wings and a head of its own; they were, in fact, a swarm of Nervous Apprehensions; troublesome little insects enough, and well-known elsewhere, but which now, for the first time, found their way into the grove.

Iduna ran away from them; she shook them off; she fought quite bravely against them; but they are by no means easy to get rid of; and when, at last, one crept within the folds of her dress, and twisted itself down to her heart, a new, strange feeling thrilled there, a feeling yet known to any dweller in Asgard. Iduna did not know what to make of it.

"'Beware of nervous apprehensions, Sarah Shaughnessy,' my mother would cluck at me, like little black feathers that become vile pests, they'll twist down into yer heart. If we look too closely at ourselves, losing sight of how great and grand the world around us is, all we'll find are nervous apprehensions.'"

Mrs. Bennett hugged Nicolas close in her warm arms for several moments. Her dress smelled of bread flour and a rich musk of fresh-tilled earth. "Don't reflect too much on the difficulties in front of you, my sweet boy. Have hope. 'Ave faith. Always 'ave faith. An' 'ave care that one dark bird doesn't become many."

When Lord Sulla, the somber High Chancellor of the City of Relic, stalked into Halen Ward's personal chambers, Nicolas instantly thought of the cautioning words his mum had shared with him on that sunlit, May afternoon three years earlier. *Have care that one dark bird doesn't become many.* But everything about the High Chancellor made it hard for Nicolas to keep those little, black-feathered, nervous apprehensions from twisting down into his heart.

Lord Sulla was an unsympathetic and sallow man with a sloping forehead, weak chin, and thin cheekbones that all came together at the tip of his long and pointed nose. He was dressed in official, long, grey robes of state, reminding Nicolas of something he'd once seen a parish priest wear one Saturday morning. Nicolas had been playing by himself among the time-scoured tombstones near the "Giant's Grave," an odd assembly of ancient rocks located on the north side of St. Andrew's parish church in Penrith. Mr. Bennett had let him play in the yard around the church until the start of a christening service at 1 o'clock, and Nicolas had been in the middle of patting the soft, bright green moss growing atop one of the yard's aged tombstones when he'd seen a priest hurrying down the narrow path alongside the standing stones of the Giant's Grave. The priest wore a black cassock whose length mostly hid the worn-out trainers on his feet; but something seemed amiss, and it took Nicolas a moment to realize the priest wasn't also wearing a surplice, the outer robe of white that usually covered the black cassock. The black robe by itself looked strange and gloomy. The half-attired priest had smiled and waved to Nicolas before walking out of the small churchyard's gate and disappearing inside the white storefront of Peaky's Barbershop, the same barbershop in fact where Mr. Bennett and Nicolas had their hair cut. Mr. Bennett later joked the priest must have wanted to keep his surplice free of cut hair so he wouldn't bathe the infant's christened head with "hair and holy water."

Like the priest Nicolas had once seen, the piously unhappy High Chancellor was also clothed in a full-length black cassock, a low-spirited and dismal frock, but here the general similarity ended. The High Chancellor's robe was belted with a broad band of satiny, emerald green cloth instead of the green rope Nicolas had seen around the priest's waist, and while the priest's garment had had no other adornment, Lord Sulla's robe was piped and trimmed on every hem with elaborate stitchings of gold, red, green, white, blue, and purple threads. The lavish embroidery at the bottom of the robe depicted six castle keeps, each with a large, golden key sewn in front of their outer walls. The cuff of the left sleeve was decorated with likenesses of open books, parchment rolls, and quill pens, but it was the needlework around the cuff of the right sleeve that caught Nicolas' closest attention. This sleeve depicted a modest and vacant throne with some kind of small bird perched on its right armrest. Behind the throne in vague outlays of purplish and blueish shades with flecks of grey and red was the imprecise image of an enormous dragon. Suspended from a weighty gold chain hung around Lord Sulla's long neck was a large, six-sided lock made entirely of iron, corroded and frozen with rust.

"Laird Ward!" the High Chancellor said as if it was a demand from a person in charge, not a greeting.

Aldus gave a slight nod and kept his seat. "Compliments, your Grace, but may I kindly remind your Grace, that I only warrant the named-title of Ward, when I am within the walls of my own gatekeep? I'm sure you remember, of course?" Aldus' tone was restrained, conciliatory, but his mild criticism of the High Chancellor's decorum worked its intended effect. Lord Sulla *pfffed* his lips, clearly flustered.

"What? What? Ah. Yes, yes, of course I *remember*, Laird Aldus, habits, Laird *Aldus,* habits are called habits for a reason, and I am most accustomed to seeing you where you *properly* belong, in your *own* gatekeep." The man's wedge-shaped nose twitched like a nervous rat's as if he were trying to smell Nicolas, but for the moment the conversation stayed between the two nobles. "Indeed, I must admit I was alarmed to see you at the trial of those vile carrion, those War Crows. Highly unusual and a dangerous precedent to set, would you agree? Besides, I am quite sure your own gatekeep has no lack of important matters to address."

Aldus did not move and still did not rise from his seat. This seemed to further fluster the High Chancellor.

"I genuinely thank you for your concern for the well-being of St. Wulf's-Without-Aldersgate, your Grace. I admit my keep's jurisdiction *does* have an endless list of matters to address. As do we all these days. But my gatekeep's grimlock and wardens are all capable and efficient administrators. Surely it is those who look to the gatekeep's daily tasks who know what, or who, it needs better than *you*—" Aldus, having said the word 'you' with a touch of stress, also left it hanging in the air for a second longer than necessary, "or I do. In fact, there are days when I suspect they might fare better without my bungling interference; as if I might disappear and the gatekeep would remain properly kept." The greatest of the Commissioners of the Forfeited Gates thinned the lids of his good eye, and Nicolas noticed its color turn blue-black. "Might you agree, your Grace?"

"May the endless heavens save us from your absence, Laird Aldus," was Lord Sulla's proper but hollow response, a noncommittal and flat remark from a man whose attempt at a frontal assault had been neatly rolled up on its flank. The High Chancellor gave ground and attempted to rally. "I only suggest you'd do best to stay near your own bench where you are most keenly valued, Laird Aldus, but that is only my opinion. An opinion of the *City*, an opinion of the First Kingdom, I might add," he quickly said, emphasizing his position as custodian of the empty throne.

Lord Sulla now threw a distrustful and mean-spirited look toward Nicolas. He appeared wary of Nicolas; the boy's unexplained presence provided an opportunity to try once again to scold, perhaps accuse, Aldus. "Forgive me, Laird Aldus, but if I may deliberately press my inquiry: why *were* you here today? You must admit, as I've said, it is highly unusual for one laird to be present during another laird's passing of judgment." His sharp nose gave a haughty, knowing sniff. "Such disregard for proper tradition may suggest an abuse of power, or of secretive influence, or any number of unseemly notions. *I*, of course, wouldn't share in any of that scandal mongering but there *are* others, many others, who might," he said smugly. The High Chancellor had a twitching, arrogant look on his face.

Aldus smiled a cheerless smile and chuckled.

A fleeting, unhappy grimace spasmed across Lord Sulla's face, his smugness gone.

"You're right on both observations, your Grace. My presence in Laird Halen Ward's courthall was both highly unusual and could have had the appearance of impropriety. Although I'm not sure *who* would hold that view as you suggest. However, it so happens I was *invited* as an attendant guest by Laird Halen at the last moment. He sought my counsel on other urgent matters and thought we might both gain a better, combined understanding of the immediate War Crow threat if I spectated at today's tribunal. I'm afraid we did not, or at least *I* did not gain any insight, but I was, and still am, happy to make myself available. I warrant we must all be willing to look to each other for ready support and advice in these troubling times. Indeed, these are increasingly strange and worrying days, are they not?" Aldus abruptly stood up, gathered his beard in his fist and tightened his gaze on Lord Sulla. "On *that* particular point, your Grace, might I impose upon *you* for a moment and seek answers to two questions I have?"

The High Chancellor's face became ashen. He looked like a cornered animal—a pale-brown stoat, a weasel-like creature Nicolas had once seen in the stand of woods on the far side of the Bennett's sheep pasture.

At the time, perhaps two or three years before, Nicolas had sat propped against the English elm his father had named the "Red Deer Tree" when Nicolas had spotted a stoat nosing around a shrew's small burrow, snuffling for a little, furry victim to eat. Abruptly, the stoat had flattened onto its belly, trying to hide in the rotting leaf fall piled between the tree's exposed roots. Too late, it had sensed some unseen danger. There followed an instant, loud, wild impact, a riotous burst of feathers and fur that stopped almost as quickly as it had begun. When it was over, a long-eared owl had been sitting upright atop the dead stoat's body, its eight-daggered talons buried in the body of its prey. Nicolas hadn't moved. At least he didn't think he'd moved but the owl saw him nonetheless and had turned its ginger-orange eyes in his direction. Then, as suddenly as it had appeared, it was gone. The rapacious bird had snatched up the stoat's limp body and had flown into one of the nearby oak trees to roost in an abandoned crow's nest.

Nicolas could now imagine the High Chancellor crouching like a weasel-like stoat on the litterfall of a forest floor, sensing doom had come. His nose twitched uncontrollably, and his eyes blinked in a jerking frenzy. He was not a man accustomed to others' questioning and certainly not any implied accusation. There was a distinctive sense of threat in Aldus' entreaty. Nicolas couldn't yet tell why it was there, but he suddenly realized each of Aldus' responses had thus far ended in calculated questions. Each question set like a small trap meant to bait Lord Sulla.

"As you please," the High Chancellor replied in a dry, thin voice. The arrogant hunter knowing he had become the hunted.

Aldus, enjoying it, took his time. He repacked his pipe, drew a pinewood taper from the spill vase, lit the taper in the fire, and relished several pregnant moments more hovering the burning stick over the pipe's bowl as he coaxed lazy clouds of smoke that smelled of baked stone fruit, filling the chamber's close air. The suspense, deliberate, was as strained as a fast frigate would be with its moonraker sail hauled up in a strong wind. The High Chancellor of the City of Relic looked as if he might snap like an overwrought mast under the strain.

Aldus peered low over his hand that grasped the pipe's bowl and through the smoke's shadow he said, "If you please, your Grace, has Marshal Arminius' Third Legion returned to the City or to the Gate of Noble's Bane, or has he sent word of any plans to return?" He sat back, shrouded in clouds. "I haven't received any official dispatches but I've been otherwise informed that he and his five hundred might have returned unannounced."

Lord Sulla's taut face didn't change at all. It remained stretched and wary. Aldus' comment of having been otherwise informed. An intended reminder of spies other than the High Chancellor's, caused Lord Sulla's right eyelid to flutter on its own with an anxious tick. Nicolas could see the thin man's eyes dart around as if to somehow physically discover the trap Aldus was certain to be setting. "Permit me to find out," was all he finally said; this, as a slender thread of stretched wire.

"Hmmm… Yes, please. At your convenience, of course. Thank you, your Grace."

Aldus sat there quietly.

After nearly a minute more of uncomfortable silence had passed, Lord Sulla finally erupted. "Your second question! Your second question, Laird Aldus?"

"Oh, yes, yes. Of course. My apologies once again, your Grace. I had forgotten I proposed to ask two questions and presumed our interview was at an end. Thank you for your kind reminder. You can see what kind of mental bungling my gatekeep's administrators must endure from me. Yes, yes. Thank you for the thoughtful prompt."

Lord Sulla's tongue clicked angrily against his spindly teeth.

"'Tis a minor question perhaps but one of some personal importance to me that I shall not share at this time. Be that as it may, there is a boy, currently imprisoned in this gatekeep, Benjamin Rush is the lad's name. At one time he was an invited guest of mine under the Law of the Forfeited Gates, but for some reason he was recently arrested while in the City, cruelly beaten by bailiff men, and brought here for detention. I mean to raise the issue with Laird Halen Ward and with the other Commissioners, but might you know why or how this unfortunate incident came about?" As Aldus spoke, each of his words became more sharp, more measured.

The High Chancellor froze; nervous ticks instantly ceased. The hunted stoat pressed further against the forest floor. It seemed he couldn't tell if he was being directly accused of something or if this was another kind of clever trap. "Of course not," he snapped, anger and suspicion in his tone. "I have little reason to be informed of every arrest and treatment of insignificant, small boys. I imagine there was rightful basis for what was done, but I really have no idea."

"I did not say he was a small boy, your Grace."

The stoat's face paled. "What? What?"

"I simply said he was a boy, your Grace; a lad, but not a small boy."

The High Chancellor's lips slowly curled back in twists, powerless fury flashing in his eyes. Nicolas imagined Aldus' talons sinking into the High Chancellor's flesh. "Pardon me, Laird Aldus," the stoat hissed, his teeth clenched. "As a boy, I presumed he would be small."

The two men held each other's gaze for a while.

"As I said, an unfortunate incident, your Grace. A mistake, I'm sure. Thank you for indulging me."

"Will that be all, Laird Aldus?" Lord Sulla was almost panting, bloodless as a stone.

"Yes, your Grace. That will be all."

The High Chancellor whirled for the door, almost tripping in a near-panicked rush. "I expect I'll see you at Council within the week!" he spat acidly over his shoulder and slammed the door shut before Aldus could say anything more.

The door's bar-latch had barely dropped shut before the Laird of St. Wulf's-Without-Aldersgate burst out into a fit of laughter that deteriorated into a disorderly bout of fierce hiccups. Nicolas wasn't sure what was funny but the genuineness of Aldus' laughter, and the comical convulsions of his hiccups, caused him to laugh, too.

"What's so funny?" he finally asked as the now-irritated old man crossed his arms and folded himself over in his seat in an absurd attempt to rid himself of the hiccups. They stubbornly remained in full force and before there was time to regroup, the chamber's door again flew open. As the baritone knell of a heavy bell tolled four times from somewhere within the bowels of the gatekeep Halen Ward, the grave and commanding Laird of the Gate of the Deep and the Deputy Viceroy to the Commissioners of the Forfeited Gates, stalked in with storm and fury, and flung his considerable weight into the chair behind the desk.

"I have the lethal beaks of crows stabbed into every cleft and crack of this gatekeep!" He boomed. "Damn their heartless existence! Curse them all, they're here! They're *here*, Aldus. As sure as I've warned our robed brethren, the damned War Crows are here but no one pays any attention!"

Laird Halen, a weathered but warlike man, sat there irritatingly, glaring at Aldus as the old man's grotesquely loud hiccups shelled the room's silence. "For the love of all salt and sense, can't you control those infernal explosions, man?! And what wave of madness caused you to provoke Lord Sulla? Don't give me that eye, Aldus. His Grace rushed past me in the stairwell like a chased spring hare, sniveling and arguing with himself without so much as a nod in my direction. I swear you're like water freezing in a rock; your cunning and calculations will splinter our unity and fracture this entire kingdom if you're not careful!"

At last the violent hiccups stopped. Laird Halen spat into a brass bowl near his feet.

Aldus had sat there, ludicrously sucking in enormous gulps of air and lingering pipe smoke, his eyes watering. He looked very much like a wall-eyed fish dying in the bottom of a boat. Finally, with his composure somewhat regained, he sank back exhausted and flopped a weak hand in response to Laird Halen's criticisms. "True unity is formed by testing, Laird Ward. Resolve is tempered by opposition. I'm quite sure Lord Sulla will soon recover. In the meantime," he said, turning the bright blue of his good eye toward Nicolas, "we all have a few things to discuss, including what needs to be done to help Master Bennett, this simple boy about whom you've been so uncertain."

Nicolas could feel his cheeks redden. He hoped the two men would think it was the fire's heat.

Aldus wiped his eyes and chuckled optimistically. He puffed out a satisfyingly large smoke ring that curled itself into a figure-eight. "This dear boy, Laird Ward, happens to have been a former guest of mine, a lawful guest of St. Wulf's-Without-Aldersgate, and—" here, Aldus paused and placed a dramatic hand on Nicolas' shoulder, "he happens to be a Dragon Nightfall."

"What?! *Him*? This boy?" said Halen Ward, chucking a scowling, disbelieving chin toward Nicolas. "He's a stripling! Probably couldn't even wield the weight of an Iron Knight's arming sword, much less confront the brutal, blood-and-meat ferocity of a wicket-keeper dragon."

"You might be right. I haven't seen Master Bennett ever lift a sword or kill a *wicket-keeper* dragon," Aldus said unphased. "I *do*, however, have it on very good authority that this stripling, as you say, *killed an overlord dragon.* And no wicket-keeper either! *The* fourth generation overlord dragon. *The* Shadow Thief, Árnyék Tolvaj."

Laird Halen's mouth gaped open. His eyes shocked, he stared at Nicolas as if to look through him. His voice, now restrained, was thick and chillingly sober. "An overlord dragon," he whispered in awe. "It was *him*? This one? Not the bladesmith boy everyone talks about? But how?"

"Ranulf son of Renfry was only one of his companions, but *Nicolas* was the one who actually killed the dragon." Then, in a low and deliberate tone that swelled the sense of authority Aldus' words shifted to Nicolas, he added, "Remiel, one of the Kohanim, one of the last Clokkemakers from the Hollow Fen, was there when it happened, Laird Halen. A terrible thing it was, but it's true."

Nicolas lowered his eyes, gazing into the fire. Aldus' reference to Remiel made him feel uncomfortable and remorseful.

Aldus walked over to Halen Ward's sea desk and jabbed a long finger atop a disorderly sheaf of unrolled papers, containing ancient maps of Telluric Grand, of the First Kingdom's shifting borders, of the Outlands, the Dolman Tombs and beyond, and mariners' maps of the long-battered coastal waters of the Cold Sea. "The High Chancellor and his toady advisors are staring blindly out the front door while thieves are sailing through the back. You're right, Laird Ward. War Crow raiding parties are coming fast this way from the Land Beyond the Fogs. Damned innumerable blood hordes, taking advantage of our niggling distractions and rumors of far-off terrors. Their violence and death are going to wash ashore and if they're not soon stopped, their scourge of murder and ruin will destroy us all while we look the other way." Aldus now pointed the same long finger at Nicolas. "*That* is why *he's* come, I'd wager. That is why I believe he's here."

Nicolas could feel his heart hammer tightly in his chest. His empty stomach growled and his breath came in short, tight sips.

"This boy is Nicolas Bennett," announced the ancient Laird of the First Gate with an outspread hand, "a Wren of long-told prophecy and a Dragon Nightfall of the First Order. He has come to make war. He has come—" Aldus Ward lifted his chin high, "He has come to *kill Crows.*"

CHAPTER 11

Only a Boy

"Confound you, Aldus! You must be stark ravin' mad! War Crows will tear that lean boy limb from limb, consume his entrails, scrap his flesh, rip him to pieces as easy as an osprey rips apart a coalfish."

Laird Halen, with a commanding quarterdeck voice that could be heard amid a howling storm, was a man accustomed to issuing orders and having them obeyed. "Anyone can see that, man! It's as obvious as the nose on your face and I won't have any of it. I won't. I don't care what you call the lad. A killer of dragons, or a baiter of bears—that *boy* is not goin' anywhere. It's the law of the Forfeited Gates." He slammed a fist into his hand. "We're bound by the same charge as Wards. To obey the Articles of the Gate, to close with and destroy the King's enemies, to provide for and protect all *guests*, and to defend the City from without and from within. He's now my *guest*, Aldus, just as he was yours an' my duty is to protect him, not throw him out, not to guide him into the clutch of savage butchers and slave traders. Here he *is*, an' here he'll stay."

The aged Laird of the First Gate swung his chair to face his equal and sat there puffing furiously on his pipe until the bald crown of his head was drowned under rolling reefs of grey-white smoke. "There is no other way, my lord," he said slowly, gravely, letting each word ebb the smoke, "and it's exactly because of *who* Nicolas *is*—and *who* he *isn't*—that gives him a unique advantage, an advantage that we might easily overlook at our own peril. And at the peril of the City, at the peril of the

First Kingdom." Aldus waved his hand in the air and continued building his own wind-gauge of raw temper. "And why, pray tell, is something *more* threatening just because it's obvious? I say it's the obvious things that tend to pose the *least* danger. I have little worry reserved for those persons and things I *can* see. It's those things I *can't* see, mind you, those things that lurk about in the shadows," here he plunged spread fingers into the cloud of pipe smoke, "things masked, disguised and moving under false colors; those things I can't weigh and measure and figure out, *they're* the ones that cause me the greatest concern, my lord. They ought to cause *us* the greatest concern as well." Bleached corral-colored banks of the pipe's thick haze again washed over his head.

"Bah!" said Laird Halen and thumped his desk.

"Here's an obvious thing for you, seeing you're so inclined to be deceived by obvious things you *can* see," Aldus said puffing out a rolling sheet of smoke like a sail in full wind, "why have the six Grey Legions of Talon Knights been gathered and deployed these past many months when the spies who first reported the threats on which our War Marshals relied have all disappeared or been quietly executed for petty crimes? Where are the invading armies of beast-men, bane-elves, and witch-goblins who were supposed to have broken through our borders?"

"There's been fighting, mind you," growled Laird Halen stubbornly. "I've seen the wounded and dead brought back to the City an' so have you, Laird Aldus."

"Yes, so've I, but the numbers are too few for full-war actions. Terrible but too few. Mere skirmishes, yes; great battles, no."

"Bah," said Laird Halen again.

"Each gatekeep has been left without its attached legion of Talon Knights. Ask yourself, Laird Halen, why have we and the City been stripped of the might and power of our warlords at the exact time a vengeful blood-storm sails in from the east, from across the Cold Sea with black wings?"

Halen Ward scowled at Aldus for several seconds. Nicolas watched the face of the grim Laird of waves and coasts as he weighed different explanations, throwing them away until at last the great man peevishly pounded his heavy fist on his sea desk and came back to the most obvious reason of all. "Because of *threats*, Laird Aldus! Because of threats, I say. As clear as six fathoms in calm water, the First Kingdom is beset by a rising tide of threats on *all* borders! There might be Crows at my shores, but there are confirmed sightings of disgruntled giants heading northwest, bands of long-knives roaming the Wilds, and sorcerer caravans gathering in the High Plains of Shadows. Timber merchants talk of tree blights souring strong oaks, and farmers up from the south say they've been magically cursed with nothing but black rams in their folds and lone magpies in their haylofts. Perhaps these don't amount to the enemy armies we at first thought, but we're beset by *real* threats on every side, not unseen conspiracies devised in your own mind. Real threats require real measures—the force of arms, I say! Any man can see that." As if the matter was settled, Laird Halen sat back in his chair and folded his long arms over his thick chest. He impressed Nicolas as an honest and practical man; to Halen Ward, the thought of conspiracy and inner treachery was strange and repulsive.

Aldus sighed and slumped back in his chair. He regarded the friendly glow of the suspended oil lamp hanging immediately overhead with a hollow eye. The tone of his voice became quiet, almost as if he were speaking to an upset child. "Threats, my lord? I would kindly remind of you of the threats you recently held inside your own dungeons and who you judged at your own bench until you had them thrown, literally, I might add, from your gatekeep. *War Crows,* their miserable blood hordes and whatever hell that follows them, are the *real* threat roosting on our windowsill, hammering away at a now-very-thin plate of glass. Once a nuisance of occasional raids, but a nuisance that has become a scourge, and the scourge will be our ruin long before witch-goblins and fenris wolves pour through the Black Forest. War Crows are an ocean-borne army of dripping black feathers and bitter salt that are here *now*! You heard what that vile Crow chief spat out, '*the Murder brings war.*' Yes, there are real threats, Laird Ward, and war is indeed upon us but as you rightfully said the immediate war is 'stabbed into every cleft and crack of this gatekeep.' Like it or not, someone or several someone's have deprived us of our regular defenses when we need them the most; some destructive or deceitful plot desires that we look the other way as the *Murder* invades our shores like the plagued bloom of a red tide."

Aldus leaned back, placed a hand on his forehead, and stared at the stone ceiling. Long minutes went by. Quietly he finally said, "I would trade a thousand fenris wolves outside the firelight for one wolverine inside the tent."

Halen Ward peered at Aldus from under the wiry brush of his peppered eyebrows. The hard lines of his face relaxed even though the stern Laird didn't smile. "Fine. Fine, Aldus," he relented. "You've been right too many times for me to second-guess a reliable trade wind such as yourself. I agree to agree." He scratched at the iron-grey scruff on his chin and spread an open palm atop the stack of maps on the desk. "Even so, it's hard for me to think there's some twisted traitor's hand in all of this; but I'll admit to sometimes having too simple a view of the intrigues of those who seek power. I suppose stranger things have happened." He pinched a fold of skin at the bridge of his nose. "Thanks be to the throne, the Forfeited Gates have survived them all. We'll survive them again, I imagine." Gradually, a deep, furrowed scowl settled over his face. He leaned forward, eyes dark and narrow. "Do you think the High Chancellor has anything to do with this? With turning our attention elsewhere?"

"Perhaps," Aldus replied vaguely, rubbing his forehead. "I honestly—I don't know." His voice was tired and he went back to smoking his pipe. This time he rocked back against the rearmost legs of his chair and aimed his smoke rings around the suspended oil lamp as if playing an upside-down game of ring toss.

"May I ask something?" Nicolas said. His heart was beating fast, nervous, afraid to say anything at all but still needing to say something. He had sat quietly in his chair in front of the fire all this time, wondering and fearful as to how he fit into what all he'd heard. Terrified at what Aldus had said about him being there to kill War Crows and struggling with a thick knot in his dry throat.

"What, what?!" Surprised out of his reverie, Aldus fumbled and nearly dropped his pipe. He laughed and with an expectant look said, "But of course, Master Bennett! My most kind apology; we've been so busy crossing our words, we've forgot who is standing in between them. Ask away! Ask away! It's time we gave your questions some answers."

"Might I have something to eat?"

Both men looked at Nicolas blankly as if it took time to make sense of what he'd asked. Halen was the first to react. He nodded and as he did so a naïve smile finally found its way onto his face. It wasn't the kind of smile one would call overly warm or even kindly, but it was a smile nonetheless and in an odd way, it made Laird Halen seem a bit more like Nicolas' gruff Uncle Winston than a hawkish sea captain piloting a man-o-war.

"Of course ya may, lad." Halen pulled a rope bell near his desk and within seconds in ran a steward, barefoot but dressed neatly in a white tunic with a blue coverlet. The boy, near to Nicolas' age, was carrying a bowl of pickled golden plover eggs for Laird Halen and set them on his desk with a tin of coarse-ground pepper. "Thank 'e, Tom. Jump to an' fetch a hot hash of red taters an' black puddin', and bring in three cups of mulled wine with the food. I imagine we'd all welcome something to drink."

"Here, here," said Aldus in agreement, tugging his beard.

"Thank you," Nicolas said. His stomach growled loudly. Embarrassed, he felt himself turn red but hoped the men wouldn't notice. "I haven't had much to eat, sir."

"I see you're on familiar terms with Laird Aldus, Master Bennett. I'd welcome the same consideration if we're to share private counsels on matters as dark as those we seem to have before us." The Laird of the Gate of the Deep bowed his head. "Call me, Halen, or Laird Halen. Whichever you like. If you are who the Laird of the First Gate says you are, and of that, I'll admit I'm not yet entirely certain myself but I'm willing to be convinced, I'm afraid you've seen a rougher side of my gatekeep than was your due." He cleared his throat, visibly awkward, and said, "I'm sorry for that. These days we don't see many innocent visitors by way of land. Even in less dodgy times it's uncertain; solid ground is the domain of other gatekeeps. Mine's the Cold Sea and coasts an' whatever the tides might bring. Many of my guests, guests of the Second Gate, arrive by sail through the Bay of Wrath, the narrow gulf leading from here to the Cold Sea and the eastern waters. We largely deal with spice traders and freight merchants, or country nobles who've paid for a traveling passage up from the south so they can avoid unguarded roads in the Woodcutter's Forest and brigand bands who hide among the rocks of the Crinkle Crags, a barren stretch of stony hills in the middle of the Southern Fells between us and the Lowlands. A lad such as yourself, appearin' from the sea but without a ship, interruptin' a lawful execution as only a king might do and knockin' on my gatekeep's southern portal claiming to be none other than Ranulf son of Renfry, is proper cause for rumor and concern. I hope you understand that. Still," Halen Ward said, managing a stroppy smile, "I'm glad my sentry didn't crack your skull open. I'll have to make sure his gaffer adds twelve extra pecks to his pay. My Master Grimlock, Odibrand Dred, sent word he'd seen you pass by on the docks. You were being led by a page for the Second Watch, I believe, and Odibrand was satisfied you weren't any hazard. He has a shrewd sense about these things and I trust him entirely. By right counts, you should've at least been quartered in one of the guest cells. I'm sorry for that an' I intend to look into why you were sent down to the passage tomb." Halen Ward thumped the table. "That's a vile an' dangerous place, lad. It's certainly no place for guests or even those who're held for questioning. In truth, I wish that dreadful passage didn't exist," he glanced at Aldus, "but it has had its purposes."

There was a light knock on the door and in popped Tom the steward, balancing a wooden tray that held three, tall cups and a hard bread trencher steaming with mash potatoes and sliced rounds of crisp, black sausage, something like the black pudding, the blood sausage, Nicolas' mum would sometimes serve with Sunday breakfast. Laird Halen nodded toward Nicolas and the steward served him first. By the fifth mouthful, Nicolas began to feel the warmth of the food and the mulled wine—a watery, mild wine spiced with cloves and ginger and raisins—fill his belly. The two men said nothing, letting him eat in silence.

Several short minutes later, with Nicolas wiping the last bits of pork grease from the corners of his mouth, Aldus Ward knocked ruffled ashes from his pipe bowl and repacked it with moist leaves. "Wherever or however you'd like to begin, Master Bennett, Laird Halen and I will do our best to answer."

"Might I see Benjamin?"

The smile left Halen Ward's face. Aldus gave his fellow Laird a quick, hard stare.

"Benjamin Rush?" asked Halen curtly.

"Yes, sir—I mean, yes, Laird Halen—Halen."

"He's a thief, a snatcher."

Aldus quickly raised his hand and glowered at Halen, his good eye flashing sharp flecks of gold and blue. "Give us a chance to speak on that point privately, Nicolas," he said without averting his stare.

Nicolas nodded respectfully and pressed forward with his next question. "I saw Adelaide, Adelaide Ashdown. She's here. I'd like to see her again if I may… may I?"

Halen Ward's smile didn't return. He twitched his nose and rubbed at his stubble. "Makes no difference to me. She's a refusal of the Barrow Cloister but she's been helpful to my men." He cocked his head as if remembering a minor detail. "She keeps a goat as a pet, I'm told. Odd girl. The watch officers say she can be cheeky and kicks you if she's upset." He waved his hand. "You may meet with her if you like, Master Bennett."

"Thank you. Aldus?"

"Yes?"

"Where is Ranulf? Adelaide told me people are saying wicked things about him. Is he alright? May I see him as well?

Laird Aldus sat back, tugging his beard. "Might I suggest something?" he asked, looking compassionately at Nicolas. "I know you'd like to reunion with your friends as soon as you can. Makes perfect sense, Nicolas; a perfectly reasonable request. But there are… circumstances. Yes, circumstances, and if you'd be so kind as to indulge me, I'd ask you to be patient. I promise to arrange for a get-together shortly."

Nicolas felt profoundly disappointed. He suddenly realized that while adventure and the fantastical nature of Telluric Grand had urged him to return, his heart had mostly been set on seeing his friends again. The blow was a hard one.

"I understand," he said. Nicolas was tired. His head and body hurt, and even though the food and drink in his belly had helped brighten his spirits, loneliness and anxiety were slithering their way back inside his soul. Ominous talk of war and armies and desperate strategies, watching and listening to the two, great Lairds quarrel, made the quiet boy from Plumpton Head, England, deeply unsettled, frightened. Lost, he stared into the fire and thought about his grandfather and as he did, he remembered a conversation he'd once had in the gloaming fallow. It had taken place during the last light of day, encircled by a high hedge of Celtic maple trees near a small peat home hidden in a moorish, mystical place called the Hollow Fen. Nicolas had been, and remained, one of the very few living who'd met and spoken with a real Kohanim, a Clokkemaker. He's a powerful, ancient Wisp by the name Remiel.

"You are young," the Wisp had said to Nicolas. "You are young like your grandfather was once young, and like he once was, it is your youth, with the confidence and hope undamaged by man's Time, which are your best weapons. These, Nicolas, are far greater than those weapons which are forged in steel or wielded by great men of war."

Nicolas clenched his jaw and felt a burst of unexpected strength inside him push back against the fear and loneliness. His grandfather had been here. His grandfather had first come when he was Nicolas' age. He'd squired for a great chieftain, founded the City of Relic, won the borders of the First Kingdom, and fought for those who could not fight; in a world linked magically to his own Nicolas' grandfather had been a celebrated warrior king, but once-upon-a-time, even before that, he'd also been a boy, a boy just like Nicolas. A quiet, English boy who'd found he had an age-old will of iron hidden inside his chest and a desire to help others even if he seemed the least likely to be able to help. *Just like Jack was*, Nicolas thought suddenly. A catch in his throat relaxed as quickly as it had come. The thought of Jack snapped the anxiety inside his heart like a dry branch of kindling. His soul felt ancient but his heart felt new. Resurrected.

Without looking away from the fire Nicolas firmly said, "I don't know much about these War Crows, and I've no idea how to help, but if I can, I'll do my jolly best." He looked at Aldus then at Halen. "I want to help. My grandfather would've helped."

Aldus clapped his hands. "Aha!" he said, his good eye sparkling.

"Grandfather?" asked Laird Halen with a frown. "Who's yer grandfather, lad?"

"Um… my grandfather—Grandfather Bennett."

"Where is he? In the City somewhere or serving in one of the legions?"

Aldus looked keenly at Nicolas and winked. "All that later, Laird Halen. You and I have much to discuss, including a bit more about Master Bennett, and we must quickly call a war council but *first* let's acknowledge your brave guest's wishes. Let's set him on the road to help us, as safely as we can, I might add."

"He's only a boy!" Halen protested.

"A boy who knows *where* he is," again Aldus winked at Nicolas, "and a boy who knows *who* he is. Boys have been kings, Halen. They've borne the weight of crowns and kingdoms, and kings. Whether they be boys or not, they protect their realm."

"He's a king now is he?"

"Perhaps. Perhaps less, perhaps more."

A pensive, thoughtful silence followed, Aldus allowing Laird Halen to accept what he was saying, Laird Halen wrestling with the right of what Aldus had said, and Nicolas breathing a bit heavy, feeling a wild pressure in his chest like the kind he'd felt the first day of school at Hunter Hall.

"Alright, Master Bennett," Halen finally said, lifting his unshaved chin, "if that's what you want, I won't stand in your way. I respect your courage although I don't agree with you. I can't fathom how a lad such as yourself, clearly *not* a king—no offense intended—can help. The First Kingdom must meet War Crows with the mass and force of Talon Knights, not boys. Axe to sword and hammer to shield, but I imagine Laird Aldus and I will set that particular disagreement to rights. In the meantime, if there can be found a way for you to help, I swear you'll have the full provision of the Gate of the Deep."

Laird Halen made a fist and struck it against his chest. "Mark my word, Master Bennett," he said darkly, "your ambition places you in harm's way. Those brutes I executed today, they were survivors from a recently defeated blood horde; even in defeat War Crows are relentless and it is rare to capture any. Their hellish race, the great *Murder*, is a savage, primal nation of butchers. They are as dangerous as starving fenris wolves and as remorseless as northern orcs. War Crows *do not parley.* They *do not show mercy.* They sail and live to kill and enslave. They are nothing but carrion crows, Master Bennett, an' when they're done killin'," Halen Ward said with glistening black and angry eyes, "they *eat* whatever remains."

CHAPTER 12

Unexpected Help

"Slipped bights an' cracked 'awsers!" grumbled the aging, little man, swinging his short, hairy legs over the side of his little cot. "I was seven bells in ta the best sleep o' me cursed life, an' I'm turned out o' the sweetest fiddler's green so I can mop about in the marnin's wee 'ours ta get *you* a decent set o' oilskins. Is that *right*? Is that what the fuss is about?" He smacked his thick lips, snorted like a penless pig rooting for truffles, and spat, entirely missing the chamber pot that sat not more than a foot away.

The little man's name was Bidlebee, or Ol' Marm Bidle-da-bee as he was widely and somewhat affectionately known throughout the gatekeep. A grousing, nagging, pestering, mother-hen of a gate steward, the senior-most of a handful of gate stewards who were scattered throughout the Gate of the Deep. Bidlebee's assigned gate was the Stern Gate, a relatively comfortable post and the seaside gatekeep's only access into the City of Relic. Bidlebee was master of quarters, whose duty it was to supervise provisioning of his assigned gate's guard, distribute supplies, oversee repairs, superintend accommodations and meals for each twelve-hour watch shift, and to harass and harangue the two storemen under his authority without ceasing. Both of them more storeboys than storemen, and who were presently in the gatekeep's infirmary, having recently eaten from the same cut of putrid meat taken out of the same salt-beef cask. Like his fellow stewards, the little man took pride in his post but somewhat greater pleasure in a night's fitful sleep. Nicolas had had the disagreeable task of waking Bidlebee, doing his bravest best to gently poke at the snoring steward and to kindly ask if the little man might have a spare cloak Nicolas could borrow. Provoking a response, much less waking the soundly snoring steward, had taken several long minutes and finally, a few not-so-gentle jabs with Nicolas' finger.

Sitting on the edge of his smelly straw mattress, the stout little man curiously reminded Nicolas of a wild boar, or better yet, a wild boar's piglet given the man's queerly small size. Bidlebee's head, a bristly thick block of a head, seemed to take up nearly a third of his body, while his neck and shoulders, as broad and as thick as his head, were connected in such a way that it looked as if they must all turn in unison when Bidlebee turned his head. His fore and upper arms were beefy boughs and excessively hairy, even hairier than his legs which comprised the shortest part of his person making him look quite top-heavy, constantly tippled, and always at the ready for a forward charge.

Scratching absently at a furry armpit, Bidlebee drowsed and spluttered. His breath smelled of sour pipe smoke and bitter alcohol. An empty jug of fuddling swill, the likely cause of his exceedingly sound sleep, sat against his hip. "Say agin 'ho sent ya an' what I'm to do." Bidlebee's dull eyes shut again even though his squally-haired eyebrows remained lifted. He belched and farted at the same time.

Nicolas, for his part, was doing everything he could not to laugh and not to rudely hold his nose although the little man's sleeping quarters stank like green egg yolks and Aunt Harriet's unsocked feet. "Laird Halen—Laird Halen Ward sent me, sir. One of his pages brought me here, told me to wait for a guide into the City, and Laird Ward," Nicolas said, remembering how to correctly refer to a gatekeep's Laird, "instructed me to ask for a traveling cloak or something of that nature. My escort said I should come in here and wake you. I hope that was alright."

"Awright? O' course it's awright iffin' Laird Ward says it's awright." Bidlebee rubbed his eyes and wagged his fierce head trying to focus his bleary eyes on Nicolas. "Yer but a lad! Thought you was someone bigger. Ya 'ave a strange tongue. What'd ya say yer name was?"

"I didn't, but it's Nicolas. Nicolas Bennett."

"Well Master Bennett with a strange tongue, I've a perfect kit ta give ya, an' ya can keep it; no need ta barrow. No need to dip in ta ma ledger's supplies, neither. Me two storemen 'appen to be a twin o' foolish lunkheads, gettin' sick as blind kittens after eatin' from a rancid beef barrel while sopped with fiddlin' ale. Both lads are 'bout yer same size by the looks o' it. Wezel keeps a long-cloak 'e don't use unless there's a n'rthren gale. It's hooded an' that'll do fer yer weather wear. Fezel 'as an extra tunic, trousers an' boots if ya like, an' some cord for a belt in a chest you'll find by 'is 'ammock in the common room. Here!" Bidlbee said, tossing Nicolas a short belt dagger he'd scrounged from under his mattress. "The world's a kinder place if a lad 'as a quick blade at the ready."

"Thank you."

"Tsk. It's me job. An' now it's me job to go back ta sleep." Bidlebee yawned ferociously and waved a hand toward the door. "Yer welcome ta wait in the common room fer yer companion. A fire should be goin'. Stoked it meself at the last bell." The little man pulled his little legs back into his bed and rolled over, a boar piglet of hair and stench nestling back into its crib of straw. "An' lad," he muttered sleepily as he pulled the blanket over his shoulders, "may thar be a followin' sea at yer back, friends at yer side, an' salt in yer enemies' eyes."

About twenty minutes later, Nicolas was sitting by himself in the common room, grating a fire with a now-and-then prod from a bent andiron he found leaning against the great hearth.

He'd quickly discovered the clothing Bidlebee had offered; all entangled in a heap of grimy clothes between two, small, mattresses stuff with straw and shoved against a far wall. Nicolas had pulled on a pair of Fezel's stained and ratty trousers loose enough to wear over his own, dropped a worn yet mended tunic over his shoulders, and wrapped himself in Wezel's long weather-cloak, a thin affair of beaten, scrap leather but oiled and supple. After some hesitation, Nicolas untied his Malham boots and replaced them with a pair of stained, front-laced, ankle boots. Reluctantly, he hid his own boots underneath the rest of the clothing and swore to himself to get them back before they were discovered. Finally, finding a short loop of hemp cord in Fezel's small chest, he belted his trousers and tucked the dagger inside his trousers. Nothing now but to wait.

Nicolas felt nervous. His stomach was still settling the salted porridge and ale he'd eaten a half-hour before. Thirst, hunger, and the weary ache in his head and body were no longer foremost in his mind. There wasn't any thought of a faraway Christmastime or of moonlit snow covering the quiet sheep's pasture. There was little room in his thoughts for much of anything, little room except for a single, overshadowing thought.

Out there beyond the gatekeep's long, arched causeway, waiting expectantly for the grey morning's eastern light lay the City; the First City of the First Kingdom's long chronicle, the silvered and long-storied City of Relic. Whatever journey's beginning that might be lying in wait for him within the shade of its high walls filled his restless mind.

Indeed, the world's early dawn seemed to be waiting, waiting expectantly for *him* once again.

The evening before, Nicolas had finally had a bite to eat as the first dimming rays of fallow lowered the light in Laird Halen's high chambers. Just after the ring of two bells, the first dog watch of the evening guard shifts, while the two Lairds continued to bicker and wrangle over "the next move," as Halen Ward kept putting it, his mind a chessboard of right angles, structure, and rules. Nicolas, happy to watch and listen, had been happier still when the end-of-day food had arrived. There'd been a juicy joint of pork roasted with parsnips, peppered crackling, and something much like the jaffa cakes Nicolas would sometimes beg his parents to buy three little cakes filled with orange jam and topped with a thickened cap of cold maple instead of chocolate. The two older men had yattered on, only pausing to slurp down bowls of pea-n-potato soup and several glasses of wine. Nicolas, stuffed, exhausted and aching, and finding himself nodding in and out of consciousness, had trailed behind Tom out of Laird Halen's private office and into an adjoining, smallish antechamber. Within it there was a slung hammock, a single stocky candle sitting atop a rickety table, and a frayed bell-cord hanging over one end of the hammock.

"This is my lord's chamber," Tom told him. "He only uses it during full quarters when war's afoot or when he's 'ad too much wine. Sleep as you like. Pull that line if yer in need, an' I'll see what's about."

Nicolas had groped his way into the hammock and had fallen into a dreamless sleep until the ring of four bells. The gatekeep's turning of the morning watch, what Nicolas would have known as six o'clock in the morning, reverberated throughout the gatekeep's great halls, chambers, stone pockets, and long passages.

"Ni-co-las… Ni-co-las… A-wake," he heard Adelaide say, her wonderful voice sounding strangely like the ring of eight bells in St. Andrew's Church on a Sunday morning.

He awoke with a snap, his thoughts jumbled, his mouth dry, his feet cold. Tom, or someone, had removed his boots while he slept and had thrown a heavy blanket over his shoulders. He could hear the muffled tramp and shuffle of moving soldiers along with the impatient bellows of sergeants and gaffers outside the antechamber's door as one watch relieved another. He was alone.

Nicolas rubbed his groggy eyes and swung himself out of bed. He tottered to the door, focusing on the slit of weak light lining its threshold. He found the door's sliding bolt and ring-handle, and cautiously opened it just enough to peek around the door's frame and into the lengthy hallway beyond. There stood a pair of guards at post outside another door some yards away; they both saw him and grinned grins of missing teeth but said nothing. One knuckled a morning salute. Nicolas ducked back inside and walked over to the smooth-worn cord hanging over the hammock. A hesitant pull and another once again with a little more spirit. He didn't hear anything and wondered if the cord wasn't working until Tom's loud knock struck the door.

"Ya called?" The steward-boy had asked from the other side.

"Yes, please—yes, yes, I did." Nicolas realized he hadn't planned on anything more to say. He was awake but aside from that, he hadn't any idea of what to do next; it sounded daff to come out and say that, so he'd stuck with the obvious. "I'm awake now."

The door opened and Tom stepped in. "I hope you don't mind, Master Bennett. I was told to leave ya be but I took yer boots off whilst you was sleepin'. I thought it might be more comfortable an'," he said with eyes darting past Nicolas to the hammock, "I was a bit concerned about their soles tearin' my lord's sleepin' 'ammock. They're made o' very hard hide tho' I can't rightly place what animal was used to make 'em. Is it a horned-beast's skin?" Nicolas had looked blankly at the steward who'd waved his hand in dismissal. "Never-ya-mind, Master Bennett. None o' my business. I'm prattlin' on like a maid. Didja sleep well?"

"I did, I think—Was, was a girl in here?"

"Shouldn't a-been!" Tom had said, surprised disapproval clouding his face. "If one o' them scullery hens was botherin' you, Master Brooks, jes you let me know an' I'll sort it out wit' the Master Cook. They shoulda been busy enough without no need to go snoopin' about after the dog watches—them's the late night gate watches. They're a titterin' flock o' gossipin' ninnies, an' they 'ave *no* business leaving the scullery after grimlock, after the witchin' hour."

"Oh no," Nicolas quickly said, "nothing of the sort. I just thought I heard my friend's voice a few minutes ago. She's a… a Healer. She's here in the gatekeep."

"Humpf. I've not seen any o' their kind within the Laird's offices. If yer not feelin' well we 'ave an infirmary; no windows, the air's unwell, an' the hay's damp, but the salted porridge is hot—hotter than this, I'd say." Tom had smiled crookedly and had held out a square wooden plate holding a ladle-full of lumpy, grey porridge; there was also a tin mug containing a cool, dark, toasted-brown liquid. "That said, our mornin' bitter is the best brewed in all six gatekeeps," the steward boy had said proudly. "Everyone says 'tis so."

"Thank you." Nicolas took a sip. The drink was earthy and sour almost as if some fruit rind and bread had been left to spoil in a bucket. Tom's eyes were wide with expectation; Nicolas had braced himself and considerately had drunk a mouthful, willing it down his throat. "Brilliant."

Tom had flashed a grin. "Top marks! Top marks!"

The porridge was a sticky situation. Nicolas had crunched his way through the large salt crystals sprinkled on top of it and had gummed his way through most of the grey masses of gluey oats. He'd drunk as much of the ale as he could manage, much to Tom's obvious satisfaction. Shoving a last bite in his mouth, Nicolas has said he was "quite full," which came out sounding more like, "quite fōō." That accomplished, he'd asked about Aldus Ward.

"I believe Laird Aldus left the gatekeep an 'our ago. He provided instructions to let ya sleep until you woke and then start ya off toward the Stern Gate. It'll have a guardroom an' its master of quarters should'a been instructed to provide you with a long weather-cloak an' some different boots or footwraps if ye haven't got any," Tom had said eyeing Nicolas' Malham boots which sat in a corner.

"Am I to enter the City then? Do you know where I'm supposed to go?"

"Laird Aldus didn't say but he *did* say you was to wait there. Wait for a guide or a page or someone. He sounded like you'd know who it was." Tom had given Nicolas an encouraging wink. "I'd submit Laird Aldus is a man to trust, Master Bennett. I've never 'eard o' him bein' nothin' but wise an' charitable… at least to those he likes an' trusts, an' I think he likes an' trusts you." Tom had wiped his nose. "That's quite a lot of compliment, comin' from a Laird of a gatekeep, ya know."

"Yes, yes, of course, you're right. Thank you, Tom."

A page from the First Watch had soon appeared and, at Diggory's same harried pace, had led Nicolas through a warren of brightly lit hallways, shadowed corridors, and ever-ascending, ever-descending stairwells until they'd come to the Stern Gate's guardroom.

"In there," the page had said. Several gate guards were standing around; none of them had moved to help.

"In there?" Nicolas had echoed hesitantly. He'd put his hands on his waist and tried to catch his breath. "I'm to go in there?"

"Aye, in ya go," the page had said merrily. "I've satisfied me duty an' delivered me package. I'd rather not celebrate it by 'avin' me ears boxed by bein' the one to wake Ol' Marm Bidle-da-bee."

"*I'm* to wake her?"

"Good 'eavens, Master Bennett! Ol' Marm Bidle-da-bee is *not* a *her*. Bidlebee, that's the fellow's right an' proper name, is jus' called Ol' Marm on account of—" the page's enormous smile revealed a tongue poking through gaps left by two missing teeth. "Ha! I 'aven't got a *clue* as to why Bidle-da-bee's called 'Ol' Marm.' May-haps the ol' fella's like some ol' ship. We say ships are 'hers' tho' I don't rightly know why we do that neither 'less it's because they provide whatever we need even tho' they fuss an' creak an' groan like a hen-house o' ol' biddies. Ha! By the king's empty throne! I swear I teach meself somethin' new every day!" The boy had slapped his bony knee in self-delight and off he'd went humming a merry tune, leaving Nicolas to wake old Bidlebee entirely at his own peril.

Having survived his encounter with the irritable gate steward, Nicolas could now hear Bidlebee snoring again, a long sucking rumble, gasp, and shudder—silence—a rumble, gasp, and shudder—silence. So intent was Nicolas on the dreadful rhythm of Bidlebee's snore, he failed to hear the door to the common room open behind him until a boot's heel caught and scraped the buckled threshold board. Nicolas spun around.

"Holy hair knots an' ham fat! So 'tis you after all, Nicolas my boy! Not that I'd doubt his lordship, but *seein'* is somethin' apart from knowin' and it *is* lovely to see ya, laddie," said the tall man whose frame filled the doorway. The tall man was wearing the same leather pack, the same weather stained hood and long cape, all black, coarse cloth, over the same rough-sewn shirt tucked into the same broad leather belt, with the same old, but now much more threadbare pair of trousers jammed inside the same pair of muddy boots as when Nicolas had first seen him outside the Cider Press Inn over a year ago.

"Mr. Westenra!" Nicolas shouted, his eyes lighting up. The two had once journeyed along a dark forest road together and as one, had entered St.Wulf's-Without-Aldersgate at the end of a long, baleful night, a grim traveler returning to the City alongside a peculiar boy in search of the Laird of the gatekeep.

"'Mister,' ya say? Ha! Yer still as strange as the day we met, Master Bennett. No, I'm no master. Nor no mister as it must be said in the land where yer from. I'm only Albrec. My title's my axe an' my watch-word is 'Fire an' Iron.' No more, no less." The tall man smiled warmly and chuckled. "Great gander gaffs, lad. It's good to see ya. Give us a hand!" The man and boy gripped hands and Albrec rested his other hand on Nicolas' shoulder. "You were such an *odd* lad on odd business that night, poppin' outta the woods like the fairie folk, titterin' for directions like you was in the middle of a merchant-fair. I hadn't any idea at the time," he said, a deep look in his eye. "The first time we met you was lookin' for the Laird of the First Gate, an' *this* time—" he squeezed Nicolas' shoulder and gave him a long, thoughtful stare, "this time the Laird of the First Gate came lookin' fer *me* because of *you*. Odd business. C'mon, my boy, let's sit by the fire an' have a quick word before we're to go."

"It's you? You're to guide me then? To take me—to take me into the City?"

"Of course, it's me."

They both sat on the long bench in front of the fireplace. The tall man withdrew a long-stemmed pipe from out of his cloak and filled it with clay-brown pipe-leaf kept in a leather pouch which hung from his belt. "Ya sound as relieved as Laird Aldus did when he asked me to do it." Silky bolts of smoke flowed upward from the pipe's chipped bowl. "I guided ya once so I suppose that must give me first rights to do it again but there's no need to sound so comforted. This'll be a stroll lad. A mere doddle." He snapped his long fingers together. "We're visitin' parts of the City I *know*, streets I grew up in an' hail from."

"The Dreggs?" Nicolas asked, calling to mind what the tall man had told him so long ago.

"Aye, the Dreggs." Albrec sat there puffing his pipe and gazing into the fire for a few minutes. "This way o' course—through the Gate of the Deep—isn't my usual path of travel. It's damp an' cold an' salty, and it isn't a gatekeep I much pass through. It's mostly for seafaring folk, eastern traders, an' the like. I tend to keep to my own parts which mostly takes my path through the Traitor's Gate to the west, or when I've strayed below the Southern Fells I come up through Laird Aldus' gatekeep." Albrec swung his head about the no-frills guard room. "Laird Aldus keeps a more… *mystifyin'* gatekeep than this one, I'd say." He glanced at Nicolas and grinned. "Don't know exactly what I mean to say by that, but it's true nonetheless. Laird Aldus is, well, he's an unusually *ancient* one, somethin' about him… In any case, that's where he found me or at least where his Master Grimlock—hmphff, odd that I don't know his name after all this time—him an' his great war-beast, Basileus, found me. I thought I was on my own errand, but here I am!" He thumped the bench and laughed. "Truth is, never thought I'd see you again, lad. You *are* a peculiar one, Master Bennett."

"Yet here I am," joked Nicolas lightly, tapping his toe on the stone floor. His earlier nervousness vanished the moment Albrec had arrived. He'd been the first person Nicolas had met during his first journey into Telluric Grand and it was a gut-feeling about Albrec, and the simple honesty of the tall man's donkey, Cherry Pit, that had encouraged Nicolas to set out to find Laird Aldus. Here he was again to lead the way, and for that, Nicolas felt enormously pleased and grateful. He felt safe.

"Yes, indeed," Albrec said. "*Here* you are." The tall man leaned forward, upended his pipe's bowl and knocked its curled cinders atop grey pillows of ash piled at the front of the hearth. "Might I ask you a direct question, lad?"

Albrec's voice wasn't demanding; it was friendly but a touch nervy.

"Yes, sir."

"No, no, sir, for me, lad. Call me Albrec, by yer leave, Master Bennett, I'd be pleased if you call me Albrec," he said even more generously.

"Yes, Albrec."

The tall man straightened his back and fixed his face with a firm look. "I remember how ya handled yerself that night on the road from the Cider Press Inn. That Wisp's shadow-presence woulda made almost any man's stomach twist an' churn, but you, you held fast." He rubbed a calloused hand thoughtfully against the stubble-growth on his cheek. "Laird Aldus explained a bit to me 'bout yerself—I've heard strange tales, lad, an' seen stranger ones still, but by the king's throne, yer an *oddity* on all counts. A Dragon Nightfall the Laird says—says it was *you* that killed the Shadow Thief. That's high-an'-heady stuff, lad. Some are alive who've killed wicket keepers, but not a breathin' soul can claim to have killed an overlord dragon. Not sayin' I doubt his lordship, but—but what I'm gettin' at is *why*? *How*? Why is it that ya seem to be only a whip of a boy yet stand in shoes no man's feet can fill?" Albrec seemed about to say more but the serious look on his face faded and he left it at that. "Just a question, if yer willin' to answer, Master Bennett."

Nicolas abruptly had the mental image of being a much younger boy, perhaps only four or five years old, and asking his father what the word 'earth' meant. Peter Bennett had chuckled and said, "Shall I describe every grain an' scrap of sand an' rock or shall I simply say it is the thing upon which we're born ta live an' stretch our legs an' die? What if, instead, I just describe a single rock, my boy?" He'd swept Nicolas up into his arms with a playful twinkle in his eye. "Imagine that place we went on 'oliday last summer—up along the Scottish coast ta see the sea caves hidin' under Cullain Castle; we were headed north out of Girvan, an' I said, 'Look, lads!' ta you an' yer brother, an' I pointed at a great rock-island stickin' up in the outer Firth of Clyde? Do ya remember that? I told ya boys it was called the Fairy Rock an' it had a lighthouse an' an ol' tower-'ouse on it that we couldn't see very well. Do ya remember, Nicolas? Well, the earth is like that rock, lad, it's like the Fairy Rock, sittin' high an' mighty amid an infinite ocean of blue, under a limitless sky. The earth's round like that rock's round. It's hard an' sure like that rock's hard an' sure, but the earth is tragic as well." He had planted a kiss on Nicolas' cheek. "The earth is our home, Nicolas, but not for always. We live on it, we climb its mountains, we defend its shores, we fish in its seas, an' when the time finally comes, we're buried beneath it. Just like they've discovered stone coffins on Fairy Rock, but all that's momentary. Life's as quick as a sneeze, lad. We truly belong somewhere else, an endurin' home, high and away among the skies far above as Reverend Walker 'as told us." Mr. Bennett smiled at Nicolas and ruffled his messy hair before setting him down. "Does that make a bit of sense, lad?"

Now an older Nicolas, but still a boy even so, looked at Albrec and found new significance in his father's words. "I'm not sure I can describe *every* reason, Albrec, but maybe I can describe one reason that makes the other reasons make better sense. There's, there's something I feel inside me…" Nicolas' words were measured, finding their way as he went. "It feels like it's made up of a lot of parts, too many to really describe I guess, but they fit together just right. They feel so mixed, yet they all lead to one thing.

"For a long time, part of me was lost—and—and I didn't even remember every day to remind myself of what part that was—but it was there. A hole inside. I guess I felt lonely because of it. I guess somewhere inside I hadn't found my hard-and-sure thing to stand on yet." Nicolas shook his head. "I love my parents." And in his head he could hear his mum say, *Yer blessed, Nicolas, how blessed you are!* "I'm blessed," Nicolas said, "but I guess I've always felt like I was… I dunno—meant for more. My brother—my brother, Jack—he once said to be as 'free as you can' and he was… he was free."

A secret place inside his heart suddenly opened and Nicolas stopped and stared at the fire. "He was brave, too," he added. "*I* want to be that brave. The part of me that felt lost also feels like I've found it again when I'm here. Feels like I need to be here to keep it from being lost again… and if I'm discovering a new feeling because I'm here, then it also feels like I owe something… like I owe it to my grandfather and maybe to Jack somehow… to do the best I can."

Nicolas stopped, embarrassed. He glanced at Albrec to see if the tall man was laughing at him, but Albrec's face was unmoved, intent. A burning log popped loudly and made Nicolas jump, making him feel silly.

"Brave ya are, lad," Albrec finally whispered, his mouth was a thin, stern line. "Brave ya are. Yer honest, too. That's more rare than bravery sometimes. Well," the tall man said, standing to his feet, "thank ya for openin' yer mind, Master Bennett. Makes a man feel better to know the mettle of those 'e's goin' into battle with."

"Into battle?" asked Nicolas. "I thought we're heading into the City."

"We are, lad. All battles 'ave a beginnin', an' if what Laird Aldus says bears true, which I think it might—what lies ahead is the beginnin' of a battle, war even, tho' we'll pray that doesn't happen. This particular beginnin' lies in the City of Relic, an' *that,* Master Bennett, *is* where you an' I are headed."

Nicolas licked his tongue against his now-dry lips. Whatever he'd said about bravery a few moments before seemed less certain, but he didn't want to look foolish in front of Albrec. "What, um—what shall I bring?"

The tall man looked him over. "Grab that rat-chewed sun-hat," he said, pointing back at the dirty pile of clothes between the two mattresses. Lying forgotten on the floor was a broad-brimmed, straw hat, at least what was left of a hat, one meant to be worn on sunny days out on the broad landing leading to the gatekeep's arched causeway. Rat's had gnawed most of the hat's brim but it was still serviceable. "Drop yer hood back an' put that thing on yer head. I'll go ahead of ya, and you'll follow no less than ten minutes later. I want ya to be seen enterin' the City alone. If anyone's spyin' as ya leave the gatekeep, they'll think yer alone an' they'll think they can recognize ya easy cause yer wearin' that barmy hat." He put a hand on Nicolas' shoulder. "Listen close now. Once yer within the City walls, take the first merchant road to yer right. Follow it for a stone's throw until you see a stand of hazel trees to the left. It's only a short distance after enterin' the City's wells. There's a fresh spring of water among those trees where travelers an' pilgrims can rest an' fill their water skins. Stop there an' I'll find ya. After that, no one will know to be lookin' for a man an' a boy together."

"Is someone looking for us?"

"Perhaps. I don't know. Laird Aldus said to be cautious so I'm applyin' a bit o' caution. No need to worry, lad. Keep to yerself an' follow my instructions, the rest 'll take care of itself. Like I said, it'll be a doddle."

"Albrec," Nicolas said as he jammed the dirty, yellow hat on his head.

"Aye?"

"What are we going to do in the City?"

"It's not *what* we're goin' to do, Master Bennett. It's *who* we're goin' to see."

"And who's that?"

"Yer friend, of course. The bladesmith. Ranulf son of Renfry."

Nicolas didn't know what to say, but the thought of seeing Ranulf again, especially with Albrec at his side, relit a warm glow of courage inside of him. Adelaide had made it sound like Ranulf might be in trouble or at least might be headed for trouble. He was in the City after all and if Ranulf needed him, Nicolas wanted to be there to help.

"Albrec?" As much as he wanted to see Ranulf, he wasn't necessarily eager for Albrec to leave him alone and like most boys do, like most children do, Nicolas kept talking to create a last few moments of delay.

"Aye?" the tall man said again as he took a quick look outside the guardroom's door.

"The man snoring in there, Bidlebee, he said something to me before he went back to sleep."

"Eh? He did? What was it?" Albrec looked at Nicolas closely.

"He said, 'may there be a following sea at my back, friends at my side, and salt in my enemies' eyes.' I didn't know what to say back. I hope I wasn't rude. What did that mean?"

Albrec lifted his eyebrows, tucked his pipe back inside his cloak, and slung his pack over his broad shoulders. "He said that, did he? Ya weren't rude by not answerin', Master Bennett. There wasn't nothin' to say back. That old man simply gave you a blessin', tho' it's not one commonly used."
"Why isn't it commonly used?"

Albrec took a deep breath and looked straight into Nicolas' eyes. "Because," he said gravely, "it's only given when the Second Legion's departin' this gatekeep for battle. Now follow me out onto the landin', lad. Ya can wait there among the guards as if yer an attendin' storeboy. Once I've been gone for no less than ten minutes, yer to follow. Understood?"

"Yes," Nicolas replied. His stomach felt tight.

"Very well." Albrec straightened up and swung the door wide open but paused before striding outside. "As I said long ago, all I've ever known is Fire and Iron. *You* tho' I could see Fire and Iron in you as well. I was sure of it when we first met, an' here we now stand, lad. Here we now stand."

With that, the tall man walked out into the morning light, and the boy followed.

"Why is it called Dragon Dead Day?" Nicolas had once asked.

When he'd asked this Nicolas been standing in the shadows of a cold mid-morning light, looking out through the arch of a barrel-vault gateway; a gateway that led from the back wall of St. Wulf's-Without-Aldersgate which then led out across a high causeway of cobbled stone and into a City of wide-known legend; there lay the First City of the First Kingdom, the City of Relic; a city borne out of a long-ago act of sacrifice, sprung up from the fountain of a fabled spring; this, a stronghold for a kingdom, a refuge for its peoples, and—something Nicolas had yet to discover in a time yet to come—a monstrous gravestone for an ageless evil.

"You've arrived on a holiday," came the reply to his question. Laird Aldus' young scrivener, page, and jack-of-all-things-needing-attention, Master Brooks, had been standing next to Nicolas that long-ago morning. "Today is the three hundred and fifth day of the year. It's Dragon Dead Day," the monkish boy had said. Pushing his spectacles up the thin bridge of his nose, Master Brooks had handed a red-petaled flower to Nicolas. "These are Dragon Poppies. People wear them on Dragon Dead Day," and Nicolas had stuck the blossom's stem in his sweater.

That frosty, sunlit morning had passed by over a year ago; a late autumn morning when the quiet boy from Plumpton Head had set out to find a true giant, only to meet three unexpected and soon-to-be-loved friends; off to experience the greatest adventure and the most difficult instant act of his young life; a grievous moment in which he'd sacrificed the life of a mystical Wisp to create a twinkling's deception that had saved the lives of many, tens of thousands perhaps. Beginning on that long-ago, year-ago morning, Nicolas had discovered parts of himself he'd never known were there. He'd found an enduring and steady resolve inside himself. A resolve buoyed by a willingness to believe, anchored by innocence, and driven by a readiness to do the impossible. He'd found the resolve of his grandfather. A man who'd once been a servant and then a king.

Now, on a very different morning, one on which he was to set out again into the City of Relic but this time to fetch a friend, Nicolas found another measure of resolve. A brother's resolve. Jack's resolve.

A strength of mind that accepted the reality of limitation, of frailty, of youth, yet pressed on. Pressed on with a brave, smiling face. "You're with me," Nicolas whispered to himself. To the Jack inside his heart who laughed his wobbly laugh, and off Nicolas stepped. On he went across another narrow-necked, cobbled stone bridge; no Dragon Poppy's petals bobbing in his sweater's knitted threads; no Master Brooks to charitably bid him farewell; no giant to see. This time a friend needed him, a brother of sorts.

So off Nicolas went, the Wren once told of in an ancient poem of ruin. A boy, and yet, a king-perhaps-to-come.

PART III

A Thornbush Hung with Rags

If I should die, think only this of me:
That there's some corner of a foreign field
That is for ever England. There shall be
In that rich earth a richer dust concealed;
A dust whom England bore, shaped, made aware,
Gave, once, her flowers to love, her ways to roam,
A body of England's, breathing English air,
Washed by the rivers, blest by suns of home.

And think, this heart, all evil shed away,
A pulse in the eternal mind, no less
Gives somewhere back the thoughts by England given;
Her sights and sounds; dreams happy as her day;
And laughter, learnt of friends; and gentleness,
In hearts at peace, under an English heaven.

The Soldier
Rupert Brooke

CHAPTER 13

False Coal

Long before Nicolas found his way to Telluric Grand, in a time when the borders of the First Kingdom were still muddled in war-ravaged, obscure lines, a woodland forager lived by herself in a small cottage about a day's walk to the southwest of the Gate of the Deep. From time to time she would take dozens of small hand-sacks full of wild hazelnuts or sweet chestnuts in her hand-barrow, over the sea gate's great stone archway, and into the sprouting City where she would sell them for a groat apiece or twelve bronze pecks.

The clever woman discovered few folk who passed through the Gate of the Deep turned left toward the Iron Quarter and fewer still kept straight on the road that led to the King's Castle or to the City's open lands, the sprawling commons of short-grass where intermingled herds of tribute cattle and sheep and goats grazed in protected peace. Most folk who came through the Gate of the Deep arrived from the bottle-green saltwater of the Cold Sea; they were thirsty, rowdy folk, and while some were eager to sell their merchant goods in Weaver's End or food stock in the Buttery, a great many noisily followed the broad, sandy lane to the right, the inviting road that led them to the Dreggs.

The Dreggs, for all its ruinous squalor and hazard, boasted the best alehouses within the City's walls; dodgy places where one could merrily exhaust six months of shipboard pay in splurges of drunken and wagered excess before staggering upstairs to flop into flea-infested beds with other wasters for little more than two groats. Mousecatcher Lane was the broadway road that led to the Dreggs, a much-worn thoroughfare unrolling to the right and north of the Gate of the Deep near Relic's inner wall. At the time when the forager woman began bringing her nut harvest into the City, Mousecatcher Lane was already a worn, ruttish affair, packed with grit and dust except for one brief stretch of bogged mud and gluey clay.

Her barrow empty and having little else to do one bright, spring day, the clever woman decided to follow the source of the boggish, sticky mud. "There's always secrets to find in a water's birthing cradle," she'd said to herself and soon after noticed a tame, sweet-water spring bubbling up from a deep cleft in a large, fractured, grey rock, its faults and fissures festooned with colorful dwarf snapdragons. The cracked rock crowned a gentle embankment that rose up from the roadbed some fifty yards away. The rock-spring was a young one—deep winter cold from two years before had split the rock—and its murmuring gurgle of water spilled from its natural pool across the stone's gritty crest, plied through flinty rifts and clefts, and swanned down the slope of the knoll. The curious water ambled its way further among mugwort bushes and tall, proud stems of wild garlic, until it dribbled across the shingle and dirt of Mousecatcher Lane to be mashed, mixed, and mushed beneath thousands of seafaring boots, peasant sandals, oxen hooves, and horse-cart wheels.

Clutching a handful of left-over hazelnuts from her apron pocket, the clever woman took her tool-knife and made a deep notch in the skin of each nut. She plugged the scored nuts inside earthen holes she'd bored into the rock-crowned embankment in the shape of a bow-like crescent and when this was done, she whispered the simple Outlands' blessing she had learned as girl when her father and brothers were planting hedges around their family's Outland farm.

May no frost touch yer roots,
May no drought wilt yer stems.
May no rain drown yer buds,
An' no saw take yer limbs.

May ye grow to the skye,
May ye yield to no men.
May ye strengthen yer boughs,
An' hold 'ands with yer friends.

After a few, brief years, a sturdy grove of hazelnut trees sprang up. The woman coppiced some of the young trees and sold the cut wood; others she carefully pruned into single, thickly knotted trunks. Taking together handfuls of other saplings, the woman interwove their branches, and when they had grown larger, she cut them as well, the branches now latticed into the frame of a small hut in which she'd made herself a new home. Her copse of hazel trees all grew strong and bore heavy yields of nuts. She no longer had any need to forage in the forest. In time the shrewd woman married a wayfaring cobbler named Bróg and they bore twin sons, Filbert and Cobnut, who played in the spring's waters and aped-about, entertaining passing travelers in exchange for bronze pecks. When the boys were old enough, the woman told them to dig a culvert for the spring's overflowing water. The boys created a useful stone channel for filling goatskins, a lower pond for watering livestock, and a solid rock bridge for Mousecatcher Lane so the spring's water could run freely beneath it. They christened their stone bridge "Whither Away" because their mum would tell stories about water-fairies, fairies in the form of pool frogs with spotted, grainy brown skin and yellowish stripes along their backs, who lived in the spring and who would sometimes leave the grove of hazelnut trees and journey to their ancestor's home in sea. The clever woman's name was Cailín and the stand of hazelnut trees eventually became known as Cailín's Spring.

Years later, when Nicolas entered Cailín's Spring, the hazelnut orchard was larger and much more hustle-and-bustle than when Cailín was alive.

The thick trees were filled with seasoned collections of golden and coppery-orange leaves, soft ovals of sunset colors, crackling in autumnal breezes or drifting onto the turfy ground below. Scatters of scribble larks were hopping and skipping among the litter and leaf-fall to the sliding whistle of migrating willow warblers, while red-breasted nuthatches capered up smooth-bark branches hunting for insects and old woodpecker nests. A jumbled line of huckster-carts edged one side of the grove where passing wayfarers could buy cheap meals of fish pasties, roasted sheep's feet, griddled pears, brown bread, seed cakes, and for the grand price of one groat and three pecks, the rare treat of a hot fig pie. A weather-stained canvas sail was spread over Cailín's aged, wicker-frame hut, a pheasant corn-dolly pinned atop the sail's pitched roof. Under the tent sat a fat, pimpled man, hawking boar-tusk charms, sprays of mugwort leaves for traveler's tea, and pipe-weed with an aroma of lemon and hazel. A perpetual cluster of crude-looking, sea-going men huddled around a fire near a horse-cart that held a tapped beer barrel on its back edge. The men were busy chin-wagging about the open sea's great perils: breachin' a hull on the teeth of shallow reefs, wastin' away in slacktide 'arbors for weeks on end, yawin' a ship in dangerous an' breakin' seas, and ghostin' their sea-vessels through the southern ocean's starving doldrums while good mates around them dropped dead o' thirst.

Amid all of this, Nicolas spotted a knot of haggling boys, three or four "snatchers" who'd slipped out of the Dreggs to barter with a few much-too-trusting herding boys from the open lands: two tin earrings for a sack of prime wool, they said; a skin of watery ale for a leather shepherd's sling, and a small bucket of stones cleverly painted black to look like coal in exchange for a warm, sheepskin sleeping mantle. Two of the taller boys, a snatcher with a large, crooked nose and a cropped ear, and a herding boy with ruddy cheeks and a stout chin who sported a goatskin cap, were quarreling over whether one of the black stones could be thrown into the fire to prove its quality as coal. The snatcher—knowing his mean trick would then be discovered—argued that if any of the stones were thrown into the fire, it'd be unfair; he'd lose no matter what. If the black rocks were only stone, the herding boy wouldn't barter with him; if they were truly lumps of coal, he'd have lost some valuable stock. The snatcher boy cunningly offered a sham solution: toss a handful of black stones in the fire but pay for the lot of them in advance. This predicament, the desire to test the suspicious looking black rocks but not wanting to pay for something he couldn't use, clearly stumped the simple herder boy. Nicolas could hear him protesting, 'thot's a load o' cobblers!' as he stalled for more time to think it through.

"Connor isn't smart, but he's a brave lad. His father trusts him with their entire second flock." At Nicolas' feet, almost unnoticed, sat a little boy even smaller than Benjamin Rush, his thin arms and legs folded under him in an odd, deformed way. A snow-white lamb,impossibly dwarfish, lay curled up in his little lap.

"You know him?" Nicolas asked, pointing to the tall herder boy.

"Connor's my friend," the boy said proudly. "He killed a wolf last winter. Maybe even a fenris wolf. He an' his father went into The Wilds to find chaga mushrooms for one o' their sick rams. A huge wolf tried to kill his father an' Connor used his sling to kill it with a single slug-stone."

Nicolas smiled at the boy's enthusiasm. "What's your name?"

"I'm Quinn."

"And have *you* killed any fenris wolves, Quinn?"

The boy laughed. "I can barely walk," he said matter-o'-factly. "Haven't got no real family, jus' Connor's. They found me an' my sister abandoned in the open lands when I was wee, an' took us in. I'm lamed so I take care o' the weak lambs." The small boy reminded Nicolas of how his brother Jack would sit on the floor, laughing and telling Nicolas to sit with him and pretend there were giants around them.

"Why aren't you over there with Connor?"

"Cause *that* boy," Quinn said pointing a finger at the tall, bent-nose snatcher-boy, "says I'm bad luck—my gammy legs an' all—so they made me sit to one side. 'Yer only fit ta play with dormice,' says he." The boy petted the little lamb on his lap, pushing his small fingers through its downy wool. "I don't mind really. Snatchers can be a bit rough sometimes, 'specially the bigger ones."

Nicolas nodded and stared at the boys. "They're arguing about that bucket of coal?"

"Aye. Las' season Connor bought a bit o' coal fer our hearth an' it turned out to be dried horse dung dipped in pitch." The boy leaned back and laughed. "He made a right bags o' that! Ya can see 'im sniffin' that piece there," he said, pointing. Connor was turning a painted stone under his nose doubtfully and Nicolas could see him trying to crush it with his hand.

"*I* think it's just a stupid stone," Quinn said with conviction, "but no one listens to a *navnløs*."

"What's that mean?"

"Apologies," the boy said shyly. "My sister left when I was still very young an' I've got no proper family. The herders sometimes use the Old Tongue from the Outlands when speakin' about certain kinds o' things, an' *navnløs* is what herders call lambs who grow up wit'out no ram o' ewe nor nobody else to look after 'em—means nameless, I think." The boy smiled but Nicolas thought he detected a hurt in his eyes.

"Oh," Nicolas said. After a few minutes, he winked at the boy. "I have an idea, Quinn. Are you brave enough to go with me over there? I might need your help."

"I will if'n ya can carry me," the boy said, setting his chin. He clutched the lamb close with his skinny arms and Nicolas scooped them up, surprised at how light they were. The boy and lamb smelled like dirt, grass, and sweet wool.

"Excuse me," Nicolas said, interrupting Connor and the tall snatcher-boy. He was nervous but surprised to find he felt slightly cross as well.

"Eh? Whaddya want?" asked the snatcher-boy sourly. He bit at one of his grimy fingernails and spat in the dirt.

"I'd like to trade," said Nicolas.

"Trade what?" The thief was wary but greed aroused his interest.

"I'd like to trade my cloak and hat."

"Fer what in return?"

"I'd like to trade them in return for letting this boy give that piece of coal a try." Nicolas nodded his head toward Quinn. He could feel the small boy give a quick shiver in his arms.

The tall snatcher-boy sniffed and crossed his arms. He looked close at Nicolas, then Quinn. He spat a wad of brown saliva into a pile of leaves and sneered. "Fine. Let the cripple try; I don't give a toss, but it's like I tol' this other lad," he pointed a finger at Connor, "if the cripple throws it in the fire, yer cloak an' hat are mine no matter what 'appens. I ain't losin' nothin'. A trade's a trade."

Nicolas nodded and set Quinn down on the ground carefully, helping to make sure the pint-sized lamb stayed in the little boy's lap. He shrugged off his thin weather-cloak and handed it and the tattered straw hat to the tall, snatcher-boy. "May I have a piece of coal, please."

"Please? Please?" the boy mocked, putting a hand to his mouth. "O' course ya may, Lord Nobby-Nobbs. Remember, I'm keepin' yer clothes whatever 'appens. All ya asked fer was ta give that cripple a try at the roc—I mean, the coal."

"Of course," Nicolas said, doing his best not to grit his teeth in a sudden flush of anger. He handed the painted stone to Quinn. "Rub it against the lamb," he whispered in the boy's ear.

Quinn's eyes lit up. He took the stone and quickly rubbed it against the lamb's oily white wool. The wool remained lilly-white.

"What're ya doin'? Stop that!" The snatcher's face was an angry, deep red.

"I never said I'd like to burn it," Nicolas said evenly, trying his best not to smile. "I simply wanted to your 'rock' a try."

"Yer a bloody clot! I still get ta keep yer cloak an' stupid hat," the tall snatcher-boy shouted, seeing there wasn't even a smudge of coal-dust on the lamb's wool. "Ya agreed to a trade, ya daft rube! Coal 'r not, the cloak an' hat are mine."

"Be gone with ya!" Connor piped in, shaking a clenched fist in the snatcher-boy's face. The herding boy, stout and physically hardened by years of rough work, had a threatening look about him—simple-minded or not, he didn't like being treated the fool. "Take yer thievin' rabble an' go back to where ya belong," he growled.

The tall snatcher-boy jeered back. "These dolts ain't worth our time. Let's go," he said to his companions, pushing the yellow, straw hat down low on his head.

"Yer on yer tod," the other snatcher-boys said to him, shaking their heads and holding up their hands in disgust. "Snatchin' outta a mean shopkeeper's fat purse, as opposed ta lyin' durin' an honest trade-n-swap is like chalk an' cheese, Clacc Blamore. One t'ing's a matter o' rights, an' the other *isn't* right. We trade, an' haggle, an' parley, but we *don't* snatch from those that're like us."

Clacc Blamore spat in the dirt. "'Those like us,' ya say. Bah! Yer all a bunch o' clack-handed clots!" The tall snatcher kicked a pile of wet leaves and turned away, the yellow hat's tattered brim fluttering in the cool breeze. The other boys from the Dreggs followed some distance after him, keeping their own company.

"Thanks," Connor said, thrusting his hand out to Nicolas. "I see you've found our little Quinn." He swept the little boy up in his arms and gave him a tickle and squeeze until the boy cried for quarter. Connor set him down again and turned back to the other herders.

"By the way," Nicolas said, kneeling next to Quinn, "I once had a brother. He, um—he left me, too. Do you still think of your sister? Can you remember her?"

"Aye, a bit. Some memories come, 'specially at night when the lambs are quiet an' the stars are out."

Nicolas rubbed the lamb's head and looked around the autumn-colored grove. "My mum used to tell me stories about hazel trees. She'd say a boy named Fionn MacCumhail once cooked a fish that got magical wisdom from eating hazelnuts dropped into a sacred pool by nine hazel trees." Nicolas scrunched his face, trying to remember. "I think the cooking fish spattered oil and Fionn licked his fingers or something like that, anyway he became magical too." He shrugged and looked back at Quinn. "But my dad always said hazel trees are like family; their branches can be wound together when they're young, and once they grow older and stiffen up, or even die," he added close under his breath, "their branches stay that way—woven together." He paused, not knowing just how to say the next thing in his mind. The small herding boy looked at him, his dark eyes waiting. "I bet if you and I remember our brother and sister," Nicolas said slowly, "then they're still wound together with us no matter where they are. Means they aren't far away. You think that's right?"

"Aye, aye. I like that," agreed the little orphan boy, a grin spreading across his face. Connor, who'd stepped back over to them, looked at them both strangely but smiled as well.

"Hey, there!" said a man's gruff voice behind Nicolas. "You, lad! Looks like yer in need of some weather clothin'."

Connor's face darkened, but when Nicolas turned and saw Albrec, he waved a reassuring hand at the tall shepherd's boy. "It's alright," Nicolas said. "He's—he's my uncle."

"I saw what you did with that duffer—that boy-thief. Smart thinkin', lad, sheddin' the telltale hat an' cloak."

Nicolas and Albrec were walking together up Mousecatcher Lane mixed amid groups of tired travelers, come-to-market farmers, coin-heavy seamen on shore leave, and impatient merchants. All were making their way to the Dreggs or, if more prudently minded, keeping to the main thoroughfare until reaching the City's quarters beyond: Weaver's End or The Buttery.

"I wasn't really thinking about needing to give anyone the slip," Nicolas said, "but I guess it worked out nicely."

Albrec cocked an eyebrow. "Then why'd ya do what you did?"

"I dunno. That tall boy with the bent nose irritated me. He shouldn't have said what he did about the small boy, Quinn. The way his legs are isn't his fault. It made me angry."

Albrec eyed Nicolas keenly. "Well, it worked out smart enough in the end, what with needin' to change your look to throw off anyone who might be lookin' for you—but I'd urge ya to be careful, Master Bennett. That big snatcher-boy could've just as easily hit you as let ya spoil his game."

Nicolas hadn't thought of that either. It made him a bit nervous but also a touch more irritated with the bully. He shrugged, "I will be," he said and walked along in silence thinking of Jack.

Several minutes later, they came upon a two-wheeled potato cart stopped at an angle in the middle of the road. Nicolas moved around to its left and Albrec walked around its right side. The earthy-smelling cart was half-full of fist-sized onions, beetroots, turnips, and apple-headed cabbages. A wrinkled old man stood in front of the cart, clucking reassuringly at a blue-hair donkey harnessed within the cart's traces. The stubborn beast doggedly thrust its muzzle at the old man until he relented and fed it a handful of turnip tops from the burlap bag slung over his shoulder. When Nicolas came around the front of the cart, he caught sight of three, boorish-looking men loafing under the shade of a wild pear tree by the side of the road.

"Hey!" the largest of the three men shouted as he and Albrec moved past them. "You there! Hey, blackfrock!"

"Keep movin', lad," Albrec said in a quick voice, putting his arm around Nicolas' shoulders to hurry them along.

"Hey! Avast there!" the big man cursed. His hoarse voice carried the want of violence in it. "I'm speakin' to *you*, ya scurvy-sored blackfrock. You'd best mind yer betters when they're speakin' to ya. Stop where ya are!"

Releasing a deep sigh, Albrec came to a slow stop in the middle of the lane but didn't turn around. Instead, he moved his large hand to Nicolas' shoulder, spread his feet apart, and stared up the thoroughfare, his face a blank look. Nicolas didn't dare glance back; he could hear the approaching heavy thump and pad of bare feet from behind. Yards ahead a few, timid travelers tucked in their chins and sped up their pace, ignoring what was about to happen; the City's long-enduring and binding sense of goodwill had, some years ago, begun a long, moldering descent into indifference. Every man, woman, and child more likely to care only for themselves, turning a blind eye to what might be happening around them; seasons without a king on the throne had spawned a worsening sense of vulnerability, a leaderless hesitation, and an alarm for self-preservation goaded by deepening shadows of black gossip and rumor. As if in tune with this subtle decay from within, none of the City's bailiff men were anywhere to be seen. The road had emptied. No help was close by. Nicolas and Albrec stood alone, and even with Albrec beside him, Nicolas felt defenseless, helpless. Queasy fear surged from his stomach and felt sick in the back of his throat. "That's better, blackfrock. Jus' you stand there until I'm done 'avin' my say."

"That's right, Geoff. Make 'em stand there whilst ya 'ave yer say," urged one of the other men.

"Yeah, 'ave yer say, Geoff. Tell 'em whot for," driveled the third man.

Nicolas could smell the hot breath and body odor of the three men standing close behind them, their mouths exhaling the stench of bitter ale, scurvied gum disease, and stale pipe-weed.

"I will, that I will," said the first man, sucking at his yellow-grey teeth. "I'll 'ave my say an' this blackfrock 'ere will 'ave a listen. He'll 'ave a listen jus' like I 'ad ta listen ta the cries o' my dyin' mates as dog-eatin' blackfrocks fed 'em like ship's biscuits to those sea-worms from hell. Ya know of what I speak, blackfrock."

Albrec moved slightly as the big man jabbed a heavy, hardwood, belaying pin into his shoulder. "An' maybe *this* blackfrock will 'ave to see whot it feels like to 'ave 'is *own* bones broken an' 'ave 'is *own* flesh ripped apart while 'e's bein' eaten."

"Fobbin' boar's blood, Geoff! Yer not gonna eat 'im, are ya?" asked the slow-witted third man. "Don't seem level to actually up an' eat a man. Let's jus' murder 'im."

"Shut yer clangin' cake-hole!" the big man snarled. "I'm not gonna actually *eat* 'im, ya stupid quisby. But I *can* break a few o' this blackfrock's bones, an' you an' Evrat can gut 'im wit' yer knives. We'll let cadaver crows do the eatin' part."

Albrec glanced down at Nicolas. There was a sad expression on his face. He took in a deep breath and whistled it out slowly. Without any warning, he abruptly pushed Nicolas so hard, Nicolas flew off the roadway and tumbled into the filthy silt of a shallow ditch. Confused, Nicolas pushed himself to his knees and looked up. As quick as Albrec had shoved Nicolas out of the way, the tall man had unbuckled the leather pack strapped to his back and in what seemed like the same motion, freed from it a weathered blanket tightly rolled-up by two, pigtail cords. He never said anything. He simply gripped the rolled-up blanket by the two cords and turned to face the men.

All three were thugs, pirate-outlaws who plied up and down coastal waters in swift, single-masted cutters, boarding and burning sluggish and vulnerable merchantmen ships. They were vicious thieves and were ferocious-looking. One who had lost two fingers and part of a thumb on his left hand, held a long marlin-spike in his right hand. Another—the daft one—had no ears and part of his lower lip was gone; this caused a constant strand of drool to hang out of his gaping mouth which he kept wiping with a hand that held a cruel-looking rock. The big one, who stood there scowling at Albrec through dull black eyes, had a pair of hideous, fleshy scars running up from one corner of his mouth; at one time, someone or something had slashed his face open to the jawbone, but like an undying devil, he'd managed to live.

"Are ya goin' to beg fer mercy, blackfrock?" the ring-leader taunted darkly. He jabbed his stained club toward Albrec's face. "Are ya holdin' out yer filthy blanket like some stupid plague-beggar, hopin' it'll keep death at bay? I've a better idea. The Healers can use that rag as yer buryin' shroud once ta birds 'ave picked yer cursed bones clean." Repulsive brown spittle frothed and bubbled where the scars began. "We're goin' to *hurt* you, blackfrock. We're goin' to hear ya scream, an' *then*," he said as he pointed the blunt weapon toward Nicolas, "we're gonna hurt *'im* so you can 'ear 'im scream, too." The other two bullies stared at Nicolas like mongrel dogs.

"Always liked ta beat young lads. Like to hear 'em cry," the stupid one said matter-of-factly.

Albrec kept silent, but strangely, he raised his bedroll until it was level with the big man's eyes.

"What kind o' brainless—" was all the big man managed to say as he took a heaving step forward, his club raised.

As quick as a Bengal cat, much quicker than Nicolas would have thought the tall man could move, Albrec skipped lightly forward and slammed the wooden heel of one of his boots down on the top of the big man's bare left foot. The man staggered, several of the metatarsal bones in his instep now like crushed gravel, while the finishing arc of his club only made a weak and peculiar-sounding knock against the middle of Albrec's blanket. A shock of agony contorted his face as he tried to put weight on his broken foot. He fell heavily to his knees and bent over. Albrec instantly cuffed the end of the rolled blanket soundly behind the big man's left ear. Nicolas heard a distinct cracking noise as it snapped against skull bone; the big man's body flopped into the dust of Mousecatcher Lane like a stone dropped from a castle wall.

For a second, the other two men were dumbstruck. The middle and ends of Albrec's rolled-up blanket hadn't sagged or drooped or given way, but even more startlingly, they'd heard noises a rolled up blanket shouldn't make—they'd heard their ring-leader's wooden club make a knocking sound against the blanket, and they'd heard the end of the blanket crash against his skull. Almost at once, Nicolas guessed what had happened, but one of the men, the earless, dull-witted one who liked to hit young boys, never had time to guess.

Still gripping the blanket's pigtail cords, Albrec slipped to the right of the motionless body like a skilled pugilist and punched his left fist straight toward the man's sweaty, drool-wet face. He drove the punch from his powerful shoulders, and now there was a third, odd sound, much like one Nicolas had heard many times before as a striker's bat would whack against the hard leather-and-cork of a cricket ball. This was followed by a bursting shower of snot and spit and blood-spray. The man's nose pulped, split open, and lay mashed like a stomped beetle. In a flash, Albrec hit him again and the man's head snapped backward, sending sharp bits of two cracked teeth flying from his blood-filled mouth.

The last man standing, the eight-fingered one, had just enough time to crouch and twist like an animal, raising his eight-fingered hand to ward off any impending blow; this exposed his ribcage. Albrec dropped his right fist toward his thigh and uncoiled it, gripping the right end of the rolled blanket with the strength of his entire trunk. He swung it upward in a forceful sweep and drove it home deep inside the third man's left armpit. There was another peculiar noise, like Mr. Bennett's heavy meat-cleaver made as it chopped into chuck steak, carving it into raw hunks of stew meat. The third man let out an awful, mewling whine, dropped his spike, and tried to grip the now-bloody mess of the blanket's end. His useless left limb flopped about as Albrec, with a dark, savage look, wrenched the blanket's end out of the man's flesh and took several steps back to survey what he'd done.

The tall man from the Dreggs finally let go of the blanket's pigtail cords and reached inside the disheveled, soiled material. Out came the same battle axe Nicolas had first seen on a shadowy forest road over a year before. The axe's head was chisel-cut with a wicked, pointed beard, smaller yet more ruthless-looking than the fantastical axe heads of make-believe stories. Its foot-and-a-half long shaft was wrapped in discolored leather, burned in some places and scored by cuts in others. Its ends were sopped in fresh blood and skin bits, and Albrec rocked its weight easily in his calloused hand.

"Yer wicked sea-brigands an' low criminals," he said above the sobs and grunts of the two, barely conscious and gravely wounded men. "Yer outlaws of the First Kingdom an' confederates of devilish War Crows. What 'appened long ago on the *Day of the Passage Tomb* was fair vengeance for what the Crows an' yer kind did to the innocent people of Galloglass." Albrec's voice became aloof, detached, as if his mind was in a faraway place, a desolate and painful place. "Ya butchered defenseless fathers an' mothers, an' threw their wee ones into the Narrows. Ya 'ave blood on yer hands an' ya have no souls. Yer mates' own pride was the cause of their doom; they foolishly thought yer monstrous butchery meant you were strong." Albrec spat at the ground, shaking with anger. "Ya foolishly thought you could sack the Gate o' the Deep. But she lay waitin' fer ya with her teeth an' claws an' salt an' death." His look tightened; his voice cold. "The three of ya are dead men, but I'll not kill you today. I'll let the bailiff men find ya; they can serve yer warrants an' I'm sure they'll finish cuttin' the livin' parts from yer soulless bodies. My name's Albrec Westenra—remember it!"

The old man with the potato cart had been standing stock-still the whole time. He stared at Albrec. Nicolas at first thought he might be angry or shocked and offended by what he'd seen. He wasn't. When Albrec looked up, the old farmer pushed his right sleeve up past his elbow. His arm's sun-burned skin was crinkly and liver-spotted except where it had been branded; there was a large burn-mark in his forearm's flesh. Nicolas could see connected lines of a strange, yet oddly familiar, constellation. "Beware the Fire," the old man said in a low voice and dropped his sleeve.

Albrec nodded in reply. "And guard the Iron." Then turning to Nicolas, he said, "Faring well, Master Bennett?"

Nicolas was a bit numb. "I—I think I am." He stood, shook out his arms, and hoped Albrec couldn't see the wobble in his legs. "What was that… what was that about, Albrec?" he asked.

A sad expression once again passed over the tall man's face. Without answering, he snatched up his bloody blanket, retied it carefully around his axe, rebuckled his pack, and shifted the kit lightly onto his back. Albrec glanced at the greying sky and shook his head. A heavy cloud bank was beginning to edge its way over the City's high. The gloaming light dimly silhouetted sentries who were moving about the wall's parapets, changing the guard. "These days so many men are false coal. False coal. Even inside the City things are no longer what they once were."

Albrec Westenra looked sharp at Nicolas, his eyebrows drawn in a grim crease. "Ever more my brethren and I find ourselves much akin to sheepdogs, watchin' close over the innocent as wolves move among 'em. Ours has always been a hard life, mind you, meant to stand fast against a greater evil, but times have changed. Seems that greater evil we once fought has been revived; its once powerful dominion now altered into splinters an' shards. Those wicked fragments 'ave been cast wide into a winter's dark wind; they've set root in the hearts o' men, elves, an' giants. They've set root an' rotted into malice 'n spite 'n cruelty. A baleful harvest o' nightshade, 'tis." Albrec lifted his hand into the sudden breeze that was whipping its way up Mousecatcher Lane. His voice became vague, distracted. "Strange, 'tis. Once a great, black mountain, we thought the ancient evil had long been shattered, broken into millions of harmless rocks; but *those* rocks, those rocks became false coal, disguised, untrue." He lowered his hand until it pointed to the men who lay blubbering in the roadway. "An' this kind of false coal is among us all, hard to spot, hard to oppose, too many to count; better dealt with by the edge of an axe."

Nicolas didn't know what to say. He wasn't sure if Albrec had said this last thing to defend what he'd done or if he was talking about something greater, something beyond his understanding. The tall man's eyes seemed to see through the wounded outlaws. Almost a full minute passed by in silence. A worried merchant scurried by them, eyes wide. His shoulders were hunched over a leather bag of weighty coin that clinked dully against his chest; the pecks, groats, and heavier half-nobles inside, sounding much like the dull tramp of faraway, hobnailed boots.

"But no matter what I or my brethren do," Albrec suddenly boomed, his voice now clear and hard, "it's paid for with blood, an' the sheep we defend don't seem as grateful as they might should be." The tall man spat in the dirt as the merchant hurried around a bend in the road. "Bah! None of it was ever 'bout no gratitude anyway. Didn't do what I've done for that."

As soon as he said this, his weathered face eased. He laughed and winked quick at the old man, then smiled at Nicolas. "Nuff ramblin' on in the open. Dust yerself off an' let's stretch our legs as best we can. We've hazardous business to attend. 'An you, Master Bennett, you've a friend to find."

CHAPTER 14

Rotted Wood

The Dreggs, one of the City's four, great quarters, had not been a deliberately planned affair.

In the year 793 R.R., a year of far-reaching and stabilizing royal legislation under King Caranack the Deceived, true and friendly giants from the north were granted exclusive license to own blacksmith shops, known as 'Chancellor Blacksmiths,' which anchored the business of the City's Iron Quarter. Also in that same year, the first foreign silk merchants were admitted as members of the toffee-nosed Warp and Weft League and gathered in the Weaver's End; and thirteen fat bakers clenched fat hands together to organize the royally endorsed Moral Guild of Lardymen, their goods and bakeries thereafter located in The Buttery. The First Kingdom had begun to thrive as its crown City thrived; with most dragons and enemies at bay, it had become a more unified realm, its administrators and officials soon sprouting up by the dozen.

Like a royal storehouse of raw grain, the wealth and protection offered by the flourishing City of Relic also attracted and sometimes created what King Caranack's High Chancellor, the snobbish Lord Thrax, called "base and pestilential rodents"a fast-growing rabble of unskilled workers, Outland peasants displaced by long decades of war or famine or miserly landlords, and an abundance of the various, unwanted human consequences of a fattening feudal society. The City's pastoral open lands shortly became an unruly and dangerous warren of haphazard tent towns and tavernesque-hovels until one fine spring day when the chief tax collector from His Majesty's Exchequer's office was killed while attempting to seize a poor soap maker's single boiling pot. The unfortunate and soon-to-be-doomed soap maker, the lowly, third son of a noble's Old Tongue tutor, had made the regrettable mistake of using his rudimentary education to write a brief petition to the Clerk of Pells, Foul Clenger, politely asking for the repeal of the unpopular Soap Tax of 813 R.R.

By the August Grace of His Royal Majesty, King Caranack, to Your Excellency, the venerable Clerk of the Pells, Foul Clenger, health and sincere affection, etc.

My lord, if it may suit and please Your Excellency, I hereby humbly and contritely propose and advise that His Majesty's most proper and good Soap Tax doth, by some cruel and involuntary oversight, combine in itself, and that to a considerable extent, two of the most objectionable elements in taxation: such be that duties are laid upon all the raw materials of soap manufacture, and then a heavy duty, both mischievous and exceedingly vexatious, being thereafter levied upon the marketable commodity of soap itself, such that the effect of the regulations under which the Soap Tax is collected is to encourage soap smuggling and to shut out all improvement in the legitimate manufacture and trade of soap merchandises.

Therefore, being that I am wholly dedicated to the cleanliness and health of my own obedient family and to the sanitation of my fellow and equally compliant but lowly neighbors, most of whom are remarkably foul-smelling, malodourous, and unpleasantly fragrant. I respectfully, meekly, and urgently petition you, as agent of His Majesty's Exchequer, the Right High and Mighty and Good and Gracious Lord Halibash, to repeal, annul, and herewith to cancel said Soap Tax if such a repeal may be done with the leave and sanction His Royal Majesty, King Caranack, may the endless heavens forever bless his inestimable kindness and sympathy.

This, given in the protectorate of our Most Noble City of Relic, by my hand on the fifteenth spring day of Mercedonius, the third month of the eight hundred and thirteenth year of Relic Rule, your ever dutiful and faithful servant, Miles Enwezor, soap maker and peddler.

The peevish Clerk of the Pells immediately passed the modest soap maker's request along to the Exchequer, Lord Halibash, relishing the thought that Lord Halibash would surely squash the soap maker, his family, his smelly neighbors, and his neighbors' neighbors like hapless earthworms. True to his bovine temperament and the guess of his spiteful clerk, Lord Halibash, a squinty sot with large lips and a nose like a ship's rudder, glanced at the soap maker's petition, became self-importantly enraged, and ordered his chief tax collector to immediately seize all the soap maker's belongings on the suspicion he was trading in untaxed soap goods.

On the day the chief tax collector was killed, the incensed soap maker's wife, who happened to be a water carrier of unusual height with an exceptionally strong upper body, had her stout wooden, water buckets at her furious disposal. In defense of her husband and their pitiable belongings, she used those buckets like two, crashing cymbals. The Exchequer's tax agent fell dying, the imprint of a bucket on both sides of his cracked head. To add further insult to fatal injury, a resourceful pickpocket nicked the dying tax collector's tax-purse. The expiring man's upper body having fallen conveniently across the public pathway while his lower half lay inside the soap maker's miserable home. Upon hearing of this outrageous assault on one of his own agents, Lord Halibash loudly, and with great nasal explosions, protested to the High Chancellor, Lord Thrax, who, despite his personal loathing of the Exchequer, instantly seized upon the opportunity and ordered large gangs of cudgel-swinging bailiff men to permanently cleanse the open lands.

Mobs of vagrants, drunks, ale-peddlers, pocket-thieves, dodgy Gammeldags, orphans, and scores of underprivileged and under-coined families were herded to the site of what had long been understood to be an age-old slag field that stretched under the tall shadow of the City's southeastern wall. This hastily erected slum-quarter was speedily enclosed by tall wattle fences, supposedly erected to keep cows and sheep and goats from wandering off the open lands. At various times various monarchs exerted themselves and the royal treasury with attempts to rehabilitate and assimilate the Dreggs into a safe, quiet, and clean quarter of the great City but such efforts always ended in failure. Some modest improvements were made and remained, but the Dreggs, as it came to be known, was the farmyard "pig sty" of the City of Relic. As Hemmet the Friendless, the fortieth sovereign of the First Kingdom—a sinewy and hard-fisted man who held the throne from 859 R.R. until 875 R.R.—incautiously said when his counselors complained about the populace of the Dreggs, "Pigs are priceless. Let them run a bit wild and give them mud and filth and waste. In return, they'll furnish you with grease, meat, rennet, bone glue, and even their own skin. Besides, what would our celebrated Kingdom do with its slop if we didn't have our pigs to eat it?"

During the past many years without a sovereign on the throne the City's pig sty had slowly worsened still more. The

Dreggs consisted of jumbled ghettos of cheap tenements, stifling alleyways, filth-sodden gutters, Healers' charity hospitals, bloody knacker's yards, bawdy public houses crammed with casks of ale, cheap beds, and vulgar customers, and plaster-sided workhouses—so-called Bampfylde Houses for the poor—where those who were able-bodied could earn five pecks a day and two meals of barley bread, pickled pork, and yeast dumplings by breaking stones, crushing bones for fertilizer, or picking half a stone-weight of thread with large, metal spikes from castoff ropes.

Buildings and streets within the Dreggs had been constructed on top of what had long been known as Pauper Holes. Ancient catacombs bored through rust-colored limestone that led to a once-sacred-but-long-abandoned labyrinth of damp warrens, inhabited by giant sea spiders that hid under flowstones and ambushed unsuspecting hairy earwigs, long-legged centipedes, and cave slugs, or sometimes larger meals. Before the Dreggs had taken its shape as a recognized quarter of the City, a few of its poorest citizenry had made their homes in these lightless grottoes but never strayed far from their openings. That changed with the official settling of the Dreggs. Among the many royal decrees issued in an attempt to bring better order and living conditions, rag-and-bone men who had long been licensed to collect household and vendor rubbish in the streets of the Iron Quarter, Weaver's End, and The Buttery for a small fee. Rubbish that was carted to a large, gated culvert under the City's eastern wall and disposed of in the river far below, could now pursue their occupation in the Dreggs, and for an additional, once-weekly, royal chit for a flagon of watery ale, collect the dead or barely-breathing bodies of the homeless and dying poor, those many unfortunates who were without the comfort of family and friends, those who were no longer able to 'live on the rough.' As is the case with most well-intentioned policies, little practical direction was given and no one knew what should be done with the perishing and the perished once they'd been collected; left to their own limited devices, most rag-and-bone men carted the unfortunates deep inside the Pauper Holes where they were left to rot or eventually to die alone and unseen within those dark, wet tunnels.

The crowded, main entrances to the Dreggs, not counting dozens of small "sprite holes" cut through the wattle fencing, were marked by enormous stone columns called the *Lech O Wahanu*, Stones of Separation, in an old but still remembered tongue. Nicolas remembered seeing one of these great boundary stones from a far way off as he, Benjamin, and Adelaide were walking toward the City's Iron Quarter on a mid-autumn morning over a year before.

After the violent encounter with the sea-brigands, Nicolas had been wracking his brain, trying to come up with something to say to break the silence as he and Albrec now worked their way toward the Dreggs. "What's that?" Nicolas finally asked, pointing to the boundary stone they were approaching, a great, pitted column of greenish-hued gritstone rising up one side of Mousecatcher Lane.

Albrec at first didn't respond; the look of his face suggested his mind was still in some other place.

"Does it mark the entrance?" Nicolas asked.

His second question brought the tall man to a stop. A yellow dog ambled past them, its nose sniffing the dirt. "Aye. It does." Albrec scowled. "It's where most poor folk an' the unguilded laborers live, where they can work their trade without a by-yer-leave from Lord Sulla. The High Chancellor an' the rest o' the City 'aven't much interest in the Dreggs, except that it stay where it is an' it's people stay inside it. Those outside the

Dreggs relish the ale we brew, the leather we tan, the meat we butcher, an' the slaked lime we make, but they've little concern for much else. If it wasn't fer the Poor Laws, there'd be little way to pay our ale-conners, bailiff men, pinders, an' hedge wardens. Every odd year, the Dreggs levies a local tax for itself. We call it the Floaties Tax after the extra bits o' yeast that float in a pint of ale but it doesn't earn much. Most people in the Dreggs are honest blokes, they've families an' work hard at what they do, but they live on the lower rungs of the City, an' those lower rungs come with dung an' mud an' snatchers, an' sometimes squiffy, violent beasts that rut about lookin' to cause needless trouble." Albrec spat and adjusted his pack. "The best way to see the Dreggs is from over yer shoulder, Master Bennett, but most o' those who are born here, live an' die here. I'm a lucky cove, though. I found me a way out."

A crinkly tanner pushed past them with a single-wheel handcart piled high with stiffened skins of wild boars, brindle elk, and roe deer.

"How did you get out?"

Albrec gave Nicolas a curious look. Unsmiling but not unfriendly. "I'm a Holocaust Man," was all he said and turned and strode past the Stone of Separation.

Mid-afternoon in the Dreggs was a lively time.

People and creatures of all sorts roiled through warrens of tightly packed streets, lanes, alleyways, and echoing courtyards. Shabby dressed children darted here and there scooping up dog and pigeon dung to sell to the bubbling tanneries that lined the half-moon of Tanner's Court. Round-hipped washerwomen came and went, picking up or dropping off piss-pots that sat on street corners or inside private, shallow alcoves. Sooted charcoalers lugged packs of split birch, alder, and oak on their way to the ash-caked kilns running along the winding sides of Frideswood Lane. Strapping ropemakers twisted fibers of straw, linen, jute, and wool, beating the laid rope with heavy, wooden mallets under long, narrow, awning-covered ropewalks, each formed in ranks at the far east end of Littlegate Street. And fouled scavelmen, shouldering shovels, scrapers, and hoes attempted to scour muddy, streetside ditches and gutters, booting and shoo-ing away roving chickens, pigs, dogs, and the occasional cow or goat; all of this amid the raucous shouts, grunts, squawks, screeches, barks, yelps, crows, and cooing of countless people and animals.

Albrec, with Nicolas close in tow, picked his way northward, up Mousecatcher Lane, dubbed Titmouse Lane by those who lived in the Dreggs, until it took a steep ascent and flattened broadly into Frewin Court, a broad, public arcade crowded with costermongers' vegetable carts, pie-sellers, egglers hawking pigeon and chicken eggs, fishmongers with rods of impaled, drying trout, watersellers, a stone pulpit for criers and heralds, and an array of stocks and hanging scaffolds ready for their next quarry of snatchers, bandits, and murderers. From there, the two struck northeast onto Blood Cart Street, a slick roadway congested with hungry dogs and curly-coated pigs that ate spilled offal from nearby slaughtering stalls; from this, quickly left into the refuge of a shadowed, narrow alleyway that went by the name Hangingshaw Way, a slender gap between the high, ochre walls of a meat butcher shop to the left and a tallow shop to the right. The alleyway's lean path tightened further, bottlenecked almost to the point of a single man's shoulders before it widened into the dead-end of a dreary and rough looking courtyard. The courtyard was unlit and empty except that at its center stood a large, three-sided arrangement of tall posts connected at their top by heavy crossbeams; what would have looked like a triangle from one of the many dark tenement windows above them. The structure's wood was a discolored bluish-grey and emitted the slight smell of earthy decay. Just beyond the posts, as opposed to the other high, doorless walls of the courtyard, stood a wide and open entrance out of which spilled a rich bath of lantern light, harsh laughter, and bawdy shouting.

"Yer friend'll be inside there," Albrec said with a jerk of his head. A weathered and warped sign hung above the entranceway; a scrappy, painted picture of a blue, three-legged horse with a headless man holding its lead rope.

"What is it?"

"Just a tavern with some beds to let in the floors above it. It was one of the first drinking halls that sprouted up when the Dreggs came about, t'is a rough place called the Quiet Man, owned by an old bag who goes by the name of *Ženská*. She's from the north, north of the Northern Voda from among a people ruled by Oleg the Mystic. They're horse people, a fierce folk who love their stout ale an' shaggy ponies more than they love gold. They're welcomin' enough if they think yer strong an' can 'old yer own ground." Albrec grinned. "My kind of people, that."

"And you think Ranulf's in there?"

"I don't think, Master Bennett, I *know*. I saw 'im in there but a day ago an' he didn't seem in any shape to leave," he added, a note of sadness detectable in his voice.

"Is he hurt?"

"No. Wouldn't say that, but I *would* say he's hurtin', if'n that makes sense." Albrec laid a hand on Nicolas' shoulder. "Watch what ya say, Master Bennett, an' the manner in which ya say it. We need to help Ranulf as cautious as we can, drawin' no more attention to ourselves than we must. The fewer who know we're here an' the fewer who know why we've come, the better. With luck, he'll see his way to join us an' we can leave this place together."

"Why—why wouldn't he want to leave?"

Albrec rubbed the scruff of his chin. "Well, sometimes pain makes a person feel helpless an' sometimes anger seems the only way to stave it off. Yer friend's hurtin' an' he's angry."

"Why?"

Before Albrec could answer, there was the shattering of glass, a few hard blows and pinched grunts, and a frowzy and wild-looking man came tumbling out of the lit entrance, thumping to a hard stop at the base of one of the tall, dark posts in the courtyard. A thickset woman, her black hair askew, followed quick after him, bending over the man until she was inches away from his dirty, bristly face. Her words were thickly accented, stretched, and came from the back of her throat. "Lūtz'is be za last time I see you in z'e Quiet Man!" She stood up, kicked at the man, spat in the courtyard's dust, and spotted Nicolas and Albrec. "Albrec's!" She shouted hoarsely, holding both arms open. "Why are you standing in z'e shadows? Cōme inside whar z'e drinks are!" Without waiting for a reply, the woman bustled them inside, planted them in a pair of roughly bodgered chairs that sat in front of a small fire grate, and shoved pewter steins in their hands, each brimming with a dense, brown liquid.

Albrec grunted his thanks and took a deep draught of the autumnal ale. He smacked his lips. "That takes the biscuit," he said, but then in a lower, somber voice asked, "The boy?"

The raised wrinkles in *Ženskấ's* expectant and happy forehead instantly fell. Her bushy eyebrows drew close together into a single queue of wiry hair. "Lūt me fetch 'em," she said in a conspiring way and ambled off. Moments later she returned, insistently guiding the stumbling, bleary-eyed form of Ranulf son of Renfry.

"Ranulf!" Nicolas said, standing up.

His bladesmith friend lifted his head. "Nicolas?"

"Yes, it's me. I've come back."

For a fleeting moment, Ranulf's face lit up, but as soon as it did, a clouded, deadened look folded back over it. The older boy belched and nodded as the sturdy tavern-keeper grabbed a free chair and shoved it between Albrec's and Nicolas', firmly pushing Ranulf into it. With a frown, she spun on her heel, shouting back at a loud table of men who were griping about the lack of service, "Qui'vt acting lăk a 'erd *ōv* stroppy mēlkmaids!"

Ranulf slumped deeply in his chair, unbending his legs until his black, muddy boots were closer to the fire. His long hair was unwashed and messy, mostly an unhealthy grey except for a large swath of bone-white hair, a lasting mark from when Ranulf had once been swallowed by a dreadful bog-worm as he, Nicolas, Adelaide, and Benjamin had traveled together through the foggy marshes of the Hollow Fen. Nicolas' once-sensible, reliable friend now stank of stale beer, sour sweat, and musty filth, his frayed clothes stained mottles of brown and grey. The bladesmith, only a couple of years older than Nicolas, looked overused and unwell. Nicolas peered at Albrec over Ranulf's wilted shoulders and the tall man looked back, concern clouding his eyes.

"Ranulf?" Nicolas asked quietly.

"Eh?"

"Ranulf?"

"What?"

"It's good to see you again."

Ranulf turned his head just enough to peer at Nicolas out of the corner of his eye. He didn't reply and the silence was awkward. Something was frightfully amiss. *Gentle is the hand that heals the sick.* Nicolas had often heard his mum, Sarah Bennett, whisper those words as she lightly washed his feverish forehead when he was sick or when, in those final, heartbreaking weeks with Jack, when she'd swaddled his older brother on her lap and, like he was again a newborn, rocked him back and forth. "Gentle is the hand that heals the sick, an' gentle is the heart that guides the hand," she would murmur with warm tears stirring in her eyes.

Gingerly, Nicolas reached out a hand and placed it on his friend's shoulder. Ranulf didn't shrug it off but he also didn't move. He just kept leering at Nicolas. Finally, with a deep breath, he sat upright and glared into the fire.

"Why're you here?"

Nicolas' eyes flitted to Albrec. The tall man's face didn't change.

"We're—I mean *I'm* here to… to see you again."

Ranulf set his chin. "You've seen me then," he said.

"Yes, yes I have, but what I mean is to see you. To see you, too." It was frustrating, trying to find the right words without sounding a snob. He wanted to say, *I'm worried for you. I want to help*, but those words sounded too pushy in his head, too much like saying, *I'm in jolly fine shape and you're not. Let me help set you to rights.* Instead he said, "I'm here to see you because I want to see you, Ranulf. I've *wanted* to see you. You're my friend." Nicolas spoke steadily, deliberately. "You're my friend and I wanted to see my friend again." It was hard to tell, but it looked as if Ranulf's face might have softened for a moment.

"But you left us," Ranulf said more to the fire than to Nicolas. "I thought you'd come back, but you left us. You left us for a long time."

Nicolas hung his head. "You're right, I did. I didn't mean to—I mean I meant to, but I thought I'd be able to come back sooner. I thought—I thought." He straight at Ranulf. Nicolas' eyes were clear. "I'm sorry."

"Where did you go?"

"Home."

The bladesmith shrugged. "Benjamin left, too; left the City. So did Adelaide—went off to be a fine Healer, I suppose. All of you left." He poked the toe of his boot at a large lump of charcoaled alder. "I thought things would be better at first, you know. After the other two left, I went back to the Iron Quarter, back to Straight Hammer's shop—turns out, I went back to nothing." He kicked the black wood. "The giant was gone, his pit fires cold. Looked like the place had been looted, nothing left. Looked like some sad crofter's cottage raided by thieves instead of being the renowned Crossed Hammers, the first smithy shop in the quarter to be granted letters of marque, the first to be owned by a right and true Chancellor's Blacksmith." His voice was filled with a low anger. "Rubbish. All rubbish. Nothing left to do and no one left to do it. Even my beastly uncle, Ragnuf, was gone. 'Twas probably him and his kind that pinched everything not pinned down, the cowardly sot!"

Nicolas squeezed the older boy's shoulder slightly but this time Ranulf pulled away. "I'm sorry," Nicolas said again so quietly the words almost stuck in his throat.

"Sorry? So'm I, Nicolas, but then I'm used to losing everything, aren't I? I've spent my lifetime losing. I've lost my home, lost my parents, lost my friends, and lost my trade." He leaned back in his chair, his dark and sunken eyes fixed to a thick beam overhead, and with tired indifference said, "Word spread, Nicolas. Like lightening's fire in a dry wheat field, word spread about what you'd done, that the Shadow Thief was dead. The City hosted a high feast and games festival for two weeks and every night rang the gatekeeps' six death bells at the stroke of grimlock. The living Dragon Nightfall were summoned. The few that're left, and they gathered in the King's Castle with the Wards of each gatekeep…" Ranulf paused and narrowed his eyes. "Funny," he added, "Aldus wasn't there now that I think of it." He rolled his head slowly toward Nicolas. "And *you* weren't there either. Your name wasn't even mentioned for some reason, but mine was." He smiled weakly. "So were Benjamin's and Adelaide's, but *mine* was the one everyone yoked with killing *Árnyék Tolvaj*. Everyone thought *I* had done it, that a bladesmith apprentice from the Iron Quarter had journeyed from the City, faced the overlord dragon on the high crag of the Timekeeper's Finger, and destroyed him. I became *you*, Nicolas." Ranulf's eyes were leaden and miserable. "So you see, I even lost being *myself*."

There was a sudden crash behind them as two, rough-looking men, deep in their cups and at odds over a game of blue dice, grappled stupidly with each other. Albrec glanced darkly at the commotion. "Dah!" They heard *Ženská* shout as she furiously waded into the fray flourishing a heavy poker-iron. The woman caught one patron across his shoulder and thrust the sharper end of the blackened rod into the fat of the other's belly. Both men howled in exaggerated, drunken pain as their annoyed mates pushed them back into their places with callous oaths and impatient shouts of "throw the bones!" and "cast yer lot!" and "more beer!"

Ranulf hadn't moved. He didn't seem to care about anything, but Nicolas sat there feeling gutted. "I… I don't know what to say," was all that came out.

Ranulf stared hard at him for several seconds, then sighing, nodded slightly. He looked back at the fire. "No matter," he said distantly. "Wasn't your fault really, don't know who started the rumors. Doesn't matter, I suppose. As quick as they started, other rumors started too. I was a fraud some said, a pretender who couldn't explain how I'd done it. And I suppose I was a cheat after all; didn't bother correcting those who thought I'd killed the dragon. Didn't bother saying I wasn't you." Almost to himself, in pity, he said, "Felt good, I guess. Having nothin', but feeling like I *was something*.... Lost that, too, though. As quick as the celebrations were over, I left. I happened across an *Âld* Elf traveling through the quarter in search of a metal-worker who still knew the ancient way to craft *látnok* mirrors using mercury and silver. He was on his way out of the City, setting out for the the north country, and I asked to join him. Ttold him I was trained to mix metals and could forge woven links joined with butts in the way most *Âld* Elves and *Suthrons* favor. We traveled north together, faraway. Northern orcs killed the elf in an ambush; tried to kill me, too, but I became lost." Ranulf said no more. A feathered log split apart in the flames and one of the dice-playing louts roared in disgust. The dice had rolled against him.

Nicolas' heart was so broken for his friend; sitting so close to him but so distant at the same time. "I'm sorry, Ranulf" he said once again. "I know what you're feeling; I've lost things, too, and... and I've felt alone." He regretted the words as soon as he'd said them.

Ranulf whirled on him, his jaw set in an iron line, his voice steely and desperate. "Lost things, too, have you? Lost things? What things, Nicolas? You gained *us*. You weren't lonely. You had the counsel of a laird of a gatekeep, the fury of a wisp, the company of true friends, the favor of the endless heavens. But me—*me*? I've nothing but curses. My story is one of lonely places, and I'm *afraid*." The older boy's shoulders shook as hot tears dropped off his cheeks. His voice rose. "I'm afraid, Nicolas! I've no sacred Seren Drist to place me among the exalted constellations. I've no family to call a Healer to fill no sorrow basket when I die. When I die, I'll die as I've lived, abandoned, caught up by a tusk moon to be cast away to the empty, lonely spaces between stars, forgotten and lost. Left alone in some Pauper's Cave."

"No!" Nicolas felt his own heart tearing, the force of a long-seated sadness welling up beyond his ability to stop it. "No, Ranulf. You'll *not* die! You'll not be alone. Come with me! Come with us. *Please*. Please, Ranulf, let's kill dragons together." he was reaching for the right words with the right sense of hope. "I'm here now. We've things to do. Great things. We've War Crows to kill!"

As he said this, having said it louder than intended, the tavern's common room went stone silent. An ominous scuffing of chairs and benches scraped across uneven floor planks as men moved to see who'd spoken. The fire cracked and someone coughed, but no one said a word.

"Yer ta kill *what*, boy?" A vicious man with a horrible burn scar on the left side of his face stood up amid a tight knot of other fierce-looking men. He'd pulled a dagger out of his boot, and like a stalking fenris wolf, he began moving toward Nicolas.

"Avast, Bróccan," came another voice, tightly whispered, urgent. "Look thar! That one's a damned blackfrock. Blackfrocks 're mad. No tellin' what 'e'll do."

Albrec Westenra hadn't moved but Nicolas heard a small sigh escape his mouth.

There was a pause and some faint, frustrated grumbling among the tavern's other patrons, but chairs and benches soon scraped again against the floor as men turned back to their ale and games.

"Dah," *Ženská* said from somewhere among them. "Drink z'e ale an' play z'e game, jū drōōnk toads!" Boorish laughter followed and Albrec sighed again.

"Please," Nicolas implored in a whisper.

"No," Ranulf said, his breathing shallow and forceful.

"No?"

"No. No, I'll not again go with you to kill dragons or anything else, Nicolas." His voice was harsh and carried a wounding malevolence. "I won't be baited with your talk of Crows. You know *nothing* of Crows and you know nothing of the pain and loss they can bring." His fists gripped handfuls of his trouser cloth and wrenched at his clothing. "By blood and death, I can be smart, too! I've my *own* ways of killing dragons, my own ways of killing Crows; I'll not be some pawn left standing in the shadows of my own life. Now *leave*! Both of you! Leave the way you came!" Ranulf leapt to his feet, overturning his chair and sending pieces of burnt wood and flying sparks scattering across the dirty floor. His fists came up wildly as if to fight and a mad sickness of hurt and anger flashed in his hollow eyes.

An ill-disposed silence swept once more across the room. The striking of soiled raindrops could be heard against the sliced-horn windows and in the courtyard outside the door.

Albrec slowly stood but kept his chin low. He never looked at Ranulf; just gave a quick tilt of his head and motioned Nicolas to move for the tavern door. Nicolas, numb all over, gazed in misery at his bladesmith friend. "Please, Ranulf," he whispered. "Come with us."

Ranulf's face tightened. Two unmanageable tears rolled down his cheeks. "Leave," he hissed.

Dully, Nicolas stood up and moved to the door. Albrec turned to face the hostile room. He smiled broadly, dark fury in his eyes. "Aye, we blackfrocks, we're *mad*," he said and followed

Nicolas out the door. They lifted their hoods over their heads as torrents of rainwater beat against their heads and shoulders. They were almost out of the courtyard when they heard a shout.

"Nicolas!"

They spun on their heels to see the silhouette of Ranulf standing in the lit entranceway. His wretched voice pressed its way through the drapes of sooty rain. "Sometimes death is the greater part of our living!"repeating something he'd once said to Nicolas as they'd walked together through a dark forest over a year before. The older boy held still for a moment then turned back inside, slamming the tavern door shut behind him. As if the door's jolting had the strength to cause ground tremors, the three-post triangle in the yard abruptly collapsed. The soaked shin of one of the posts had snapped from rot. Nicolas jumped back but Albrec didn't move. "Galloglass," he gritted through his teeth, barely loud enough for Nicolas to hear above the drumming rain. The tall man then strode into the narrow neck of Hangingshaw Way.

"What did you mean?" Nicolas asked a few minutes later as they made their way across the storm-deserted Frewin Court. He was glad for the shadow of his hood and for the rain even as cold as it was; they helped mask the confused heartache routing his insides. "Why did you say Galloglass after those posts fell, Albrec?"

"Wasn't just some posts that fell, Master Bennett."

"Oh. I'm sorry. What—what was it?"

"It was the rotten ruin of the ol' three-legged mare, the first set of hanging gallows built in the Dreggs. A place where they used to swing thieves by the dozen. Them same posts were once known all over the City as the Quiet Man."

"Oh." Nicolas, still shaken from his encounter with Ranulf, was now further disturbed by the gory history under which he'd casually walked. "But—but what did they have to do with Galloglass? Is that where the posts were from?"

The tall man stopped and peered closely at him. They were near the far side of Frewin Court, near enough to see green water coursing into the street gutters at the head of Titmouse Lane and go roaring down the hill like the watery charge of disordered cavalry. A large, dead rat floated by.

"The last one ta be hung on that cursed timber was a War Crow. He'd escaped from the bailiff men an' a crazed rabble o' citizens caught 'im an' drug 'im there fer execution. It 'appened soon after the Crows' murderous raid on the town of Galloglass but before the Day of the Passage Tomb. Fear an' anger an' retribution drove common sense from people's brains. As they roped the Crow's neck, it's said he uttered some foul blasphemy, an' as he twisted there, stranglin' an' dyin', one o' the hangmen slipped in the Crow's blood an' broke his neck by fallin' against one o' the posts." Albrec straightened up, threw back his hood, and stared at the mottled, grey sky. His face was washed and soaking wet when he looked back at Nicolas. "Men an' wood can both decay from 'avin' somethin' inside them they shouldn't 'ave. Pain an' loss an' fear can break a man like that cursed post snapped from rot."

Nicolas, exhausted from all that had happened that day, chilled from the rain and deeply troubled over his meeting with Ranulf, was confused but wanted to understand what Albrec was trying to say. "You think Ranulf's like that broken post?"

The tall man nodded.

Nicolas felt sick. "But I'm afraid I still don't understand how Galloglass fits. Is it because of the Crow?"

Albrec looked surprised and shook his head. "Ya don't know, do ya?"

"Know what?"

"It's because o' yer friend, Nicolas. Ranulf." The rain slackened as if drawing breath, then strengthened. "Ranulf was born on a small farm outside o' Galloglass. His mum was in that town when the Crows came, an' when the boy's dad seized up 'is hayfork to come to her aid, it's that town in which they died, torn apart by the hands of a murderin' blood horde. Torn apart by Crows."

CHAPTER 15

The Woodmare of a Sylph

Within sight of the Stone of Separation, Albrec held a long arm out and brought them to a stop. The tall man sniffed the air. He appeared to be looking around for something.

They'd passed very few who were still out in the drenching downpour: steady night watchmen with short, hard cudgels of ash, and a handful of other dim, dogged figures moving here and there along fast-emptied streets and snaking byways. With the whipping storm had come the onset of fallow in the Dreggs. A low-spirited, murky dusk that caused shops to be shuttered, stalls to close, and lock-bars to drop behind shut doors. As Nicolas and Albrec had hurried back down Titmouse Lane, the crisp day blowing to its cold, wet end, most sensible folk were collecting themselves and scurrying off to an assortment of homely dwelling places: smoky hovels, infested tenement homes, congested charity hospitals, or rough and noisy inns and alehouses. There, they all shook the dampened chill from woolen cloaks, leather cowls, hats, wimples, and shabby tunics, and thrust their bare hands toward the warmth of countless hearths with countless fires crackling inside countless fireplaces. Dogs barked, oxen lowed, and pigs drowsily mumbled as they sorted themselves out, nestling into the trampled hay of fusty sheds and half-sheltered, fetid stable yards.

The soaked and deserted evening carried no promises other than greater darkness and more rain. In spite of this, Albrec kept looking for something or expecting something amid the wet gloom, but Nicolas, standing close by him, couldn't tell what it might be.

"A'ha!" the tall man exclaimed and without further explanation darted to the right down Cockrowe West, a slip-shod, jarringly cobbled thoroughfare with tight clusters of empty pie-maker booths, bread maker boxes, and cured fish shops hedging its high curbs.

Nicolas, half-consumed by unhappy thoughts after his encounter with Ranulf, was slow to follow, taken off-guard by Albrec's unexpected change in direction, and he splashed along several steps behind the black-robed man. "What is it?" he managed to ask, sputtering droplets of rainfall from his chilled lips.

Albrec didn't answer, instead treading steadily along the narrow lane with long, loping strides over quick gullies of flashing, dirty water until coming to an abrupt stop in front of a poorly lit, triflingly small shelter. The lean-to was nothing more than a three-sided awning of draped canvas, stretched and clumsily tacked between two large, brewer's barrels. Beneath the sad sail of weathered cloth crouched a crooked little man, poking a crooked little twig at a crookedly close-assembled stack of sticks arranged between two rocks. Charcoaled rags of torn linen were piled in the middle of the stick-stack, and an engorged, vivid spark was busily eating into the black of the ragcloth; as little flames took hold, bits of burning linen fell to the bottom of the stick-stack in which lay curls of birch bark. The crooked little man carefully placed a thin but wide pane of split oak bark on top of the stack, sheltering the glowing cinders and harboring them from the wind and lashing rain as they grew into flames. The smell of incense, something of meadowsweet, lavender, and wet woodlands, smoldered out of a cleverly whittled knot of yew wood at his side.

"Come along, my pretty," he was murmuring in a sing-song voice. "Come along. This skulky wind might o' made a right bags o' me grille, bōōt it won't be actin' the maggot with yer tender rouge. Come along now! Come along, my pretty! That's it. Come along!" and when Albrec and Nicolas approached "Haven't got any beef ribs o' sheep's feet, nor pies, nor pickledy-dickledy cabbage, mind ya," the crooked man squawked without looking up.

"But I'd guess you've a few slices o' cheese to toast, 'aven't ya now?" Albrec asked. "A few slices o' cheese to toast fer a travelin' man an' 'is boy?"

"Ha, ha! That I do! That I do!" sang out the man as he laid the ends of a blackened bakestone on the edges of both rocks. From a shabby, waxed bag he withdrew a long, thin blade, a small block of crumbly, white cheese wrapped in white cloth, and a half-loaf of bristle oats bread. From both he sliced two, generous portions and arranged them carefully on the smooth bakestone. Out of a small clay pot near his muddy boots he took a healthy pinch of coarse salt and crushed fennel seeds and sprinkled a dusting on the toasting cheese. From another dark pot he withdrew two, cold-smoked kippered herrings by their tail-fins, and after they'd been skewered over the smoggy fire for several minutes, laid them out on the crusted oat bread followed by a layer of the bubbling cheese. "Seven pecks apiece! Seven pecks apiece!" he piped out and clapped his bent hands.

Albrec fished inside a leather purse and dropped a groat and two pecks into a jar of vinegar while the crooked man tilted his head to the side, listening as each coin splunked through the surface of the brownish liquid. "A groat, a groat, yes, a groat'll do! A stout groat wit' a wee lad an' a wee lass fer company!" The crooked man looked up, sightless, ivory, translucent eyes staring somewhere far beyond Nicolas and the tall man. He pointed a curved finger at the food. "Take yer pick, lad," he whispered as if he could see Nicolas standing there as plain as day.

Nicolas studied the griddled bread, the toasted cheese, and the caramel-grey kippers. He scooped up the smaller of the two, politely aware he hadn't paid for either of them. "Thank you."

"Well done! Well done," glibbed the happy cook, his milky eyes almost disappearing behind a swell of wrinkled, grinning cheeks. "The greater takes the lesser. The greater takes the lesser." He swung his creased head toward Albrec with a now-serious look. "I know *you.* I know you, Westenra. Yer a steely blackfrock. A Holocaust Man ya are! A Dreggish-ne're-do-well who does well, but yer *more* than that, too, more, oh yes, yes! Yer more an' ya don't yet know it, do ya now?" The crooked man's face broke into a great smile and he began to laugh with delight. The drizzling wind shifted and the little man caught a lungful of smoke, buckling him into a ricking fit of damp coughs.

The tall man, a grave look lying deep inside his shadowed eyes, gave the crooked man a minute to recover. Albrec adjusted his hood, the storm now at its height was nearly spitting rain sideways. He put an arm around Nicolas' shoulder and stooped more closely under the lee of the sailcloth. "Aye," he said. "I thought you might be *One*, ol' man." The tactful caution in his hoarse voice was further muted by the noisy downpour. "Ya are *One*, ain't ya?" Nicolas wasn't sure what Albrec meant by One, but with the howl of the storm and the beat of the sailcloth, he also wasn't sure he'd heard him correctly.

"Eh? *One*?" the little man spluttered with a final cough. He wiped his lips and smiled an unusual smile of brilliant white teeth. Slowly he swung his head back and forth; his large ears waiting for any sound that might come from either direction of the storm-blackened lengths of Cockrowe West; there was not a soul in sight, not a soul to be heard. The living world had all vanished beyond dark shrouds of cold rain, closed windows, and fast-shut doors. The crooked man stretched his long, curved fingers over the little fire's merry warmth. He cocked an eyebrow and gazed aimlessly, blindly up over Albrec's broad shoulder. "*One* is it? Aye, One it *is*. As ya rightly say, Westenra, I am One."

"Can ya help us then? Will he be safe? Is it safe to leave the Dreggs? What can ya see?"

"*See*? Ah, yes. Yes, I can *see*," the crouching man crooned wistfully as if the idea of having sight occurred to him like a philosophical curiosity. Smacking his lips, he settled himself and passed a hand over his sightless eyes. "Seeing? Seeing? Aye, that's whôt I *do*; it's what I've *done*, Westenra, from time outta time. Can't rightly say I 'see' t'ing's in the prim sense o' the word, but seein' is what I *do*, what I've always done. Oh, I've *seen* many o' t'ings. Great t'ings, little t'ings, wicked t'ings, an' wonderful t'ings. Doors an' windows an' places an' spaces that're *shared*, ya might say." He winked a blind eye at Nicolas. "Ol' towns, ol' woods, ol' caves, ol' castles, ol' graveyards, an' rooty root cellars. Oh, I've seen many t'ings, Westenra. Seen beginnin's an' ends; I've seen thar an' here, an' now yer askin' if I can see a very *small* t'ing, a '*whot's down the road*' t'ing."

The crooked man's gentle laughter was unoffending, generous, and honest and he poked a twig at the spritely blaze. "The smallest t'ings are apt ta go unnoticed, ya know," he punched his strange face in Nicolas' direction, his pasty-white eyes roaming nomadically over him, his brows scrunching in crossed lines. "The smallest t'ings… the *smallest* t'ings," he repeated solemnly. "*You*—you, laddie. Yer a 'One' too, I see. Not a One' lak me—bōōt. One' even more than I; a different One; a small t'ing… A *Wren* p'rhaps?" he said, whistling the last word through his teeth.

Nicolas was startled. "I, I—I don't know." He glanced at Albrec for help but the tall man's face was almost entirely shadowed within his deep hood. Nicolas could just see the glisten of his eyes looking keenly at him. "I don't know what to say."

"N'ermind!" chuckled the crooked man, waving his bent fingers. "N'ermind, laddie." He settled back down and clapped his hands above the fire. As if on command a pillaring gush of sparks leapt up, dancing like hundreds of frolicking fireflies. "*See*!" he ordered them, and to Nicolas' amazement, the firefly embers raced about, assembling and displaying themselves into smallish but recognizable constellations: a long roadway, a boy and tall man on the road approaching a throng of people, and some kind of arched bridge beyond that. "*See*!" the crooked man barked again, and again the fireflies darted about, rallying and constellating, forming into a ring of large, ominous birds with outsized beaks and stiff head-feathers. A thimbleful of lustrous embers stayed apart, however, hovering above the others, as if unnoticed and waiting until two of the large, wicked birds reeled into the middle of the circle and began stabbing at each other with furious eruptions of sparks. Down the small group of hovering embers now came, instantly forming into a bird no larger than a farthing coin, driving itself into the heart of the two, fighting birds and blasting them apart. The ring of birds instantly disintegrated, magical embers no longer, colliding and fizzling in a chaotic sizzle; spent and dying, each cinder returned to its natural course, drifting dreamily upward; a few with just enough glowing life left to escape into the diminishing rain but most burning out before they touched the sailcloth awning.

The crooked man's shoulders slumped with a heavy, unseen weight. His head bowed. "Safe to leave," he said as if it were unimportant. "As you've asked, it's safe to leave, Westenra.

Beyon' that tho'—" he raised his narrow chin and stared straight at Nicolas with a peculiar, sightless passion, "—beyon' that, I *hope* but I cannot yet see. I cannot see if'n *he* is safe." He held out his long fingers, lightly touching Nicolas' cloak. "You've 'ad the *dream*, 'aven't ya, laddie? You've 'ad the darkest of dreams."

As if he'd felt an electric shock, Nicolas remembered the terrible dream he'd once had during a long night spent in St. Wulf's-Without-Aldersgate, what now felt like so long ago; a strange dream in which there was a massive door and lock, a cavern lurking behind it, and within that, an immense and evil creature chained in shackles of bronze and steel; heaps and piles of dead and dying men, a large square of iron hung on the massive door with strange words beaten into it that told the grim histories and names of those who had already died and those who were going to die. *We are the dead*, he'd heard their many ghostly voices grieve. *We are the dead*, they'd said over and over again. "Yes," Nicolas said. "Yes, I've had a dark, dark dream."

The little man nodded slow. He shut his blind eyes. "Go then. Safe as ya travel an' may the endless heavens be with ya, Nicolas, Nicolas the *Wren*."

By the time they passed the Stone of Separation, the fearful rain had spent itself into a drizzling, erratic mist. The sky was as black as a tomb and the road before them, muddy and slimed with patches of greasy clay, was a vague, ribbony, brown streak. Here and there a late-night wanderer passed them by, everyone keeping to their private purposes, wary of the possible cruel intentions of whatever cloaked and shaded figures might loom out of the confused night's damp air.

The tall man's pace was rushed. He bent his cowled head against the mist and laid his broad shoulders against the nightfall's sharp winds. Nicolas did his best to keep at Albrec's heels, splashing and sloshing his way along spongy wagon-wheel ruts and gooey black puddles. His feet were chilled and he hugged himself, rubbing his arms for warmth, giving his head a snap every so often to clear his face of gathered droplets. Their trek back toward the Gate of the Deep felt much longer than it had earlier in the day.

The dim glow of a lantern gradually came into sight, bobbing and dipping its fuzzy eye midair as a rain-smeared, smudgy glow. Shapes materialized in its weak light as they drew closer: a poorly dressed ploughman, his wife gripping the lamp's handle and a long goad-stick in one hand, three shabby children, a dreadfully tired-looking ox, and a two-wheeled, wickerwork-sided cart. The cart's left wheel, having slid off the swamped roadbed and into the bank of a shallow, submerged gully, was gripped in sticky, water-logged mud as deep as its hub, and the ox, its long yoke-shafts all askew, couldn't find enough true purchase on the road's slippery edge to drag it out. The ploughman's ragamuffin children stood knee-deep next to the embedded wheel, doing their best amidst quick whispers to clear the mud away spoke-by-spoke while their mother petted the ox's wide, gummy nose and spoke gently into its laid-back ears. The anxious ploughman, his modest, worn-out coat drenched with mud and grime, was toiling back and forth between his children's work and the yoke-shaft on the far side, lifting and pushing in sequence in a vain effort to free the cart and set it right again on Mousecatcher Lane.

"Ha'llo!" called Albrec.

With a jerk of their heads the struggling family froze in unison; their guarded white eyes stared meekly out of the murk.

"Ha'llo!" Albrec said again, spreading his arms in a show of empty, non-threatening hands. "Seems as if yer in bloody straights. Need some 'elp, mate? I'd be glad to lend a hand."

The ploughman glanced to his wife, who gave a hurried but wary nod. Turning to Albrec, he straightened his back to his full height. “I’d bite me arm off fer a bit o’ kind help, stranger.” The farmer had a bent nose and wiped it with the last bit of mud-less fabric on his upper sleeve. “T’would be downright good o’ ya, iffn’ yer so inclined.”

Albrec stepped further into the lantern’s light feeble blush.

“Beggin’ yer pardon,” started the ploughman in surprise and dropped his chin to his chest. “Had no idea ya was a blackfrock, m’lord. Apologies.”

Albrec laughed and spat rainwater out of his mouth. “M’lord? Since when are any o’ my kind, lords? I won’t ’ave it. Yer placin’ me far above my station. Just a common coat, this.”

“*We* know what ya do,” the man said with honest firmness. “We know what you an’ yer brethren ’ave done an’ what ya’ve sworn to do. ’Tis a noble thing, that. A thing beyond what most landed lords ever come close to doin’. No need to delay yer travels w’t a dodgy cartwheel, m’lord. May the endless ’eavens bless ya all the same.”

Albrec paused, tilted his head and let out a hearty laugh. “He speaks w’th a silvered tongue! Trust me, the black cloth don’t convey no nobility, my friend, an’ if we can’t help those who truly need it, then what business ’ave we in wearin’ it?” His generous smile split the hoary mist. “The boy an’ I can lend our backs an’ ’ands, an’ I swear on my lost mum’s grave, may she rot in warm pig’s piss, that we’ll get yer cart an’ kit back on the roadway proper!” Pushing his sleeves past his elbows, Albrec leapt into the ditch next to the ploughman’s amazed children, giving each a playful punch to the shoulder and smearing a silly bit of mud on his cheeks while rolling his eyes and sticking his tongue out. They all laughed, and the oldest took a finger of mud and flicked it on her younger brother. The boy laughed louder and aped Albrec's antics. Taking a stave of unfinished oak out of the back of the cart, Albrec shoved it as hard and as deep as he could beneath the mud-interred wheel. "Yer wheel looks to be made o' winter-elm," he shouted. "Should take the strain if we all work at once. C'mon now!" He and the three children laid their shoulders and hands into the wheel's spokes and pushed upward.

The ploughman, speechless for a moment, yelled back excitedly, "C'mon then!", and jumped to the yoke-shaft nearest the middle of the road, throwing his weight on top of it. Nicolas, taken up with the cheerful and sudden action—a welcome relief to his soul after the despair of Ranulf and the foreboding brought on by the crooked man's words—came close after the ploughman, gripping the yoke-shaft with both hands and slinging his body's weight downward. There was a reluctant slurping, lapping, drawing sound as the muddied wheel moved an inch. Again they heaved and pulled. Again the wheel moved and lifted by a thin finger onto the flat stave of oak wood.

"Gee! Gee!" urged the farmer's wife, exhorting the drenched ox, a grey bull of the milking shorthorn variety, to swing its weight and massive head to the right. With a final stagger and pitch, the mired cartwheel abruptly sucked free of its squelchy tomb; it spun drunkenly in empty air and followed the cart's liberated lurch onto the comparative firm level of Mousecatcher Lane. The children cheered, "Oh, father! It moves! It moves!"

"Thank'ee, thank'ee," the ploughman gasped between deep gulps of breath. "I'm indebted to ya, I am."

"Bollocks!" Albrec replied with a sly wink and leaned back to pull in a lung-full of the night's cold air. "No debt to repay, my friend. My—my lad an' I," he said, grasping Nicolas warmly around his shoulders, "had a badgered time of it earlier today tryin' to help another who was in need, but our friend's wheel stayed stuck, so ta speak. You've given us a chance to set things back in balance, so it's mine to say, thank'ee." He shook the ploughman's hand.

"Yer right kind an' good," was the man's choked response. "Lost our plot jus' this last week; snivelin' landlord said our harvest levy fell short, but 'twas a bald-faced lie. He's increased our duty each year, everyone's duty each year, piously claimin' it's needed to fill the charity grain bins, but it's a filthy load 'o cobblers! He lives as fat as a winter-fed pig, an' the number o' poor increase only because the filthy sot keeps takin' land from those of us who can work it." The man's weary face was pinched, his eyes wet with more than mist. "Hard lines, 'tis. Hard lines fer those unwillin' to bend a knee. I won't be another man's slave." He jammed a balled, frustrated fist into one eye and cleared his throat. "Apologies, m'lord. You've no need to hear the blubberin' of a simple crofter like m'self. You've far greater burdens to carry than I'll ever know. You blackfrocks are willin' to lose everything fer the sake of nothin', nothin' 'cept the gratitude o' those ya save. Yer a king among men, I say." He set his chin and seized Albrec's hand in a calloused grip. "Thank'ee, thank'ee, m'lord. May the endless 'eavens bless ya an' yer boy." With that and not a word more, the ploughman's wife gathered up the soiled hem of her coat and herded their mud-spattered children and herself into the cart. The ploughman stepped alongside his ox's left shoulder, tapping the long goad-stick against the beast's rear quarter. "Come up, come up," he said, putting the short-horn bull in motion, and on they went, swiftly lost in the damp black, but for a while the faint and haunting lullaby of the woman's voice could be heard singing softly to her children.

"The woodmare of a sylph," Albrec said in a hushed, absent voice.

"The what?"

"The woodmare, the echo of a man's own soul." The tall man turned to Nicolas and looked him in the eye. "The sylph are a kind o' fairie folk. They're never seen but are said to sing songs that echo the meanin' of a person's soul." He glanced after the ploughman's vanished cart, the roadway now silent except for the patter of occasional drops against sodden mud. "Somethin' 'bout her voice, Master Bennett. Mournful tune, that. Somethin' in 'er voice."

"The song said something about a bird but I didn't catch it."

"What? Oh, that. That's an ol' lullaby 'bout a Mistle Thrush. Says the Mistle Thrush 'as been silent fer too long, makin' the fairies cross, but now comes the time when the Mistle Thrush 'as somethin' to say, an' the fairies beg it to make its nest low to the ground, 'mong the tall grasses, so they can hear its secrets." Albrec stopped speaking; he stared again into the black mist.

"What does it have to say, Albrec? The Mistle Thrush, what did it have to say?" Nicolas asked. The mention of the bird brought to mind another bird, a bird with the unusual name of Magnus Mungo Macaroobie; not a bird at all really but a *kelpie* trapped in the shape of a Mistle Thrush Nicolas had once encountered on a unexpected wooded path, a path that led to the peculiar home of a peculiar, little man, a peculiar home that had a small, iron door that led to Telluric Grand.

Albrec had a curious and intent look in his dark eyes. "Says the king 'as come, the king 'as come. Never you mind, Master Bennett. 'T is only a child's lullaby, a nursemaid's foolishness to soothe cryin' babes." The tall man snapped his hood back over his head and hunched his shoulders against a fresh rush of stinging wind. "Strange as this day's been, we've a bit more to go an' the night only grows darker. Step quick! Let's be on our way."

They didn't speak again nor meet anyone else until they'd reached the neck of road adjoining Cailín's Spring. The mist had slackened until nothing more was left of the storm than lingering fog shrouds heaped in low-lying places and woven among the copse of hushed hazelnut trees. Nicolas could see a large fire lit off the side of the roadway, its flames whipping and thrashing about in the gusting night air while wavering shadows of burly men huddled around its warmth.

"Halt!"

Most of the shadowy group of men stood up, swinging helmet-capped heads toward Mousecatcher Lane, Nicolas and Albrec, shadows themselves at the edge of the light.

"You there! State yer business." The barked commands had come from another helmeted figure, a large man with broad shoulders and a dark, leather cowl who stood further away from the fire along the near edge of the road, gripping a tall pike fitted with a sweeping axe-head.

"Comin' from the Dreggs," Albrec said back sociably, lifting up his large, empty hands. "Had a bit o' business to attend. Caught up with this mangy lad in Poxy's Pub off Littlegate Street, hidin' under a table, 'e was, 'avin' run from 'is sworn duties like a chick tryin' to crawl back in its shell." Albrec roughly smacked the back of Nicolas' head which left Nicolas' ears ringing.

The shadowy cluster of men around the fire laughed. "Poxy's Pub! Ain't that yer mother's home, Simon?" one called out, producing another round of laughter and affable swearing.

"Shut yer manky mouth, ya dosser," the guard growled back. "Sworn duties, eh? An' whot might those be?"

Albrec took several steps toward the guard, and in a low voice said, "Fire and iron," his black cloak flapping in the breeze.

"Demons an' dragons," one of the other men said, letting out a low whistle.

The roadside guard squared his big shoulders. "A blackfrock, eh? Thought you an' yer kind 'ad been ordered outta the City." His growl was still there but now with some uncertainty. "Will! Will!" he barked over his left shoulder. One of the shorter men standing near the fire walked over, swinging a nail-studded bailiff's cudgel. "Ain't the Lord Sulla ordered all blackfrocks outta the City last year, Will?"

"Aye, that 'e did."

"Well, this fella's wearin' one o' their cloaks an' sayin' 'e's one o' their kind."

"He does, does he? What's 'is name?"

"Dunno; 'aven't asked yet."

"Well then ask, ya fool."

"Don't like it when ya call me a fool, Will."

Will tapped his club roughly against the guard's helmet. "Then don't play the part, ya onion-eyed pignut."

The large man growled. "What's yer name, blackfrock?"

"It's Albrec. Albrec Westenra."

All the other men, except for one who remained hunched near the fire, moved closer to the roadway; cruel-looking truncheons, cudgels, and long knives now visible in their shadowed hands.

"Westenra?" the man named Will asked, his voice suddenly pointed and sharp-edged. "Picked up a threesome o' stinkin' sea brigands earlier today, beat an' mauled like victims o' a *farlig* jamba. One o' the clotpoles died 'fore we could lock 'em up in the Warden's Hold. Mentioned that same name yer sayin', the name Westenra, 'fore breathin' 'is last. You the same Westenra?"

"Aye," Albrec said in a flat voice. "I am."

"An' yer a blackfrock, ya say?"

"Aye, that's what I said."

The man named Will paused, frowning. His peevish eyes narrowed to mean slits. "No 'arm meant, stranger, but orders is orders. Iffin' yer a blackfrock, yer supposed to keep outside the City's walls. High Chancellor says so."

"Aye. I know it."

"But here ya are."

"Aye, here I am."

"'An what 'bout 'im? The boy?" Will asked, pointing his club at Nicolas. "Ya say 'e's sworn to yer service?"

"Aye. I say that 'e is."

Will nodded and leaned coolly against the large man holding the bladed pike. He picked his teeth with a sliver of wood and as he did so, the other men moved slowly across Mousecatcher Lane forming a loose semi-circle. A log broke in the fire sending up a spray of bright sparks. *Safe to leave*, the crooked man had told them earlier. *Safe to leave*, he'd promised, but Nicolas was frightened.

"Don't want ya to think we're not grateful fer catchin' those damned outlaws, Westenra, but we've specific orders tellin' us to keep a sharp eye out fer a man an' a boy. A man an' a boy travelin' together, tryin' to sneak outta the City together; 'aven't seen no other such man an' boy since settin' up our post, but here we now are. Got a blackfrock, a blackfrock *inside* the City, who says 'e came lookin' fer a runaway, a runaway *boy*. An' here we now are wit' a *man* an' a *boy* sneakin' along the road." As one, the troop of bailiff men stepped forward and began closing the distance between themselves and Albrec and Nicolas. There was nowhere to go.

With the slightest movement, Albrec spread his feet apart and sighed deeply. One of his large, rough hands came to rest on Nicolas' shoulder who tensed so tightly he couldn't breathe. Nicolas glanced at the tall man's hard face. It was half-hidden within his cloak's black hood but the part Nicolas could see had the same sad expression from earlier that day; the same expression he'd seen right before Albrec had beaten those other men senseless, killing one of them.

Death was coming.

"I am *Ansgar*! I am a Throne Shield. I am a Sovereign Protector. I am *Eodur Nihtweard* of the First Kingdom, and I say this boy and this man are guests of the Gate of the Deep! Laird Halen Ward has declared them his guests in my presence and by the Law of the Forfeited Gates, it is the *sole* privilege of the Gate's Laird, who is the Deputy Viceroy and council member of the Commissioners of the Forfeited Gates, to take their lives or to let them live."

As if by magic, there stood Ansgar. The archer, a high Captain of the King's Guard, had been the only figure who had remained, sitting by the fire, and now he flanked the bailiff men. The tall warrior's outer coat had been thrown off and the silver circlets clasping his purple cloak to his leather chest guard flashed and gleamed in the firelight. His forearms and legs were armored with embossed, black leather greaves, and his long shirt and coif of chainmail was iron-grey, made of double-butted, small ringlets. Ansgar's great war bow was in one hand, his pointed helmet in the other.

Will spun around in a mean crouch. "You've no license to give orders, ya filthy archer! We've no king, an' yer post 'as no master. You may 'ave a seat by our fire, but *I'll* be the only one tellin' my men who lives an' who dies."

Without moving and with little emotion, Ansgar said, "My first arrow will pierce two, blackfrock. They'll be sure to rush me after that, but I'll send another two to their early grave before a fifth finds my knife gut-deep in his belly. What say you? How well do you swing your battle axe? Swift enough for the other four?"

The sad look on Albrec's face lifted a bit, allowing for the crease of a grim smile. "Aye. I do," he said. "An' each o' these City toads 'as seen what my battle axe can do even before I take it outta its roll."

The man named Will swung his head from side to side, glaring wickedly at Albrec and Ansgar. "Nine 'gainst two? Yer both mad as turd-eating dogs." He jerked his chin toward the large guard holding the bladed pike. "I'll 'ave Simon 'ere shove 'is pole up yer—" Will's head abruptly snapped back so hard, Nicolas thought the man had suffered a seizure. He hadn't. An ashwood arrow jutted out from beneath his right eye, its goose feather fletching fluttering from the impact with flesh and skull bone. The man died on his feet but his death throes made him stagger, opening and closing his mouth in silent cries. His spasming fingers clutched instinctively at Simon's sleeve before sinking to his knees in the slick mud. A final breath wheezed from his gaping, slack mouth. He would have then fallen onto his pock-marked face, except the end of the arrow's shaft kept him propped up: a dead man kneeling in the mud.

"I was wrong," Ansgar said with some surprise as if he were contemplating a riddle. "I thought I could skewer two with one shaft but I didn't account for the back of his helmet stopping my arrow. No matter! The next ones I let fly shall find the softness of their throats."

Several minutes later, a hard-looking Holocaust Man, an unyielding archer and high Captain of the King's Guard, and an utterly spent boy from faraway Plumpton Head, England, crossed the narrow-necked, cobbled stone bridge that led them back into the Gate of the Deep.

CHAPTER 16

Fairie Rings and Death Pits

"Ah, awake at last, are you?"

The warmth and darkness of the heavy bearskin felt safe. The voice, muffled beyond it, was dimly familiar but sounded like it was from somewhere far above; couldn't quite place who it was. Nicolas, who hadn't meant to wake up in any case, lay there numb, the whole of him wavering in the gauzy vagueness of in-between. Almost-but-not-yet consciousness, his body perceiving sensations of reality but his mind still flighty with wild dreams of lovely elfin fairies fluttering carelessly in and out of splendid little doors fixed between tree roots, sober earth-gnomes scurrying industriously in and out of tidy burrows of rich, dark soil, and wizened little *broonies* drinking agreeably from saucers of sweetened cream left on hearths by mindful homeowners.

Now came a gentle poke and prod. "Awake, are you?"

The voice clearer now. Fairies and gnomes and brownies disappearing, spiriting back through elfin doors, down earthy burrows, and up sooty chimneys.

Nicolas scrunched his face tight and stretched it before pushing back the bearskin, allowing a draft of unwelcoming cool air inside his snug refuge. "Yes. Yes, I'm awake," he muttered.

"Good then." Aldus Ward clapped his hands lightly. "A spot of a nap can be worth its weight in dwarfish silver, I'd say, at least the kind of silver mined by those northern clans of dwarfs whose halls are carved within the high Graystone Fells; a rare marbled silver, that." The Laird of St. Wulf's-Without-Aldersgate looked away and tugged gently at his curly beard, absent in thought like an old man who's lost his way recounting a story.

"What is marbled silver?" Nicolas asked, sleepy but curious, intrigued by the thought of mining dwarfs.

"What? Oh! For another time, Nicolas. I'm sometimes a rambling ninny." Aldus smiled kindly at Nicolas, the old man's blind left eye a milky orb of absorbed firelight and sightless clouds, his right eye bright blue, specked with sharp twinkles of gold and emerald. "I'm glad you've been asleep these past few hours. It was exactly the marbled silver your spirit needed. Long day, 'Twas, and you held up remarkably well." The bright blue inside Aldus' seeing eye slowly diffused and became a soft grey. "I'm sorry about Ranulf," the aged Laird said. "It's a sad and wretched thing, but you must be careful not to blame yourself, Master Bennett. Loneliness and anger are fenris wolves that've gnawed at the poor lad's soul for quite some time; Ranulf needs to deal with them from within, and when he finally does, I believe he'll need you even more than he needed you yesterday. He must let go of all that has happened to him, all that he has wanted, once loved, and thought he could or should be, and however strange it may sound, he will find he needs to forgive *you*."

Aldus dipped his head slightly. His great beard settled like lamb's snow on his chest and his voice deepened with the kind of melancholy born out of long wisdom. "You see, Nicolas, *who* you are, and more than that, who you *were* and what the four of you experienced together, put Ranulf in a position where he'd chosen to leave behind everything else. He chose believing in you. He knows deep in his heart that choice was worth it; that there's something very special about you. The others know it, too, but our Healer and young snatcher have a different sense of it, I think." Aldus again tugged at his beard's curls. "I imagine Ranulf thought his choice would lead to instant changes, an abruptly different life, and it did, but those changes were losses, not gains, at least for the time-being they have been. Letting go of those expectations when you left and didn't return, forgiving you for that. That'll be the greatest part of Ranulf letting go. And when *that* happens, Master Bennett, he'll need *your* forgiveness, too. No, no." Aldus held up a hand in mild protest before Nicolas could speak. "No, I don't mean to say *you* hold anything against him, but he'll hold it against himself. He'll hold his own actions and words against himself; he'll be crushed under the weight of his own measure of disloyalty and weakness, that's what he'll feel anyway, and he will desperately need you to give him what he won't be able to give himself."

"Forgiveness?"

"Yes, but simply to say I forgive you is not enough, they are simply words after all. The *reason* must fill those words; they must be, and must especially be for Ranulf, love. He'll need to know you love him as a friend and as a brother, Nicolas. Love forgives. He hasn't anyone or anything else and won't have anything else. And when that moment comes, when you are able to let him know that, to *see* that in your face, the terrible bites and wounds that loneliness and anger and reproach have torn from his soul will truly begin to heal. He'll find the peace he seeks."

Aldus' words were a comfort, and Nicolas wanted badly to be convinced; his heart was heavy with the anguish he'd seen in Ranulf's eyes and heard in his voice. "I—I… It hurt to see him, Aldus. It… *hurts*." There was a shattering emptiness inside, an emptiness he'd rarely felt; perhaps had only felt once before when Jack had passed away. A hard lump choked his throat. "He said, Ranulf said, he'd die abandoned, Aldus, lost in the empty, lonely spaces between the stars. Why?" Nicolas' voice caught but with a deep breath and long, shivery sigh, he mastered himself. "*Why*, Aldus? Why didn't he just come with me. I was right there."

Aldus stared at him for several moments, then reached out and squeezed Nicolas' arm. "And there you'll remain, my boy. Beneath it all, Ranulf can feel that; a noble part of him knows you wouldn't abandon him, and with time…" Aldus smiled, the field of bright blue returning to his good eye, "with time, he'll discover he's part of *your* constellation."

Nicolas blinked. Tears were there, ready to fall, but he willed them away. For the moment, just a moment, he wanted to talk about something else.

"Where are we?"

"Haha! Ever the sensible one, Master Bennett. We—*you*—are back in the Gate of the Deep. It's a little-used guard room near to where you first entered the gatekeep, I believe," Aldus said, looking around. The unfamiliar room was long and narrow with high-beamed ceilings and a large fireplace at the far end around which several people were huddled. The fire's light winked around their silhouettes. His eyes, still unfocused from sleep and emotion, couldn't make out who they were just yet. He heard the muffled sound of laughter. Some kind of game being played between those sitting around the hearth. Nicolas had fallen asleep on the lower bunk of a stacked set of couchettes and pushed himself onto his elbow to get a better look.

"Are we safe?" he asked, his voice hushed, guarded.

"Aye." Aldus looked at the knot of figures who were lightheartedly jabbing each other and trying to speak in stifled tones. "Yes, we're safe, Master Bennett, although it was touch-and-go there for a while."

"Ansgar, Ansgar the archer helped us."

"That he did. That he did."

"Why?"

The old man chuckled. "Because of me, of course." Aldus had a shrewd look in his eye. "I, shall we say, *suggested* that he help if he could, and he did. Ansgar is a high Captain of the King's Guard, a very special kind of warrior intended to act as the king's personal bodyguard. Of course, there are times when they can also be assigned to guard a king's proxy, a stand-in or representative for a king, as they often have in the past when a king has sent out a vice-regal envoy or herald during a time of war and great battle. But over these past several years, the High Chancellor, Lord Sulla, has steadily gnawed at the empty throne like a worming nine-eyed eel. Not long ago he began assigning members of the King's Guard as his attendant guards every time he stepped a foot outside the City walls, even if his errands took him no further than into one of the Forfeited Gates."

Aldus turned his face into the shadows, his voice dark and low. "The High Chancellor is a cunning man, Nicolas. He's deftly twisted his position as Viceroy to the Commissioners of the Forfeited Gates into a greater half-truth; the Commissioners, against my vote and the vote of Laird Halen, recently proofed a warrant by the Earl Marshal that the High Chancellor is now the empty throne's chief viceroy for *all* purposes outside the City of Relic." The aged Laird of St. Wulf's-Without-Aldersgate leaned toward Nicolas. There was the faint smell of cherry cavendish pipeweed on his whispered breath. "These days only continue to darken, my boy. There are sinister threats and schemes afoot I cannot yet unravel. I merely grasp at hanging strands—the tinker's attempt on your life in the Woodcutter's Forest over a year ago, the recent arrest of Benjamin, the outcasting of Adelaide, and the strange events surrounding Ranulf since you left. Strands, all strands, Master Bennett, but strands that are hung from the same black loom, dozens of warp threads waiting to be bound together by some unseen and devious heddle stick. But *who*, who wields the stick?" Aldus asked vacantly. By this time, he was tugging gently on his beard again, his gold and emerald-flecked eye seemed to look through Nicolas. Alone in private thought, he remained quiet.

"Is it the High Chancellor?" Nicolas finally asked, trying to be helpful. The thin-cheeked, pale-skinned Lord Sulla had worried Nicolas from the moment the man had burst into Laird Halen's chambers.

"Perhaps, perhaps. I've honestly wondered the same thing, and by the king's throne it makes sense on the face of it. But there's something more, too. Something more…" though the old man would say no more of it just then. Instead, he abruptly stood up. "Come now, Master Bennett! We've much more immediate things to discuss in the short amount of time before the sun climbs out of its own bearskin. Dawn is in the offing and you and the others must be well-away from this gatekeep by then."

Nicolas took a deep breath, gave a final yawn, and threw back the comforting security of his own bearskin. "Is there anything to eat?"

"Haha! Boys, in my meager experience, are almost always hungry creatures. By the fire, Master Bennett! By the fire there is a sideboard with smoked fish, rye bread, and beer or a pot of ale, or there should be if the inexhaustible Benjamin Rush has left any for anyone else."

"Benjamin! Benjamin Rush!" Nicolas exclaimed, leaping at the smallest figure who sat at the end of a low bench by the fire, and bear-hugging his friend from behind.

Benjamin whuffed, short of breath, so Nicolas quickly let him go, all smiles and laughing.

"Pinch, punch, first of the month!" Benjamin said, whirling around and playfully cuffing Nicolas' shoulder.

Instantly a long-forgotten memory of Jack popped in Nicolas' head, his older brother calling out *white rabbits!* after doing the very same thing to him when he was much younger. Nicolas threw an affectionate arm around Benjamin's neck and buried his face in the young boy's wild shock of dirty hair. It smelled of sour leather and old dirt, but it was *Benjamin*, it was Benjamin Rush at last. "Ha! A flick and a kick for bein' so quick!" Nicolas said, lightly flicking the other boy's ear.

"Ouch!" Benjamin sat there gingerly touching his ear.

"Oh! I'm so terribly sorry, Benjamin," Nicolas said gravely. At arm's-length he could now see that what had looked like smudges of dirt were instead strands of dried blood webbed across the younger boy's earlobe.

"No matter," the young snatcher-boy said shyly. A mile-wide grin replaced his injured look. "I almost forgot the bloody thing hurts."

"What—what happened?"

For a moment the snatcher-boy was quiet, then almost as if he was giving a bit of advice, evenly said, "A couple o' scroungy-lookin' bailiff men nicked me a couple of weeks back. Thought I'd been done in at last for slippin' out of the Buttery with a long stick full of crispbread biscuits and my pockets a mess full o' jam roly-poly, but no such luck. The scroungers said nothin', only boxed my ears hard, an' dropped me in the bottom of the Weedy Onion well, an old dry hole near the Dreggs where they keep ner'-do-well's until they can stock 'em, beat 'em, or hang 'em. Weren't so bad really, 'cept for the cold an' wet an' some dead fella who'd been left lying down there to rot. Ha! Hearin' myself say it now, maybe 'twas a bit bad!" Benjamin laughed at himself, his bright eyes twinkling in the firelight. "They tossed down some burnt crusts of barley bread and I had me a bucket of rainwater, so I made out like a king for a few days. Must've been a week ago, they finally hauled me up, boxed my ears again and brought me to this gatekeep where I was tossed inside an old root cellar with not a tuber left in it that the rats hadn't eaten! Before they left, one of the bloody clotpoles stamped the heel o' his boot onto my little finger; said everyone should see how crooked I am." The young boy held up the little finger on his left hand as if it was a museum curiosity; there was an unnatural bend at the second knuckle and it was tied against a slender splint of wood with a strip of dirty linen. "Strange really; never told me why I'd been nicked or why they were beatin' me, so I set my mind to play the same game an' held my tongue, too." Benjamin stuck out his tongue and jokingly bit down on it in mock defiance. "Truth is, those fly-bitten hedge-pigs kept askin' stupid questions 'bout *you*, Nicolas. Strange things like where you were from, how ya knew Laird Halen, how ya came to know a Wisp an' Straight Hammer, and whether you were a sorcerer." The smallish boy laughed delightedly. "I gave 'em nothin' and kept mum which made 'em mad as a chased spring hare. I figured they were looking to nick you, too, an' I wouldn't have it, you bein' my friend and all."

Nicolas smothered Benjamin in another tight hug, doing his best to keep the sting of guilt off his face and tears out of his eyes. "My friend," he whispered earnestly. He felt the boy shudder slightly on his shoulder.

"My friend," Benjamin replied and hugged him back tightly.

Nicolas finally let him go. "But you're here *now*; you're here now and you're safe. And after all this time! It *is* good to see you, Benjamin Rush."

The younger boy's cheeks colored, his irrepressible smile again spreading from ear to ear. "And it's good to finally see you again, Nicolas Bennett. I *knew* you'd come back. You said you would."

"Silly birds! You boys are such silly birds."

Nicolas had been so focused on Benjamin, he hadn't seen Adelaide sitting quietly nearby on a pillowed pallet on the floor, a deep green traveling cloak over her head, with her little goat, Cornelia, asleep on her lap.

"Adelaide!" Nicolas turned and looked at the others who were gathered around the hearth. Tom, the steward-boy for Halen Ward was there. So was Albrec, as was Ansgar, who nodded stiffly at Nicolas.

"Reunions!" Aldus said, pleased. He laid a hand on Nicolas' shoulder. "Tom! Pass along those remaining kippers and that last chunk of bread for Master Bennett. We've a few things to discuss, but we have a few minutes before the Laird of the Gate joins us so first thing's first." The steward-boy did as he was asked, also passing along a mug of weak beer which Nicolas thought tasted pleasant when mixed with the sharpness of the rye bread and the smoked and salted fish. Tom turned his attention back to Albrec and Ansgar who were playing a Game of Twenty Squares. Ansgar was enjoying a string of lucky rolls and kept capturing Albrec's pieces in the combat squares, sending them back to the beginning. "Devils and death-tokens!" Albrec groused as another of his pieces was forced to begin its journey over again.

"Battle," Ansgar said as he moved one of his pieces forward, "is more about strategy than it is about strength."

Albrec rolled the pyramid-shaped die, moved a piece two squares, and scooped up one of Ansgar's. He grinned and winked. "Aye, strategy trumps strength, unless strength smashes strategy in the mouth."

With that, Laird Halen Ward suddenly strode into the room, showers of cold water droplets scattering off the oiled skin of his great cloak. "Damned storm picked up again." He gave Tom a sharp look. The steward-boy hopped up, hastily moved a large, tavern-style chair near the hearth's warmth, and poured a deep mug of brown ale which Halen half-drained as he plopped down in front of the fire.

"Hardly damned," Aldus said. "Storms are the shrouds of the endless heavens and those who'll soon be leaving will need them; they'll need to move in shadows until they're well away from meddling eyes."

"For the love of all salt and sense, Aldus, can't you ever leave a man to his grumblings without driving him mad with prudence and good sense?" His weary eyes landed on Nicolas. "And our Wren? How's the winged boy this fine mornin'?"

Aldus, who was just beginning to prime his pipe, shot a quick look at his fellow Laird and then at Tom, who was standing nearby at-the-ready with the pouring pot of brown ale. Laird Halen seemed to catch the older man's meaning and with barely a wave of his finger dismissed Tom from the room. "Don't go wanderin'!" He shouted after the steward-boy as the door shut.

"I'm fine, thank you," Nicolas replied, swallowing his last swig of beer while thinking how disapproving Mrs. Bennett would be if she knew what he was drinking and how secretly amused Mr. Bennett would be.

Halen jerked his stubbled chin toward Benjamin. "And you? I see yer on the mend."

"I'm splendid, m'lord." Benjamin stood, wiped crumbs from his mouth, and bowed. "I've had nothin' but fine food, fine quarters, an' fine treatment since bein' escorted to your generous gatekeep, m'lord."

"Careful, snatcher," Halen growled but Benjamin grinned back in such a silly way, the look on the man's large, craggy face relaxed. "They shouldn't 'ave done that to yer finger, boy," he said quietly as he stared into the fire. "The king's justice may hurt, but it should never hurt out of meanness. They weren't *my* men." Benjamin nodded self-consciously and sat back down. Halen acknowledged Ansgar and Albrec but said nothing more.

"Well then, now that we're acquainted, fed, and somewhat rested, let us speak openly about what needs to be done. I fear there is little time." Aldus Ward gathered his robes and found a seat between Ansgar and Nicolas. He took up a blackened poker-iron and drew a rough circle in the ashes near their feet. "This is the City," he explained, obviously excited by the opportunity to draw a map. "And this is the king's road running south from my gatekeep. The Cold Sea is over here to the east," with this he drew a ragged shoreline roughly north to south, "and here is the Lonely Road," he said, dragging the tip of the poker through the ash in a general west-to-east bearing that ended as it touched the shoreline. "As at least some of us know, the Southern Fells lay below, to the south of the Lonely Road, and include the Crinkle Crags *here,*" he jabbed the poker to the southwest of the intersection of the Lonely Road and the main king's road, "and the Hourglass Hills *here.*" He hovered the poker in the air, drawing an imaginary line roughly parallel to the south of the Lonely Road.

"Yer Crinkle Crags are too far from the roadway, Aldus," Halen said. "Their bluffs run sharp up against the road; makes it easy fer highwaymen to use 'em to rob unwary folk."

"It's an imperfect map made of *ash*, Laird Ward," Aldus snipped back. "Of *course* it's not to scale. I'm only intending that we all understand where things stand—by and large, that is, so there's as little confusion as possible. Now, if you please, Laird Halen, can you share with us your latest dispatches?"

The large man shifted uneasily in his chair, emptied the last of the brown ale and wiped his lips with the back of his sleeve. "Latest dispatches, eh?" He eyed Albrec and Benjamin suspiciously. "You already know what they are, Aldus."

Patiently, as if to a stubborn school-boy, the aged Laird of the First Gate said, "I know that *I* know what they are, but there are those here who don't." His seeing eye gleamed a deep, glossy blue. "We've discussed this, Halen. This is the best way, the only way, this is the *necessary* way. Now please," Aldus opened the palm of his hand "If you don't mind."

"Very well then." The Laird of the Gate of the Deep narrowed his deep-set eyes. "The bulk of the Gate of the Deep's Second Grey Legion and its War Marshal, Lord Cadwallon, rode south months ago on the direct warrant and orders of the High Chancellor. They were to set guard over the kingdom's southern border and join themselves with the First Legion which was posted further to the west. The few reports I've since received from Lord Cadwallon have been dark and troubling.

"On the Legion's movement south 'n west, its first and second troop-battles had running fights with bane-elf *furies*—far-ranging war patrols mounted on great-tusked boars that had stolen their way through the Woodcutter's Forest, north and to the west of the Lonely Road." Halen jabbed a stiff finger toward the map of ashes, "Somethin' that hasn't been seen or heard of for many long years past. To add to that, several of the War Marshal's hunting parties, even those led by local folk or his *Âld* Elf scouts, have been shot at and attacked, shot with poison-tipped orc arrows, arrows fletched with the stretched skin of black adders." Ansgar's mouth hung open and his head jerked back in surprise. Laird Halen narrowed his bushy eyebrows and leaned almost imperceptibly toward Nicolas. "Such evil arrows haven't been seen since the Great War of Giants, Wisps and Men, that, ages ago. It's thought the lore was long lost, to make an arrow twist an' turn its flight so that it strikes its victim like a snake, but it hasn't." Halen sat up. "An' there's more too. There are reports of fiefs in the Outlands that've lost livestock to roving fenris wolves an' there are dark rumors that a hive of necromancers has returned to Càrn Mairg in the High Desert of Shadows. Children are said to be disappearing from remote farms as if the Black Hârcă, that baleful-rot of witch-flesh thought to be long-dead, has again crept out of her mountain cave and is using her long arms and sharp, curved nails to reach through cottage windows at night and snatch wee ones outta their beds while they sleep." Laird Halen's look was murderous, his voice hoarse with anger.

"Three separate scouting companies have also reported skirmishes; last week, six more men-at-arms were killed, this time their chainmail shredded like cotton shirts, mauled to death by giant *farlig* jamba-bears—an evil breed of jamba long thought to have been driven back into dark corners and caves within the Black Forest or to the icy steppes beyond the Northern Voda. Men who've survived these encounters, all hard men who're no strangers to the blood and spit and slaughter of battle, have also recounted the inexplicable presence of War Crows among the attacking enemy. Strangely, they say the Crows are alone or in pairs and appear to be leading the assaults but vanish when actual fighting begins, the stone-cold opposite of how War Crows normally react to violence. None have been captured or counted among the dead. Other than a few black feathers, they say, there is little witness except for the word of our men. The High Chancellor is convinced the legionnaires are conjuring feathered ghosts out of fear."

Laird Halen spat with disgust into the fire and stared at Aldus. The Laird of the First Gate nodded slightly, encouraging him to continue. "Two days past a secret message was brought to me by one of Lord Cadwallon's houseguards; the man had ridden hard, only stopping to change mounts at the Cider Press Inn on the king's main road. He handed me a small piece of parchment and a blood-soaked scarf of burlap. Inside the scarf was indisputable proof of what the scouting reports had said. 'Twas the head of one of those that're called Tongue-less."

Both tall men, Albrec and Ansgar, sat in stony, hard-faced silence. Adelaide hugged Cornelia, whispering gently in the goat's ear, as Benjamin let out a long, low whistle.

"What—what is a Tongue-less?" Nicolas asked, his eyes wide.

"It's a devilish kind of corpse-loving Crow," Laird Halen said flatly and spat again. "A War Crow whose tongue has been deliberately cut-out so he tells no secrets. The black-feathered bastards use them as messengers… and assassins." Nicolas remembered the huge, tattooed man who he'd unintentionally set free from the executioner's block by the sea cliff days before. His chest felt tight and cold. "This particular headless, Tongue-less, Crow lost his filthy life when 'e was caught sneakin' inside Lord Cadwallon's tent. The War Marshal's houseguards killed him. It's thought he'd been sent to murder Lord Cadwallon, not steal secrets."

"Or maybe he was goin' to eat him!" Benjamin interjected. "People say they eat flesh an' it rots the tongues outta their skulls."

Nicolas couldn't help himself. "Why kill Lord Cadwallon?" he asked and even as he said it, the question sounded impertinent, pointless.

"*Why?*" Halen repeated after scowling at Benjamin. His voice was gravelly and sullen. "Why? Who knows, Master Bennett? Could be to incite panic, to cause confusion, or perhaps for sheer bloodsport an' the taste of flesh." The Laird of salt and storm leaned forward and stabbed an iron finger at Nicolas. "But I think all that's as meaningful as a nobleman's fart, boy. I think there's only one *true* reason and one reason alone."

"The Murder," Ansgar interrupted quietly.

Laird Halen nodded grimly. "The *Murder*. The secret message Lord Cadwallon's man brought to me had but one thing written on it, *The Murder comes*—a black fleet of blood-drunk Crows unlike anything we've ever seen!" He growled, smashing his boot into the map of ashes, sending embers and charcoal flying. "Those muck-spitting Crows have been blinding our eyes with a sea-spray of bane-elves and *ferlig* jambas while they're busy forming a great, unseen storm on the horizon at our backs. They've got us looking at every border of the First Kingdom except the one with shores an' waves an' black longboats full of War Crows. That ruttish, fen-sucked, piece of Tongue-less filth was sent to slaughter the War Marshal of *this* gatekeep," Halen slammed a ham-sized fist against his knee, "to chop the head off the Second Legion. The Legion that guards the City against whatever the tides of the Cold Sea bring because *this* time the tides bring the Murder. *The Murder comes*! Our throne-hall stands empty and the Murder comes!"

No one said anything for a while. As safe and warm as the fire and the guardroom felt, a bitter despair grew inside Nicolas. There'd been a sense of desperate hopelessness in Laird Halen's voice; despair barely veiled by the lord's steely callousness, a pitilessness fashioned out of many dark and close years filled with blood, salt, and good men dying.

"Albrec?"

"Yes, my lord?"

"A couple of days ago, before I sent you here to join Nicolas, you arrived at St. Wulf's-Without-Aldersgate and shared some news with my Master Grimlock. Would you now mind repeating what that was?" Aldus' voice, though calm, held an unsettling sound of foreboding.

"Aye. I will." Albrec sighed deeply, gave them each a brief look and stared at his large, roughly used hands. He spoke slowly. "I'd come up from the Lowlands on other business, dark like most other business these days, and instead o' takin' the king's road, I stayed within Wistman's Wood, the wild woodlands that stretch between it and the coast." His toe kicked at what remained of the ash map. "I'd come about even with the Spit-n-Roast, the spiny peninsula that stabs out into the Cold Sea, formin' the southern shore of the Bay of Wrath, an' I was beginnin' to make my way back northwest t'ward St. Wulf's-Without-Aldersgate, when I saw 'em." The firelight wavered. The tight, hard lines in his face deepened.

"Saw what?" Ansgar asked firmly.

"Fairie rings. I saw three, black fairie rings."

Nicolas watched Benjamin's eyes grow even bigger than when Laird Halen had mentioned the Tongue-less War Crow. "What are black fairie rings, Albrec?" Nicolas asked the tall man, half-afraid to find out.

"Some folks in the Outlands say they're rings o' mushrooms formed by witch-goblins who dance in circles before castin' spells. Some say they're magical elvish rings guarded by giant toads that eat children who become lost in the woods. Durin' those long seasons of terror when overlord dragons an' their wicket-keeper spawn roamed freely, simple folk thought the rings were places where a dragon had slept." Albrec grimaced and gritted his teeth. "But that's not what I saw. I didn't see no rings made from dancin' witches, nor guarded by toads, nor made by sleepin' dragons. I saw three cursed circles o' scorched, dead grass, an' in the center o' the circles were deep pits with greasy smoke and the sick smell of burned flesh comin' outta them. The woods 'round was silent an' I watched fer a long time before makin' up my mind to have a closer look; I knew what I would see even tho' I've never seen nothin' like it this close to the City. Best I could tell, the bodies, alive or dead, an' who they were, I don't know, had been thrown into the bottom o' each pit an' torches had been thrown in after 'em to cook 'em, to harvest the spell."

"That is dark, evil magic, blackfrock," Halen spat, gripping the arms of his chair.

Aldus nodded in agreement. His aged face was drawn, his bright blue eye suddenly tired looking and ashen. "What Albrec saw was how a blinding spell is cast. A *vraja orb*, an ancient, magical incantation meant to blind an enemy."

"War Crows?" Ansgar asked.

Laird Aldus looked at the archer. "Yes. It's obvious the War Crows are using it as a final strategy before their invasion, but it wasn't them who cast the spell. They are a vile and violent race but their strength doesn't lie in dark magic and this is an incantation known only to a few."

"Then who?" Halen asked.

"I have some thoughts, but now isn't the time for speculation. The important thing is we have undeniable proof the War Crows are planning something far greater, far more ruinous and devastating than anything they've tried before, even greater than when they were defeated by the Fourth Grey Legion years ago…

even greater than what was crushed on that terrible day, the Day of the Passage Tomb." As he spoke, the old man had turned his good eye toward the flames in the hearth, his voiced sank and he seemed to drift into some far-off thought. "They have help," he said dimly as if he were alone. It wasn't until Adelaide mumbled something that Aldus appeared to be aware of them again. "What was that?" he asked the young Healer gently.

"Nothing really," she said, petting the small, dappled goat curled in her lap. "I was just speaking to Cornelia. Told her it'd be alright." Adelaide looked up, a cross determination flashing in her eyes. "It will, won't it?" The look on her face reminded Nicolas of the first moment he'd ever seen her, disheveled, her flushed cheeks wet with angry tears, a painful welt on the side of her mouth, and a single Dragon Poppy bouncing at the tail-end of her hair's long braid. She'd been furious, uncertain of herself, perhaps, but indomitably, righteously angry. She now had that same look again. "You've got a plan, don't you, Laird Aldus? Those terrible Crows hurt Ranulf—they killed his family—they're causing all these bad things to happen and they're coming to kill all of us, too, but you've got a plan, don't you?"

The old man tugged at his long beard and smiled. "As a matter of fact, I do have something of a plan, Miss Ashdown."

"Well," Halen said impatiently, throwing himself back in his chair, "for the love of all salt and sense, Aldus! What's the plan?! The Grey Legions have been scattered like dead leaves on a failing wind. Bane-elves and fenris wolves roam at-large. Vermin-ridden Crows play us like fools and now we're told they've some darker sorcery at their employ. I see little left to plan except to bolt shut every gatekeep's door, mount archers atop the outer walls, call up every last man-at-arms, sharpen our swords an' axes, an' wait for hated, black feathers to blot out the eastern sky."

Aldus dipped his chin. "Barring the doors and manning the walls is, of course, wise counsel, Laird Halen. The Commissioners of the Forfeited Gates must be prepared for the worst. Every tide that rises brings those black longboats a closer to our shores, but I would cautiously suggest we have something else to offer. Something our enemies haven't yet taken into account."

"Dammit, man!" The Laird of the Gate of the Deep pounded a fist on his knee. "Speak up! What is it?"

Aldus' blue eye sparkled. "It's *Külon Tuz*. The overlord dragon known as the 'Separate Fire.'" Everyone's face was shocked with disbelief. Laird Aldus ignored them. Instead, he knowingly turned and looked straight at Nicolas. "Or as the War Crows call it, the Worm of Crows. *We*, my good company, have the Worm of Crows."

CHAPTER 17

The First Lesson

Nicolas left the Gate of the Deep from the same place by which he'd entered it.

After a few hours of troubled sleep, Tom, Laird Halen's steward boy, had swiftly guided the silent company through a warren of increasingly narrow and dark corridors, some descending and some ascending, until Nicolas' nostrils had again filled with the reek of decaying seaweed and a lingering stink of foul wind. As they'd passed the cold chill of murky side-chambers and corridor openings, he had kept a keen eye out for the piggish watchman but all remained quiet and still. They moved as shadows among darker shadows.

"Up ahead," Tom had said at last, pointing toward the grim-rust outline of a large door. "Out through the Butcher's Bill an' you'll be a stone's throw from the cliffs to the east. Crack on now! Mean John *Belly* Morely is this door's steward," the boy had said with a sly grin. "At this hour he's likely to be deep in 'is cups somewhere's, drunk on fuddlin' swill, an' fartin' like a cabbage-stoofed pig." One by one, Albrec, Ansgar, Nicolas, Adelaide, her little goat Cornelia swaddled snug against her chest, and Benjamin, struggling to stifle his laughter at Tom's comments, filed through the barely open door; free at last underneath a cold night sky. The swelling pitch of a leaden dawn drove upon a bank of low-slung clouds that had gathered on the far horizon. "May there be a followin' sea at yer backs, friends at yer sides, an' salt in yer enemies' eyes," Tom whispered.

The heavy door scraped shut. The hanging man door-knocker clanked once against its iron cleat.

Setting out at a swift trot, the small band stayed close and hurried away from the exposed heights of the First Kingdom's sandstone cliffs.

Dawn revealed a stark seascape of steel-grey. Squalling blasts of easterly winds thrust up and over the cliffs' edges, spitting a bitter confusion of rain and frigid spray that chased the anxious company to the south and west, driving them as if it knew where they were to go. Far ahead Nicolas could see a thin, staggered line of stunted, wind-shaped trees standing as dauntless bannermen, bent forward in advance of the front of a thick line of battle. To the seaward their twisting, grey trunks were stripped bare, exposed and savaged by years of savage squalls and far-reaching storms. What branches these few trees had were all pointed inland. Tattered flags, they were, affixed to gnarled poles, facing the thick, front ranks of corkscrewed spruce, knotted alder, and curled pine aligned some distance beyond them; a many-miles-wide stand of wild, wet forest known as the Wistman's Wood, the timbered borderland stubbornly rooted between the sea cliffs and the king's main road to the west, known for its rare, broad-capped red mushrooms, its frightening abundance of black-scaled adders, and its rocky forest floor.

Fist-like gusts of frost-mauled wind struck down from the north, hurtling and skittering along the rocky ground, causing Nicolas to stumble when they caught him crossing dodgy patches of slick, bruised moss. Overhead the purpled sky seemed unusually near, bunted with drapes of violet haze and great curls of bone-grey clouds. Adelaide, Benjamin, and Nicolas pulled their hoods further down, scrambling wildly for the cover of the far-off trees while the tall man and the archer brought up the rearguard, their broad backs hounded by storm, wind, and the ashen wash of an illuming eastern sky.

Once among the dense ranks of wood, needle, leaf, and pine cone, the powerful crash and boom of the Cold Sea's surf began to thin, deadened by soaked bark, dense litterfall, and thickets of wild fern. A few strides further and the once-thunderous sound dulled to no more than a throaty rumor of wrecked waves and sallow foam. Soon the Cold Sea and the threat of black longboats racing across its green currents seemed lost behind them.

Nicolas, the first to reach the inner band of woods, stopped and shifted the shirt of chain mail hiding under his long weather cloak, adjusting its weight more evenly across his shoulders. Before they'd left the guard room, Laird Halen had called for Tom, who'd brought in a heavy-looking courier's haversack. From it he withdrew two stained weather cloaks and three padded shirts, plain brown ones for Nicolas and Benjamin and one for Adelaide, hers embroidered with swaying purple flowers and a swooping blue jay, the same shirts they had once worn under the same chain-mail the bag also held, links scrubbed bright with sand and protected by a thin rub of tallow. The bag also held a clink of metal and Benjamin eagerly shoved his arm inside, fished about, and pulled out a chipped hatchet which he held in front of his face. "Jes like she was new," he'd said, thrusting the hand-axe in his belt. The snatcher-boy next took out Nicolas' small, flat dagger hung from a cord; as he had once before, Nicolas dropped the loop over his head, the knife tucked inside his shirt against his chest. Benjamin paused and looked at Adelaide, his thin arm still in the bag. "Something from Ranulf," he'd said to her in a soft, pained way, and slowly removed a delicately forged hair dagger from the bag. The Healer nodded and gingerly slipped the slender spike of metal inside her hair's thick braid, squeezed Cornelia, and pressed her face into the goat's long pelt. With Fezel's worn trousers, Wezel's long weather-cloak, and the pair of mucky ankle boots on his feet, Nicolas had looked only a shade better than Benjamin. Two unremarkable street boys with Adelaide not looking like much more than a common farm girl. Now, among the dark, drizzly shade of Wistman's Wood, the three of them were even less a sight.

"I'll lead the way," Albrec said, stepping past Nicolas as he unslung his axe. The tall man guided them quick and led them quiet, steering them in a southwesterly direction across cold streams, through prickly thickets, and along shadowed borders of grassy meadows until the rain lifted and the early morning's nickel sky lightened to a bluish, slate-grey.

About two miles inland progress slowed to an exhausting crawl as they crept through a tight copse of timberwolf grey trees whose exposed, barkless roots were snarled into webs of slippery wood. At last, after Nicolas nearly twice twisted his ankle, they left the trees and mounted a large, bald crop of weathered stone. At the crest Albrec halted, tilting his long nose into the air; a strange eddy of bitter wind whipped up from the south, gusting, then falling off just as suddenly as it had come. The tall man pointed the head of his bearded axe off to the left into the head of the dying wind, his eyes humorless and narrow. "The black fairie rings an' bloody death-pits they dug lay among that thicket o' blackthorn trees." Nicolas looked down the hill and tried to see through the woody murk but could make out very little. The faint breeze carried a distinctive, sickening strain of sulfur mixed with a strange sweetness and the trace of something that reminded Nicolas of burned pot roast. It was horrid. He held a hand over his nose. Adelaide and Benjamin did the same.

"Why did they dig the pits there?"

The tall man shook his head. "Don't know, Master Bennett. Iffin' the pits are meant to invoke the kind o' magic Laird Aldus says they are, then I would'a guessed the Crows would dig 'em near an important place, somewhere closer to a harbor town or to one o' the gatekeeps. Strange tho'. The City is miles away, ain't nothin' near this place 'cept Grimbol's Gutter."

"What's that?"

Albrec pointed to his right, roughly north. "The tail o' Grimbol's Gutter is that-a-way, 'bout five hundred yards; it's a broad-bellied gorge with a head that begins near a tunneled drain in the southern wall o' the Gate o' the Deep. It runs south for almost a mile, an' back there." His hand waved eastward "I

t turns off to the east 'fore its dwindling tail squeezes inside the mouth of an underground burrow that spills out onto a shingle beach far below the sea cliffs. Point o' fact, we walked over the burrow part of the Gutter this last quarter-mile. That rat's nest o' bloody roots hold the burrow's roof in place." He thrust a finger north, stabbing the haze. "See that rock over there? Over them treetops? 'Tis the ragged peak o' the Rat Catcher; a splinter crag that's part o' the western lip o' Grimbol's Gutter. The City used to keep a guard's watch there for southern threats that might sneak up through these woods or through the Gutter from the sea, but the place was abandoned ages ago."

Slowly, the tall man shook his head again. "I've no idea why them pits were dug here, Master Bennett, 'cept that War Crows are all mad. Cracked as starvin' fenris wolves." He sniffed the air again. "We'll camp in the hollow below us until the darkness of fallow comes. Safer to keep still by day and travel by night even if it costs us some speed." Albrec looked his younger companions in the face. "We're entirely on our own and must be careful; woods may have fewer spyin' eyes an' ears than cities an' towns but all it takes is one slip. For now, this should be as decent of a place to rest as any other. Nothin' but crows an' moon sprites care to be anywhere near fairie rings an' death-pits."

They filed quietly down the hill and through a mixed-up mess of hawthorn and holly hedging, a kind of natural, broad furrow cut into the hill's base. In spite of the heavy damp, Albrec soon had a small fire going. Waxy pine cones and cracked twigs of crinkled gorse wood set ablaze the gummy resin inside a fat length of split pine that straddled two, debarked logs of fallen oak. The warmth felt friendly and cheering. After a brief but spirited row with Albrec over who was most lak to know the ways 'round health an' healin'," Adelaide happily fussed about, the girl quite in charge of their first camp; she set Nicolas and Benjamin to chopping leeks and ordered the two men to gather beds of needles and soft fern leaves for them to sit and sleep on. The young Healer boiled water from a nearby creek inside a soot-blackened tin filled with milk thistle roots and birch leaves she'd been collecting as they'd walked. Soon there was a rasher of bacon frying up in a large, deep pan, and once the fat had melted, Adelaide added the roughly cut leeks, two even spoons of heavy cream poured from a petite flask hidden in the folds of her kirtle, a crush of brown salt, and several strips of smoked cod out of Albrec's food pouch. Benjamin, whose eyes shone as he gabbled excitedly from the smell of scrummy hot food, passed around small trenchers of dried bread into which Adelaide ladled the smoked fish potage. For afters, the company sipped steaming mugs of the birch leaf and milk thistle tea and split a wedge of highly regarded autumn cheese from Wordwell, a peaceful hamlet located near the market village of Southerham in the Lowlands. When Albrec and Ansgar had finished their stew, they gave the soaked remains of their trenchers to Benjamin, smiling as the smallish boy devoured them both in a flash, pausing only long enough to use a last bit of crusty bread to swab up a few morsels that had caramelized in the bottom of the pan.

It wasn't long before Albrec, wrapped in an oiled sheepskin cape, was lightly snoring, while Ansgar sat silently with his large back to the grey-smoke fire, sweeping a hand-sized sharpening stone down the curved edge of his fighting knife. The three friends sat nearby in a tight triangle, knees touching, petting Cornelia, drinking more tea, and playing knuckle bones with an old set of sheep's ankle bones Benjamin kept in a little pouch stained as black as a walnut with age and long use. It was the first time Nicolas felt truly happy since arriving back in Telluric Grand although the absence of Ranulf tugged at his heart. The friends chatted and chuckled contentedly as if they were still in the Black Forest among the Caledonii people who, as Adelaide had once said to Nicolas, reminded her of earth-gnomes, only bigger and much more talkative and silly. The two boys listened in awe as Adelaide described the marble-sheathed and gold-veined halls of the Barrow Cloister; Adelaide impulsively hugged Nicolas when he told them about the cripple shepherd boy he'd encountered at Cailín's Spring; and Adelaide and Nicolas laughed and snorted when Benjamin impersonated Laird Halen growling snappishly at Laird Aldus and Laird Aldus puffing his pipe until disappearing in curls of smoke. Their merriment became a bit too loud and Ansgar shot them a stern look, holding a finger to his lips.

"Stop it now, Benjamin Rush," Adelaide giggled, her cheeks ruddy and beautiful from the fire's heat. She combed her fingers through the small boy's moppish hair. "I've missed you," she said; a protective hen. "I didn't have anyone to look after once we parted ways last year."

Benjamin winked and produced an aging, bruised pear from inside his sleeve. "And I've missed ya, too. Been in sorry, sad shape, havin' to look out fer m'self which is no small feat."

Adelaide stifled another laugh. She looked down at Cornelia and tugged gently at the little goat's soft ears. "I miss Ranulf," she blurted out after a few moments and quickly looked at Nicolas. "Oh, I know it wasn't you, Nicolas; Laird Aldus told us a bit of what happened when you went to see him, although I'm desperately hoping he'll come 'round again. Doesn't seem right, just the three of us."

Benjamin nodded. "It's why I decided to go back to the City. Heard somethin' about Ranulf havin' a hard go of it, an' I says to m'self, *have a look an' see, Benjamin Rush*. Besides, there's slim pickin's outside the City fer a lad such as m'self, no fat lardyman to kick in the shins." He winked at Adelaide, doing his best to make her laugh again. "But now I'm glad to be outside its walls again. I'm more like our blackfrock friend, I think; raised in the Dreggs but more comfortable outside the City's walls. Less likely to get my ears boxed anyway."

It was Nicolas' turn with the knuckle bones but when he'd gathered two tossing stones in his hand he paused. "The other day Albrec told me he's a Holocaust Man. I think I understand blackfrock, because of his black cloak, I suppose. But I'm not sure what he meant by being a Holocaust Man. Is it why he isn't welcome in the City anymore?"

Adelaide and Benjamin looked back at him with some surprise.

"Thought everyone knew 'bout Holocaust Men," Benjamin said, shaking his head.

"Benjamin!" Adelaide scolded. "Nicolas, Nicolas knows *other* things, I'd say, maybe different than what you and I or anybody else may know, but he doesn't have to know… well, he doesn't have to know *everything*."

Benjamin rolled his eyes. Nicolas shrugged trying to look as if he didn't care. He pitched the two small stones in the air, swiftly swept up three knuckle bones, and caught the two tossing stones on the back of his hand. "You're turn," he said, handing the stones to Adelaide.

The young Healer played the same hand but caught only one stone.

"Hard lines," Benjamin quipped, scooping up the stones. "A Holocaust Man," he began matter-of-factly, "is someone whose job it is to fight dragons. There used to be a lot of 'em," the tossing stones flew up in the air, "but now there ain't," the snatcher-boy's quick hands found five knuckle bones and the stones fell neatly on the back of his hand, "no more ancients livin' in the Pauper Holes, I wager."

"What do you mean?"

"What do I mean 'bout what?"

"What you just said about ancients. Aldus mentioned something about them once. Made it sound like they were some kind of old wise men."

"Old 'nuff to be wise, I'd say, an' not all of 'em men if the stories are true. Can't rightly say if any more are alive, tho' I've got a mate I could ask who still lives in the Dreggs. He's been in the holes a time or two. He'd know, that one."

"Ancients lived in the Dreggs?"

"Some did, I s'ppose." Benjamin laughed at himself. "Guess I don't know much about 'em neither now that I turn my mind to it. Thought I did but no one's ever asked before." His face scrunched up. "Can't say I've ever heard *anyone* say much about 'em in the proper sense other than ancients are, well, ancient. The fishmonger wives say they've been 'round almost as long as when Telluric Grand was first crafted outta the endless heavens. Strange lot, them. Wizards o' necromancers dependin' on who ya ask, but what I *do* know is that there are some or *were* some, who lived in the Pauper Holes in the Dreggs even before the Dreggs was the Dreggs. Have ya any more of that pottage, Adelaide?" He looked wistfully toward the fire.

"You know I don't, Benjamin Rush. You nearly scraped the black off the pan when you were finishing your supper."

The smallish boy laughed. "That I did! An' if I could bite the pan an' save my teeth, I would. Hard lines, I guess. Anyway, like I was sayin', the ancients," Benjamin gave such a melodramatic flourish with his arms that both Nicolas and Adelaide covered their mouths to stifle their laughter, "filled the Pauper Holes with magic an' old powerful spells. Uncommon influences, is what the old fishmonger wives say 'bout it but I think they're all chock o' block full o' thralls an' curses an' enchantments."

It was Adelaide's turn to roll her eyes. "That's what *you* think, is it?"

"Don't rightly know but neither do most folk, Adelaide. What I *do* know is them Pauper Holes attract death, an' death follows bewitchments like a Wild Hunt of heath hounds chase a mid-winter's night."

Adelaide hrumphed in disgust. "Those dreadful holes don't attract death, Benjamin, and you know better than to speak of such things as Wild Hunts while we're still in these dreadful woods. Fenris wolves are a dark enough thought without mentioning those other things." Benjamin crossed his arms and sulked. "Pauper Holes only seem that way because rag-and-bone men don't bother to call Healers for those who're left to die alone. It's horrid. They toss them away like rubbish; it leaves a stain of dark pain and loneliness in those places. I've seen it—" She put a hand to her stomach. "I've—I've felt it when I was still with the Cloister; there was a sense of loss and misery I could feel. Others made fun of me, said it was a bit of bad fish I'd eaten, but it was real! Once a month a Healer of the Second Order would take some of us *newyddiadur*—*nuisances* is what we're called in the common tongue, and we would each carry a sorrow basket filled with white lilies and purple chrysanthemums or lilac snapdragons."

"Would you sing the song?" Nicolas interrupted. His mind was taken with the gossamer memory of a moonlit evening in the stillness of the Hollow Fen when Adelaide had first told him about sorrow baskets. She'd been standing in the doorway of a Wisp's humble peat home and had sung the ageless lament of Healers who come to take away the suffering of grieving families. More than a few times since Nicolas had returned to Plumpton Head, when the Bennett family's home was dark and quiet in the middle of the night, he could hear Adelaide's warm voice in his head. Aching dreams of Jack would become less painful.

"No. I've only sung it that one time," she answered, her eyes timid and downcast. Benjamin looked confused. "Only a *Bendith Duw,* a real Healer, is supposed to sing it and then only for the dead," she said.

"You *are* a real Healer."

"I hope so." Adelaide pulled gently at Cornelia's velvety ears. "In any case, we'd go with a Healer of the Second Order and she'd sing the song at the entrance of each Pauper Hole after lighting a single shepherd's candle. We'd wait until the flame had died out before we'd move to another hole." The three friends sat in silence for several moments, the game of knuckle bones now forgotten.

"And there are ancients in those holes?" Nicolas asked.

"We never saw any. Not sure what they look like really."

Benjamin shrugged and returned to playing knuckle bones and Adelaide, who seemed lost in her own thoughts, sat back, letting Cornelia suckle sleepily on her little finger.

Nicolas waited for his turn to play. "You said there aren't a lot of Holocaust Men anymore because there aren't any more ancients living in the Pauper Holes. What do they have to do with Holocaust Men?" He felt a bit awkward pressing the issue but he wasn't any closer to understanding who Albrec was—what a blackfrock was.

Both tossing stones fell off the back of Benjamin's hand before he could grab a single knuckle bone. "Guess I bodged that one right proper," he snorted. "Aye. No ancients, no Holocaust Men. That one over there," snapping his chin toward Albrec, "is probably one o' the last ones; can't say I've seen too many others. It's said some Holocaust Men started out as weaklings; weak orphans given over to die, I guess; they'd be abandoned in the Pauper Holes and an ancient would find 'em an' raise 'em in the darkness. The fishmonger wives say them holes go deep, deeper than dwarf mines, deep down to where skins of molten iron float on lakes of fire, an' that's where the ancients would raise 'em. That's where their axes are made, it's said, not by no common smithies who live in the light of day; an' the black cloaks they wear are spun from the hair of those killed by dragons." By this time, Benjamin's own eyes were wide in wonder. "Blackfrocks're raised to fight darkness, to fight fear, to fight fire; the ancient raise 'em to fight dragons!"

"Fire and Iron," Adelaide muttered quietly.

Ansgar suddenly loomed over them, his sunken eye sockets in deep shadow under the ashen sky. "I think it best we all get some sleep now. The blackfrock you're so busy discussing is right.

These next few days will be hard, dangerous work, traveling by night with little comfort or safety until we reach, if we're *lucky* enough to reach, the War Marshal's battle encampment."

Without another word, Nicolas, Benjamin, and Adelaide, who tucked Cornelia protectively under the doublings of her deep green weather cloak, curled down where they sat, and as quick as tossing stones fall, they were each asleep.

Sitting once more with his back to the fire, the tall archer continued to scrape his sharpening stone slowly along the arc of his knife's edge, whispering to himself in a language Nicolas wouldn't have understood.

When fallow arrived hours later, when the night's first constellation, the twelve green-starred arch of the *nocte portam*—the *night gate* as it is more commonly known—had edged above the treetops surrounding the hollow, they all quickly drunk what was left of the tea, divided a salted piece of dried meat, and gathered up their few things in tight bundles. Off they went, Albrec in the lead and Ansgar last in line, careful to smother what remained of their fire by scattering wet, blue-green pine needles over its smoldering cinders.

The next night and day were mostly as promised, hard and tiring but thankfully uneventful. Wistman's Wood was not well-traveled and had almost no footpaths except for Smygler's Run a stone's throw to the south: a hard-to-find narrow ribbon of pebbled earth running east-to-west from the sea to the king's main road under the overhang of steep embankments, through tunnels in thorny thickets, and along hidden corridors within tight stands of knotted trees; it was a secretive smuggler's route but one that if taken would have added further danger to their already dangerous journey. Instead, the five companions spent their first night of travel wriggling, writhing, and pushing their way tediously through the woods, careful not to place their feet on heaps of fallen leaves or their hands in the darkest crooks of curled roots, sheltered places where nests of adders might coil. Not much was said as they straggled along and when it was, it was huffed in gasps and loud whispers. Their second day of rest came under a knitted canopy of intertwined, dwarfed oak trees, chock full of knots and twists, and bulges and bumps. The trees had grown in a rough circle, their branches leaving a kind of latticed opening in the middle that reminded Nicolas of a chapel's atrium.

As Benjamin dropped his kit on the moss carpet, he looked at Nicolas with an impish grin, raised his arms like the trees, and in an absurdly low voice sang out, "*A moanin' mob of moorish men whose bends an' bows have bent too much / Lift up their limbs in protest loud while gaspin' grip their graspin' touch!*" His silly rhyme brought smiles all around, even to the grim archer who'd hung back in the shadows for several moments, checking to see if there was any hint they'd been followed.

No more rain had fallen but the sky remained a lifeless counterpane of sluggish clouds; a cold wind eddied through the trees and nibbled at their fire's flames as the morning's dew, with some fog to boot, wetted everything around them. Each of them huddled round the fire's smoky warmth, deeply wrapped in weather cloaks, looking much like a quintuplet of odd rocks. Albrec, in a very un-rock-like way, blew smoke rings that smelled of mulberry pipe-leaf. Their breakfast consisted of two, griddled loaves of flat barley bannock bread turned out with crisp slices of cured pork and smoked cheese. Albrec filled their mugs with dark beer, each eating and drinking their fill in a drowsy, weary silence.

Unlike the morning before, Nicolas felt tired in body and spirit. No games of knuckle bones or easy banter entered his mind; by this time, Benjamin must've felt the same. The smallish snatcher-boy, a bit tippled from an extra mug of Albrec's autumn beer, sat there slow-winking, occasionally jerking his head, trying to stay awake. The long night's march, a woeful sum of perhaps ten miles among misshapen trees and grab-along brambles, mostly in silence, weighted with nervous thoughts of poisonous snakes, orc arrows, fenris wolves, and monstrous War Crows, had left Nicolas subdued and exhausted; glad for the fire, glad for the rest, and heartened only by the nearness of his friends and Albrec and Ansgar.

"Fire destroys."

Nicolas had the odd sensation of staring so fixedly into the flames, another's words seemed almost to come out of the amber-rouge of its embers and coals.

"Aye," came the affirming response. "Aye, an' in that, we find light." It was the tall man and the archer speaking to each other.

"You've heard the Three Lessons then?" Albrec asked.

"I have," Ansgar said quietly and dipped his chin. "That is the first."

"So 'tis."

After several moments of silence between the men, Nicolas couldn't help himself. "What are the Three Lessons?" he asked, not sure if he wanted an explanation of each lesson or whether he was asking what they were altogether.

Albrec looked at Ansgar and raised his eyebrows, but the vigilant archer turned his head and gazed off into the grey in-between's of the trees. "What are they then? Why they're basic notions, Master Bennett. Guides if ya will; wise counsel first given by Fenyw Doeth to her son an' daughter, Dechrau an' Diwedd, in the gloam of the first fallow, just as Time began to turn his great wheel across the face of Telluric Grand, when the moon was still white and new.

"I first heard 'em when I was only a lad. Didn't 'ave no dad nor mum, livin' in the Dreggs on nothin' but pinched bread an' gutter water, tryin' to run from what I was meant to do. I remember feelin' dicky one cold mornin', not up to my usual ways; a mate had tol' me the bailiff men were lookin' to nick me. I could steal salt outta the sea back then an' I started lookin' for a place to lay up fer a while. Ran up Bagford Street; cut through a yard or two over to Wright Road to shake 'em, but they wouldn't be shook. For whatever feverish reason, I ducked through a ditch-pipe to Capener's Close."

Albrec picked up a stick and stabbed at the fire, stirring the glowing wood. The flame leapt up and he sat watching it for a while. "Never been there before," he said as if to himself. "A broad alley of carpenters' shops, smelled o' wood dust an' glue. Seemed light an' airy to me, not fouled with stink an' piss an' rubbish like the rest o' the Dreggs. I hadn't a plan, so I walked along watchin' them work the wood: shavin' it, cuttin' it, shapin' it, polishin' it—takin' it from somethin' raw to somethin' brilliant." He held up the stick; a tendril of smoke rose from its charred end. "I'd forgot what I was doin' an' before I knew it, a bailiff's man caught me by the shirt." Nicolas glanced at Benjamin who was gawking at Albrec and rubbing his sore ears. "They'd 'ave beat me for sure but instead, a big man suddenly stepped outta a shop carryin' a heavy wooden hammer. *Leave off,* he orders the bailiff's men. *Leave off or I'll use yer front teeth fer me chisel.* They grumbled an' said he must be sloshed to meddle with a no-good, thievin' scrub, but they let me go; guess they didn't like the look o' that mallet he was carryin'." Albrec grinned and winked at Benjamin who smiled back.

"The big man tol' me to come inside. Tol' me to go sit by his fire. I did as he said an' remember fallin' asleep right away. When I woke it was dark, close to grimlock I'd say; the fire was bright an' the big man was at his table hummin' a tune as he whittled a piece of soft wood. A young woman who musta been 'bout ten years older than me—as beautiful a woman as I've ever seen—was there. She was his daughter an' he called her Sophia. She'd wrapped me in a blanket while I was sleepin' an' had a hot bowl of turnip soup for me to eat when I woke. I drank it down an' musta eaten a whole loaf of rye bread; felt smashin' well, as whole as I'd ever felt. Never'd had a war, hearth to sit by, nor no bowl of fine soup, nor no bread given to me instead o' taken. I was a cheeky lad. Wanted a home an' someone to call family, so I up an' asked Sophia if she could be my mum. Hoho!" Albrec slapped his knee and held a rough hand over his mouth.

"She flashed a lovely smile an' said nothin'. She don't speak, the big man tol' me, but it don't mean she hasn't anything to say. Sophia's a rare one, a *Siaradwr Nefoedd*,' he explained. 'I found her years ago when she was very young while I was out gatherin' wood on the edge o' the wilds, just inside Hawkshead Forest west o' Traitors Gate. There's an old grove of apple trees there, full of golden apples as big as your head an' butterflies as large as me hands. It's said them trees 'ave a mind o' their own. As long as a fella don't take an axe to their trunks, they'll kindly drop fruitless branches as thick as a giant's arm.' The big man stopped whittlin' an' sat back as if he'd forgotten I was there. I've only known one bloke who was daff enough to chop down one o' them apple trees, he said. He was from south, down past the Lowlands, with broad cheeks an' a flat nose an' stank like a wet goat. Went in with an axe an' never came out. The big man went back to whittlin' for a bit then went on 'bout Sophia as if he'd never stopped. I heard a little bubble o' laughter an' there she was, an infant girl, layin' all by herself in a wickerwork of applewood boughs. There was a small brook nearby an' it looked as if her cradle had sprung up from its mossy banks; I couldn't tell. She had on a soft gown of green an' silver, an' she was 'bout covered head to foot in purple an' gold butterflies, laughin', she was, an' speakin' to 'em in some tongue I'd never heard. Not a soul was in sight, nor did anyone appear as fallow settled into the darkness of night; I took the wee lass home to my wife, may she remain blessed, but the moment I left the grove with her, Sophia went mute and has never spoken since. My wife said she was a *Siaradwr Nefoedd*, one o' them born from fairies an' starlight. She's the one who named her Sophia."

By this time Nicolas, Benjamin, and Adelaide, who'd otherwise been about to fall asleep curled around Cornelia, were listening raptly to the tall man. His face somber and thoughtful melancholy. He snapped the stick he'd been holding in his hand and tossed its parts in the fire. "After that the big man bid me goodnight an' went off to bed. Sophia stayed behind to stoke the fire an' as she was sittin' on her heels in front o' the hearth, I swear I heard her speak. To this day I can't rightly say what I heard was the common tongue, but whatever she was speakin', I understood the words. Her voice was like water movin' among rocks. Fire destroys an' in that, we find light. This is the first lesson, Albrec Westenra, she said, though I can't say how 'twas she knew my name. The next night after the big man went to bed, she tol' me the second lesson, an' on the third night she tol' me the last one." The tall man leaned back and closed his eyes. "Those were the only words I ever heard her speak. 'Twas not long after that I returned to where I'd come from an' became what I am, what I was supposed to be."

The moment Albrec finished saying this, a damp stick in the fire snapped, and Adelaide, to almost everyone's surprise, screamed.

Ansgar, the Throne Shield, the *Eodur Nihtweard* of the First Kingdom, whirled about and leapt to his feet, his great war bow in hand. In almost the same motion, the skilled archer let fly an arrow, the quivering shaft disappearing into the gloom of the woods beyond them. "Look to your axe!" he roared at Albrec, his noble face dark and savage.

A bane-elf, an unnatural deformity, suddenly crashed madly against the stout trunk of an oak nearest to Adelaide. The wicked creature spat and hissed as it convulsed madly on the ground, struggling to tear out the arrow protruding from between the swollen sinews of its pale neck; a deathly gash now slick with the beast's infected, yellowish blood. Just as quick, Nicolas could see five more bane-elves racing fast toward them out of the grey, wooded murk. They seemed like gruesome wraiths, phantom demons born of the hollow shadows between the trees. Albrec's head lowered and his long face relaxed into a strangely sad expression. Throwing his black cloak over his broad shoulders, he shook out his scarred battle axe and grasped his long knife. "Fire and Iron," Nicolas could hear him whisper. And as one, they sprang forward, the Holocaust Man and the Throne Shield, their sword, knives, and axe pushing back against the malevolent fury of attacking bane-elves.

As if he'd abruptly fallen asleep, Benjamin Rush suddenly curled on the ground close to Nicolas' feet, the edge of the small boy's cloak cast dangerously into the fire's nearby coals. The snatcher-boy lay there senseless. In the flash of a moment's ferocity, he'd been cruelly bludgeoned; a bright stream of blood poured from a gaping head wound, flowed over the boy's stunned eyes, and into his open mouth. A bane-elf crouched over Benjamin. Its mouthful of needling teeth yawning wide above the small boy's exposed neck.

Nicolas, numbed by shock and fear, stood there frozen.

And yet, amid shrieks and shouts and the swiftness of violence going on round him, a hard, cold shiver darted up his spine. It tingled through his skull and shocked the skin of his face. Nicolas could taste a slight, metallic tang in his mouth. He could see each, grey tooth in the bane-elf's mouth. He could feel his heart nearly come to a stop and he could feel his lungs fill to bursting. It was rage he felt. A raw and bitter rage consumed the once-Wren and Dragon Nightfall.

In horror, anger, devotion, Nicolas screamed. It was feral and uncontrollable, and as it ripped from his throat, he threw himself forward to protect his friend.

But even as he did, the bane-elf bit down and bit down hard.

CHAPTER 18

THE DYING OF THE LIGHT

For the hundreds of years during which St. Wulf's-Without-Aldersgate has existed, it has possessed a small, seldom seen archive. It is a curious collection of various reports, records, histories, and chronicles many of which are inscribed within the linens, parchments, and goatskins of a bizarre assortment of scrolls and books all packed, higgledy-piggledy, within Laird Aldus Ward's personal study.

Sundry items are detail and preserve a vast array of subjects; such subjects one might expect from such a peculiar place maintained by such a peculiar man. There are great narratives of military histories and migrations of peoples and races, ghastly descriptions of anatomical oddities, mostly those removed during the dissection of witch corpses and some of which are accompanied by gruesome drawings in bright colors, extravagant poems of heroic tales and deeds, aromatic lists of rare spices such as winkle-sumac, a spice which has a flavor so tart, persons who eat it are unable to stop drooling for two days, nearly impossible puzzles contained in books just as impossible to open. These, in fact, are said to sprout legs and walk away if the reader comes too close to discovering their solutions. And sketches and explanations of the mechanics of clockwork without ever the mention of Time. There are tiny, glimmering books with covers like moth wings; some like the Madagascan moon moth, some like the giant leopard moth, some the cinnabar moth. These tell of fairies. There are twine-bound stacks of earthy chapbooks thick with ballads, poems, myths, and stories of the Outlands. There are dozens of richly colored, leather bound books swollen with sumptuous illustrations and overlong registers that herald the history, kings, battles, and increase of the First Kingdom. There are books and scrolls and records and accounts of great men and women, both bad and good, ancestral clans, lines of blood, and inheritances. There are also other non-bookish things like the carving of an elvish hieroglyphic in a large fragment of petrified wood, all that remained of an long-extinct sigillaria tree. And the spiraled horn of a giant eland filled with colorless tourmaline crystals used for the study of light. Yet among the thousands of jumbled scrolls, books, and eccentricities, there are a small number of texts that possess the tales and secrets of age-old and sacred things.

Some of these, a few, large, leathery books clasped shut with broad straps and studs of rock-iron, contain frosty legends of giants and long-lost mines dug deep under the mountains of the Dolmen Tombs. Another considerable tome, this a hefty, earthy volume with wild bindings woven from the shaggy bark of woolly oaks, describes the vast single-root colony, peculiar coppery leaves, and fabled first seed of the rare Eldur trees that grow at random throughout Telluric Grand. While a very few unique scrolls, each the size of a giant's thigh, made of single rolls of supple parchment filled with sinuous and willowy calligraphy, this in a dialect said to be the original tongue of the ancients, lay protected inside caskets of stained acacia wood; these parchments alone whisper hauntingly about the primordial *Beginnings* of all things. Yet there are even more, just as unusual bits of writings found deeper still within the library of the Laird of the First Gate.

There are those cocooned within a dull layer of dust at the back of a hard-to-see cubbyhole. They are made of carved lumps of wicket-keeper dragon bone, strange bits of bone that softly click and tick and snap if one listens closely. There are curious symbols and letters engraved on the bones, inscriptions that, if viewed under the flush of a green-flame candle, uncannily move in related circles, circles resembling the varied wheel trains of clock gears, dangerous oddities, these *etzem*, locked safely inside two, bronze cylinders made of metal wrought from a dead king's hoard of old coins. In one cylinder is a set of bones white as alabaster; these murmur hints and inklings of the secretive and timeless *Kohanim*, formidable Wisps known as Clokkemakers. The Clokkemakers are otherworldly beings few of whom are now left, who walk among men yet remain part of the endless heavens. In the other cylinder are slate grey bones, fissured and pitted; these crack and hiss of those Wisps who long ago fell out of Harmony, the ghastly *Shedu*, vengeful storm demons left to wander aimlessly across the face of the earth, lost, void of shape or form, who can only be seen as horrifying chasms of awful darkness.

Perhaps the oldest of all, mingled here and there like footlights along a shaded forest path, are five, twice-folded codices wrapped in soft, red goatskins. Glossy sheaves that smell of honey and mint, threaded in their gutters with plaited cords of silk and tipped at the corners with deep blue enamel. Their bright covers are fastened with delicate loops of hand-spun silver-thread and when the loops are opened, the pages of these strange records emit a muted glow as if self-possessed of starlight. They are the only written records in all the First Kingdom that speak of *Âld* Elves.

Each is called a *Cynecynnes Boc*, a *Book of Ancestors* that, if read in the common tongue, would be little more than a dissatisfying and tiresome sequence of elvish names. But in the elvish tongue, a tongue known but to few men, these individual and family names contain *everything* there is to know:

constellations, songs, places, folklore, experiences, teachings, births, deaths, histories, and, embedded within the fantastical account of elvish lifespans, even the bendable framework of Time itself. These remarkable sheaves, containing only lists of names, of course, also speak of the Great Crossing. How, when sunlight was still crisp and new and undiminished by the wane of countless days, *Âld* Elves first appeared from over the southern seas, from far beyond the furthest horizon of the warm, vast Suthron waters, from distant, extraordinary lands, uncharted and never seen by mortals. Sweeping savannahs of sun-bathed grasslands known as the *Ælfheim*. In the long ages before the First Kingdom was formed, before the Great War of Giants, Wisps, and Men, elvish lords and their noble companies began arriving in Telluric Grand, gliding silently up the broad Suthron river *Ælfflōd* in elegant longboats sculpted from emerald wood; they came in boats without sails, the *wiðoutan merehrægl*, not bound by currents or draughts of ocean wind but carried across the water on cradles of loamy seafoam, skillfully harnessed daylight, and clever elvish spells. The ancestry books of names, the enduring lore of *Âld* Elves, are rich with beauty, magic, skill, and long life. But elves, as splendid and noble of a race as they have always been, also possess a terrible capacity for base wickedness and corruption. Thus it has been that some names in the Books of Ancestors have been crossed out.

Like a poisonous cane toad hiding in the shadows, there is a little-known sixth codex. It is concealed in a corner behind three, high stacks of well-worn grimoire, ancient books devoted to the enquiry of amulets, charms, potions, and spells, especially those used to combat warlocks and bloodless *draugar*, the dreaded *again-walkers*. This codex is mildewed, wettish and slick, and emits a foul smell not unlike the fevered sweat of a dying person. Unlike its brethren, this bloated toad-of-a-book is called the *Eardwreccan Boc*, the Book of Exiles. It is folded three times and bound in stretched, black frog skin; there are no gutters neatly threaded with plaited, silk cords; its corners are not tipped with blue enamel; and it can only be studied in short bursts, the longer it is left open, the more light it seems to devour from around it. Elvish names that have been struck from the ancestry rolls are said to appear in the *Eardwreccan Boc*. They are spitefully written as if by the dark magic of a malignant, unseen hand. Most are remnants of names, once lengthy and pleasing, now shortened into chains of harsh letters, abrupt and vulgar-sounding. Others, whose ink has hemorrhaged into disfigured stains and blots, are nearly unreadable and grotesque-looking. And still there are others, these but a few, that are the most spoilt and mutilated of them all. Their guttural letters run in ruts of harsh scratches and scrapes, almost cuts. Piercing through them are many hurried black strokes; pitiless marks made as if to cross out these names, as if to forbid their utterance and obliterate their memory and history from the race of elves. These all were once *Âld* Elves. High elves who forgot beauty, who forgot the *Ælfheim*, who allowed their eternal hearts to decay, who succumbed to desire and treachery until all they were and all they'd known became lost. Elves driven mad by covetousness and cruelty and hate. Elves ruined in spirit, corrupt in body, malevolent, cunning, and faithless.

These are known as the *Brecðan*, the Broken, although that name is hardly ever spoken even behind locked doors or in front of brightly burning hearth fires. When pressed, most folk will cast a wary glance over their shoulder and whisper the familiar name Nicolas had already heard: bane-elves.

Time had almost seemed to come to a stop for Nicolas. It had stretched into a slow-moving scene of shock and terror.

The bane-elf crouching over Benjamin was wiry and starved-looking. Its leathery skin and scabbed body seemed almost insect-like with abnormally elongated forearms (which some bane-elves used much like a second set of legs when running), sporting rows of small spines used to pin struggling prey. Nicolas watched the creature's long fingers bury their dirty, curved fingernails into the flesh of the limp snatcher-boy's arms; bright beads of blood sequined around the wounds like tiny circlets of rubies. Its grey head seemed stretched, almost triangular in some vague way, with a hairless scalp covered in pale, veined, and rough skin. Its once healthy, emerald-green eyes were virtually useless, nearly blind, their almond-shaped orbs now dull and cloudy. Beneath its eyes were two, long nostril slits excitedly quivering with the tempting smells of its young victim. To Nicolas' horror, the lower part of the bane-elf's face disjointed, the lower jawbone thrusting forward unnaturally to reveal ranks of stained teeth whetted into thin, jagged barbs. Glistening webs of sticky saliva globbed at the corners of the *brecðan*'s black mouth as its jowls repeatedly clamped shut like the chewing mandibles of a giant mantis.

Nicolas hurled himself at the dreadful thing, blind with rage and terrified all in one moment, and as the thing's needle-like teeth began tearing into the skin of Benjamin's neck, the dreadful scene Nicolas had been watching suddenly and confusingly changed.

One moment the bane-elf was there in front of him, but in the next moment the vile beast was entirely gone—vanished. One moment Nicolas was madly lunging forward, screaming insensibly in anger and fear and panic, and the next moment his face was buried deep among bristling hairs of a thick, coarse matt of shaggy fur. The tangle of hair felt warm and wet and smelled musty, stinking in the same way as when Jasper would come charging into the Bennett's boot room after romping through the pasture and woods, drenched with rain. Whatever owned the woolly fur was as solid and as enormous as the trunk of an oak tree. When Nicolas' full weight collided with it, his head and neck absorbed the impact leaving him slightly stunned. He staggered backward in a daze, passing his hands weakly over his face. From somewhere close by came a last, inhuman shriek of pain and death followed by a profound sense of stillness; this, only punctuated by the panting of those who still lived and a hurried succession of choked sobs. Nicolas' jellied legs sank beneath him. He fell back on the cold, damp earth and stared widely at the low, colorless sky. The clouds were a desolate, watery paste, smudged and stubbornly mean-spirited; not a hope of glad sunlight anywhere.

"Der 'e is!"

A great shadow with the vague outline of a bear's head leaned over Nicolas, who pressed himself against the ground, twisting his head, squinting, trying to adjust his eyes. "Haha! Der 'e is! An' 'e's alive. Thot 'e might o' got squashed." The great shadow laughed and straightened, the bear's head flopping back lifelessly. "Goot as new but older, too, I see." Nicolas lifted his head. A sudden sense of relief caused his temples to throb but the fuzziness in his head began to clear. "Haha! Dat Grief, 'e must still like you."

"Bardölf!" Nicolas exclaimed.

"Aye, 'es me." The huge man stood there much as Nicolas had first seen him on the Lonely Road in the Woodcutter's Forest over a year ago, his flat teeth flashing in a broad smile, his massive war hammer balanced loosely in his hand.

It was Bardölf, a kind of shepherd of bears. A Jamba keeper.

"Der are few who would dare charge an angered jamba an' none who did would live." His smile broadened. "But ya jus' did, didn't ya. A rar' t'ing, a very rar' t'ing."

Not knowing what to say, Nicolas looked at the mountain of shaggy fur next to Bardölf. "Grief?" he asked and as he did the mountain turned. With a head the size of the Bennett family's stove, paws as large as dinner plates, claws as long as steak knives, and a colossal body that seemed the size of his dad's old Land Rover 110, the jamba-bear was a force of savagery and it was that wildness that had saved Nicolas. Nicolas stood up, twigs and leaves clinging to him, and without thinking—much as he had once done long ago—he reached out his hand and, while doing his best not to tremble, gently touched Grief. The great jamba-bear tilted its massive head. Its dark-brown eyes looked right at the boy from Penrith, England, for several, long seconds and with deliberateness, it nodded.

"A rar' t'ing," Bardölf said again in a low voice.

Grief abruptly stood up, towering above them, and moved off toward an old, bent alder tree and leaned against it to scratch its back. The staunch tree shivered and shook as the giant *ennlig* jamba-bear chafed its body against the cracked, grey bark. It wasn't until then that Nicolas realized Ansgar had been holding his war bow fully drawn, only releasing the tension on the nocked arrow after Grief had moved away. Albrec stood close by the tall archer, breathing heavily and holding his battle axe loosely by his side, its blade smeared with bane-elf skin and blood. Adelaide was kneeling on the ground a couple of yards away as Cornelia bleated and licked a raspberry-colored welt the size of a copper one-penny on her left cheek. The young Healer's hair was tousled and she looked frightened. She'd been viciously cuffed during the fight but it didn't look as if the pain had yet registered. The corpses of two bane-elves lay nearby, one with its grey head split open and the other with its throat slashed and face smashed into pulp. *Bardölf's hammer*, he thought.

"Adelaide?" Nicolas said, trying to make sense of what had happened so quickly. The fixed look on her face frightened him; the few sobs were coming from her. She scrambled toward him on all fours. In a sudden fit of action, she was trying to reach Benjamin.

The smallish snatcher-boy was sprawled on the ground in front of Nicolas, the least noticeable of them all, having been covered in a spray of mud, leaves, and feathery ash from the scattered fire. His lips were like bluish veins, his eyes closed, his cheeks were colorless. The boy's arms and legs looked disturbingly confused as if he hadn't any control over them. Benjamin's small chest didn't seem to be moving with the breath of air.

"Benjamin!" Adelaide cried, scudding to a stop next to him. She floated over him, her head jerking about, her hands searching for hurt and injury. There was nothing to be found except the nasty gashes in his neck from the bite of the bane-elf. "Benjamin Rush!" she shouted, holding his face in her hands. "Benjamin Rush! You wake up this instant, d'ya hear me? Benjamin!" Adelaide looked wildly at the others and at Nicolas. "What do I do?" she whispered in a hoarse voice as she cradled the smallish boy's head.

Nicolas shook his head. His mouth was dry, not even enough saliva to swallow, and there was a haunting, familiar pressure in his chest. He dropped down on the other side of Benjamin. His left hand rambled around on the ground next to him, unconsciously gathering bits of wood and rock and mud he began to arrange in a very specific and peculiar way.

"What do I do? What do I *do*?" Adelaide repeated in breathless rushes. She moaned and pulled Benjamin's head against her chest, rocking him back and forth, a shielding metronome of anxiety and helplessness.

Vacantly, Nicolas looked down at a small stone his fingers had found. The rock was smooth, flat, and was unnaturally rectangular. With it, a single memory—a *feeling* more than a memory really—squeezed out everything else around him. For a moment, he wasn't there anymore. He wasn't sitting in a cold, twisted corner of Wistman's Wood. For a moment his mind, his heart, were elsewhere. Finally, though, Nicolas answered, three words without any sound. Words made only by the slight forming of his tongue and cold lips. An answer Adelaide wasn't able to hear.

"Death is coming," he said and dropped the stone.

Four months after the Bennett's holiday to Tantallon Castle, Christmastime had arrived at Plumpton Head. It came guardedly without its usual high spirit of warmth and laughter and hope. In mid-December, Jack had left the Bennett family's home and had moved into a small, neatly made bed inside the Children's Ward of the Cumberland Infirmary in Carlisle. His sudden weight-loss and labored breathing had spelled the need for machines, tubes, needles, and constant care. In spite of it all, Jack's deep, grey eyes had remained bright, especially in those moments when Nicolas was able to visit, and on one visit just two days before Christmas Eve, they'd even sparkled.

There had been an unexpected surgery to deal with a complication the week before and Jack had been placed on a ventilator. For once, he was unable to joke with his younger brother because of the hose in his mouth, his already waning voice now replaced with the hypnotizing whoosh and hiss of the breathing machine. This all came with more wires and tubes and complex-looking apparatuses, and more low beeps and small lights than before. Nicolas had thought his brother looked like someone out of a science fiction movie.

A white, plastic writing board lay on Jack's stomach, and when Nicolas had arrived to visit at ten-to-three in the afternoon, Jack began scribbling something with a black felt marker, his eye's lighting up like shiny, wet marbles. Sarah Bennett settled Nicolas into a chair near Jack's bed and after a long kiss to Jack's forehead left to find two cups of hot tea.

Jack pushed the board toward Nicolas.

The words he'd written were in an uncharacteristic, shaky scrawl, but the letters were clear. *The hills alone unchanged from span to span.* Jack lifted his eyebrows as if to say, "D'ya remember, Nicky?"

Nicolas nodded, remembering the day he, Jack, and Mr. Bennett had visited the strange stone in the woods beyond the sheep's pasture.

Jack's eyes shone even out of the deadening drowsiness of sedating medicine. He grasped Nicolas' hand and dropped his head back on his pillow. With some effort he lifted it again and used a corner of his bedspread to wipe the board clean. *I'm free*, he wrote. Again he lifted his eyebrows, a weary but peaceful look.

Nicolas wasn't sure what his brother meant, but he nodded once more, wanting to be encouraging. The expression on his face gave away his confusion.

You don't need to carry me, Jack wrote before once more falling back against his pillow. This time he closed his eyes. He looked calm, almost as if he'd fallen asleep.

Nicolas had sat there silently for several minutes. He could hear nurses' voices murmuring in the corridor, the ventilator's rhythmic swish, and the faint hum of the overhead neon bulbs. "Jack?" he whispered.

Slowly, his brother opened his eyes. They were as bold grey as a winter storm whipping over the Irish Sea.

"Jack?"

Jack Bennett squeezed Nicolas' hand, gave a feeble smile, and closed his eyes again.

Nicolas, feeling so terribly alone, sat there listening to the sounds of silence.

"You're a Healer. A *Bendith Duw*."

Panicked, Adelaide's eyes stay locked with his.

"You're a *Healer*, Adelaide," Nicolas repeated, insistent. "You *know* you are. I'm a, I'm a, well, I don't know yet what *I* am, but I *know* you're a Healer." Nicolas tenderly picked up one of Benjamin's hands and intertwined their fingers. "Benjamin *needs* you, Adelaide. He needs… he needs… he needs you to *carry* him." Nicolas' mind began to drift again.

Adelaide choked back a fresh sob. Her unblinking eyes were wide and wet, her face creased with nervous doubt.

For a distracted moment, Nicolas thought he could hear the low pull and whoosh of a breathing machine. Or maybe it was Grief's deep-toned *whoofing*. Maybe. "You can do it. This, *this* is when you come face-to-face with who you've always been." The words sounded like something his father would have said. Nicolas touched her cheek, not knowing what else to do. He seemed to be looking through her. "This, this is what your heart was always set to do." These last quiet words came with an abrupt, detached feeling. Nicolas wasn't sure anymore if he was speaking about Adelaide or himself.

A large hand seized his shoulder. Standing next to him, Bardölf the Jamba keeper added something in a thick, strange language—the Old Tongue—a language Nicolas dimly remembered Adelaide having told him was still spoken somewhere in the Outlands. A wild language.

The young Healer glanced feverishly from Nicolas to Bardölf. She looked protectively at Benjamin, brushed the hair off his forehead, kissed his pale skin, and without looking up again, nodded. “Yes,” she said, her soft voice accepting but firm.

Without a word, Albrec walked over, knelt beside her and scooped up Benjamin. Together, the young Healer and the tall man moved toward a small stand of leafless birch trees as Cornelia followed discreetly at their heels.

“What happened?”

Bardölf looked down at Nicolas. “Eh?”

“I’m not sure what happened. I—I remember trying to get to Benjamin and… and I think I must’ve tripped into Grief instead.”

The Jamba keeper chuckled, his eyes twinkling. “Ya didn’t trip, boy. Ya were chargin’ like a mad badger.” He chuckled again. “’Twas a rar’ t’ing to see. Dat bane-elf was takin’ a bite outta the little one, an’ I t’ink Grief thought it was *you* bein’ served fer supper. He smashed that evil t’ing so ’ard it flew way o’er dar.” The huge man jerked his bearded chin toward the edge of the oak grove. A crumpled heap of grey flesh lay crushed against the crinkled base of a dwarfed oak. The force of the jamba-bear’s blow, and the impact with the tree, had broken every bone in the bane-elf’s body. It’s remains looked like a clomp of black knot fungus.

Bardölf leaned close and smiled grimly. His brownish teeth were broad and flat and his breath smelled of Welsh onion and black radish. “I’ve seen ’im—dat king o’ Jambas—movin’ about in battle, smashin’ an’ thumpin’ an’ tearin’ through man, orc, an' wolf alike, but I never seen 'im kill wit' so much rage. I t'ink dat jamba-bear was protectin' *you*, Master Wren."

Before Nicolas could think of anything to say, Ansgar strode up. He'd been checking the bodies of the other bane-elves, slitting necks to make sure they were all dead. A practical safeguard borne out of an old fable; thought to be dead of grievous wounds inflicted by a brave farmer who'd defended his one milk cow, the injured bane-elf suddenly leapt to its feet, back to life, clawing and biting the farmer's cow until the farmer struck it down a second time, this time cutting its throat. From this, the old wives would say, came the well-known Outland's proverb, "Better a twice-dead enemy than a once-dead friend."

"Are you hurt, Master Bennett?" The tall archer looked him over carefully. "None the worse for wear, I'd say, after living through an attack of bane-elves, only the second I've ever seen in my life to be honest, and I've *never* seen a jamba-bear do what that one did." Ansgar turned, dipping his chin to Bardölf. "I am Ansgar. I am a Captain of the King's Guard." Bardölf grunted, pinched and blew his nose, but said nothing. "Thank you for your help," the tall archer continued, glancing toward Adelaide and Albrec both of whom were kneeling low over Benjamin's body. It looked as if they were speaking but Nicolas couldn't hear what they said. "Thank you for your help. For the jamba-bear's help. May I inquire, who might you be?"

Bardölf gave his nose another pinch and spat. "I'm me," was all he offered. The Jamba keeper leaned indifferently on the upended shaft of his great war hammer while Grief, still scrubbing his coarse fur against the alder tree, let out a great yawn that closed with an intense, mewing whine. Bardölf smiled. "An' dat, dat es Grief."

"Bardölf's a—he's a Jamba keeper," Nicolas said. His throat was dry and raspy. There was a lingering numbness inside.

It felt like it was Jack over there, lying beneath Adelaide and Albrec. He felt the same way he had felt every time they'd had to leave Jack after visiting. He wanted to be strong, to appear routine, to be the grandson of a grandfather who was once a king. Nicolas did his best to re-focus his mind. "I've met him. *We've* met him, once before, a year ago," he explained to Ansgar. "Over a year ago. There was a terrible tinker-man who tried to—Benjamin was Bardölf… Bardölf came out of nowhere and killed him. Not Benjamin, of course, but the old man, and the next day Grief came. Well, he didn't *come*, I suppose. He more showed up. I went out of the cabin in the morning and he… he… it…" The rapid jumble of words was like trying to speak while chewing a mouthful of jelly babies. The words stuck to Nicolas' teeth and tripped his tongue. He imagined his dad cocking an eyebrow, telling him to finish chewing and to start over again. He paused and swallowed dryly several times. He couldn't think of what else to say. He turned to Bardölf and asked, "Come to think of it, how'd you know we'd be here?"

Bardölf, who had been giving the tall archer a long and wary look as Nicolas rattled on, finally appeared satisfied. His familiar chuckle came from deep in his chest. "Done wat I been doin' since I was a wee cub keeper: followed da nose of a jamba-bear. I've known jamba-bears ta smell ripe, red autumnberries 'alf a day away. Me an' Grief were paddin' along Smygler's Run when dat jamba-bear caught the filthy rot o' bane-elves. Their black mouths drool when they're huntin', makes 'em smell lak 'erring boiled in tar. Dat Grief came straight fer yer camp, crushin' everyt'ing in 'is path."

"So you were looking for us?" Ansgar asked.

"Aye, dat we were."

Suddenly a shrill cry of "*hallo the camp!*" rang out of the shadowed spaces between the oak trees. With it there was the loudening crash and clatter of metal on metal, staccato clops and strikes of hooves on stone and rooted forest floor, and snorts and gusts of winded horses. A blade-thin herald of no more than fifteen years, wearing the crimson colored coverlet of the Gate of the Deep, burst from out of the wooded darkness. He rode high on the bare withers of a delicately-shaped, dappled mare. "*Hallo the camp!*" he cried out again, the boy's face turned upward to project his tinny voice. Upon catching sight of Grief, he pulled hard at his reins with a startled look of fright. This caused his roan mare to turn sharply and nimbly drop her hindquarters, abruptly bringing them both to a full stop. The skinny boy's Adam's apple, a ludicrously enormous lump, bobbed up and down in his long neck. Clearing his throat with a whimper, he choked back his panic and shouted, "His Excellency, Lord Cadwallon!" The herald lay his right hand on his chest and bowed his head toward Ansgar, the most familiar looking person in the grove and certainly *not* a jamba-bear. With that, a party of roughly forty, sweat-drenched coursers and heavy destriers thundered into the middle of the small clearing.

In the midst of the war party, helmetless but arrayed in plate armor of blue steel, rode a lean, hawkish-looking man whose long, salt-grey hair—ashine with droplets from the morning's stewish fog—hung over his face like a bead curtain. The man tucked some of his hair behind his ear with a gauntleted hand, revealing a bony face half-mutilated by battle scars, including the skeletal cavity of an eye socket where his left eye had once been. Like a bird of prey, his head snapped back and forth allowing his remaining eye, an unfriendly orb of brown and yellow, to take in the scene around him. He rested his gaze a stroke longer on Nicolas than on the rest.

"Still alive, are you?" the man mused, his flinty voice almost unconcerned. The question was neither demanding nor curious.

Nicolas, unsure of what to say or how to say it, said nothing.

Lord Cadwallon, the War Marshal of the Second Grey Legion, a man whose sword had slain enemies of the First Kingdom for the past two-and-forty years stood high in his stirrups and looked away into the deep glooms of Wistman's Wood.

"Still alive," he repeated to himself, his voice harder but still indifferent. "Alive yet not long for the grave."

Minutes later mounted sentries had been posted in the trees, no more than a spear's length from the clearing's edge. These, somber, grim war-fighters all, covered in mud-spattered armor and boots but with spotless swords, axes, and lances. Riderless horses were picketed to nibble at tuffs of wood-sedge while several of the men-at-arm's piled together the fire's scattered embers and coals, threw fans of dead bracken and brushwood atop them, and encouraged the quickening curls of breeze to coax them it into a bright blaze. The eastern sky had sallowed into a sickly mottle of laurel green and dirty yellow, its bloated clouds flogged into long ranks of dark, storm furrows. The morning's dew shrank from the earth and the fog slunk away; it recoiled into low scrapes, dells, and dark gullies as if lying in wait for the passing of another salt-laced storm.

Nicolas, standing between Ansgar and Bardölf with hands out-stretched over the warming flames, watched Albrec make a few strange signs over Benjamin's forehead before leaving the snatcher-boy in Adelaide's care and joining the rest of them around the fire. He said nothing but caught Nicolas' eye; the tall man's lips were pressed tightly in pity and concern. He shook his head ever so slightly. Nicolas' insides were hollow and queasy; an enormous sense of loneliness, of helplessness. He couldn't help but think of home, of his mum and dad. He thought of Jack, of the Children's Ward in the Cumberland Infirmary. For a moment, he imagined rushing over to Benjamin, grabbing the small snatcher-boy and saying *don't go*. But he didn't. He just stood there, his feet lifeless weights. He felt sick and swallowed hard against the painful lump in his throat.

"Master Bennett," Lord Cadwallon said, his right eye sharp, his usually hard voice trimmed with uncharacteristic, ever-so-slight tenderness, "you *are* Nicolas Bennett, are you not? Yes? Good. Alright then. We have short work to do, Master Bennett, aye, we *all* do." The War Marshal's imperious voice now returned, his narrowed eye piercing each man round the fire. "'Twill be bloody chancy work, mind you! Work that's likely to find us all in worse shape than that boy lying over there near death; our toes pointed toward the endless heavens and tongues lollin' out of our mouths like old rope. But we'll do it all the same!"

The hawkish lord withdrew a small item, folded in a linen wrap, from inside his breastplate. "Days ago, I sent a coded warning to the Laird of St. Wulf's-Without-Aldersgate and warned him the Murder is *coming*. His raven brought this back to my field quarters last night." His long fingers unwrapped the linen gently as if something was alive inside its folds. He held out his hand. A leaf, a coppery leaf as thin as parchment paper, rested upon the linen alongside a small scroll tied with a black ribbon. Lord Cadwallon tucked the scroll between two fingers and stared at the strange leaf. "I've seen battles, wars, and blood, but I've—I've never seen an Eldur leaf separated from an Eldur tree before," he said, his voice thick and hoarse. The War Marshal tipped his hand and let the leaf fall unceremoniously into the fire. Ansgar and some of the men gasped in protest but the half-blind warlord raised a black, gauntleted hand, causing them to fall silent. At first, the leaf curled as if to burn but like a butterfly unfurling its wings to take flight, it suddenly swelled and fanned out, its veins and edges glowing with pulses and currents of strange light.

"Pull it out," he ordered but then kicked a man-at-arm's shin when the man moved to obey him. "Not you," he growled. "Him. Pull it out of the fire, *Master Bennett*."

Nicolas' mouth was bone-dry. He looked about and found a bent stick near his foot, and with it, raked the coppery leaf out of the coals. The leaf looked almost identical to the one he'd found so long ago. The leaf the crow had brought to his bedroom window, the leaf that had brought him to Telluric Grand the first time. He picked it up without thinking. It was warm like a kitten is warm, and although he couldn't have explained it, Nicolas thought the leaf felt alive.

Lord Cadwallon nodded his narrow head. "So *'tis* you," he said. "Can't say I've seen much stranger things than a boy who's a Dragon Nightfall," he corrected himself "a *Wren*, Lord Aldus wrote, a Dragon Nightfall *and* a Wren." He cocked his head: a rapacious bird-of-prey spying a field mouse. "And *are* you, Master Bennett? *Are* you those things?"

Something in the lord's voice smacked of danger, wariness. Nicolas looked from Albrec to Ansgar to Bardölf but they all just stared back at him. He looked at the peculiar leaf resting in the palm of his hand; its veins had somehow faded, had been absorbed, leaving a shiny, mirror-like surface, a surface in which he could see the vague reflection of his face. Nicolas looked older than he'd remembered looking. Perhaps not, perhaps only more careworn. "I—I am. I'm—I'm a Wren," he answered more to himself than to Lord Cadwallon, his unconvincing words hanging in the air like the remnants of a feeble echo. His mouth felt even drier than before.

The War Marshal's pitiless, yellow and brown eye glared at him for several, slow seconds. Finally, the hawkish man's thin lips curled into the scarred semblance of a horrid smile. He laughed a sharp laugh. "Well, then, *that* settles that. I'm too old and have given too much bone and skin to the battle's butcher to quibble 'bout whether a boy can kill a dragon." He paused and looked in the direction of the posted sentries. His cheeks dropped. He grasped both hands to the hilt of his long sword. As if a formal council of war had suddenly been convened in that forlorn clearing in Wistman's Wood, the War Marshal of the Second Grey Legion cleared his throat and threw his shoulders back. His voice became full of authority and power.

"I've defied the warrant of the High Chancellor! I've broken with my legion and have abandoned the lawful orders of my post. These men I've brought with me have done the same—others would have come but I forbade them to. Disgrace or no, my orders still carry the sentence of my sword, and they obeyed me." He smashed a clenched fist against his chest. "But *these*—these few have come; they've come freely to their own wreck and ruin, and they've done so with my blessing. They've done so based on the report I shared with them yesterday evening. The Murder is coming! My spies and those of Laird Halen have seen evidence of it, yet pleas for a change in our kingdom's stratagem have fallen on deaf ears." The War Marshal ground his teeth and spat into the fire. He looked savagely from man to man. "Something wicked eats at us from within, but by the endless heavens and the salt of the Cold Sea, I swear I'll not let that malignancy keep my sword dry in its scabbard! I've come to make war! I'll die with bloody feathers on my blade and Crows' flesh in my teeth if I must, but a plan we must have. Our own blood must buy as much death as we can manage. Then, perhaps, against all hope, with black ships filling the Bay of Wrath and the heart of the Second Grey Legion lying lifeless in the blood-soaked tide, will the High Chancellor relent and change his pigheaded mind. But to do this—to kill as many Crows as we can before we die—we *must* have a plan."

Lord Cadwallon grasped the small scroll he'd been holding and spread it open. "I've never known Laird Aldus to speak falsely or to offer empty advice, but it's the second part of his message that has been a puzzle to me, a greater puzzle even than how a boy came to be a Dragon Nightfall." Again, Nicolas heard something twist in the lord's voice, a slight change of key perhaps, suspicious and ugly. "But perhaps *you*, Master Bennett—*you* who seem to somehow be the key to this Crow's-rot of an unpleasant riddle, can shed some light on the rest of Laird Aldus' dark message."

Nicolas glanced round the forbidding circle of humorless and warlike men. They looked back with curiosity and demanding expectancy. Grim looks from hard men. "I'll do my best, sir."

"Good. That's good because the message sent by the Laird of St. Wulf's-Without-Aldersgate says, *Give them the Wren—Give them the 'orm of Crows.*"

Several minutes later, despairing minutes in which Nicolas had spoken rapidly, earnestly, but above all, without any shred of real hope, each face around the fire had become as cinder-grey as the ashes accumulating at their feet. He'd dutifully explained the plan as best he could; the plan Aldus had proposed before they'd left the Gate of the Deep. But without greater numbers from the Second Grey Legion, and with the most critical part of the plan still left unanswered, what was left of the scheme seemed to be in tatters, useless scraps of a daring, impossible strategy.

As Nicolas finished, he looked toward Adelaide and Benjamin. He hung his head. The young Healer had been bent closely over the snatcher-boy, shading his wilted body with her own. Nicolas could just perceive the slightest rise and fall of the boy's small chest. He couldn't tell if Adelaide was crying or quietly singing. As if she felt his eyes on her, she met his eyes. Her skin looked so pale, her lips full yet grey, and her scar a marble white accent of peculiar beauty. Without another thought, Nicolas moved as if to go to them, but Adelaide quickly held up her hand, stopping him where he stood. The young Healer closed her eyes, arched her back, and drew in a long, deep breath; strangely, as she did so, Benjamin also breathed in deeply. After several moments, she looked at Nicolas again. Her eyes were now as dark as coal but somehow lovely, too tender. "Go," she mouthed. "I must stay. *You* must *go*." Her slender finger pointed northward.

Nicolas, shivering with a chill, nodded. He turned back to the war council. Alone.

Lord Cadwallon, the storied War Marshal of the Second Grey Legion, exhaled loudly and broke the hangman's silence. "Well then," he said, his tone flat, dull, "we've all come too far, we're too committed, to turn craven and run like welps. Besides, there's nothing but a company of outlaws now standing round this cursed fire anyway: a blackfrock exiled from the City, a Throne Shield with a kingless throne, a dying boy, a Jamba keeper, and a War Marshal and his house guards who stand in violation of the High Chancellor's strict orders." The hawkish man drew his sword and held it close in front of his face, staring distractedly at the blade's scored edges. "Nothing left for any of us to do except arrange our souls among the stars."

A great shadow moved across the clearing. Whatever honest light the morning's sun had shared was now blotted out by rising ranks of impenetrable clouds. The approaching storm consumed the eastern sky.

The warlord's raptor-eye flashed cold and unyielding. His horrid, scarred smile returned. "Get the horses," he growled and spat. "We've Crows to kill."

CHAPTER 19

Worms for Crows

"Külon Tuz..."

The aged Laird of the First Gate and the greatest among the Commissioners of the six Forfeited Gates, had uttered those two words several nights before; he did this in a hushed, slow way, reflecting on each syllable as if to dislocate them from each other. "All of this," he sniffed, "... all of this began long years ago, Master Bennett. It began with the killing of the overlord dragon called Külon Tuz, or *Separate Fire*, by those who speak the common tongue; the creature was a second generation, overlord dragon, the corrupted offspring of that greatest of all evils, the first dragon, Komor Herceg."

The fire's flames failed. They slipped away under the blackened belly of a heavy bole of yew wood as if they'd been summoned back to an underworld. The room became gloomy.

Aldus Ward hunched over, huffing his long pipe until shifting ribbons of smoke encircled his head like white, gossamer snakes. The fire leapt bright again as the yew wood cracked in half as if a gate of the underworld had opened. The old man sniffed and sniffed again. "*That*—that ghastly *maggot* of a dragon is the same one known as the *Worm of Crows* by those murderous butchers from across the Cold Sea, from the Land Beyond the Fogs. To this day, they revere the beast and fear it at the same time. They believe it can reawaken or some awful lore like that.

"I think they desire more than the City of Relic, Nicolas; more than the First Kingdom. They want to find Külon Tuz, or whatever they think there's left of the damned thing, and they want to parley for its powers. You *do* remember, don't you, Nicolas? What I once told you about the history of dragons? Good then, smart lad. *We* must now use it against them. Invent armies where there are none, so to speak. *You* must help us use that foolishness against them. I have no one else. *We* have no one else." He fanned his bony hand toward the others. "They'll follow you, Nicolas! In spite of their doubts and fears, they'll follow you. They sense there's something more to you than what can be seen." The aged laird smiled a kind smile and chuckled. "You're a Wren after all." He sniffed yet again and blew his long nose into a kerchief that appeared from out of his sleeve. "Damnable damp in this damn place! Haven't any conceivable idea why Laird Halen doesn't keep a fire roaring brightly in every chamber," he said, cross. "Seems as if the mighty Laird of the sea prefers his saltwater cold."

Before all this, Nicolas and Aldus had been sitting silently in front of the fire for several minutes, each tending their own thoughts in silence. The others had since scattered themselves around the room on benches and the floor, wrapped within cloaks and blankets, meditating on what shortly lay before them; all but for Halen Ward who'd left for his own quarters in anger and disgust. "*That's* yer great scheme, is it, Aldus?!" he'd bellowed once Aldus had shared his plan with them, a plan for how they might destroy the Murder of Crows while they were still on the shingle beaches of the Bay of Wrath. "I'd rather us all be hacked to pieces under a Crow's axe on the walls of this gatekeep than to do what you've suggested! It'd be more merciful. I won't allow it!" Exasperated, Aldus had champed down on his pipe's stem, puffing furiously until a rosy blush glowed from within the pipe's bowl.

In truth it was, in every respect, a risky plan, and an incomplete one in its most important aspect; a plan none of them liked and about which all of them expressed snappish criticisms or nervous doubts.

Nicolas alone had sat there quietly, saying nothing.

Amid their protests, the Laird of the First Gate had hmphfed and frumped, becoming annoyed. Finally, he'd scathingly suggested, "you'd all just as well then find your own damnable corner and dream up your own damnable plot, or, by the endless heavens, make your own damnable peace with being food for Crows." At that moment a burst of high flame had flashed in the fire basket and his face, for a moment, seemed to lose its age. No one had said anything since.

Casting a clever eye toward the others, Aldus leaned toward Nicolas. His white beard draped the English boy's shoulder like a wispy December's snow, his voice conspiratorial. "They're all absolutely right, you know. Square as pegs. It's a stark-raving, mad plan. There's every estimation it could end in dreadful failure, *but*—but I also hope it can *work*, Nicolas. It must work! I've already sent word to Lord Cadwallon, and I've," Aldus abruptly paused; he looked as if he didn't quite know how to say what he wanted to say. "I've messaged another, as well. Another who can help us. But *you*, you and your companions, must do everything to make the War Marshal's camp as quickly as you can. Not a moment to lose. The Lord Cadwallon's a hard but sensible man. He'll see there's no other way, and most importantly, he'll bring some of his men with him—the more, the better, quite frankly, although I'm afraid not enough will come even if the entire legion left its post." Aldus Ward heaved a heavy sigh but sat up and squared his shoulders. "We must steal ourselves, Nicolas. We must hope against hope. We must lay our shoulders against the horse-less plow and together we must push. We must scrap; we must fight!" His eye was a brilliant blue, specked with amber and flashes of silver.

Nicolas sat there, muddling through everything. He wanted desperately for a surge of courage to course through him, for a wave of daring to move his heart. But none came. "So these other, these *other* dragons, then, the ones you mentioned earlier, the ones that're in some tunnel far beneath us," this he said almost soundlessly as if his words might pierce through stone and water and dark, "they're like that one from *before*? They're like that one I saw rip the bull apart? The one Remiel killed?"

Aldus suddenly seemed so ancient, weary. "Yes."

"Oh."

"They're like that one, Nicolas. It's what made them so horribly, mindlessly deadly on the Day of the Passage Tomb. A shocking and frightful day, that." The old man's voice blunted. He had no taste for what he was saying. "Only, only here, there are *three* of them, of course, and they're also," The august Laird of St. Wulf's-Without-Aldersgate winced and gripped his side as if recalling some long-obscured pain. Twisting, he desperately gripped Nicolas Bennett's knee. His brilliant, gold-flecked eye fastened on Nicolas' own. His breath expelled in ragged wheezes. "I shan't lie, my boy. I shan't tell you what you might want to hear. I shan't tell you you'll live, that *any* of you will live. These wicket-keepers, this brood of dragons, they're much bigger and faster, they *slither* in ways other dragons don't; wormish really, and above all else, they've been starved, they're *hungry*."

"Bearach!"

Lord Cadwallon's lean frame betrayed the raw force of his voice. He stood in his booted stirrups and shouted again over the heads of his men. "Bearach, damn you! Someone fetch that stuffed cloak-bag of ox guts and get him up here! Bearach, you fobbing, fat-fuddled scut! Get yer vile-smelling arse here now!"

The war party—all mounted but for Bardölf who, keeping with Grief's great ambling strides, trotted along at a surprising speed—had come to a stop within a half-moon circle of the tangled branches of several blackthorn trees. Nicolas could hear muffled laughter from several of the men-at-arms, each falling silent as a monstrous hulk of a man mounted atop a monstrous hulk of a warhorse, road slowly to the front of the column. What little armor he wore, a worn breastplate with riveted cracks, a loose steel collar, spaulders covering his immense shoulders, and greaves on each lower leg, was dented, scored, and spoiled with blots and stains of filth and rust. Ropes of dirty hair hung in uneven braids down his back. The spiraled locks of his beard were wild and frayed. The man's heavy arms were bare: swollen muscle of pulleys and cables that easily carried his great war-scythe. He reeked of acrid sweat, sour wine, and sour breath. Other men jostled to move out of his way as he rode toward Lord Cadwallon. Nicolas, for his own part, shivered as the man walked his horse slowly past him; Bearach's small eyes met his own and for what seemed like a long time, he could not look away.

"By the King's throne, Bearach! You're as fouled as a ship's biscuit after a year long's voyage." More muffled laughter.

The monstrous man grunted, blew his large nose, and smiled, not stupidly, but as one might do if the effort of forming words wasn't worth it. The insults were a friendly hail, a father's welcome.

"The widely admired Laird of the First Gate has a plan, Bearach. A plan! That one there," Lord Cadwallon pointed at long finger Nicolas, "has laid it out for us all like a platter of roasted boar ribs at a king's feast. As I see it, the Laird's devilish plan means we'll all end up as dead as cracked crabs on the sand!" Hoarse cheers went up from some of the hardest men. "We'll meet the cursed Crows as they ship their black boats on the shores of the Bay of Wrath. We'll stab and thrust and slash until we've killed a bellyful of Crows or until they've killed all of us!" More throaty cheers mixed with guttural curses. The likelihood of death had a strange, seductive certainty to it; a bizarre sense of touting a life lived by how fiercely it would end.

Bearach grunted again, this time in agreement. He looked over his shoulder at the War Marshal's company, his malodorous smile wide, his eyes cruel and narrow. The men huzzahed and hailed their company's most infamous, savage warrior.

The hawkish Lord Cadwallon grinned meanly, warming to the barbarity of his own words. "Death! You're made for *death*, Bearach! I've seen you skin the faces of northern orcs, rip apart the jaws of fenris wolves, gut bane-elves like bloated fish, and cleave the skulls of their great boars as if cracking walnuts!" Shields were thumped in praise. "And *you*, Bearach, my outlaw champion, my glutton for blood and war, are needed again today! Death needs you today!" More swords and axes struck shields. Hoarse cries of *Bearach*! *Bearach*! rolling up and down the column.

The War Marshal of the Second Grey Legion waited for the salutes of his men to die down. Silence would build and shape the words to come. "But *you'll* not be on the beach, my old friend," he continued in a low, grave voice. "You'll not be there to kill any Crows." He paused, looking over his entire company. "You'll not die among us."

Men-at-arms nearest their lord leaned forward to catch these last, rushed words. There followed a murmuring, confusion, and some sense of betrayal among the war party. "You'll stand *alone*, my ruttish oath-of-toad! Alone but for three, very devilish, very quick, *dragons*." Every man's murmuring stopped as if the wind had died.

Lord Cadwallon's decision had been made.

The bait was to be Bearach.

Bearach's war scythe swung loosely in his hand. His shaggy head moved slightly, weighing his odds. "'Tis a foolish waste, m'lord."

"I know."

"I'll be dead as soon as dat damn gate es open."

"I know."

The war scythe stopped swinging. Bearach grunted and spat onto the trunk of a blackthorn tree. He shook his head. There was absolute silence. "An' after I'm dead, after I'm in da belly o' one o' dem dragōns, who's gonna make de dragōns go to de beach?"

Lord Cadwallon glowered at the great war-fighter. His armor-jointed hand gripped the handle of his sword. Even with wits a bit duller than most, Bearach had hit upon the most singular, fatal flaw in Aldus' plan; and the monstrous man had said it aloud, he'd said it as a challenge. Bad enough that someone, anyone, should be sacrificed just to open the drain's gate. Bad enough to think of those wormish demons pouring out of that dark, forgotten hole, but once loosed, there was no way to drive them along Gimbol's Gutter, no way to force them onto the beaches below the cliffs, no way to steer them against the oncoming tide of War Crows.

To deliberately release the dragons, to do it knowing they might turn and wreck disaster on the gatekeep or tear ravenously into the exposed countryside, shredding, slashing, mauling, and devouring. 'Twas a fatal flaw, utter madness. Madness against which Laird Halen had cursed, madness that had eaten away at what little hope there was, madness the hawkish War Marshal of the Second Grey Legion could see coming even without both his eyes. Yet what else was there to do? With the City's Grey Legions scattered throughout the kingdom, distracted and unfocused, doom was fast riding the tides to the shores of the Bay of Wrath whether by the claws and teeth of dragons or by the axes and war hammers of Crows. At least there *was* a plan. However thin a chance it had to work, it was *something*, and for Lord Cadwallon, a man of action, of melee and blood and death, it was better than wasting in camp with the arrows of War Crows in his back.

"Damn yer eyes, Bearach! You'll ride up that bloody ravine and you'll unloose those bloody demons or die trying! Those profane spawn of Separate Fire *will* smell blood, I tell you—*Crow's* blood; they'll hear swords on shields and screams of dying men. They'll *come*, Bearach." Lord Cadwallon stood in his stirrups and turned. "They'll come, damn you!" he roared out over the heads of his men. "They'll come, and while we wait, we'll do some *killin'* of our own and then we'll do some *dyin'*. We'll hold that black-winged excrement on the beach and wait for those dragon dogs to lay waste to 'em!"

A keening wind snapped among the branches. Horses' hooves stamped impatiently but aside from this, Nicolas heard not a sound. Nothing from the assembled men. No beating of shields, no boasting, no dark oaths sworn by warriors-come-to-battle, nor salutes to their martial lord.

"I've my family livin' outside the City's walls." Finally, a cautious voice, an anonymous voice venturing from somewhere at the back of the column.

"Mine, too," came another, bolder, closer to the front. "My missus an' boy are alone. What of them?!"

"Crows at our fronts an' dragons at our backs!" Another even closer.

"Madness!" cried one more.

Hear, hear! others barked as Doubt and Uncertainty hissed nervous babble into the men's ears. Like a wound's sharp stabs of pain, genuine dread and rebellion lay not far behind.

The lean warlord sat there, bracing himself against the grumblings and outbursts for several more seconds, a black look on his face deepening; he waited for there to be a sufficient weight of shame. "Damn yer eyes! Damn yer eyes an' curse upon you all!" His harsh words knocked down the protests in mid-sentence. "Shame upon you all! Shame upon the Hand-from-the-Deep. Shame upon this Legion! I see nothing but a gaggle of toothless hags and nursery wags where men-at-arms should be. This is a black-mark day for the City. A black-mark day for the First Kingdom, that its legionnaires should shy from a fight out of fear."

Heads quickly hung in awkward embarrassment. Hard-bitten war-fighters who'd faced countless foes together but who'd now shuddered at the thought of claws and teeth and hot breath slicing through flesh, fell silent. Silent except one.

"'Tis not fear, m'lord. Them dragons, them dragons will look to take lambs; they'll not seek out rams wit' 'orns. Why should they come to the beach where they know spears an' knives an' arrows await them? Why should they not fly into the countryside?" This stubborn question remained, and the man who spoke, an older, grizzled warrior who had long served as Lord Cadwallon's first aide-de-camp, spoke it in earnest, each word deliberate with counsel, not tinged by panic or reluctance. The old soldier wasn't afraid to die, only afraid to fail, afraid that his lord would fail, to die uselessly, overwhelmed by Crows, waiting for a reinforcement that would never come.

Lord Cadwallon glowered at his secondary. He wrenched the reins inside clenched fists and opened his mouth.

"I'll do it!"

No one moved. As if a headstrong pupil had spoken out of turn, all eyes,wide, expectant, waiting for sure-to-come wrath, remained on the interrupted War Marshal.

"I'll do it," Nicolas repeated.

He was seated behind the Marshal's skinny herald, astride the other boy's dappled mare. Nicolas could hear the boy gasp and could sense him tensing, stiffened against the inevitability of his lord's angry response. Nicolas, however, plunged ahead. "I think there's a way to draw those dragons through the gorge and onto the beach."

Lord Cadwallon, along with every man in the war party, slowly turned his full attention to Nicolas. His yellow-brown eye narrowed; it was dour and cold, the scars on his face discolored in a flush of aggravation. His words dripped sarcasm. "You'll do *what*, boy?"

"I'll unlock the gate. I'll make sure the dragons go to the beach."

There was muttering along the column and one or two choked laughs.

"Would you, now?" The War Marshal of the Second Grey Legion settled in his saddle, a strange blood-lust filling his single eye. "Then enlighten us, *boy*. Since we're to commit ourselves into your all-wise surety, pray tell us: what splendid scheme would a *Dragon Nightfall* possibly possess that might spool three, frenzied dragons along a stony gorge and into a killing field?"

"I have a plan, sir, but I'm not sure… Well, I'd like to see the gorge first if I may. I'll need a horse, too; a fast one preferably." In hushed tones, Nicolas explained what he was thinking.

Lord Cadwallon never lifted his low stare. Long moments stretched by. The wind mounted as the War Marshal's mind wheeled shrewdly behind his eye. "Bearach," he said.

"Yes, sire?"

"Bearach, take Master Bennett into the Gutter by way of the Trench. See that he finds his way to the grate beneath the keep's southern wall. Do what he says. I'll broke no defiance, Bearach; you'll do as ordered. Seems this boy has a *plan.* A plan inside a plan… he's more daring than any man-jack-of us."

With that the Marshal of the Second Grey Legion once again stood high in his stirrups. His rabid eye flashed toward the eastern sky. Hair beating in the wind, a black banner's ribbon of reckless valor, his voice was gravelly and hard. "Blow your horns and ride with me! If not to life, then to legend! Level your blades and let those who eat and drink tonight do it with songs of you on their lips! The storm comes and Murder comes with it!"

Like a wolf hound he was away through the trees, his heeled dogs of war close behind him.

"I'll do it."

Those three words, repeated over and over again, had been clattering around inside Nicolas' head like loosed ballast stones until the moment he'd dismounted, picketed the dappled mare, and cautiously rounded the last, man-size boulder, coming face-to-face with the tunnel's enormous maw.

"Stone the crows, it stinks!"

Nicolas had caught the tunnel's smell long before; the same sulphuric, blistered stench that had engulfed him the night he spent in the passage tomb, the night he'd unknowingly spent lying just above the fetid breath and depravity of three, trapped, wicket-keeper dragons.

The tunnel's half-hidden entrance, which served as an outlet for the monstrous drain running far beneath the southern wall of the Gate of the Deep, was shut fast by a wrought grate of thick iron bars, its metal discolored and filthy, corroded and unwell, slick with stinking mold and scaled with large scabs of weeping rust. Nicolas counted no less than half-a-dozen giant, black slugs. Evil-looking worms, none less than six inches in length, clinging to its latticework, feeding on its mildew and rot. Several of the grate's bolts were loose or missing as was one of the great hinges that had once been anchored deep in the rock casing. The remaining hinge along with an alarmingly decayed lock-bar appeared to be all that held the grating in place.

"I'll do it," Nicolas whispered again, grim. A cold, grave-like stillness settled inside his chest.

He looked around and found a stone about the size of a rugby ball. Taking in a deep breath, he smashed the stone down against the grate's lock-bar. Sparks flew and the jarring noise echoed crazily among the boulders in the gorge. Nicolas did this several times, each time holding his breath in a suspended, clenched panic, awaiting some dreadful sound from far within, but none came. After a time, the weakened bar gave way, its clasp bolts snapping like rotted twigs. Nicolas, gasping and light-headed, pulled at the grate, but it still didn't move.

He fixed a firm foot against the outer rock casing and, for reasons beyond his understanding, yelled, "*Death is coming!*" which excited a fresh swell of panic in his chest as he threw his full weight backward. Again, the grate refused to move. "Death is coming!" he grunted again, and again and again he heaved against its iron bars. The metal whined and complained but would not move. The last, unbroken hinge, unyielding in its own decay, kept the grate tightly shut.

Out of breath, Nicolas' heartbeat thumped madly inside his ears; his arms were like rubber and the burn of the tunnel's corrosive air had made his eyes bleary. He collapsed to the ground and looked up. The sky was heavy, a blurry wash of leaden clouds, whipped white haze with black streaks. His hands began gathering bits and bobs of rock and pebble and arranging them in a precise order. *Now what?* The boy from Plumpton Head thought, choked with distress and anger. *They'll be dying on the beach and I can't get the bloody gate to open!*

Still panting, Nicolas pushed himself to his knees and stood up.

It was then he noticed a small thornbush a few yards off to the left of the tunnel's grate. Like the Glastonbury thorn in Somerset once was, it was a scrappy thing with a smallish crown of bent sticks and grasping shoots sprouting from a knotty trunk of dull bark with carroty cracks. Much to Nicolas' surprise, in a place full of stone and stench and death, the thorn tree stood in full bloom, ornamented with petite flattish flowers, each with five white petals. A mottled assortment of small, weathered rags were tied to its many branches; the sight caused Nicolas to think of some old, tattered beggar leaning on a stick, and he stood there, childishly watching as the rags flickered and flapped in whips of wind blustering down the Gutter, 'til a bit of living activity caught his eye. There was a skipping, hopping movement as if on cue, an actor had hopped onto stage out from leg curtains made of cloths and twigs.

Along the length of a stooped branch appeared a large-ish and strangely familiar bird with grey-brown upperparts and dark spots across its chest and belly. It cocked its head, peering at Nicolas with shiny russet eyes before letting out an abrupt, loud song peppered with fluted squawks. Lingering echoes bounced off surrounding boulders in slow delays as if the boy and bird stood inside the domed mausoleum of the Dukes of Hamilton.

Having sung its brief hymn, the thrush seized at a shabby, blue-green rag near its feet, jerking and pulling and wrenching, until the rag came free and fluttered to the ground. The bird glanced at the fallen rag, then at Nicolas, and repeated all of this several times. Like a thundercrack, it hit Nicolas, *untie one, ya bloody wazzock*, so he did. He gave his fussy guide a sidelong peek while reaching for a nearby strip of scarlet cloth. The thrush gave a vigorous bob of its head and snatched at another rag. Together they worked, fingers, claws, and beak flying along, creating a large pile of messy cloth at Nicolas' feet.

"Now what?" Nicolas asked.

The mistle thrush glared at him and with a beat of its wings landed near the rag pile. As neat as a pin, it began arranging the scraps of fabric into a long line.

Nicolas snapped his fingers. "Well aren't you a clever clogs!" He beamed and leapt to the front of the line, tying the rags end-to-end. Before long, he had something like a rope in his hands, and with a resourceful thought about the ploughman's ox on Mousecatcher Lane, scrambled away to fetch his horse. After double-knotting the clumpy rope to the iron grate, Nicolas made it fast to the mare's saddle, whispering to the horse with a level of calmness that surprised him. "I owe because I'm free, dolly, and *that's* that." The mare looked at him with her large, brown eyes and pushed her soft muzzle against his hand. He smiled. "And *that's* that," he said again, swinging himself onto her back.

The thrush, curiously familiar, had since recovered its perch in the thornbush.

"Magnus!" Nicolas shouted with joy, remembering. "Magnus Mungo Macaroobie! Is it really you, you ol' codger?"

The thrush angled its head as if thinking, pecked at the branch beneath its feet, bowed, and with its head kept low did an odd shuttle backward, disappearing behind branches, blooms, and prayer rags.

"Say hello to Baatunde!" Nicolas called after it, feeling all the brighter inside, a long-sought sense of belonging and certainty washing over his heart.

These past eleven years an' a day, I've been waitin' fer you, Nicolas. The boy could hear the stout little man's voice and the silver bells chiming at the braided ends of the Caledonii's long moustache. His mind's eye could see the odd, little treehouse in the woods, he could smell the potatoes, sweet onions, tiny leaves of thyme, and bacon gravy, and of course he could feel the rough metal of the small, iron door. *Ye are* where *yer supposed ta be an'* when *yer supposed ta be… an' when ye return*, Baatunde had kindly said, *I'll be 'ere, an' Magnus will be 'ere*, this followed by silence. Then, and now, *What do ya say, lad?*

I'm a wren, was Nicolas' simple reply. *I'm a wren.*

He squared his shoulders and looked ahead, mapping his way among the boulders, away from the tunnel's grate and down the curving neck of Gimbol's Gutter. Nicolas tapped his heels against the mare's flanks and tensed when she sprang forward. The rag-rope snapped taut, jerking at the saddle beneath him, straining, stubbornly holding, and then at last came the shrill shrieks and shivers of chafing, rasping metal, twisting, turning, barking. The pin of the rusted hinge splintered, and with a crack of breaking bone the grate suddenly shot free, clanking noisily behind them across stone and shingle, leaving gobbets of jellied slugs in its path.

Nicolas pulled back on the reins and looked behind him. A gratified smile spread across his sweat-stained face. He'd done it. The horrid drain now stood open, and in the queering light of the storm-sky, it looked like the yawning mouth of a blind corpse. A trickle of black ooze wept from its lower lip.

For the first time, an unwell sound came from deep within its shadowy throat. A faint and miserable sound. Then another. Drowsing whines. Spitting. Cold teeth grinding and gritting against each other. Long, hooked claws scratching and scraping against cracked and fetid rock. Cruel hissing.

For a moment, the darkness lay hushed and the wind died.

Gimbol's Gutter held its foul breath.

Then, like the ripping and tearing of gristle and flesh, there came a loud, fleshy sound, the wrenching chafe of stirring bodies. Huge, slippery bodies, bloated, discolored. Colossal maggots worming feverishly from out of a greasy carcass; three, hideous wicket-keeper dragons, depraved beasts of grief and violence and ruin. Nicolas had seen such a dragon a year before on the rainswept heights of the Timekeeper's Finger, seen what destruction such a beast could do, how it slashed and tore and devoured. Everything in him turned small and terrified.

His smile now gone, his eyes filled with alarm and dread, Nicolas bucked his heels hard at the mare's belly and threw his shaking arms round her graceful neck. He pressed his face against her warm, earthy coat.

"Death is coming!" he shrieked madly into her mane. "Death is coming!"

And it was.

The dappled mare's first nimble hoof-falls saved them.

Like a fox before the hounds, she sprang into full flight, bounding deftly between giant steles of ancient stonework and vaulting over a battered deadfall that blocked their way. The grate, clanging behind them, held them back for but a moment. A fouled anchor caught in the cleft of a split rock but she heaved her chest against it and the rag-line snapped.

Coming clear of the rubble, the first three furlongs of the Gutter's floor ran steep yet smooth, scoured by years of storm wash. Avoiding scattered patches of grit, the mare's dark grey hooves found good, stony footing. She practically flew down the course of balded rock as if racing lead at the St. Leger Stakes in South Yorkshire. With ears laid back, neck arched and legs stretched out in a flat dash, the smallish horse made short work of those first six hundred yards. Those first twenty seconds when, given the violence of the tortured uproar behind them, Nicolas were sure they were lost. Food for dragons.

The mare's swift strides were long and even, rhythmic, but even so, the thought of falling from the saddle evoked a nightmare of horrible consequences. In a fit of terror he'd only once known, Nicolas clenched his arms about her neck, heedless of the painful flogs of wind and mane thrashing his face. He tucked his chin and shut his eyes, letting the horse have her head, even as a knot of fear in his throat willed her to run faster. The sounds close behind them were an abomination: ravenous slavering, spitting, hissing, the gnashing and grinding of countless teeth, and the rasping and chafing of slithering, sinister bodies.

Nicolas' plan, the plan now working so well, had been a simple one.

Bearach would lead Nicolas down through the "Trench" and into the gorge before retreating back out again; he would then take a position atop the lip of the root and earth entanglements that covered the Gutter's tail as it dove beneath Wistman's Wood, burrowing its dark way to the shores of the Cold Sea. The great warrior would wait there to rendezvous with Nicolas and to post a last-stand defense should the War Crows overwhelm Lord Cadwallon's company on the beach too quickly. Nicolas would make his way to the tunnel's grate as the War Marshal's herald would ride a pack pony in haste for the old watch tower atop the Rat Catcher's crag. If all went to plan, Nicolas would open the grate releasing the dragons and use himself and the mare as bait to draw them down the ravine. When passing the Rat Catcher, he would signal the herald who would mirror-signal Bearach nearly a thousand yards away. Swiftly, word would be passed along to the men fighting on the beach to let them know the dragons were coming. Until then Lord Cadwallon's small company would have to batter themselves against the landing War Crows. A brutal sacrifice for the sake of trickery. Once the signal had been passed, those still alive would feign defeat and fall back to the hollow where Gimbol's Gutter emptied onto the shoreline, doing their best to find shelter among the black, sea-soaked roots on its outer edges. By then the dragons would be rushing out of that miserable hole and everything, and every*one*, in their path would be killed and consumed, friend or foe alike. With the blessing and favor of the endless heavens, Nicolas' plan would lure the War Crows into the hungry jaws of doom.

Without praise or censure, the scarred War Marshal of the Second Grey Legion had listened silently as Nicolas had laid out his plan; there had been a strange look in the man's eye, Nicolas couldn't tell if it was admiration or sadness. Ansgar and Albrec argued to stay with Nicolas, but after realizing their axe and war bow would be put to better use amid the fighting on the beach, they both laid grave hands on Nicolas' shoulders, conveyed their brief goodbyes in silence, and rode after the War Marshal's company on borrowed steeds, Bardölf and the giant Grief loping along by their side.

Thus far, Nicolas' gamble had worked.

As the Gutter bent its course to the southeast, coming even with the Rat Catcher's watchtower, Nicolas turned his head and hoarsely screamed a warning to the herald. He and the roan mare had gained some little distance from the dragons but he dared not sit up and risk loosening his grip around her neck. Afraid his shout wouldn't be heard or understood, he looked over his shoulder, but a split second later there came the flicker of silvered light reflecting off the herald's polished buckle. The warning was being passed to Bearach!

As Nicolas and the mare fled down the last open bit of the Gutter, its smooth floor turned more skittish, shingled with splinters of stone and flotsam from seasonal, high tides. The mare's hooves slipped and skidded as they raced on, but the game horse kept her head, snorting and champing her way through each dodgy step. The slender opening for the Trench came in sight and just beyond it the baleful maw where the Gutter thrust below tree roots and into the earth.

Somehow, even above the dreadful clamoring behind him, Nicolas could hear the vague shouts, screams, and curses of men fighting on the beach ahead of him. With luck, Lord Cadwallon and his men should be collapsing back to the Gutter's seaside opening. Buried deep under the choking terror in his throat and tightened chest, Nicolas felt the slightest stir of hopefulness. Within the next minute the three, pitiless dragons would be vomiting out of the Gutter and onto the beach, seizing and consuming the unsuspecting War Crows, wolfing them down as snakes among chicks.

Nicolas only needed to get out of their way.

In a few seconds, he and the mare would dart back up the narrow Trench as the wicket-keepers swept by into the Gutter's underground burrow. By that time, the irresistible smell of blood and butchery on the beach would have replaced Nicolas for bait.

But it was here, with the sudden, sick despair of a soldier who unexpectedly sees death coming, that everything went terribly, terribly wrong.

Trying to make a sharp turn, the mare's hooves began skating across a loose sheet of scree and small bits of driftwood. Her momentum and loss of footing nearly threw her onto her shoulder. She scrambled and kicked powerfully to regain her grip, lurching hard to the left and right. This caused Nicolas to lose his hold round her neck. He snatched wildly for mane or saddle or rein, but everything escaped his hands. For a moment, he tossed roughly about on the mare's back, until his chest slammed against her sharp withers, knocking the wind from his lungs. A heavy lifelessness flooded into his arms. As if a curse had somewhere been whispered against him, in a dreamlike moment of disbelief, near hysterical with fright, Nicolas, the once-Wren and Dragon Nightfall, fell heavily to the ground. The dappled mare continued on, galloping up the Trench without him.

Sorely bruised and alone on the stony ground, Nicolas suddenly thought of Jack. He could see his brother, sitting on the floor of the Bennett's living room, pretending everyone else were giants. Jack, laughing and bright, even in the Children's Ward. Nicolas wished Jack was there. Wished he was there, hand-in-hand, to show him how to be brave, how to be still and at peace, because in that peculiar, fleeting moment of time, Nicolas knew he was going to die.

"Nicolas? Nicky? You awake?"

It was Jack's voice. As sure as if he was there, it was Jack's voice. Nicolas closed his eyes and could see him; it was one of his favorite memories, one he often thought of when he felt overwhelmed. Jack would be lying on his stomach in the Bennett's living room, the evening's light shadowing his slim face, looking up at Nicolas who'd inevitably fallen asleep on the settee. It'd be one of those days when nothing was on the telly and their mum and dad would be cooking dinner and reading the newspaper. Jack would have opened his favorite book, a birthday gift from Grandfather Bennett; a worn-out, first edition hardback with the original price of *£3.50 net* stamped at the bottom of the jacket's inside front flap. "A book about rabbits," Jack would simply say with a playful grin and away he'd go, leading the boys' imaginations through dark warrens, over sun-cast hillocks, and along banks of chalk streams until the rhythm of his gentle narration would lull Nicolas to sleep.

"You awake?" Jack would eventually ask, knowing well his younger brother was asleep. Nicolas would stammer out a groggy objection but would struggle to wake up; Jack always woke him for their favorite part.

"They're about to bring the dog, Nicky," he'd say, eagerly rubbing his hands together.

"Why do you like that book so much?" Nicolas had once asked after the good rabbits had yet again thwarted the much more powerful bad rabbits.

Jack had shut the book and rolled over onto his back to stare at the ceiling. "I wish I was a rabbit, I suppose. Running about, havin' adventures, an' usin' my brains to outsmart everything else. I guess I also like when the weaker ones beat out the stronger ones." He'd held his slender arms above his head and turned his thin hands back and forth.

"I like that, too." Nicolas had balled his fists and scrunched his nose, "but I wouldn't need no dog to do it. I woulda boxed that general rabbit 'til the ol' wally cried."

"Aha, my Lord Wellington the pugilist!" laughed his father, who'd just walked in to tell them dinner was set. A plate of Mrs. Bennett's Cornish pasties, a recipe from her mother's side of the family that Mr. Bennett uniquely enjoyed with a large spoonful of clotted cream. "To be sure, strength is good when it's there, Nicolas, but Jack's book reminds me of something your grandfather always said about one of England's greatest battles—one where strength and heart wasn't quite enough. 'The English brought the arrows, but God brought the mud,' he'd say. Using yer brawn as well as yer wit is like bringing the arrows *and* the mud, my boy. And I agree with ya both," he'd said with a grin and a wink. "I like the weaker ones beatin' out the stronger ones, too. Now go wash up!"

Now, in this most awful moment, Nicolas thought of Jack, laying on the floor with his book, his grey eyes twinkling as the farmer's dog flew amongst the bad rabbits, confounding them in terror and disarray. It was, after all, that very memory which had given Nicolas his own plan.

And every time Jack had read the story to him, Nicolas had been afraid the dog would catch the rabbit.

"Get up!"

A deep voice boomed above him like the shock of close thunder.

"Get up!"

The boy from England looked up and there, swaying several feet above his head, was Bearach's great war scythe—the sickle of a tusk moon come to take him home to the endless heavens.

The brutish man's small eyes, however, weren't looking at Nicolas. They were staring out beyond him, crazed with blood-lust, fight, and battle. "Grab dee handle!" He bellowed, his eyes never straying from the horror rushing down on Nicolas.

So Nicolas leapt up and grabbed it.

Up he swung with dirt, mud, and the hoary roots of alder trees in his face.

And after him came the scissoring jaws of the first wicket-keeper dragon, the quickest of Komor Herceg's terrible watchdogs, the dragon's slathering tongue flickering between cruel teeth, sensing Nicolas' sweat, his fear and terror. Like its brothers, the dragon's skin, a stretched, scaleless, rubbery membrane, was blanched a watery pallor from long years without sun; its slitted eyes were waxen and nearly blind, unused even to the ashen light of a storm sky. The beast's thin hide had shriveled away from great daggers of its claws, those long, cruel carving knives it had stropped against dark, wet stone for ages. As the monster sprang toward Nicolas, its nostrils flared with rabid memories of pulped man-bones. Ruddy chunks of scarlet flesh and mangled armor. This morsel of meat dangling above it was somehow familiar in its smell. A recent scent that excited the dragon's appetite to a feverish pitch. The smell of sleepy, unaware bait.

Nicolas, whether in terror or shock, never looked down.

Instead, as Bearach pulled him upward, the grotesque head of a War Crow suddenly appeared in front of him. It took Nicolas a disturbing second to realize the Crow's head was disembodied, the grisly remains of a sneaking scout whose last view had been light flashing off the blade of the legionnaire's war scythe. Bearach held the macabre thing in his other hand as he lifted Nicolas to the forest floor, and when the wicket-keeper's gaping mouth was mere inches away, he hurled it at the dragon. Like an enormous asp striking at prey, the creature's pitted tongue darted out, curled around the Crow's head, and sucked it inside its hideous mouth.

The distraction took just long enough.

The other two dragons, one a fattish worm that fed on giant shrews scraped out of the drain's damp walls, the other a nasty whip that had attempted on more than once occasion to eat its fattish brother, arrived and slammed into the lead wicket-keeper, biting and snapping at its pallid haunches, enraged with a hunger now turned mad by the strong blood-smell drifting up through the Gutter's dark burrow. Roaring, the three beasts slashed and tore viciously at each other, but their brawl soon gave way to the insatiable craze of hunger. Fresh meat to be eaten.

Streaming strips of ripped and bloody skin, mindless of pain or threat, the three plunged into the burrow beneath Wistman's Wood.

Nicolas had been forgotten.

CHAPTER 20

Some Corner of a Foreign Field

For quite some time, Nicolas lay there alone.

After making sure he was unharmed, Bearach had run through the woods to the beach to join his comrades, but Nicolas stayed where he was, his mind descending into a deep pool of emptiness. He felt disconnected from his body, from the smell and sight of the dark trees about him, and from the distant cries and screams of dying men. As if submerged beneath water, he gazed vaguely up at the muted haze of storm clouds overhead and he didn't notice the drumming of heavy raindrops on his skin.

He was alive.

He wasn't supposed to be, but he was.

His fall from the horse and the certain realization he was about to die had left Nicolas dazed and in a strange dreamlike place. Every so often, his body would shudder. His breath was shallow. His mind wandered. Through shadowy mists, over stormy bluffs, inside dark burrows and down forest paths. Benjamin, Adelaide, and Ranulf wandered with him. And there was Jack dressed in some silly lamb's wool jacket—waving, beckoning, then fading.

Time passed. The sky drove its cloud flock across the heavens. The light changed and the rain lessoned to dull plops and splashes.

Nicolas rolled over onto his knees, gripped a thick, wet root, and shook his head like a waking sheepdog. With his feet leaden and dragging, his mind restless. Nicolas forced himself through the few hundred yards of woods until he stood on a low bluff above the Bay of Wrath.

What he saw was unlike anything Nicolas had ever imagined.

Here, the beachhead was narrow, a bony strand of black sand strewn with tumbled rock, water-logged debris, and driftwood. Past the first line of green-grey breakers the water became particularly dark, dropping abruptly into a channel ideal for deep-hulled smugglers' cruisers or, as it was that day, a fleet of tar-black longboats. It was these Nicolas first noticed as he came to the edge of Wistman's Wood.

The longboats, each able to carry fifty War Crows, were a jumbled mess in violent disarray. More than half had been capsized, their carved, black sterns propped high above the cresting waves, looking much like ill-fated remnants of a drowned forest, or their upturned, tarred bellies bobbed low in the water like a plague of dead frogs; others had been outright smashed with little left to resemble what they'd been: masts askew, feathered sails in rags, hulls ruptured, and oars splintered into bits of tender. A handful had escaped noticeable harm but these drifted about stupidly, lengthwise to the roll of the surf, no hand on their rudders, no pilot in their prow. These longboats were the first dead Nicolas saw.

After that, he noticed the bodies.

Those afloat in the surf didn't look at all like men. They were drowned birds, hacked and chewed into bizarre lumps of feather, bone, and water-grey flesh. They rose and fell with the swell of the sea, a gruesome litter of limp refuse. Those who'd died onshore were even worse. Chunks and pieces here and there, bright splashes of meat and white sinew, unrecognizable and ghastly, scattered among ragged banners, discarded war hammers, and useless axes. Had it only been dead War Crows, Nicolas would have stayed where he was. But there were more.

His eye caught flashes of light.

The dying sun had found a hole in the clouds. Its lean rays glimmered off the polished shields, swords, and helmets of Lord Cadwallon's men. Their instruments of war were clustered like sets of jewels accidentally dropped in the black sand, and their bodies were among them, pierced and pricked with long, dark arrows, cut and hewn by Crow blades. The legionnaires had drawn together, back-to-back against the clay and chalk cliff, fighting to stay alive until the dragons came. Few had survived.

Looking almost straight down, Nicolas could see Bearach, battle-stained and gritty, with a thick arm around his lord, pushing the War Marshal's bloody hair out of his face, both of the hawkish man's eyes forever fixed in the blindness of death. The small number who survived were scattered about, comforting injured comrades or on bent knees, eyes vacant with numbness, looking out to sea, to the scoured, grey sky far to the east.

Far down the strand, Nicolas spotted some grotesque movement, a strange whale or scaleless fish washed ashore, he thought for a moment, and then heard several horrible, sharp shrieks; one of the dragons, the fattish one, was taking its time, snipping cruelly at the War Crows who'd managed to flee down the shoreline until the land ran out. The corpulent worm slithered greedily after the handful who flung themselves into the water, finally disappearing beneath the greasy surface like a leviathan returning to the deep. The other two wicket-keepers, having glutted themselves on the crowds of men near the burrow's opening, had pitched into the waves, chewing through those who had tried to swim back to their boats, and turning finally to the boats themselves, ripping them open like cans full of feathered sardines. The Cold Sea, full of dark life and great pools of fresh blood, felt natural to them. After a last great breach above the water, the dragons vanished into the deep.

As Nicolas' gaze ran back over the killing field, his heart seized.

A man in a long, black cloak was kneeling over a smallish-looking War Crow. The man's axe lay in the sand by his side, his hand was on the Crow's chest. But it wasn't a Crow at all.

"Ranulf!" Nicolas screamed and scrambled down over root and rock, half-falling, half-running to get to his friend.

A red bloom was spread across the bladesmith's chest.

Ranulf was dressed in a War Crow's cloak of black feathers and a jerkin of black leather, and his bright blood shimmered over wing and cloth. Albrec, who glanced up briefly at Nicolas, a vicious cut on the left side of his head which caused half his face to be covered in a phantom-mask of blood smear, leapt up, his teeth clenched in a grim line. "Death's among us all, but this boy might yet live." Catching his axe in hand, the tall man sprinted away for help.

Nicolas dropped beside his friend.

"Ranulf?" he whispered.

The bladesmith opened his eyes. They were dull, their color washed-out with hurt and the dim reflection of the grey skies above. Each were purpled and bruised, yet pinched comically at their corners as the older boy's face broke into a pained grin.

"Nicolas," he said, coughing. "Nicolas? Is it you? You've come then?"

"Yes, yes, I've come, but why're you here? What—what happened?"

"Why'm I here?" The older boy lifted his head off the sand but let if fall back heavily. Streaks of rain washed some of the grime and sand from his face. He laughed feebly. "I'm here to see *you* again, Nicolas Bennett. Didn't seem right any other way really… Besides," Ranulf wheezed and his throat burbled with a moist cough. Pale fizzes of blood settled in the corners of his mouth. "Aldus asked if… if I would…" He reached out with a gore-stained hand but it also fell back to the sand. His face turned pale, his voice steady but bleak. "He asked if I would help."

Nicolas, scooping up his friend's hand, squeezed it between his own. The older boy's hand was slippery, heavy, cold.

"Help?"

Ranulf smiled wanly and gave him an absurd wink. "Trick 'em, Nicolas. Convince 'em to land here instead of further south." A haggard wheeze came again and the older boy winced as he coughed. "'Twasn't easy. Had to kill a Crow who challenged me, *a parliament the Crows* call it, to gain their trust. Trust through blood," he mused. "And *you*—you, Nicolas, you helped. There was a Tongue-less one watchin' us—watchin' me have a go at you in the Quiet Man that night in the Dreggs. Heard what," Ranulf shuddered and wheezed yet again "What, what I said to you. Worked in my—in *our*—favor I guess." The spasm of pain appeared to pass, and his eyes, mournful and hurting, stared up at Nicolas.

Nicolas looked at the other boy's bloody wound. "Yeah, yeah I guess it did," he said quietly.

A shadow fell across them both. Ansgar stood there. He was blood-spattered and panting, his great war bow in one hand, a gore-washed sword in the other. "Come, Master Bennett," he said.

"Come?"

"Yes. A scout's arrived from the gatekeep. Laird Aldus Ward has sent word. We're to go north as quickly as we can manage. Something terrible 's afoot—you're in grave danger it seems."

"Danger? Me?"

The tall archer narrowed his eyes and, as if he hadn't heard Nicolas, looked around them at great length. They could all hear the spongy moans of the wounded, the squawking cries of gathering sea gulls, the timeless rolls of the waves, and the profound devotions of brothers-in-arms saying permanent goodbyes as the living passed into dying. "Yes," he finally said. "You're in mortal danger, Master Bennett."

"And my—my—Adelaide, Benjamin—my *friends*?" Nicolas asked. His heart felt small, weak against the dread and disquiet churning in his stomach. He was trying to make sense of what Ansgar was saying. He felt alone.

Ranulf squeezed his hand and forced another smile. He pushed his voice out, attempting to sound sure. "Don't worry, old boy. We'll all be comin' with you."

Ansgar frowned but nodded, then without anything more, turned heel and strode away.

"Nicolas?"

"Yes?"

The bladesmith's voice was now faint. He stared at Nicolas. His face suddenly looked utterly helpless, defenseless. Fear troubled his eyes and he clutched at Nicolas' hands.

Nicolas noticed the other boy's chest. There was a renewed blossom of blood; Ranulf's wounds seemed to be seeping again. "Don't worry. You'll be alright. Albrec's gone to get help, and Ansgar will go get the others. You'll be alright. You're going to be okay. You're going to be okay." In Nicolas' mind's eye, it was the Children's Ward in the Cumberland Infirmary.

The older boy shook his head. "It isn't that." With a visibly strained effort, he swallowed. "It's, it's—do you *forgive* me, Nicolas? Could you forgive me?"

Nicolas, the quiet boy from Plumpton Head, England, now on some corner of a foreign field, the boy who'd so often willed back the very tears that came running warmly down his face, asked, "Forgive *you*? There isn't anything to forgive, Ranulf. If, if anything—it's me who should be askin' to be forgiven. I'm sorry. I'm sorry I ever left. I tried to come back; I *swear* I did. I should've never left."

Ranulf's chin dipped in a slow nod. Relief. "You'll stay then?" he asked, hesitant.

Nicolas laid a shaky hand gently aside Ranulf's cold cheek and touched their foreheads together. "I'll stay," he promised, stealing half his heart against the hope that an English Christmastime would patiently wait for him no matter how long it might take. But he feared it might not.

"North then."

"Yes. North then."

"Together?"

"Yes, together. *All* of us." Nicolas' heart seized with the memory of Benjamin's limp body and the paleness of Adelaide's skin.

Ranulf's body suddenly relaxed. The blood on the older boy's chest slackened and with a deep sigh, he closed his eyes.

"Don't cry," he whispered a moment later through the raindrops on his lips.

Nicolas gutted back his tears. "My friend," he stammered to Ranulf but, he realized, to Jack as well.

"My friend," Ranulf whispered back.

Together the boys lay there on the stained black sand, hand-in-bloody-hand, as Nicolas silently pretended everyone else around them were giants.